Graham Hurley is a writer and television producer. Many of his documentary films have won awards. He is co-director of Project Icarus, a charity active in health education. *Rules of Engagement* is his first thriller.

Rules of Engagement

Graham Hurley

Pan Original
Pan Books London Sydney and Auckland

First published 1990 by Pan Books Ltd

This revised edition published 1991 by Pan Books Ltd
Cavaye Place, London SW10 9PG

9 8 7 6 5 4 3 2 1

ISBN 0330 31569 2

Printed in England by Clays Ltd, St Ives plc

For
Tom and Jack
Double Tops

The earth also was corrupt before God.
And the earth was filled with violence.

Genesis vi, 11

On mourra seul.

Pascal, *Pensées*, 211

I am not sure that releasing all of the forces which have been kept frozen for up to seventy years is going to be something the rest of the world will welcome.

Professor E. J. Hobsbawm
4 February 1990

Prelude

Gillespie, years later, remembered the moment when the RSM shook the photographs out of the buff manila envelope and spread them on the desk. The photographs were black and white and on the back they carried the stamp of the Military Police photographer. They were blow-ups from the original negs, but the grain was fine and the detail was excellent.

The RSM had pushed a couple of the photos across the desk towards Gillespie. McMullen lay where he'd fallen, a night's growth of stubble on his chin, his mouth slightly open, gravel scrapes on his cheek, a neat black hole where his left eye had once been. Something wet and dark had pooled on the dusty tarmac beside his head. A chalk circle ringed the spot where they'd recovered the single bullet.

In the absence of any comment from Gillespie, the RSM had leaned slowly back in his chair and arched one eyebrow. At the time, Gillespie had interpreted the movement as interrogative, the beginnings of that long process which might well prove inconclusive but would doubtless return Gillespie to civilian life. Only later did he realize that it was a quiet gesture of applause. Clean shot. Extreme range. Difficult conditions. Terrible light.

After a while, in total silence, the RSM had tidied the photographs into a neat pile and slid them back inside the envelope. He'd sealed the envelope, made a note in pencil on the top left-hand corner, and laid it carefully to rest in the adjutant's wire basket. Then he'd leaned back again, looking Gillespie in the eye. His voice, edged with regret, had the tone of someone saying goodbye.

'Shame you're such a difficult bastard . . .' he'd murmured, 'we might have done something here.'

One

Five and a half years later, on July 11th, the US Navy nuclear submarine *George F. Kennan* left King's Bay, Georgia on America's eastern seaboard. In almost total darkness, she slipped quietly down the Intracoastal Waterway, and disappeared into the Atlantic Ocean.

Nine days later, she took up station at a set of co-ordinates 120 nautical miles off Hammerfest, near Norway's North Cape. There, she lurked for weeks on end, her systems idling, every moving surface specially quietened, her crew stepping softly from station to station in their blue lint-free overalls.

The men worked shifts, six hours on, twelve hours off. They watched dials, monitored the passive sonars, annotated logs, and listened curiously to the thrum-thrum of distant Soviet submarines as they pushed west through the Iceland Gap. Off duty, they played video games, kept diaries, studied for exams, leafed through old copies of *Sports Illustrated*, and thought surprisingly little about the 80 megatons of nuclear incandescence tipping the fat D5 missiles in the belly of the boat.

The Navy did its best to relieve the boredom. There was a vast library of videos – movie classics, old ball games, *National Geographic* doccos – and a good voyage would include a number of first-release feature movies. The night the reactor blew, as it happened, was the night the EO had elected to première *Rocky VI*. Sylvester Stallone was still in training on the Acapulco waterfront when the three-colour alarms began to blink the length of the hull.

Within an hour and a half, the *Kennan* was wallowing on the surface of the Barents Sea, the fire in her reactor finally under control, her power shut off, her systems largely dead. The 170 metre hull made an interesting addition to the long range radar screens in the hardened bunkers on the Kola Peninsula, and Soviet reconnaissance aircraft were climbing into the clouds west of Murmansk as dawn began to break.

At about the same time, in Washington, the President was awakened with the news. He nodded, yawned, rubbed his eyes, and reached for the telephone. The National Security Council was already in semi-permanent session over the crisis in Scandinavia and the Baltic Republics. NATO reinforcement of Europe was virtually complete. The last thing the Free World needed was a crippled Trident missile submarine drifting towards Soviet territorial waters. He lifted the phone to his ear, and punched a single button. A voice answered at once.

'Navy's blown it,' the President announced bleakly, 'as you've probably heard.'

Gillespie awoke at five, an hour earlier than normal. For a moment or two he lay in bed. The house was in darkness. Far away, out over the sea, he could hear the *whump-whump* of a big helicopter. Closer, the steady drip from the overflow on the downstairs cistern. But it was several seconds before the paws began to dig into the duvet, and he felt the tickle of warm breath on his face, he realized that the cat had somehow opened the door, jumped onto the bed, and woken him up. He reached over in the darkness and fondled the soft triangle of fur beneath her left ear. The purring dropped a semitone, and the cat began to lick the tip of his nose. The helicopter receded into silence. The overflow dripped on.

An hour later, still dark, Gillespie sat in his tiny kitchen sipping a mug of sweet tea. He was a lean, spare man, an inch under six foot, with a hollow face and a crooked smile and a grown out crew cut. He carried with him a curious stillness, and people who knew him well often talked about his eyes. They were light blue, and playful, and utterly opaque. People said it made it very hard to judge what he ever really thought. Gillespie, when it was once mentioned in conversation, had smiled and said nothing. Privately, he'd considered it a daft comment: arty, over-intellectual, and beyond comprehension. He read as many books as the next man, but the longer words were always a waste of breath.

Now, beside the teapot on the old deal table, lay an angling magazine open at a feature article on prize cod. Gillespie scanned it carefully, noting the catch weights and the tackle details, and wondering whether he should try again at the weekend. Lately, the fishing had been lousy. He and the boy had spent day after day at sea with little or nothing to show for it.

Sean never complained, never offered any hint that he was cold, hungry, or simply bored, but simply got on with it, an attitude that won Gillespie's quiet applause. He had, it often seemed, limitless reserves of stamina. He kept his own counsel. He rarely got upset. Even when Gillespie and Sandra had split up, he'd simply shrugged his shoulders and said it would be OK by him as long as he could still see them both. For years, he'd done just that. Gillespie, in a complicated world, was proud of him.

Gillespie eyed the grainy black and white photos in the magazine one final time. Big untidy men in woolly hats with shy smiles and armfuls of plump, shiny cod. Gillespie smiled, rueful, remembering his own empty days at sea, then pushed the magazine aside and padded out into the hall, shutting the cat in the kitchen with the back of his heel. He checked the message indicator on his Ansaphone. Nothing. He headed for the street.

Outside, the cold hit him. There was ice on the windows of the cars at the kerbside: clapped-out Vauxhalls, and springless Allegros, and his own rusty 'S' reg Marina estate. It wasn't much of a neighbourhood if you were looking for a good address, but the little terrace house gave him privacy and the comfort of his own four walls, and Gillespie had never been one for lingering over the view.

He set off down the street, running slowly at first, his breath clouding on the cold air, his arms and legs moving sweetly under the cotton flannel of his ancient tracksuit. He ran every morning at dawn, seven days a week. He'd done it since he could remember, since he first joined the Corps, and it had become part of his life. He pushed himself to the limit, running the length of the city's beaches, five hard miles of pebbles, winter and summer. The pebbles drained the strength from his legs, but the feeling it gave him at the end, when he stopped to recover, was quite irreplaceable. It meant that nothing during the next twenty-four hours could touch him. It made him feel somehow immortal, beyond danger, beyond compromise, beyond reach.

Gillespie turned the corner at the end of his street, and crossed the road under the shadow of the orange lamps. The city was audible around him, a low, bass hum, but the roads were still empty. He jogged the mile and a half to the seafront, gradually picking up speed until he could hear the rasp of his own breathing, and feel the first prickles of sweat at the back of his neck.

On the seafront, he paused. A convoy of Army lorries swept past him. There were squaddies in combat gear squatting on the slatted wooden benches in the backs of the trucks. Their faces were daubed with camouflage cream, and they cradled SA80 assault rifles in their laps. They wore black berets low over their eyes, gazing at him with the kind of watchful indifference he remembered so well from Belfast.

The last of the trucks whined around a corner, and was gone, leaving a faint scent of diesel on the still morning air. Gillespie crossed the road, trying to rid his mind of the image. It was history. It belonged to a past he'd left behind. And it raised questions he'd prefer to leave unanswered. Sure, he read the papers. Sure, he knew the situation in Europe was dodgy. But squaddies? On city streets? In mainland Britain?

The beach was empty. He jumped the six feet from the promenade onto the icy pebbles and began to tramp towards the distant brown smudge where the shingle became matted with scrub grass and finally disappeared altogether. Out at sea, silhouetted against the yellowing dawn, he could make out the long low shapes of three Type 42 destroyers. They were moving east at speed, curls of white foam arching back from the flare bows.

Gillespie's step faltered. Instinctively, he glanced over his shoulder, back towards the west where the deep water channel dog-legged into the harbour mouth. Emerging from the half darkness was the unmistakable bulk of one of the Navy's three aircraft carriers. Gillespie watched as the huge ship edged cautiously out into the tideway. There were two tugs, fore and aft, and a third midships on the landward side. Gillespie frowned.

The big ships, he knew, always negotiated the harbour mouth at the top of the tide, ensuring maximum clearance in the dredged channel. Yet one glance at the tideline told him that the flood had only just begun, giving the men on the bridge very little room for manoeuvre as they conned their way out towards the open sea.

The light was improving rapidly now, and as the carrier grew more distinct, Gillespie picked out the three rows of Sea Harriers lined up on the flight deck. Aft of the aircraft was a gaggle of helicopters: Lynxes, Sea Kings, and even a couple of Pumas, blotched with military camouflage. Yet here, too, something was wrong. The helicopters appeared to have been stowed at random, almost as an afterthought, like kids' toys tidied up in a hurry. Gillespie, cold now, stayed a minute or two longer, long enough to confirm that the carrier was sailing without any evident escort. Odd, he thought, as he turned and stamped the chill from his limbs, and set off once again along the beach.

Ten minutes later, he was off the pebbles and onto the scrub grass which fringed the beach at its eastern end. Normally, he turned here and retraced his footsteps west, towards the pier, but he was unsettled now, and curious, and unresolved questions drew him on.

Beyond the pebbles, the beach narrowed into a spit of land which formed a naturally protected anchorage on its landward side. Here, the local fishermen - professional and otherwise - kept their boats. One of them belonged to Gillespie. She was a sturdy, clinker-built 18-footer, with a small cuddy forward, plenty of deck room, and an inboard 16-horsepower Petter diesel. Gillespie had bought her for a song with the remains of his Corps gratuity, and had virtually rebuilt her over successive winters. Now she was immaculate, a strong, seagoing, working boat with enough navigation aids to keep out of trouble, and enough range to give him the solitude he needed. Apart from the boy, she was the centre of his life. Like his early mornings on the beach, she gave him peace.

He crested the last of the dunes at the top of the beach, and paused for breath. There were maybe two dozen boats drawn up on the wet mud, lying on their bilges, waiting for the returning tide. Parked up on the single track road was a Land-Rover. It was dark blue with Royal Navy markings. One of the Naval Provost's men, a hard-faced matelot with a revolver on his thigh, was leaning against the door of the Land-Rover. Below him, amongst the bladderwrack, stood two naval officers. One was consulting a clipboard. The other was inspecting Gillespie's boat, peering in through the salt-caked window of the wheelhouse, shading his eyes against the low sun.

Gillespie watched for a moment or two, and then began to jog slowly down the dune towards them. As he approached, the matelot stepped forward until he stood between Gillespie and his boat.

'Yeah?'

Gillespie looked him in the eye and nodded at his boat.

'That's my boat,' he said.

One of the two officers glanced up.

'Mr Gillespie?'

'Yeah?'

The officer smiled.

'We were having an argument about your Comms kit,' he said pleasantly. 'Decca or Navstar?'

'Neither. It's a Seavoice, with special mods.'

'Oh . . .' He smiled again. 'Very original.'

Gillespie gazed at him a moment, a number of questions forming an orderly queue in his mind. Finally he opted for the obvious.

'What's it to you?' he said.

The officer raised one eyebrow. 'I thought you'd have heard.'

'Heard what?'

'Emergency Powers Act.' He rapped the clipboard with the end of his biro. 'We're updating the Requisitioning List.'

Two miles away, in the bedroom of a ninth floor flat on the seafront, Martin Goodman awoke with a long, slow yawn. He opened his eyes, ran a lazy tongue around the inside of his mouth, and peered across the room. Enough light was filtering through the heavy velvet curtains to tell him it was later than he'd wish.

He lay still for a moment, listening to Suzanne's breathing. She lay beside him under the duvet, her back towards him, her rich auburn hair spilling across the pillow. He touched her lightly, his fingertips tracing the soft warm line from the nape of her neck down the slope of her shoulder.

She stirred in her sleep as he swung his legs over the side of the bed and sat for a moment on the edge of the mattress. They'd made love in the darkness only an hour or two earlier. It had been slow and wordless, gentle and deft, and at the end she'd climaxed with a low groan, and been asleep again within seconds, a smile on the pillow beneath him. People said that guilt and happiness never went together. They were wrong.

He slipped Suzanne's dressing gown over his shoulders, and padded across to the window. He parted the curtains, keeping his body between the early sunshine and the bed. There was a thin film of condensation on the cold glass. He wiped it clean. The view from the ninth floor was breathtaking: the rich green sweep of the Common, the long black ribbon of the road which skirted the seafront, the browns and yellows of the beach, and the chilly greys and blues of the sea, flecked with white in the strengthening breeze.

Goodman stood at the window for a moment longer, gazing out at the view. From here, the island on which the city was built made perfect sense. He could see the narrow harbour mouth, flanked by the fortifications, and then the sudden spread of the harbour itself, dotted with ferries and lighters and the anchored grey hulks of yesterday's warships, awaiting their final tow to the scrapyard. Goodman inched the curtain wider, peering to the right, over the mass of the Naval Dockyard, with its huge cranes and empty drydocks, away inland to the low hump of the hill. At the foot of the hill was a creek which separated the island from the mainland. Working in the city, it was easy to forget that stretch of slack water, with its eager young anglers, and its three busy bridges. But it was there all the same.

Goodman pulled Suzanne's dressing gown tighter around him. Once, the city had depended on the Dockyard, growing outwards, street by street, century by century, until tens of thousands of men regulated their lives by the wail of the Dockyard hooter. He'd seen the old sepia prints in the city archive, thin-faced men like his own father on ancient bicycles pouring out of the Dockyard gates: flat caps, roll-ups, and the gaunt certainties of life at the bottom of the pile. They'd watched an Empire come and go, these men, unquestioning, unacknowledged, badly paid, the perfect target for disease, poverty, and – at the end of it all – the night bombing raids that had reduced so much of the city to rubble. As a kid, he'd played on the bombsites, and even when he went off to University there were pockets of the city untouched by reconstruction.

But all that, in the exact sense of the word, was history. Because the city, his city, had finally severed its dependence on the Navy and the Dockyard. There was new money around, fresh opportunities, and a real appetite for growth. The city was hungry for its share of the good times, and the new mood had brought a succession of developers to his outer office in the Civic Centre. Sharp-suited young men with their oxblood leather briefcases and laptop computers. International consortia with addresses in Zurich and Dubai. Attentive personal assistants with names like Sally-Anne, and Ghislaine, who understood the commercial value of a certain kind of smile. And all of them keen to shake his hand, state their case, and offer the sincere assurance of total commitment. He smiled. For a still-young man from one of the meaner streets, he'd done well. Deputy Chief Executive of one of the country's major cities. And still only 38.

He closed the curtain again and went through to the bathroom. He shaved quickly, splashed his face with cold water, and returned to the bedroom. Quietly, he dressed. Blue shirt, dark suit, muted red tie. Only when he was about to leave did he think to check his pager. He carried it with him everywhere. He frowned when he found it missing and searched quickly on his hands and knees on the carpet behind the canvas-backed director's chair where he'd hung his jacket. Nothing. He crossed the room and bent briefly over the bed. It was underneath Suzanne's pillow. He slid it out as carefully as he could, trying not to wake her. The tiny control on the side was switched to 'off'.

He peered down at her. With the curtains closed, the room was still in semi-darkness. Suzanne stirred and rolled over. She opened one eye and saw the pager in his hand. Her sudden smile was entirely unrepentant. Goodman gazed down at her, and returned the smile..

'Naughty girl,' he said.

She looked up at him, and budded her mouth into a kiss. He leant over her, smelling the ripe, warm scent of her breath. Her hand guided his under the duvet, across the flat, firm belly, and down.

'Naughty boy,' she said.

He smiled again, and massaged her slowly, and then kissed her one last time and stood up. As he left the flat, he heard the click of her bedside radio. The first of the day's reports announced that an American missile submarine was adrift in the Barents Sea, a bare hundred miles from Russian territorial waters. With a nice sense of understatement, the resident pundit agreed that this latest crisis was, under the circumstances, 'unhelpful'.

Gillespie arrived back at his house at 7.35, too late for the meat of the seven o'clock news, and too early for the eight o'clock updates. From the Naval officers at the anchorage, he'd learned nothing more than the existence of a Requisitioning List. They'd been perfectly polite, even affable, but he knew far too much about the Service to doubt that they meant what they said. He'd seen lists like that before. He'd seen them in Northern Ireland, precautionary gestures against the total collapse of law and order. Once you made a list like that, you weren't too far from chaos.

Gillespie pushed in through the front door, collected a warm towel from the radiator in the hall, released the cat from the kitchen, and went through to the living room to switch on the TV. The living room ran the length of the house: a cool, tidy room, thoughtfully lit by spots on the wall, with a fitted carpet, and a small sofa, and an ancient leather-covered armchair which fitted him like a glove. The bookshelves were full of thrillers and military biographies and he'd hung a print from the Falklands campaign over the open fireplace.

The print was a view of HMS *Hermes* returning to the city in midsummer, framed by the harbour mouth, saluted by thousands, an essay in greens and greys and the choking, tearful euphoria he remembered so well. Sandra had met him off the ship. The marriage had been over for more than a year, but they'd laid their differences aside for a night before real life crept back with the clatter of milk bottles on the door step, and the first pot of tea, and his own overpowering need to be out and away. Sean had watched him go from the upstairs bedroom window. For once, the boy hadn't returned his cheerful wave.

Gillespie turned on the TV and stepped back to towel himself dry. A pretty girl with almond eyes was sitting on a sofa interviewing an American actor. The actor was discussing the merits of the latest Californian diet. The crisis in Scandinavia was evidently postponed for a while. Gillespie swapped channels. More schlock. He turned down the sound and crossed the room towards the small government-surplus desk beneath the front window. There was a litter of bills, and petrol receipts, and a heap of untranscribed audio cassettes from a surveillance job he'd had to abandon after the client ran out of money.

On one side of the desk, beside the telephone, was an answering machine with a message waiting. Gillespie frowned. He'd checked the machine before he'd left for his run. It was still very early for anyone to have phoned. He spooled back the tape. The tape began to play. A woman's voice. Young. Impatient. Very London. Annie. Gillespie winced. He could picture her at the other end, cursing his gruff recorded message, wondering why the fuck he wasn't there to do her bidding. The voice was huskier than usual. Evidently, she'd had a hard night. Too many cigarettes. Or worse.

'Hi . . .' the voice said, 'it's me. It's . . . ah . . . six-thirty. Just after. And there's no way I'm going to be down by nine. The traffic's unbelievable. Everyone's leaving town. So say "Hi" to the crew for me. Tell them to set up. That's technical for get ready. OK? See you . . .'

The phone went dead. Gillespie stared at it a moment, towelling the last of the run from his face and neck. Crew? Setting up? He frowned, trying to fit the words together, trying to tease out some kind of sense. He'd known the girl six months at the most. She'd said she worked in television. She was producing a big series. It would be on some network or other. It was all about the Falklands War. It would be definitive, she'd said, and she wanted a meet. She used the phrase knowingly, exhibiting it like a badge at the end of the sentence. It meant she'd been around a bit, mixed in certain circles, knew blokes from the police or the military.

Gillespie, on the phone, had been non-committal. The Falklands was way back. He'd nothing to say. Why didn't she try someone else? But the girl had been persistent, ringing back time and time again until he'd agreed to a drink, and a chat, and maybe a meal afterwards.

She'd come down within days, a tall, rangy twenty-six-year-old, mixed blood, probably Scouse and Caribbean. She was cheerful and forthright, with a big Afro haircut and a wide face and a smile she used to some effect. She was the kind of person who built bridges at once, touched and leant in close, like a good boxer, light on her feet, and deft, and quite fearless, with a sense of instant intimacy that could have been a turn-off but somehow wasn't. The way she dressed underlined it all: an ancient blue and red check shirt under an old leather jacket, faded Levis, and last year's Reeboks.

She'd arrived in a friend's borrowed Ford Escort, and they'd driven across the city and shared a couple of pints at a harbourside pub. Afterwards, she'd insisted on a meal, and he'd suggested one of the seedier Indian restaurants where the service was intermittent but the food was great. She'd told him most of her life story, and said nothing about the Falklands until the very end. Then she said she'd talked to some friends of his, old buddies from 43 Commando. She said it the way it should be said, *Four three*. These contacts of hers had all mentioned Gillespie by name. He was, they said, the man.

Gillespie, nearly flattered, had asked why, and she'd said he'd seen the worst of it. That was her phrase. *The worst of it*. Gillespie had shrugged. The phrase, he said, meant nothing, sod all. You go to war, you expect to fight. You fight, you expect to take casualties. You take casualties, you expect some of them to be friends of yours, buddies, mates you've yomped with, and got pissed with, and helped out of the shit. Sure, some of them got blown away. Sure, some of it had been hideous. But the Corps never trained you to be a public librarian. They trained you to kill. Simple as that. Kill, or be killed.

It was the first time he'd said more than a sentence or two to her, and the effect he remembered all too well. She'd listened to him very intently, eyes wide, her body bent slightly forward over the half-empty dishes. Whenever he paused for a moment to hunt for a word, she'd nod, as if urging him on, tugging out the story, line by line. And at the end of it all, she leant slowly back against the flock wallpaper, and let out her breath in a low, soft whistle, a gesture of amazement and applause. It was, for Gillespie's taste, a hopelessly dramatic thing to do. It belonged to the world of showbusiness, and phoniness, and funny metropolitan ways, but the curry had been good, and there was no denying she was an attractive piece, and next time she came down they both got drunk and she stayed the night.

There'd been other nights since. It was never predictable, always at her prompting, a message on the Ansaphone, a call from the end of the street. Happen to be passing. Be nice to drop by. Gillespie liked the arrangement. It was loose and easy and free of commitment. He liked her company, and she liked his, and the girl was funny, and bold, and brilliant in bed. She asked nothing of him except himself, and he played the game willingly, no questions asked.

Now, he respooled the machine and replayed the message. They had a loose agreement that one day he might consider doing an interview on film. Quite what he was meant to talk about was never clear, but she'd always dismissed his qualms, and said that stuff was better coming out spontaneously. Gillespie hadn't much liked the sound of that, and so he'd simply forgotten about it, assumed it would never happen. Now, though, he realized that he'd been wrong. Because here she was, evidently somewhere between London and the South Coast, planning to descend on him with her little list of questions, and her neat preconceptions, and her cameraman, and God knows who else. And all this on a day when, by all accounts, the country was on the edge of another war. At any other time, the prospect of an interview would have been bad enough. Just now, it was out of the question. The girl would simply have to find something else to film.

Martin Goodman drove north through the city, against the first of the morning rush hour. The radio was full of reports from Oslo on the expected outcome of talks between the new Socialist Government and the Soviet delegation from Moscow. The Russians had been in and out of the Foreign Ministry now for three days, and informed sources were talking about some kind of draft agreement. Quite what this agreement would contain wasn't yet clear, but the spokesman from the Institute for Strategic Studies left his interviewer in no doubt about the consequences should the new Norwegian Prime Minister make good his pledge to withdraw from NATO. It would, he said, open the northern door to the heartlands of Western Europe. It would jeopardize the NATO alliance. And it would make the Americans very nervous indeed.

Goodman followed the arguments as best he could, but it was difficult to relate the warnings of impending catastrophe to the queues of commuter cars streaming past him into the city, and the last of the mist lifting from the saltings at the head of the harbour with the memory of Suzanne still fresh and warm in his mind.

The night before, for the first time, they'd discussed a permanent life together. After they'd come back from the French restaurant, and settled down on the sofa with a cup of thick black Turkish coffee and glasses of Armagnac, he'd heard himself talking about certain kinds of colour schemes, and the merits of owning a dishwasher, and whether or not it was wise to invest in solar heating. This kind of small print had never had the slightest relevance to their relationship. On the contrary, they'd created a world on the very edges of everyone else's life, a relationship walled in by secret notes, and stolen telephone calls, and snatched hours together in bistros, and pubs, and darkened car parks. In a sense, it had been a kind of war, the two of them underground in some hostile country, their kisses and their lovemaking sharpened by the ever-present possibility of discovery or betrayal. The consequences of either were too awful to contemplate, but taking the risk somehow made him feel alive and young. It had offered a constant sense of infinite possibility, a defiance of the laws of emotional gravity that made him feel literally weightless, utterly free. He and Suzanne, their bubble, was a world away from strategy meetings about the city's five-year expansion plan, or the sewage problems posed by the new Marina Complex. It was clean, and totally unrestrained by life's normal ration of ballast.

And yet the conversation last night, with its fond domesticities, had somehow changed the mood, brought them down to earth. Some bits of it had fascinated him. About others, he wasn't so sure. The last thing he needed was another dollop of real life.

He dropped a gear, and joined the queue of traffic driving over the creek onto the mainland. Up on the hill, overlooking the city, he could see the morning sunshine glittering on the big french windows at the back of his house. He glanced at his watch. By now, Joanna would be rousing the children. With luck, he'd arrive in time to share their porridge.

*

Gillespie sat at his kitchen table, adding up his debts. The morning's post had brought him his monthly Access account, plus a final reminder on the phone bill. In all, according to his pencilled calculations, he now owed nearly £400.

He never worried unduly about money, but lately work had been thin. He picked up most of his jobs from a local solicitor, a man in his late forties called Jenner. Jenner ran a small practice from a couple of offices in one of the city's more elegant areas. He was a peaceable, mild-tempered man, with low blood pressure and an appalling dress sense. He had a small, highly organized wife, a collection of chaotic kids, and a large rambling house on the outskirts of a village about seven miles inland. Most of his work was Legal Aid, and he'd built a reputation for defending victims of the city's chronic housing shortage: young couples ripped off by unscrupulous estate agents, elderly spinsters harried by greedy landlords, students with nowhere to live but a sleeping bag. The work would never earn him a fortune, he said, but he slept well at night, and he'd come to know a great deal about human nature.

Gillespie had first met Jenner at the time of his own divorce. His gut instinct had been to give Sandra the lot, but Jenner had pulled him back from the brink of insolvency and drawn up a settlement which was both fair and honourable. The last of this business had been conducted over a drink, and the two men found themselves forging the beginnings of a relationship.

Jenner had just dispensed with the latest of a long series of law school graduates, a breed he referred to collectively as 'duds'. What he really wanted was someone with an organized mind, uncluttered by over-education or fancy ideas. Someone with a spot of self-discipline, who'd be able to pick up the ins and outs of conveyancing, and the delivery of writs, and the keeping of tabs on this and that, and the odd spot of something he called 'research'. The latter turned out to involve surveillance work, and after some thought Gillespie agreed to have a go. He'd never been over-concerned with other people's lives, but he liked Jenner, and he needed the money.

The first jobs had been straightforward. Accompanying clients to court. Taking statements from key witnesses. Holding the fort on the rare afternoons when Jenner was away. But then came the evening when Jenner invited him along on a repossession case.

When things became unpleasant, and Jenner was pulled from his Renault by a prominent local heavy, it was Gillespie who stepped out onto the pavement, loosened the man's grip on Jenner's collar, turned him carefully round, and hit him so hard that he broke his cheek-bone in two places. Jenner, while grateful, had given Gillespie a stern lecture on what he termed 'gratuitous violence'. Gillespie hadn't a clue what he was talking about, but nodded at key points and promised to send flowers to the hospital. The incident had cemented the rapport between the two men, and Gillespie had been in more or less regular work ever since.

Lately though, the jobs had begun to dry up. Not because Jenner was any less keen on his services, but because – for some reason – people had suddenly started to be nicer to each other, and no longer, it seemed, needed the services of a solicitor. Jenner, ever philosophical, had welcomed the collective change of heart. He said it presaged an altogether gentler world. Gillespie, on the other hand, said it was bullshit. Most people were animals. Only fear of the consequences kept them in line.

Now, in the kitchen, Gillespie eyed the bills a final time, and then reached for the kettle. The kettle was empty. He was about to fill it when there was a knock at the front door. He inched open the kitchen door with his foot. There was a shadow in the rippled glass at the end of the hall. Medium height. Bulky. Gillespie hesitated a moment, and then headed down the hall. When he opened the front door, he found a girl of about 25 standing outside. She was wearing a large blue anorak and was holding a clipboard against her chest. At the kerbside was a light beige Volvo estate car with the tailgate open and two men unloading silver boxes onto the pavement. Gillespie looked back at the girl on his doorstep. He was still holding the empty kettle.

'Yes?' he said.

The girl looked faintly nonplussed.

'Mr Gillespie?'

'That's me.'

'We're from Wessex TV . . .' She hesitated. 'Is Annie here?'

'No.'

'But she did tell you we were coming . . ?'

She smiled, still uncertain. Gillespie looked at the Volvo. There was a tripod on the back seat and the bigger of the two men was carefully removing a camera from one of the silver boxes. He turned back to the girl again.

'Yes,' he said, 'she did.'

'So . . .' she nodded past him, up the hall, 'can we come in?'

Gillespie hesitated for a moment, then shook his head.

'Sorry, love. No, you can't.'

The girl looked confused. Then angry. Then confused again.

'Can't?'

'Yes, love. Can't.' He smiled at her, and put a finger to his lips. 'There's a war on,' he said, 'Mum's the word.'

Goodman first saw the black Rover when he rounded the bend at the foot of the hill. It was parked outside his house. Closer, as he slowed to drive past it and then turn into his own drive, he saw the Home Office sticker on the back window, and the splatters of dried mud curving back from the wheel arches. Someone with Whitehall connections. Someone who'd put his foot down.

He eased the big Granada through the open gate, turned carefully across the square of gravel, and rolled to a halt outside the front door. The bedroom curtains upstairs were still drawn. He frowned, retrieving his briefcase from the back seat, and got out of the car.

His wife met him at the front door. She was wearing a light blue track suit. She looked gaunt, and didn't smile when he bent towards her and kissed her lightly on the cheek.

'Darling . . .' he said, automatically.

'Where have you been?'

'London.'

He stepped into the hall and closed the door behind him. The place smelled of fresh coffee and burnt toast. The door to the lounge was open, and he could hear the low hum of an electric fire inside. His wife was still looking at him.

'Whereabouts in London?'

'Clive's place.' He smiled at her again, trying not to sound guarded. 'I know, I should have phoned. I'm sorry. It all got rather late.' He put his briefcase on the small occasional table by the door.

'So I drove down this morning.' He began to unbutton his coat. 'Kids OK?'

His wife looked at him, ignoring the question.

'I thought you'd be at the Apollo, like you said. Or the Novotel.'

'No,' he hesitated a moment, 'Clive was at a conference, and we had one or two drinks afterwards, and . . .' he shrugged, 'he's just across the river at Kennington so there seemed no point in going to a hotel.'

He glanced at himself in the mirror over the telephone, smoothed his hair with one hand, turned back to his wife.

'My love . . . I'm truly sorry . . .'

She looked at him a moment, confused, began to say something, then shook her head, dismissing it all.

'Listen,' she said, 'there's a man . . .'

Goodman frowned. 'What man?'

'A man from London. I think he's Government. He's come down to see you.' She nodded towards the lounge. 'He's in there, having coffee.'

Goodman looked blank for a moment.

'In there?'

'Yes. I think maybe you'd better say hello. He's been there since five this morning.'

'*Five?*'

'Yes. That's when I started phoning the hotels.'

She offered him a small, bare smile, trying to keep the reproach out of her voice. Goodman looked at her a moment, nodding slowly, remembering the black Rover parked in the road outside.

'I see . . .' he said, 'no wonder. Poor you.'

He crossed the hall towards her, all sympathy, but she stepped quickly towards the kitchen.

'I'll put some more coffee on. I don't suppose you've had anything, have you?'

'No.'

He watched her disappear down the hall, wondering how much damage he'd done, how plausible it all sounded. Then he turned towards the mirror again, straightened his tie, and went into the lounge.

The lounge was a large, L-shaped room, the best in the house, full of light. Joanna had decorated it herself, shades of yellow and beige, with brown fleck carpet, and carefully sited wall lights, and a huge gilt mirror over the big marble fireplace. French windows on the south side opened onto a stone flagged terrace. Steps led to half an acre of lawn, and there was a sandpit at the bottom of the garden with a swing Goodman had built for the kids.

Goodman paused, and coughed. Standing in front of the french windows was a man in a dark suit. He turned back into the room. He was about 45, medium height, quietly dressed, with neatly trimmed hair, and a face devoid of expression. He wore rimless glasses, and there was the faintest hint of dark blue handkerchief tucked into the breast pocket of his suit. He stepped towards Goodman and extended a hand. Despite the air of careful neutrality, the man exuded authority.

'Good morning,' he said, 'Oliver Davidson. Home Office.'

Goodman nodded and shook hands. For the second time that morning, he did his best not to sound defensive.

'Morning. Martin Goodman.'

There were the beginnings of an awkward silence. Goodman indicated an armchair by the fireplace.

'I'm sorry you've had to hang around,' he said, 'I'm afraid you caught us on the hop.'

Davidson settled into the armchair and glanced up at him. The smile was shy.

'We did try and find you . . .' he said, 'but I'm afraid you got the better of us.'

'My pager was out.' Goodman patted his breast pocket. 'Battery problem.'

'Ah, I see . . .' Davidson permitted himself the subtlest of pauses. 'London, I gather.'

'Yes. DOE. Conference. What to do about the Poll Tax. Bane of our lives, I'm afraid. Local Government was never simple. But this . . .' he pulled a face, 'it's a nightmare.'

'I'm sure,' Davidson said, pausing again, the same inflection, the same chill edge to his voice. He picked a thread of cotton off his immaculately pressed trousers. Then he looked up. 'I'm sorry about your Mr Moody.'

'Eric?' Goodman's voice dropped a semitone. 'Yes, it's not good news.'

'Coronary, wasn't it?'

'Yes. The second, I'm afraid.'

Another silence settled between them. Eric Moody had been Chief Executive for nearly eight years, a plump, choleric man with a photographic memory and an affection for malt whisky. His first heart attack had put him in hospital for three weeks, but he was back at his desk the following month, ignoring orders to rest, and reclaiming the key files from Goodman's in-tray. His wife, a tired looking woman in her early fifties, had confided to Goodman that she expected her husband to be dead by Christmas. But he'd confounded her, and wrong-footed the medics, and his system had survived another two years of punishment before he felt the same agonizing pain scorching across his right shoulder and down his arm. The ambulance had arrived at the Civic Centre within minutes, but this time it was a massive attack, and he was lucky to survive the three-mile journey to the new hospital. Goodman had been to see him only a couple of days earlier in the tiny private single-bedded room off the ICU. He looked grey and beaten, and the consultant had already confirmed that his professional life was probably over.

Now, for the second time in two years, Goodman was Acting Chief Executive, but this time there was a good chance the job would be for keeps. From his sickbed, Moody had extended a pale, flabby hand, and wished him good luck, but the expression on his face told a different story. He'd always resented the younger man, with his competence, wit, and effortless charm, and had done what he could to ensure the job went elsewhere. But mortality had intervened, Goodman was home and dry, and both men knew it.

Davidson cleared his throat and reached down for the briefcase beside his armchair. There were a pair of combination locks and he began to revolve the tumblers. When he spoke, he didn't look up.

'May I assume you've read the briefings?'

Goodman gazed at the briefcase. 'Briefings?'

'Yes.' Davidson looked up. 'The Civil Defence briefings.'

Goodman blinked, remembering the morning's breathless radio reports from Oslo and Hammerfest. He knew about the crisis in Europe, everybody did, but he'd no idea it had got this far. A year ago, the talk had been of glasnost and perestroika. Now, barely a year after Gorbachev's death, Europe was evidently on the edge of war. He looked Davidson in the eye.

Perhaps the man was talking about yet another exercise, something Eric Moody would have kept close to his chest. Typical. Goodman nodded.

'Yes,' he said easily, 'I've read the briefings.'

'Then this will hardly come as a surprise.' Davidson snapped open his briefcase, brisk, businesslike. He reached inside and produced a thick sheaf of documents. Goodman got up quickly and fetched a small coffee table. He placed it carefully between the two chairs. Davidson laid the documents on the table. The top sheet of paper had the texture of parchment, and the word *Proclamation* was embossed in heavy black type at the head of the page. Davidson looked at him over the tops of his glasses.

'This is material available to Controllers only,' he said. 'I need hardly tell you it's highly confidential. In the ... ah ... regrettable absence of Mr Moody, you'll be Controller-Designate. If and when the time comes.'

Goodman nodded. He could feel his pulse quickening, a warmth spreading upwards from his belly. He was vague about the specific powers of Controller, but he knew they were absolute.

'I see,' he said quietly.

Davidson produced another document from his briefcase, a single sheet of paper, and handed it across to Goodman.

'You have a pen?'

'Of course.'

Davidson indicated a dotted line at the bottom of the page.

'Signature, please, for safe receipt. Oh,' he indicated another space, 'and the date.'

Goodman nodded and bent to the paper. While he scribbled his name at the bottom of the page, Davidson glanced at his watch. Time was evidently moving on.

'I'm afraid there's a great deal to do,' he said. 'You'll need a strategy conference. Your key officers. The ones on the "A" list. Heads of Departments. Emergency Services. Transport Executives. That should happen PDQ. Preferably this morning.'

Goodman screwed the cap back on his pen. His signature sat well on the document, with its august phrases about 'defence of the realm' and 'appropriate constitutional amendments'.

'Yes,' he said, 'of course.'

'And then there's the media. You'll want to keep things as

calm as possible. If you have friends in the media, television especially, it might be wise to call in the odd favour.' He paused. 'Before that though, you and I should review the transition arrangements. Procedures. Protocols. Who does what. Formalities, I'm afraid, but vital none the less.'

Goodman handed back the receipt.

'Transition to what?' he said.

Davidson checked the signature briefly, and folded the document in half. Then he looked up again. The tone was quite neutral. The expression opaque.

'To war, Mr Goodman.'

Goodman gazed at him. 'Is it that serious?'

'Yes, I'm afraid it is.'

He got up and began to tidy the documents into a neat pile before sliding them back into his briefcase. Goodman remained in the armchair for a moment longer. Through the big french windows he could see a cloud of gulls over the city's new Marina. Upstairs, there was the splash of water from the bathroom and the sound of children laughing. He looked up at Davidson but he could think of nothing to say. Davidson reached for his coat.

'Your office, I'm afraid,' he said briskly, 'pleasant though this is.'

Gillespie sat in his kitchen, watching Annie fill his kettle from the tap. Next door, in the living room, he could hear the film crew moving furniture around. Judging by their conversation, they'd decided to shoot against the back window. Something to do with the texture of his venetian blind.

Annie had arrived half an hour after the crew. She'd found them sitting in the big Volvo, the windows furred with condensation, listening to Desert Island Discs. She'd enquired tartly what the fuck they thought they were up to, and when the PA had explained it all, she'd gone straight in to Gillespie, and shut the kitchen door behind them, and refused to take 'no' for an answer.

At first, Gillespie hadn't even bothered to argue. It was his house, his war, and his memories. He was under no obligation to share any of it with anyone. But Annie, as ever, had persisted, a dog with a bone, and when she walked out of the kitchen and back down the hall and opened the front door to the crew, he'd simply let them get on with it. Too bad if they had to pack all their equipment up again. Too bad if she didn't get her precious interview.

Now, though, for reasons he couldn't quite fathom, he found himself defending his right to silence. Annie carried the dripping kettle to the gas stove, and lit one of the front rings.

'Well?' she said, blowing out the match and flicking it, inch perfect, into the bin. 'What's it to be?' Gillespie looked at her. By rights, he should have thrown her out an hour ago. Yet here she was, easing herself onto the corner of his kitchen table, fingering the remains of his breakfast, boxing him in with her incessant questions.

Much against his better judgement, he had to admit to a certain admiration. However lost the cause, she never gave up. He smiled at her.

'Well?' she said for the second time.

'Tea,' he said, 'with two sugars.'

'I meant the interview.'

'There won't be an interview.'

'Why not?'

He shook his head, more disbelief than disapproval.

'Love, I can't.'

'Won't.'

'Yeah, won't. Can't and won't.'

She wiped her mouth with the back of her hand.

'Why not?'

'Why not?' he repeated. 'Why not? Have you seen what's happening? Are you deaf or something? Blind? Have you seen the news? The last coupla weeks?'

Annie shrugged, and dug her hands deep into the pockets of her bomber jacket.

'Sure,' she said, 'I read the papers.'

'So you'll know.'

'Know what?'

'We're going to war.'

Gillespie turned away, his case stated, the argument over. Annie watched him carefully.

'Tell me something, Dave,' she said. 'Why did you agree to do it in the first place?'

'Do what?'

'The interview.'

'I didn't agree.'

'Yes, you did. You said we'd get round to it.'

'Did I?'

'Yes.' She paused. 'So why did you say that?'

He shrugged. 'I dunno.'

'Because I asked? Nicely?' She let the insinuation rest between them for a moment. He could feel her goading him. Their nights together. Her eager, expert ways. She leant forward across the table, suddenly urgent, intense.

'Dave . . .' she said, 'you told me you were sick of all the pretence, all the flannel, all the instant TV experts. That's what you said.' She paused, letting the phrases, his phrases, sink in. 'You said it was horrible out there most of the time, just like every other bloody war. And you said it wouldn't do any harm to know the truth, for a change.' She paused again, and then came back at him, softer, more muted. 'That's when I asked you what happened on the mountain. And that's when you told me.'

Gillespie listened to her, trying not to admit the justice of her argument. He shook his head.

'Listen,' he said, 'I know how much it means to you, but there's a time and a place, love, and it ain't now. Not with this going on. No way. No matter what it would do to your precious bloody career . . .'

Annie came very close, her face almost touching his.

'OK,' she said, 'I admit it. I'm ambitious. My work matters to me. I want to do something half decent for a change. Is that a crime?'

'Of course it's not. But there are bigger things at stake just now. And you know it.'

Annie withdrew across the table. The expression on her face had changed. Part mockery. Part contempt.

'Like patriotism?' she said.

Gillespie smiled at her. He liked the word. Felt easy with it.

'Yes,' he said, 'like patriotism.'

The phrase hung between them for a moment, then Annie turned away, reaching up to the cupboard over the sink. She began to take mugs from the bottom shelf, lining them up like soldiers on the dresser. Gillespie watched her.

'What are you doing?' he said.

'Making the coffee.'

'Why do you want six cups?'

She glanced round and smiled at him.

'Why do you think?' she said, heading for the door.

Martin Goodman returned to the city at half-past nine, sitting beside Davidson in the front of the big Rover. The man from the Home Office drove fast. He was inscrutable, as if his face had somehow earned a dispensation from the normal wear and tear of life. He said very little, tuning and retuning the radio for the latest updates. The Russians were taking the submarine issue to the Security Council, citing the Cuba crisis as a justification for their decision to board and search the boat. The Americans, meanwhile, were assembling a Task Force to intervene. They expected to be with the stricken submarine within the next three days. Goodman shivered. Given the crisis in Scandinavia, the implications were suddenly all too obvious. He thought briefly of Suzanne. The touch of her fingertips. The curl of her tongue. That, at least, was simple.

They drove on down the hill, across the creek, and joined the motorway into the city. There was a convoy of Navy flat-bed trucks in the slow lane, with bulky cylindrical shapes under the flapping canvas tarpaulins. Goodman eyed them as they sped past, remembering Davidson sitting in the armchair, spelling it all out, emotionless, matter-of-fact, the phrases lifted from some Civil Defence handbook or other. Transfer of Powers. Regional Commissariats. Sub-Regional HQs. When his wife came in with fresh supplies of coffee, Goodman had made his excuses and gone upstairs for a change of shirt. Already, this morning had become quite unreal, a succession of curious events removing him further and further from the life he knew and understood. When his daughter had suddenly appeared from the bathroom with shaving foam all over her face, he'd stood on the stairs for a moment or two, blinking at her, before he reached out and accepted her clammy, pine-scented embrace. She'd asked about the man downstairs. He'd said it was someone from the office. She'd laughed and blown foam in his face, dancing away down the landing, taunting him to catch her, the disappointment showing in her face when he strode into the bedroom.

Now, driving into the city, he sat hunched in the passenger seat, with his black cashmere coat pulled tightly around him, and his briefcase between his ankles, while the rest of the world prepared to blow itself to pieces.

'What about the legislation?' he said. 'When does it all happen?'

Davidson said nothing for a moment, beginning to slow to join a queue of traffic several hundred yards before the roundabout which marked the end of the motorway. The outside lane had been coned off. The convoy of Navy flat-beds swept past, a pair of police motorcyclists riding twenty yards ahead. Davidson eyed the rear view mirror.

'There'll be three Emergency Powers Acts,' he said. 'The first goes through tonight. The others are imminent. Once they're on the Statute Book, the machinery will be in place. After that, it simply remains for you to use it.' He paused for a moment, then swung abruptly into the coned-off lane. A police motorcyclist from the rear of the convoy was beside him in seconds, waving him to halt. Without slowing, Davidson reached inside his jacket and produced a pass. The policeman glanced at it through the window, nodded, and snapped a quick salute. They were still doing 50 mph. Davidson resumed the conversation. The same soft voice. The same hard facts.

'I think you'll find you have all the authority you need,' he said. 'You'll be able to do more or less anything you want. Except sleep.'

Goodman smiled, a bid to warm the atmosphere between them.

'What do you mean,' he said, 'exactly?'

Davidson turned into the roundabout and acknowledged the police motorcyclist's farewell wave with a curt nod.

'Well . . .' he said, 'take requisitioning. Your authority will be virtually limitless. You can requisition anything you like. Food. Fuel. Transport. Even people. You can take them off the streets. Out of their homes. You can put them to work. You can put them into uniform. Behind bars. You can even have them shot' – he glanced across – 'if that seems appropriate.' He slowed briefly for a pair of cyclists. 'I'll let you have the briefing paper on that one. We revised it last month. Provision for Emergency Judicial Sanctions.'

'Thanks very much,' Goodman said drily.

Davidson ignored the irony, easing the big Rover past the cyclists and then filtering left to take advantage of a short cut to the Civic Centre where Goodman worked. Goodman glanced across at him, impressed.

'Know this city well?'

Davidson nodded. 'Yes,' he said.

'Been down a lot?'

'Never.'

Goodman gazed at him, looking for some ghost of sense in it all, some glint of light between the clipped, curt responses, some hint that the man was, at the very least, human. To his surprise, Davidson obliged. He pulled to a halt at the traffic lights at the entrance to the Central Square, his gloved fingertips tapping out some rhythm on the pommel of the gear stick. The tone of his voice had turned lightly conversational. He even appeared to be smiling.

'Your friend Clive,' he began, 'the one you were staying with last night.'

'Yes?'

Davidson looked across at him. The smile, if anything, widened.

'He's in Greece for a month,' he said. 'Patmos.'

Goodman gazed at him for a moment or two, then turned his head and looked out of the window. A girl of about eighteen was trying to settle a baby in a pram. A man with a briefcase was looking at the sky. That feeling again. Events out of control. The world gone mad.

'I know,' he said flatly.

Gillespie sat in his armchair in the long, narrow sitting room. Behind the glare of the two powerful TV lights, he could just make out the cameraman humped over his tripod, and the shape of the sound recordist, bending over his dials. Annie sat directly in front of him, cross-legged on the carpet. She was bent towards him, forward over the carpet, a pose he recognized, intense, sympathetic, trying to nudge, or tease, or shame him into parting with his tiny fragment of the Falklands War.

There was a brief silence. Gillespie could hear the cat scratching at the kitchen door. Annie leant forward again, the softest of prompts.

'OK . . .' she said for the third time, 'you were a Troop Sergeant.'

Gillespie nodded but said nothing. Annie gazed at him.

'Would you mind saying that?' she said. 'For the camera?'

Gillespie smiled. The interview had been like this from the off, a succession of false starts, punctuated by half-whispered instructions from Annie. For the life of him, he couldn't understand why they were bothering to go on. It was a game he'd consented to play. For nearly half an hour he'd said nothing of any consequence. Now it was surely time to stop.

'I was a Sergeant . . .' he said wearily.

'In the Marines . . .'

'In the Marines . . .' He paused again. This time she said nothing. He sucked his teeth a moment. '43 Commando,' he said, 'B Company.'

'And?'

'And we were in the Falklands.'

There was a long silence. Gillespie could hear the purr of the camera. Abruptly, Annie rocked back on her heels and cleared her throat. Her voice was firmer, less patient. Film stock obviously wasn't as cheap as he'd thought.

'OK,' she said, 'OK, let's take it on, then. You're in the Falklands, and the war's well under way, and you've trekked across —'

'Yomped.' Gillespie smiled his nicest smile. Annie acknowledged his correction with the briefest of nods.

'OK, you've yomped across the island, and you're at the bottom of Mount Harriet, and it's coming on dark, and you're in a firefight with the Argies, and you've lost half a dozen men, and —'

'Seven,' said Gillespie. The smile had gone.

'Seven men.' She paused. 'So what happened then?'

Gillespie looked at her, refusing to accept the proffered invitation. Her voice softened, and her hands began to move, shaping a way forward through the story.

'You saw white flags, didn't you? And you went forward to

take the surrender?' She paused. Gillespie said nothing. 'The officer was shot by an Argie sniper . . .' Another pause. Gillespie looking at her, confirming nothing, denying nothing, giving nothing away. 'So the battle started all over again. Until they surrendered properly . . .' She smiled, a gleam of white in the half-darkness beneath the lights. 'So what happened then?' She paused. 'Dave . . .?' Gillespie shook his head, closed his eyes, very still. Annie leant forward again, her voice no more than a whisper. 'You said they looked really young . . . afterwards . . . lying there.'

'Did I?'

'Yes. And you said it was raining.'

Gillespie opened his eyes, looking beyond Annie, beyond the camera, at the dim oblong of daylight sectioned by his venetian blinds. He remembered the curtains of rain trailing across the sodden moorland. And the padre on his knees in the wet tussock. And the way the wind kept lifting the corners of the ponchos draping the neat line of dead bodies. They'd buried them near by. Three hours of solid digging. In the room there was a long silence. Then another voice. The cameraman's.

'Fifty feet,' he said.

Annie nodded, the mood broken, the moment gone. She tried to keep the frustration out of her voice but it didn't work.

'OK, OK,' she said briskly, 'let me ask one more question, then we're through.' She paused, turning back to Gillespie. 'The war's over. We've won. It's three years later . . .' She hesitated for barely an instant. 'You're in Northern Ireland. It's 1985 . . .' Gillespie was watching her closely now, alert, wary. She smiled at him. 'A man gets himself killed. A man called Dessie McMullen . . .' She paused again, letting the two words sink in. 'Name mean anything to you?'

Gillespie began to say something, a query, a question, then stopped. His face hardened. He nodded towards the door.

'Out,' he said, 'all of you.'

Annie looked at him a moment before getting up. He knew at once he'd over-reacted.

'Well, well . . .' she said softly. 'So it *is* true.'

Two

Mid morning, in London, video news pictures arrived down the line in the Gray's Inn Road studios of ITN. They came from Scottish Television, in Glasgow, and the footage had been shot at dawn that morning by an enterprising amateur cameraman at Machrihanish, a NATO airbase at the southern tip of the Mull of Kintyre.

In dim light, at extreme distance, the pictures showed RAF service personnel loading long cylinders aboard four-engined aircraft with American Navy markings. The cylinders had the suggestion of fins at one end. It took two men and a small wheeled hoist to carry them. They looked heavy.

The pictures were viewed by the ITN defence correspondent. He recognized the planes at once. They were Lockheed Orions, flown by the US Navy on anti-submarine patrols. About the cylinders, though, he wasn't so sure. He ran the pictures three more times before lifting a phone and dialling a London number from memory. Thirty minutes later, a cab deposited a small, neat man in a black suit outside the ITN studios. The defence correspondent met the visitor at the kerbside. They shook hands, old friends, and took the lift to the editing suites on the first floor.

The man in the black suit viewed the Scottish footage twice before stopping the replay machine on a freeze frame. The frame showed two sets of RAF technicians, both attending the mystery cylinders. One of the cylinders was in perfect profile, a blur of black letters stencilled around one end. The man in the black suit hesitated for a moment or two, peered closely at the screen, then confirmed that the cylinders were American robot underwater mines, known as CAPTORS. These mines could recognize the underwater noise signatures of Soviet submarines and surface vessels. They could release automatically and home on the target noise. They had a range of 1000 metres, and were nuclear-capable.

Seeded in sufficient numbers on the seabed across the Greenland - Iceland - UK Gap, they could effectively fence off the North Atlantic to marauding Soviet hunter-killer submarines. With elements of the US Sixth Fleet racing north to retrieve the helpless Trident submarine, it was - said the man in black - an obvious, if provocative, move.

The defence correspondent got up from his chair and switched on the light. A pile of video cassettes lay on the windowsill. News stories already a day old. American arms convoys arriving in Southampton. Royal Marines digging in above the Arctic circle. Old ladies in Streatham queueing for flour and sugar. Where did this latest footage figure in the crisis? The man in the black suit smiled at the question but didn't take his eyes off the screen. He had a curious accent, Home Counties English with a hint of New York.

'We're way down the line,' he said finally, 'way down.'

Albie Curtis had been in the traffic jam for nearly half an hour before the car phone began to trill. He sat in the big BMW, chewing the remains of his third roll-up, glowering balefully at the back of an ancient brown Allegro. Normally, at this time in the morning, he'd be at the garage within minutes. The city's business rush hour would be over, the roads would be clear, one of the lads would have a brew on, and he'd be settling into his first coffee of the day. Instead of which, he was locked into a mile or so of stationary cars, listening to Mick's trash tapes, and wondering what on earth had given him a taste for Verdi. He turned the volume down on the cassette player and picked up the phone, recognizing at once the voice on the other end.

'Mick,' he said flatly.

'Yeah, me . . .' there was the briefest pause, 'so where the fuck are you?'

Albie glanced out of the window. A youth of about twelve was selling an old lady a bunch of bananas.

'Commercial Road,' he said, 'by the market.'

'What are you doing there?'

'Waiting for the traffic.'

'At this time of day?'

'Yeah.' He paused, picking his teeth. 'What of it?'

'You're supposed to be at the garage, that's what.' Albie heard Mick sniff, and pulled a face. Another night on the white powder. Another fifty quid up his nose. Mick cleared his throat.

'Listen,' he said, 'Harry wants a word. Both of us. Bring the books round. We're due at eleven.'

The phone went dead and the Allegro, at last, began to move. Albie eased the clutch out, and the BMW purred forward. Harry Cartwright was Mick's posh accountant, the man who had taken Mick aside, and groomed him, and flattered him, and funded him, and had given him the kind of fancy ideas that had turned Mick's head. Without Harry, there'd have been no nightclub, no mail order business, no BMW, and no funny games with the razor blade and the Woolies mirror. They'd be back in the building trade, doing what they knew best: toshing up old properties and selling them on. Good steady money. The odd nonsense with a stubborn tenant. The odd visit with the dog. The odd run-in with the greedier estate agents. But nothing complicated or risky. Nothing they couldn't handle.

Recently, though, Mick had begun to change. He'd thrown out his jeans and graduated to Armani suits and an Afro perm. A big mortgage from Harry had bought him a flat-fronted three-storey period house in one of the city's new conservation areas. He'd acquired carriage lamps for the front, and gold taps for the bathroom, and a tall skinny bird called Angie who cooked weird meals and read books in French and patently regarded Albie as a relic from Mick's past. Something faintly Neanderthal. Something better discarded.

At first, Albie had viewed it all as an aberration, as temporary as a cold in the head. After all, he knew Mick backwards. They'd been at school together, got pissed together, pulled birds together, fought as a team. Mick, sure, had always been the flashier of the two, preoccupied with appearances, quick on his feet, brilliant with the chat. But when the situation got especially dodgy, on the street, or in a pub, or when they got shafted on a deal, it had always been Albie who'd sorted it out, with his small, hard stare, and his talent for real violence. The bond between them had been tight as a drum. Best friends in childhood. Mates in adolescence. But everything, unaccountably, had changed.

The traffic began to move faster. Mick's garage lay in a cluster of old buildings in the shadow of the dockyard wall. Mick had bought it on Harry's advice eighteen months earlier, scenting a windfall profit if and when a London-based property company bought up the land for redevelopment. Until that moment came, he was happy to keep the place turning over: cut-price servicing, bent MOTs, retread tyres, and the kind of glass-fibre and jollop repair jobs that most garages wouldn't touch. Albie had been installed to keep an eye on it all, a job he'd resented at first, but he'd pulled the place together, and got hold of a couple of lads on the YOP scheme, and now the garage was the one element in Mick's infant business empire that actually turned a profit. Without the garage, Mick had recently admitted, they'd be struggling.

The traffic queue rounded a corner and stopped again. An Army bulldozer was backing across the road, its metal tracks scoring the black tarmac. On the pavement, two squaddies kept pedestrians back while the bulldozer stopped and the engineer at the controls shifted gear. Then it lurched forward, over the pavement, the metal scoop lowering as it approached a chest-high brick wall. The wall disintegrated in a cloud of dust and rubble, and the bulldozer paused for barely a moment before clattering forward again, and slewing hard left, disappearing behind the remains of an old warehouse.

Albie gazed after it, the dust still thick in the air, then pulled the BMW out of the traffic queue and accelerated hard down the middle of the road. Seventy yards away was a small turning on the right which led to the garage. There was a line of oil drums across the mouth of the road, and coils of barbed wire behind. Beside the drums stood a policeman. With the policeman was another squaddie. He was wearing a combat helmet, and cradled a small, squat rifle. Albie pulled the car to a halt, and lowered the electric window. The policeman bent towards the window. Albie nodded at the bulldozer, now visible again through the gap between two buildings. Another wall had fallen. More rubble. More dust.

'What's this, then?'

The policeman looked bored.

'Emergency regulations, sir. Sorry. No entry.'

'I work here.'

Albie indicated the garage, two faded blue fold-back doors in a row of industrial units. The policeman frowned for a moment, running his finger down a list of names on a clipboard. The finger stopped.

'Ah,' he said, 'Mr Rendall.'

'Curtis. Rendall owns it. I run it.'

'I'll give you a telephone number, Mr Curtis.'

'I don't want a telephone number. I want to go to work. OK?'

He engaged gear, and eased the BMW towards the line of oil drums. The policeman and the squaddie exchanged glances. The squaddie took half a step forward, bringing the tip of the gun up as he did so. The policeman bent to the window again. He scribbled down a number on a pad.

'It's 674556,' he said, without looking up.

'What is?'

'The phone number.' He tore the sheet of paper from the pad, and offered it through the window. Albie ignored it. The policeman let it flutter onto his lap. 'Ask for Mr Prior,' he said, 'and he'll tell you what to do.' Albie gazed down at the number in his lap. Then up again. Behind the bulldozer were a couple of yellow JCBs clawing at the remains of the warehouse. There were soldiers everywhere, rolls of barbed wire, piles of timber posts, a small mountain of sandbags. Albie shook his head. It looked like a film set.

'I'm not with you,' he said, 'I don't understand. What *is* all this?'

The policeman shrugged and invited the squaddie into the conversation with a jerk of his head. The squaddie bent to the window. His breath smelled of chewing gum. He had a thick Scots accent.

'GDA,' he said.

'Yer what?'

'Ground Defence Area. Priority installations. Key points. Like your dockyard here.'

'Oh.' Albie looked genuinely blank. 'So who are you defending it against?' He paused. 'Me?'

The squaddie smiled a thin, mirthless smile, revolving the gum in his mouth. Then he nodded at the number on Albie's lap.

'I'd hurry along if I were you,' he said. 'Your wee garage is next.'

*

Martin Goodman poured the last of the coffees and handed it to the Brigadier at his elbow. The little ante-room was full now, perhaps two dozen men, some in uniform, some in suits. In a couple of minutes it would be time to shepherd everyone through to the big conference room next door. There, he'd call the meeting to order, offer a few modest remarks of his own, and invite Davidson to share his insider's view of the international situation. Quite where that might lead, he didn't know, but as the meeting developed it would be his job to trade one civic interest against another in the strange, totally unreal business of putting the city onto a war footing.

Across the room stood Oliver Davidson, deep in conversation with the harbour master. The harbour master, a gruff, pink-faced man on the edge of retirement, was making a series of forceful points, chopping the air with his hands, while Davidson's eyes roamed across the room, ever watchful, ever alert. Nearer were the city's Police Chief, Nigel Quinn, and the local manager of Network South East, Alan Prosser. Quinn and Prosser's kids played football together in a tyro league side, and the two men shared the odd game of golf.

By the window, deep in conversation, were Tony Belling, the Flag Officer's ADC from Naval Home Command, Dave Jenkins, the city's Fire Chief, and Henry Bishop, the senior Education Officer. It would be the latter's job to decide if and when to close the schools, item fourteen on the agenda that Davidson had already slipped from his briefcase and left on Goodman's desk.

The Brigadier touched Goodman lightly on the arm. Goodman smiled his automatic smile.

'I'm sorry?'

'The Reading Conference,' the Brigadier said for the second time. 'I don't recall your face.'

'I'm not surprised,' Goodman said, 'I wasn't there.'

'Oh?'

'No. Eric went.' He paused and smiled again. 'I'm standing in. He's off sick just now.'

Fiona, Goodman's secretary, appeared in the open doorway at the end of the ante-room. Goodman caught her eye at once. She semaphored an urgent phone call. He acknowledged the signal with a nod, made his excuses to the Brigadier, and slipped quietly out of the room. Davidson, still listening to the harbour master, watched him go.

Down the corridor, Goodman stepped into his office and hurried across to the big desk by the window. He picked up the telephone and bent to the mouthpiece. He was slightly out of breath.

'Hello?'

For a moment, there was no reply. He could hear voices in the background, shouts. Then the sound of a tannoy. Something about Malaga and Rhodes. Finally, a voice, urgent, in his ear. He tensed at once. Suzy.

'Martin,' she began, 'I'm at the airport.' She sounded breathless and upset, either fear or anger. He closed his eyes, and tried to sound as calm as he could.

'Darling . . .' he murmured.

'Listen. Tell me, for Chrissakes, what's going on?' He frowned. The tannoy had started again, louder, in the background. All flights to Corfu had been cancelled.

'I'm sorry,' he began, 'I . . .'

'Listen. I've only got a minute or two, but I need to know.'

'Know what?'

'Martin, don't treat me like an idiot. Our planes have been requisitioned. All of them. They say they're flying troops out. Bringing families back.' She hesitated for a second. 'Why should they do that?'

Goodman passed a hand over his eyes, suddenly very tired.

'Manoeuvres,' he said, 'exercises. It happens all the time.'

'That's what they say.'

'Who's they?'

'The people in Handling. I don't believe them. And neither does anyone else.'

'And?'

'And you'll know what's really going on. I know you'll know.' She paused. 'Martin . . .?' Goodman opened his eyes. In a minute or so he'd have to walk back along the corridor, and call for attention, and start to usher people through to the Conference Room. There'd be options to explore, plans to draw up, decisions to make, limits to put on this action or that. And over it all they'd have to draw a cloak of secrecy, a blanket of denials, of white propaganda, of calm civic assurances that business was trickling along as usual, that nothing had really changed. It would all be lies, his lies, and sitting here, on a still-warm morning in late September, he realized that he'd started already, with the one person to whom he'd given himself entirely.

'Suzy . . .' he began.

There was a movement in the open doorway. He glanced across. Davidson stood there, the sunlight glinting on his rimless glasses. He smiled a thin smile and looked pointedly at his watch. Suzy began to talk again, the urgency edged with panic. She'd just come down from upstairs. The VIP suite was packed. Anyone who was anyone was going to Canada. Why? Why? Why? Goodman leaned slowly forward in his chair, emptying his voice of affection.

'Listen,' he said, 'we'll talk about it tonight. Usual time. Usual place. OK?'

He put the phone down without waiting for a reply, and stood up. Davidson was still in the doorway. Goodman looked at him a moment, then nodded at the phone and pulled a face, a gesture of helplessness.

'Mother-in-law,' he said. 'Bit of a state.'

By the time Gillespie arrived at the boat, Sean was already aboard, stowing his rods aft and unlocking the folding covers over the inboard diesel. Gillespie had shut himself in the kitchen, as soon as the film crew had started to dismantle their equipment, and phoned the boy at Sandra's. Sandra had answered the phone, ever patient, passing on Gillespie's brusque message. Gillespie had recognized Shaun's grunt of acknowledgement in the background. Eleven o'clock. Top of the tide. Back in time for tea.

With Sean organized, Gillespie had waited for the last of the crew to clear the front room. The young assistant had offered to restore the furniture the way they'd found it, but Gillespie had shown him the door with a jerk of his head, and the assistant hadn't stopped to argue. Only Annie stayed behind.

At first, he assumed she'd gone. He'd changed quickly into wellies, and a thick old sweater, and jeans. He'd retrieved a block of peeler crabs from the freezer, and a bowl of rag worms from the fridge. He had his rods, and his gutting knife, and he'd fetched the big conger gaff from the shed out back. Not because he expected to catch anything bigger than a plaice, or sea bass, but because he'd recognized instinctively the need to organize himself, to take several deep breaths and try and wash away the anger inside him, diluting it to manageable proportions, making himself safe to be with. Only then was he ready to leave.

Annie was waiting for him by the front door. He half expected something meaningless, like a token apology, but she looked as cheerful as ever, even amused.

'Off to sea again?' she enquired. 'Getting away from it all?'

Gillespie didn't bother to answer. Now, with the house his own again, it didn't seem to matter so much. If he felt anything, he felt betrayed, but that was a long conversation, and he didn't propose to offer her the satisfaction of beginning it. They looked at each other for a moment, the obvious question unvoiced. Then she smiled.

'Don't you want to know how I found out?'

'No.'

'Is it true?'

He looked at her for along time, then shook his head. Not a denial but an expression of disbelief.

'Don't you ever give up?' he said.

Her smile widened. 'No.'

There was a pause. She came very close. The old technique. The old temptation. She reached out and adjusted the neck of his sweater. She was wearing thin leather gloves that smelled faintly of Gitanes cigarettes. In spite of everything, he still loved her eyes. Huge, brown, moist. If he had any talent with a knife and a palette full of oil paints, that's where he'd begin.

'*Was* it you, Dave?' She waited a moment or two for an answer, but Gillespie said nothing. 'Not going to tell me?'

'No.'

'Will you ever tell me?'

'No.'

'Mind if I keep trying?' She kissed him softly on the cheek. 'Off the record?'

Gillespie gazed at her. There were a million ways of resolving the situation. He could throw her out. He could sit her down and list all the occasions when he'd been foolish enough to mistake her curiosity for friendship, her endless list of questions for simple, innocent conversation. He could lecture her on cheap advantage, and breach of faith. He could even phone her boss and make some kind of official complaint. Breaking and entering. Intent to rob. Instead he shrugged, and reached for the door latch.

'No,' he said, 'if it turns you on.'

Down on the foreshore, Gillespie parked the Marina and transferred his tackle and bait to the boat. Sean had by now primed the engine, and was untying the forrard strop. With Gillespie at the helm, it was his job to walk the boat carefully backwards until there was no danger of the prop fouling on the tangles of weed on the bottom. Only then would Gillespie slide aside the cover on the ignition button, thumb the diesel into life, and ease the boat towards the open water.

Sean joined him at the wheel. Pushing the boat out had raised the colour on his cheeks. He grinned at Gillespie but said nothing. Most weeks they met at least twice – once at weekends for serious fishing, and again during the week when Sean would drop by his father's house in the evening and share a take-away. The arrangement was totally informal, whim rather than habit, and pleased them both.

The last couple of years, after a rather stiff period of more orthodox fatherhood, Gillespie had begun to treat Sean like an adult, a mate, someone to laugh with, and ponder with, and share mutual enthusiasms. It sounded like a big jump from the old relationship, but it had worked at once, especially out at sea, where they divided the work and the rewards between them, each relying on the other, a genuine need and an absolute trust. Much of the contact between them had quickly become monosyllabic, choice rather than laziness, and like any close relationship, it had developed a repertoire of physical gestures: grunts, and grins, and long, slow shakes of the head to indicate a general bewilderment at the state of the world.

Recently, Gillespie had begun to wonder whether the boy shouldn't move in. He'd discussed it with Sandra, who had no objection, but when he broached the subject to Sean, late one evening after a brilliant day's fishing and a particularly fiery Chicken Vindaloo, the boy had shaken his head at once, and said that things were just great the way they were.

At the time, his reaction had struck Gillespie as surprisingly emphatic, and he'd been tempted to enquire why. But after a day or two's reflection he'd decided that the boy probably felt a duty to stay with his mother, that she deserved a little respect and affection from at least one male member of the family, and that therefore he had no right to leave home before he had to. Whether or not this interpretation squared with the truth was anybody's guess, but it suited Gillespie to believe it, and if he was really honest with himself, he realized that he, too, preferred it that way. His suggestion that Sean might move in had, after all, been ill-judged, a product of a glorious day at sea, and too many cans of Guinness. He felt, deep down, safer alone.

At the harbour entrance, where the shingle spit curled shorewards and the ebbing tide tugged at the lines of mooring buoys, Gillespie throttled back and tucked the boat behind a big motor cruiser, outbound from the anchorage. The cruiser was broad in the beam, about forty foot overall, and lay low in the water. On deck, aft, two men were lashing down a collection of tin trunks. One of them was wearing flannels and a blazer and what looked like lace-up brogues. From the cabin, came the chatter of women's voices, upmarket and shrill. Evidently there was also a dog aboard.

Gillespie eyed the cruiser for a while, but it was Sean who put the obvious conclusion into words.

'They're off,' he said. 'Doing a runner.'

'Think so?'

'Yeah. Look at the way that bloke's dressed. Never been to sea in his life.'

Gillespie nodded. The man in the blazer was studying a knot with intense concentration. Finally, he unpicked it, threw both ends down on the deck, and disappeared briefly inside. When he stepped back into the sunshine he was carrying a tumbler of something tawny with ice cubes floating in it. He caught sight of Gillespie and Sean, puttering slowly along in the cruiser's wake. He raised the glass in mock salute, acknowledging Gillespie's answering wave with a shouted toast. Sean frowned.

'What did he say?'

'Haven't a clue.'

Gillespie looked sideways at Sean, expecting a grin, but the boy's face was quite expressionless. He was still staring at the motor cruiser, and at the man with the now half-empty glass. Gillespie throttled back a notch or two, letting the diesel idle while the first of the ebb tide caught the boat and swung the bow seawards, towards the harbour mouth.

'You up to date with all this? Everything that's going on?'

Sean nodded. 'I watch telly,' he said, 'if that's what you mean.'

'Make sense to you at all?'

'No.'

'Me neither.' He hesitated. The current was stronger now, urging the boat towards the open sea. 'You worried?' The boy nodded again.

'Yes,' he said simply, 'I am.'

Albie Curtis double parked the BMW in the cul-de-sac outside Mick Rendall's house, walked across the newly swept cobbles, and rang the front door bell. When no one answered, he rang again. Finally, he heard footsteps inside, and the scrape of the safety chain. The door opened and Mick Rendall appeared. He was wearing a new pair of scarlet track suit bottoms and a Nike singlet. His face was pink with exertion, and his chest was heaving. There were dark blotches of sweat on the singlet. He opened the door wide, and motioned Albie inside, mopping his face with a towel.

Albie walked through the hall, and stepped into the lounge. The lounge was big, running the full depth of the house. The walls were pale green, hung with full-size Athena prints. Oriental rugs dotted the polished wooden floor. One end of the room was dominated by a rack of hi-fi equipment and two Quad speakers. The other end housed a full-length sofa in buttoned black leather.

On the floor, in front of the marble fireplace, was a rowing machine. Beside the rowing machine was an open carton of orange juice and a paperback about Commando exercises. Albie glanced at the paperback but made no comment. Mick Rendall stepped into the room behind him. His breathing had slowed, but the sweat marks were spreading over the swell of his small pot belly. Albie nodded at the carton of juice.

'You're supposed to drink the stuff afterwards, not before.'

'Very funny.'

'You'll spew otherwise.'

'Thanks.'

'Pleasure.'

Mick picked up the carton and began to gulp down the contents. Albie watched him, remembering his other flirtations with physical exercise. A couple of days' jogging when marathons became fashionable. Sunday football on the Common when the local team hit the First Division. And now this: two hundred quid's worth of chrome tubing and fancy suede handles. It was a joke.

'Where's Angie?' he said.

'She's gone.'

'Gone?'

'Yeah.'

'You mean *gone*?'

'Yeah.'

'Oh.' Albie paused. 'Why's that, then?'

Mick shrugged, affecting indifference.

'I dunno,' he said. 'Some arsehole.'

Albie scowled, genuine concern.

'You want me to find him . . .?' He paused, sliding the shaped plastic seat on the rowing machine backwards and forwards with his foot. 'Or do you want to do it yourself?'

Mick shrugged again, towelled the last of the moisture from his face, and walked through to the kitchen, leaving the question unanswered. Albie followed him. The kitchen was German, hi-tech, and very expensive. Another of Harry's little loans. He stood in the doorway, hands on hips, no messing.

'Listen, mate . . .' he began.

Mick filled the kettle and shook his head.

'No,' he said, 'leave it. She's not worth the bother.'

He put the kettle on the ceramic hob and pressed a button. Then he leaned back against the dishwater. He looked shattered.

'You get the books?'

'What?'

'The books, Albie. The stuff for Harry.'

Albie frowned a moment, then remembered the conversation on the car phone.

'No,' he said, 'I didn't.'

'You didn't?'

'No. I couldn't.'

'Why not?'

'They've closed the garage. Taken it over.'

Mick stared at him.

'I'm not with you,' he said. 'You mean it's not open? Eleven o'clock in the morning?'

'No. And by lunchtime it might not be there at all. So they say.'

Mick blinked. He pulled at a tiny gold ear-ring, his latest affectation. He seemed to be having trouble with the shorter words.

'Who's they?' he said.

Albie gazed at him. For the second time that morning, he was lost for an answer.

'I dunno . . .' he said at last. 'That's the problem.'

Martin Goodman opened the Conference at the Civic Centre at six minutes past eleven. He sat at the head of the long table, the blotter neatly squared in front of him, the long rows of faces receding towards the far end of the room.

He prefaced his remarks by expressing regret that Eric was, in a hopefully inexact phrase, *hors de combat*. He knew that the ex-Chief Executive had many friends around the table, and he was sure that they all wished him well.

There was a murmur of agreement. Several of the older heads nodded more emphatically than was strictly necessary. Eric, by and large, had made allies of these men, with his deft political touches, and his earthiness, and his generosity with the decanter of malt whisky that he kept on the filing cabinet in his office. They'd liked him because he was the right age, and the right generation. They inhabited a world of shared assumptions and common goals. They'd spent most of their professional lives determined not to rock the civic boat, and if there was any reservation about Martin, the new face at the head of the table, then it was because he was young, untested, and was rumoured to be rather more ruthless in the pursuit of efficiency than might have been strictly necessary.

Goodman, who was aware of this, ended his opening remarks by acknowledging the weight of responsibility that had so suddenly descended upon him. For the time being, he said, he'd be known as Controller-Designate. After the passage of the appropriate legislation, his powers, and his obligations, would be immense, but without their patience, and support, he – and the city – would be utterly helpless. There were more nods around the table, more murmurs of approval, but Goodman sensed that the consent, this time, was conditional. His lieutenants were reserving judgement. He had a great deal to prove.

Davidson was next. Unlike Goodman, he stood up, easing his chair back from the table, and letting a silence descend on the room before clearing his throat and fixing his gaze on a spot midway down the table.

Speaking without notes, he offered a brief summary of the international situation. As everybody knew, the crisis in Europe had already ripened weeks before the dramatic appearance of the crippled Trident submarine in the Barents Sea. The real source of it all had been the upheavals in Moscow back in the winter, after Gorbachev's second coronary. Even now, the political picture was still fogged with uncertainties, but it was clear that the hardliners were back in charge, with a mandate of their own to crush nationalist movements at the edges of the Empire, and restore the kind of monolithic Communism that Gorbachev had been at such pains to dismantle.

In places like Georgia and Armenia, remote from Western Europe, and no threat to NATO planners, the more brutal of the counter-insurgency sweeps had gone largely unreported. But up in the Baltic republics, and in Poland, the Western media had taken a lively interest in the weeks of rioting in Riga and Tallin, the tanks rolling through the streets of Warsaw, and the huge security operation in Gdansk that followed the mysterious disappearance of Lech Walesa.

There'd been rumours of mass deportations to a new Gulag, and reports of firing squads at work in the more remote areas of Eastern Poland, and every morning there were yet more interviews with the boatloads of Lithuanian refugees appearing at Swedish ports along the Gulf of Bothnia.

No one in the West was quite sure whether Poland merited yet another world war, but the recent election of a new Government, a novel mix of Green politicians and had complicated the situation still further. The n. Oslo were, in Davidson's phrase, babes in the wood, . openly welcomed the top-level Soviet delegation that was st.. locked in bilateral discussions. Quite where these talks would lead was still a mystery, but the courtship was so abrupt, and so evidently promising, that it had shaken the Western Alliance to its foundations. Indeed, said Davidson, there were certain elements on the Scandinavian Desk in the Foreign Office that were already braced for a formal declaration of non-alignment that would take Norway out of NATO, and thus enable the Soviets to turn the Northern Flank.

This possibility was menacing enough in itself, but it compounded a situation that had been developing in Central Europe since the early summer. Three months back, intelligence intercepts and satellite reconnaissance had confirmed that the Russians were calling a halt to their programme for dismantling Intermediate Nuclear Forces. Indeed, in some areas – in flagrant breach of the Geneva Accords – they'd actually begun to deploy the latest Gorki III rockets, a weapons system that Gorbachev had denied even developing. In secret top-level exchanges, the Soviets had offered various informal assurances that these deployments were purely temporary, part of the crack-down against the dissident republics, but as the data continued to pour in from Fort Meade and GCHQ, it became obvious that the Soviets were adopting an offensive posture along the length of the Central Front. Troops, armour, mobile formations, and dense screens of anti-aircraft assets echeloned in depth all the way back to the Soviet border, a naked display of force that could never be justified by the suppression of internal rebellion.

Thus, three weeks ago, the American decision to reinforce Europe, stiffening the resolve of an increasingly neutralist Bonn. And thus this morning's announcement from Downing Street that the last of the UK's Territorial Reserve would be mobilized and away by the weekend. The current situation, Davidson concluded regretfully, had all the appearances of a time warp. Post-Gorbachev, it should never have happened. Yet here we all were. Back in the coldest of wars. Praying for some end to the terrible momentum of events.

At this point, Davidson paused and reached for a glass of water. His exposition had been masterly. He'd led them through the chronology stage by stage, calm, authoritative, the narrative carefully sauced with confidential detail, a name here, a document there. He'd paid them the compliment of trusting them, of opening the doors of Central Government and the intelligence community, and offering them a passing glimpse of what life was really like inside. With his low-key delivery and careful Whitehall prose, he'd asked for – and earned – their total attention. In the silence that followed his opening address, a voice spoke up from the end of the table. It was Nigel Quinn, the city's leading policeman, a man who had the reputation for drawing the essence out of any situation. Soon, Goodman would ask him for an assessment of the Law and Order implications of the task before them, but first Quinn wanted to be quite certain of his bearings. Strange country. Difficult terrain.

'Mr Davidson,' he began. Davidson acknowledged him with a smile. 'Be frank. Where are we now?'

'Today?'

'Yes.'

'This morning?'

'Yes.'

Davidson nodded, and paused for a moment, as if savouring the last sweet in the packet.

'It's difficult to be sure . . . but from my end of the telescope I'm afraid it looks very unpleasant.' He paused again, searching for some kind of reference that everyone around the table would understand. Finally he found it, in the shape of the last Civil Defence exercise that they'd all been obliged to attend, three days in a Command Bunker in Reading, tussling with a scenario that led inexorably towards nuclear war. The Exercise had been code-named 'Hard Rock'. Davidson gazed round, unblinking. 'In "Hard Rock" terms, gentlemen, I suspect we're at Zero minus three. And Zero, for those with perfect recall, was when the Americans went nuclear.'

Mick and Albie were twenty minutes late for their meeting with Harry Cartwright. Cartwright's offices were in the oldest part of the city, a stone's throw from the Camber Dock, and he'd only taken the place over at the turn of the year. It was an old Georgian building, sympathetically converted, and Cartwright had written off the cost against the cachet his new address gave an already thriving business.

Now he sat behind a large, antique desk, piled high with papers and correspondence. He was a small man, dapper, punctilious, with a thin pencil moustache. He had a thin, weak voice, and pale green eyes, and he had built an entire career on people's readiness to underestimate him.

He glanced up as Mick and Albie stepped into the room. Cartwright waved them both into chairs in front of the desk, and returned to the file that lay open on his desk. Endless columns of figures, most of them in red.

Mick settled into the chair nearest the desk, and pulled at the knife-edge creases in his new Jaeger trousers. He told himself he felt much better after the session on the rowing machine. His head was clear, Albie had managed to remember most of the key figures he needed from the books in the garage, and in any case he found it difficult to believe that little Harry Cartwright, with his size six lace-ups, and his damp, flabby handshake, would pull any real strokes. Sure, they'd bombed on the mail order business. Maybe the world wasn't quite ready for his brand of provocative night attire. And sure, the R&B club had been unlucky with its choice of bar manager. But criminal records were two a penny these days, and in his heart of hearts he still couldn't believe that the personable young Geordie had stitched him up to *that* extent. No, Harry's abrupt phone call had been about something else. A new opportunity. A fresh investment. Some kind of joint venture that would take him even further from the shadow of the council tower blocks he'd once called home. He smiled across at Albie and sprawled a little deeper into the buttoned Dralon. Albie ignored him, staring out of the window without a flicker of interest.

Cartwright glanced up. He rarely bothered with formalities.

'These are terrible figures,' he said. 'You have outflows of eight thousand a month. That's a median figure over the last two quarters. This last month it's twelve and a half. Your VAT is five months late on the mail order business. And you haven't even started to make returns on the club.'

Mick shrugged. 'That's down to you, Harry. You're the accountant.'

'I need a little co-operation, my friend. All I get are bills.' He paused, not bothering to look down. Evidently he knew the figures by heart. 'You owe the Revenue nine and a half thousand. You owe your suppliers half as much again. The firm that fitted out the club ring me daily. I tell them you're owed.' He paused. 'Am I lying?'

'Yeah,' Mick said automatically. 'Yeah . . . I am.'

'How much are you owed?'

'Thousands.'

'How many thousands?'

Mick sniffed and looked away, the gesture of a gentleman unprepared to discuss specific figures. Cartwright composed his fingertips together, unimpressed.

'Technically, you're bankrupt,' he said. 'In law, I should order you to stop trading.'

For the first time, Mick frowned. He knew things were bad, but bankruptcy was something new.

'Bankrupt?' he said blankly.

'Yes.'

'You kidding?'

'No.'

Mick glanced across at the figures on the desk. Upside down, they made no sense, simply a list of jottings. He looked up again. Cartwright was studying him closely. To his intense irritation, he began to feel uncomfortable. He shrugged again, affecting indifference, but his tone betrayed him, rising a semitone as he struggled with the implications of Cartwright's cold analysis.

'What about the garage, though?' he said. 'What about that?'

'Ah . . .' Cartwright looked thoughtful. 'The garage.'

'Yeah, the garage.' Mick looked across at Albie. Albie was rolling a cigarette. 'Tell him, Albie, tell him about the garage.'

Albie looked up, as if surprised by the question. He licked the edge of the Rizla paper, and sealed the cigarette with the thumbs of both hands.

'Tell him what?' he said at last.

'Tell him how well we're doing. Tell him about the bomb we made last month.'

'Ah . . . last month.' Albie nodded. 'Yeah . . . we did OK.'

'OK? OK?' Mick uncrossed his legs, and pulled himself upright in the chair. 'OK?' he said for the third time. 'You call five grand a week OK?'

Mick paused, while Albie produced a Zippo lighter from the pocket of his bomber jacket and lit the cigarette. Cartwright, a dedicated non-smoker, blew his nose.

'I understand your garage has been requisitioned,' he said at last, returning the handkerchief to his pocket. 'That could make things a little difficult.'

Nonplussed for a moment, Mick said nothing. He'd hoped to keep the news from Harry until the thing could be sorted. He hadn't a clue how he'd found out so soon.

'Yeah . . . well . . .' he said, 'gotta be illegal, hasn't it? Gotta be. You can't just close things down like that. It's against the law. Gotta be . . .' Cartwright looked at him.

'We're going to war, my friend,' he said, 'the law's on their side. They're defending the realm. I'm afraid it's a sign of the times.' He paused, the voice softer, even sympathetic. 'It's gone, Michael. As a commercial venture with any relevance to this,' he tapped the file on the desk, 'it's no longer a realistic proposition.'

Mick frowned again, refusing to accept the logic of what Cartwright was saying.

'But how can they do that?' he said. 'Who do we fix? Who does Albie talk to?' He glanced across at Albie for support. Albie was lost in a cloud of shag tobacco. He looked back at Cartwright. 'Give us a couple of hours,' he said. 'Give us until tonight.'

Cartwright reached forward and slowly closed the file. The action swept aside Mick's protests and moved the discussion on towards an inevitable conclusion. The initiative now lay entirely with Cartwright, and Mick knew it. Cartwright sat back in the big chair. He looked, if anything, reflective.

'Friends of mine had faith in you, Michael,' he began. 'You came highly recommended, which is why I took you on. You were said to be quick on your feet. Sharp. Good eye for the right openings. Which is why my friends trusted you with so much money.' He smiled, the smallest adjustment to the thin, tight line of his mouth. 'You also had a reputation as a fighter, someone who didn't recognize failure, someone who could turn any corner.' 'The smile widened, intimate, encouraging. 'Now's the time, Michael, now's the time . . .'

'How much time have I got?'

'Forty-eight hours.' He shrugged apologetically. 'People want to realize their assets. Understandably so.'

Mick nodded. 'And what happens if . . .?'

Cartwright got up, sparing him the rest of the sentence.

'My friends will send in the bailiffs.'

'In where?'

Cartwright paused a moment, then glanced down and re-opened the file. The address he wanted was on the head of the page.

'16 George Street.' He looked up, the smile wider than ever. 'Or have you moved from there?'

Joanna Goodman was out in the garden, hanging the last of the morning's washing on the rotary dryer, when she heard the opening jingle of the hourly radio news through the open kitchen window. She normally made a conscious effort to avoid news broadcasts of any kind, weary of a world where planes were always crashing, icecaps melting, and half the nation's kids ending up in cardboard boxes under Waterloo Bridge. But over the last day or two, she'd found it impossible to ignore the growing drumbeat of events in Europe. She was no historian, but she knew enough about the last war, her parents' war, to recognize the way things were going. Regardless of the insanity of it all, regardless of the certain prospect of death, or disfigurement, and huge dollops of human misery, the thing just seemed to happen all the same. Only this time, it would be far, far worse.

The first item offered an update on the Americans' wretched submarine. Other warships were heading north. The Russians were already in the area. The wind and the weather were pushing the submarine towards Soviet territorial waters. Washington had warned Moscow that any interference would be met 'in kind'. Flashpoint was predicted for the day after tomorrow. She shook her head at the neatness of it all. The perfect Hollywood plot, scored for oblivion and full orchestra.

Going inside, she began to open a tin of baby-food. Lamb dinner with cauliflower. Charlie spotted it at once, and began to reverse the spoon, careful, deliberate movements of his tiny hands, a trick learned barely days before. She eased back the flap of the tin, and reached for a saucepan. The news-reader began an item about the Pope who, predictably enough, was praying for peace. Thousands had packed St Peter's Square while diplomatic representatives from many nations had joined the congregation inside. The American Ambassador, Scott Harrimann, had evidently been notable by his absence, and afterwards someone had released one hundred white doves. Stupid, thought Joanna, spooning the pale yellow mush into the saucepan. Stupid, stupid, stupid.

The news-reader ground on. Advice from Canberra for Australian nationals in the Northern Hemisphere to return home. Extra flights from Heathrow, courtesy Qantas. An undertaking from the IRA to observe an unofficial ceasefire for the duration of something they rather quaintly called 'the current troubles'.

Charlie's lunch began to bubble on the stove. She stirred it slowly with a wooden spoon, thinking yet again of the quiet, softly-spoken man from London who'd arrived so unexpectedly. The man who'd knocked at her front door, and showed her a Home Office pass, and enquired apologetically about her husband. The man who'd sat only feet away, there in the lounge, nursing a lukewarm cup of coffee, and filling in the missing clues from last week's *Sunday Times*. Even after Martin had arrived, as shattered as ever, she was no closer to knowing who the man was, or why he'd come calling so early. Except that he was Government, and mysterious, and important enough for Martin to be unusually deferential.

She closed her eyes, oblivious for a moment to the torrent of news from the radio. Martin had begun to worry her. Recently he'd become so visibly detached, so obviously in a world of his own, that she'd started to wonder about his sanity. He seemed incapable of sustaining the simplest conversation, of offering her anything but the most cursory of answers. His bedtime stories for the children, the precious hinge around which their days closed, had become so brief as to be pointless. He'd also started drinking heavily, big measures of gin topped with a spoonful of tonic, and she'd yesterday found an empty bottle of Panadol in the swingbin in the bathroom. The tablets had been extra strength, and she was quite certain he'd emptied the entire bottle in less than a month.

At first, she'd thought of confronting him, of asking what the matter was, of trying, somehow, to help, but whenever she'd managed to steer the conversation in the right direction, he'd spot what was coming, and ease himself off the sofa, and head for the drinks cabinet for a refill, or towards the telephone for yet another call that couldn't possibly wait.

Their sex life, too, had begun to suffer. It had never rung the loudest of bells, but they'd been fond together, and she enjoyed the feeling of his body over hers, his smell, and the way he collapsed so completely when it was all over. It made him somehow young again, and helpless, a near-adolescent, briefly needful, briefly hers. Lately, though, their lovemaking had virtually stopped, a consequence, she vaguely assumed, of the gin.

The man on the radio was at last bringing the bulletin to a close. A spokesman for the motoring organizations was warning about the possibility of fuel shortages. Drivers planning long journeys should take appropriate precautions. Joanna hesitated. She stopped stirring the babyfood for a moment and gazed at Charlie, wondering whether the crisis justified taking the children away somewhere, to her mother's perhaps, in Wales, or to the country. Charlie beamed back and lifted the spoon. She was lucky. He loved his food. She reached for his bib and tied it carefully round his neck. She emptied the food into a bowl and tested the first spoonful with her tongue. Then she began to spoon it gently into his mouth. She began to sing at him, very low, very soft, the way she used to when he was the tiniest of babies. Charlie gazed up at her, and reached out, fascinated by the noise. She fed him more of the lumpy yellow mush, and he swallowed it slowly, quietened by her singing. She ran out of words, and began to make them up, nonsense phrases, yummy and mummy and tummy . . . teddy and steady and ready . . . love and above and dove. The last phrase made her think briefly of the Pope, and the crowds in the Vatican square, and the image of the white birds fluttering upwards. And then she thought again about Martin, and the sight of him walking across the gravel towards the strange man's car, and the ever-courteous wave of farewell as they drove away towards the road. Her voice faltered and died, and the child gazed up at her, his mouth half open, wondering at the tears pouring down her cheeks.

Later, composed again, she phoned her mother in Wales. Her mother assured her that the caravan was ready and available. They'd all be welcome, any time.

Annie McPhee pulled her borrowed Escort into the car park of Wessex TV and killed the engine. The studio was barely a year old, a low, squat two-storey building, unpainted ribbed aluminium cladding on a simple steel frame, one of a handful of off-the-shelf designs generated by the recent explosion in regional broadcasting. The builders had taken a record four months to complete the structure, and the architect had assured the Board that his design could easily be converted into a supermarket, or a carpet warehouse, with the minimum of effort. In the ruthless new world of multi-channel broadcasting, agreed the Company Director of Finance, you couldn't be too careful.

Annie retrieved her satchel from the car boot and walked across the car park towards Reception. She'd been working at Wessex TV for a month now, using the studio as a production base while she drew up preliminary plans for her documentary series. She'd taken the idea to Wessex at the turn of the year, attracted by the reputation of their Programme Controller, Duggie Bullock.

Bullock was a big, bluff, plain-speaking Yorkshireman, an ex-producer of real class with a fine record for carefully crafted, hard-hitting topical documentaries, and an instinctive talent for making what he termed 'mischief'. One of the many casualties of the break-up of the ITV system, he'd come south in search of autonomy and some kind of programme base. Wessex TV, with its three-counties transmission area and its hundred or so employees was no bigger than any of the other new regional TV outfits. But certain members of the Board were keen to dilute the usual schlock with a stylish news operation and the occasional showpiece series. Bullock had the experience to provide both. His brief had therefore been simple: profits and profile. The former had been axiomatic. Wessex TV was no charity. But the latter was equally important. The Company wanted to earn respect as programme makers, and the Chairman had made it clear from the outset that he was keen to make a splash in the world of international broadcasting. There were local businessmen on the Board, he said with a twinkle, who quite fancied the idea of a trip to Cannes, or New York, or any of the countless other festivals which dotted the broadcasting calendar, and he was quite certain that Bullock would come up with the appropriate ideas. Providing the subject was right, and the sums made reasonable sense, the Board would back him all the way.

Annie McPhee, with her push, and her grin, and her impressive track record, had therefore made her pitch at exactly the right time. She'd left the BBC after a particularly vicious row with her Executive Producer, wisely taking with her a handful of programme files. Two of the latter had dealt with various aspects of the Falklands War, and she'd often asked herself why no one had yet produced the definitive series about that extraordinary episode. There'd been plenty of in-depth documentaries, sure, and a couple had been truly excellent. But there was still room, she was certain, for something larger, something truly comprehensive, something which would put the whole giddy episode under pitiless review, and reveal it for what she considered it was: a blatant exercise in self-interest by the current ruling class, fogged by jingoism, cloaked in all kinds of phoney exhortations about freedom, and democracy, and the inalienable rights of a handful of kelpers. As such, the project fitted neatly into Annie's preconceptions about post-imperialism, and the covert workings of the British Establishment. From the start she'd been keen to construct a series that would open the public eye to the realities of State power.

Her initial meeting with Bullock had gone well. She'd liked the man on sight. He was solid, and gruff, and witty, and difficult to bullshit. He was familiar with her work, and knew at once what she was after. The idea made perfect sense for Wessex TV, home of the Task Force, and he anticipated no problems underwriting the production budget with pre-sales abroad. But he warned her from the start that his acceptance of the idea would come with strings. She'd have to be careful with the editorial line. She'd have to sustain and develop her thesis with new and carefully researched material – interviews, incidents from people on the ground, people who'd been out there at the sharp end. He wasn't interested in disappointed politicians with axes to grind, or acres of young widows with a couple of fatherless kids. He wanted to be shocked, yes, and angered too. But there were to be no short cuts.

After that first meeting, Annie had withdrawn to London for a couple of days, sobered by the exchange. She didn't argue for a moment with what Bullock wanted – it simply confirmed all the good things she'd heard about him – but she was by now too experienced to underestimate the size of the mountain she had to climb. The Falklands had begun and ended as a media war. The raw material at her disposal had been under intense scrutiny from the very beginning. Could she *really* find enough new gems to sustain a series?

At first, she'd thought no. Then Bullock had phoned up and offered her a modest development budget, enough for her to trawl around for a month or so, following up old contacts, probing key bits of evidence and witnesses, and trying to assess whether, in the end, she could deliver what Bullock wanted.

The first month had gone badly. Admirals gave her fifteen minutes between meetings and refused to add to the record. A left-wing radio journalist talked darkly about 'incidents' during the latter half of the campaign, but shook his head when asked to elaborate. Tory politicians lectured her about national self-respect, and about a chain of events they'd already distorted beyond belief. And a young diplomat from the Foreign Office's South American Department declined to comment on wilder rumours about missing briefing papers, bungled analyses, and disregarded intelligence intercepts.

Then, after five weeks' work, came her first real lead, an ex-Marine in Plymouth who'd abandoned the Service, and was driving a taxi for a living. She'd found him through a mutual friend, and she'd taken him to lunch in a pub near the Millbay Docks. He was a sensitive, embittered young man, old beyond his years, still scarred by what he'd seen, by what he'd been part of. Some of his stories she'd frankly disbelieved, but time and again the same name cropped up. Someone they'd all respected. Someone who'd been in the very thick of it. The man who'd copped the roughest deal of all. Gillespie.

Annie pushed in through the double glass doors at the front of the studios and entered the newsroom. The newsroom occupied most of the front of the building, a wide, sunny, open-plan space jigsawed with desks. Here there was room for the secretaries, and copy girls, and half a dozen on-screen journalists who wrote and edited their own material, tapping out their scripts onto the linked computer screens that fed directly into Duggie Bullock's office at the far end of the room. In an outfit as lean as Wessex TV, Bullock doubled as Head of News and Current Affairs, a post which gave him hands-on control of the nightly news magazine, and satisfied his appetite for sharp-end involvement. As Annie knocked on his door, he was studying from a ratings report, a list of figures compiled weekly which told him how many viewers he'd pulled, and what kind of disposable income they represented. The South was a wealthy area, and judging by the smile on his face, the latest figures were evidently excellent.

Bullock glanced up from the report and motioned Annie into the office. Over the last few weeks they'd established a comfortable working rapport – mutual respect with slightly fatherly overtones – and Bullock enjoyed the whiff of radical London that always accompanied Annie's little visits.

'How's things?' he asked, pushing the ratings report to one side and waving her into a chair. Anne pulled a face.

'Terrible,' she said.

'Oh?'

'Gillespie didn't deliver.' She corrected herself. 'Wouldn't deliver.'

'Why not?'

'I'm not quite sure. I think he's a bit shy.'

'Shy.' He savoured the word for a moment or two, turning it, inevitably, into a question. '*Shy?*'

'Yes. When it came to it, he backed off.'

'That surprise you?'

He looked at her, direct, appraising. She realized he'd guessed the answer before he'd even phrased the question. There was no point trying to flannel the man. He'd been there before.

'No,' she said, 'he blamed it on the situation . . . the crisis . . . but no, I'm not surprised.'

Bullock nodded, and turned away from her, gazing out of the window. He appeared to be totally unconcerned. Indeed, she sensed he'd lost interest in the subject altogether.

'You were down there this morning,' he said after a while, 'down in the city.'

'Yes,' she said, 'of course.'

'How was it?'

She looked blank.

'OK,' she said, 'same as usual.'

'Any sign of . . .' he shrugged, '. . . atmosphere? Tension?'

'Not that I saw.'

'Queues for food?'

'No.'

'See anything of the demo?'

'Demo?'

'Families against the Bomb. Mid morning. War Memorial.' He paused. 'Broken up by our NF friends.'

'Really?'

'Yes.' He fingered the portable keyboard on the small metal trolley beside his desk. Lines of green copy appeared on the screen. He read out the details. 'Four men in hospital. Two of them detained.' He smiled. 'Both Poly lecturers.'

'Arrests?'

'None.' He keyed in more copy, shifting his body slightly in the chair so that Annie could look over this shoulder at the screen. She scanned the lines of type. Police appealing for special constables. Hospital administrators cancelling all non-urgent operations. Supermarket limits on the purchase of certain foods. Rumours of petrol rationing. He glanced over his shoulder at her.

'Interested?' he said.

Annie frowned.

'I'm not with you.'

'No?' He paused, then cleared the screen of copy with a single stab of his middle finger. His chair slowly revolved towards her. He looked thoughtful.

'I'm still game for the Falklands,' he said after a moment or two, 'and I go along with most of your thesis.' He paused. 'There's only one problem.'

'What's that?'

'I think we might have the wrong war.' He nodded back towards the now-empty screen. 'Down the road is one of the biggest cities in the south. Things look grim. It's an obvious target. In a day or so, if things get worse, anyone with any sense is going to be packing their bags. That's maybe a hundred and fifty thousand people. With nowhere to go.' He smiled at her. 'So what are our Masters going to do about it?' He turned towards the screen again. 'With me now?'

Mick and Albie left Harry Cartwright's office at a quarter to twelve. After confirming the forty-eight hour deadline for the repayment of Mick's principal debts, Cartwright had softened the blow a little. He'd accompanied them both to the door of his office, where his secretary stood waiting to show them out of the building. They'd all paused a moment, Mick subdued, Albie impassive, Cartwright wholly in charge. He'd reached up and patted Mick on the shoulder.

'A new scheme, Michael,' he'd said, 'a new idea. But something with a little substance to it. Eh, my friend?'

Now, sitting outside in the BMW, Mick permitted himself a sigh of relief. His debts were huge. It could have been much worse. Something would come up. Bound to. Albie pulled the big car out into the stream of traffic heading in towards the city centre and glanced across.

'Where to?' he said.

Mick glanced at his watch.

'The Ensign,' he said, naming a pub by the waterside. 'We need a drink.'

'What about the garage?'

'Stuff the garage.'

Albie looked across at him.

'The Ensign is the other way,' he said.

'I know.'

Albie shrugged and pulled the car into a tight U-turn, leaving a thin film of rubber on the newly-laid tarmac. At the end of the road, he braked sharply and turned left, into a garage. Mick glanced across at the fuel gauge. It was nearly empty. He leaned back and adjusted the recline on the seat, enjoying the smell and the assurance of the firm black leather. For some reason, he felt better already. Maybe the session on the rowing machine. Maybe the scene they'd just been through, sitting in with Harry, and getting his bollocks chewed off, and walking right out of it all, intact. A young attendant walked across to the car. Albie lowered the electric window and nodded at the four star pump.

'Fill her up,' he said.

The attendant hesitated a moment, and glanced over his shoulder. An older man in a suit was watching him from behind the cash desk. The attendant looked at Albie again.

'Sorry, chief . . .' he began.

Albie frowned.

'Yer what?'

The attendant smiled uneasily. 'I said I'm sorry. Five quid's worth. That's all you're allowed.'

Albie looked at him. 'I said fill it up,' he repeated. 'All right?'

'I can't.'

Albie reached for the door handle and began to get out. Mick leaned across, restraining him. He knew the youth from way back.

'What's the matter, son?' he said. 'My credit run out?'

The youth, who was edging uneasily backwards, looked relieved.

'No,' he said, 'it's the same for everyone. Five quid's all we're allowed to sell.'

'Who says?'

'The Guvnor.' He jerked his thumb in the direction of the office. 'New rule.'

'Until when?'

'Tomorrow. Or the next day.'

'And what happens then?'

The youth began to reach down and unscrew the filler cap.

'We close down,' he said. 'Because there's no more fuel to be had.' He looked up again, and shrugged. 'Same all round.'

It was nearly midday at the Conference Room at the Civic Centre before Davidson dropped his bombshell. He'd been talking in some detail about the relationship between Central Government and the Regions. He'd confirmed that authority would shortly be devolved to Regional Commissioners, and through them to

Regional Sub-Commissioners. He'd pointed out the precise geographical limits to Martin Goodman's authority as Controller, responsible to one of the Regional Sub-Commissioners. But it was only in response to another question from Nigel Quinn that he got to the real meat of the issue. It was a moment that everyone in the room would remember for a very long time, and in a sense, Goodman realized, it explained exactly why Davidson had come south in the first place.

Nigel Quinn's question was about the ESRs. ESRs were Essential Service Routes, designated lengths of trunk road and motorway which would be closed for periods of time and reserved for exclusively military use. These roads criss-crossed the country, north-south, east-west, and an important part of the network lay on the south coast, providing safe passage for personnel and military supplies to the Channel ports. One of the most vital ESRs connected the city to the nuclear weapons dumps in Wiltshire, and Nigel Quinn wanted to know how often the city's major link to the mainland would be closed. There were only three roads off the island, he reminded Davidson, and the traffic implications were not inconsiderable. The Navy's request for a two-hour closure at midday had already caused chaos.

Davidson accepted the point with a smile. He regretted that he lacked detailed information about the Navy's demands on the ESRs but he was sure that Tony Belling, the Flag Officer's ADC, might be able to help. He understood that the Navy had in fact been ferrying in nuclear depth charges for days, using hired trucks from commercial companies, but once a State of Emergency had been formally declared, Davidson felt sure that the Navy would need to organize more orthodox convoys, which would require regular closure of the motorway. Belling, to Davidson's right, nodded agreement and began to get to his feet, but Davidson put a restraining hand on his shoulder, and smiled apologetically, and said that he had one more matter to address.

The Government, he said, had been concerned for some time with the difficult issue of population movement. Under certain circumstances, the planners felt that the principal danger to law and order would be the massive outflows of people from major centres of population. Alarmed by the prospect of a real war, families living in, say, London, or Birmingham, would understandably feel the urge to get away. To the west, perhaps, or to the countryside.

Now the consequences of such an exodus would be deeply disruptive, and the Government would therefore be doing everything it could to persuade the population to stay at home. Special TV programmes had already been recorded pointing out the difficulties facing families on the run. Sympathetic newspapers had been primed to run feature articles about food shortages, and fuel rationing, and the likelihood of sixty-mile traffic queues. There'd be further appeals on local and national radio for listeners to stay at home, keeping a roof over their heads and a neighbourly eye on others less well able to fend for themselves. All these measures would help, but the exodus was still bound to happen and the Government accepted that, in the end, there was little else they could do about it.

He paused here and looked around. There were, he said, exceptions to this rule, a handful of key cities where accidents of geography and the requirements of the military dictated a rather harsher line.

Davidson hesitated again, and took a mouthful of water. Then he looked up.

'Certain cities, to be frank, are easier to isolate than others,' he said. 'Yours, gentlemen, happens to be an island. And it happens also to house the country's biggest naval port.' He smiled. 'It's no secret that there are sensitive military installations on the mainland, and certain other assets that we need to keep from . . . ah . . . unnecessary contamination.' He hesitated again. 'There are nearly a hundred and fifty thousand people in this city, and we feel that the national interest will best be served by . . . ah . . . everybody staying put.'

There was total silence. Then a voice from the far end of the room. The obvious question. The thought in everybody's mind.

'You mean seal the city off?'

Davidson looked down at the meeting, the rows of faces turned towards him, the pens frozen over the newly issued foolscap pads, the shock turning to incredulity.

'Yes,' he said at last. 'That's exactly what I mean.'

Three

In a small, windowless office of the Soviet Naval Ministry on the Oktober Prospeckt in Murmansk, a meeting took place that afternoon between two men. One of them was the personal assistant to Admiral Bilyanin, the high-flying Georgian with effective command of Russia's Northern Fleet. The other was one of the key scientists from Moscow's Lom Institute, a newly established laboratory complex on the south-west fringes of the University Campus. The Institute had been one of the Soviet Union's many responses to the Chernobyl disaster, and had been set up to explore the short and long term implications of airborne radiation.

The scientist, a young man in his early thirties, had flown up from the capital that morning, disturbed by what he saw on the way to Sheremtyevo Airport. Longer than usual queues outside the neighbourhood bread shops. An absence of kids in the suburban playgrounds. And dozens of engineers from the Home Defence Ministry, hurrying in and out of the street corner entrances to the city's many bomb shelters. Some of them carried boxes of foodstuffs. Others, piles of blankets. One, near the metro station at Borovitskaya Square, an armful of gas masks.

Now, at the table, the two men bent over a map. The map covered the area from Jan Meyen Island to Novaya Zemlya, thousands of square miles of chill grey ocean that held the key to the heartlands of Northern Russia. Territorial waters, under international treaty, stretched twenty-four miles offshore. But beyond that, Bilyanin's powerful Northern Fleet had extended the Soviet writ until only the bravest and boldest of Western submarines, embodying the very latest technology, dared penetrate. One of these had been the *George F. Kennan*. And now she was in deep trouble.

The man in uniform drew the scientist's attention to a set of arrows that had been added to the map several hours earlier. They were the work of Northern Command's senior meteorologist, and indicated the strength and direction of the wind and ocean currents that would affect the American submarine over the next forty-eight hours. One of a sequence of frontal depressions was passing through the area that very morning, and strengthening winds in its wake would push the huge hull eastwards at a rate, the meteorologist had calculated, of approximately one and a half knots. Currents in the area were pressing south-east, deep-flowing streams of ice-cold water, and the combined effect of wind and current would give the crippled Trident submarine a heading of 104° magnetic. If these calculations were correct, the *Kennan* would enter Soviet territorial waters at approximately four o'clock in the afternoon on the day after next.

The man in the uniform looked up, but the scientist from Moscow had anticipated his question and was already at work with a calculator and a sheaf of figures he'd pulled from the battered briefcase by his side. The figures had come from seawater samples taken at four-hourly intervals from the waters around the *Kennan*. The samples had been collected by fast *Krivak* class destroyers, working under the suspicious gaze of the *Kennan*'s crew, and flown by helicopter to naval air bases on the Kola Peninsula. The latest of the sample data had been radioed to the scientist when he was still airborne between Moscow and Murmansk.

The scientist keyed a last sum into his calculator and looked up. There was a hint of resignation in the slow shake of his head.

'They've had thirty hours' exposure already,' he said. 'And if these figures are correct, the radiation leak is getting worse.'

The other man nodded, impatient. His next meeting had already started, and there were three others after that. Northern Command had been on a full war footing since dawn.

'So?' he said.

The scientist paused, refusing to be hurried.

'It's difficult to be exact,' he said, 'but I'd estimate their chances of survival at less than 50 per cent.'

'And the ocean? The environment?' He paused. 'Us?' The scientist consulted his figures once again, then glanced over the map. In two days time, the *Kennan* would be less than thirty miles from the Kola Peninsula, a nuclear boil oozing radioactivity. Worse still, if his theories about the exact nature of the accident were correct, there was a real possibility that the *Kennan* might blow up, an event which would dwarf the consequences of Chernobyl. He looked at the man in uniform and shook his head.

'*Katactpopa*,' he said. 'Catastrophe.'

Gillespie and Sean returned to the anchorage in mid-afternoon. At midday, a sea fog had rolled in from the Channel, closing around them while they swung at anchor in the lee of one of the old sea forts, spooning for flatfish on the shoal banks fifteen feet below. The fishing had been moderate – a couple of nice plaice, a handful of dabs, and a stray pollock that should have known better – but by two o'clock they were both cold, the thermos of black coffee emptied, and the clammy chill beginning to penetrate the three layers of T-shirt and pullover they always took to sea.

Now, back on dry land, Gillespie drove the three miles from the anchorage to his ex-wife's house, a small red-brick semi with a tiny apron of front garden and a carefully tended privet hedge. He got out of the car and retrieved the fish from the back. He'd already divided the fish into two polythene bags. He carried the bigger of the bags towards the house. Sandra opened the door, and stood to one side, inviting him in. Gillespie gave her a nod as he passed, an all-purpose greeting that spared him the chore of actually saying anything. It was a gesture they'd both lived with for nearly twenty years, and she would have been alarmed at anything else.

She closed the door and followed them into the kitchen. She was a tall woman, two years younger than Gillespie with a strong open face, deep green eyes and a mouth that smiled easily. She kept herself fit, aerobics twice weekly, and it showed in her figure. She wore jeans most of the time, and went to some trouble to buy the perfect fit.

She and Gillespie had met in Belfast, 1972, Gillespie's first tour of duty. It was the height of the Troubles, buses burning on the streets in Andersonstown, and the women of the Falls cursing the squaddies as they stepped carefully down the streets, back to back, scanning the rooftops, hugging the pitted brick walls.

One night, in Turf Lodge, Gillespie had pulled up a youth suspected of joyriding. The youth had been barely fourteen, tousle-haired and visibly scared behind the constant protestations of innocence. The RUC were sure he'd taken an old Vauxhall from a street beside a park near the city centre. Intelligence suspected the car was earmarked for a bombing. Whatever happened, the boy was in for a painful night at the Interrogation Centre at Ballykelly.

As Gillespie and his Sergeant walked the youth to a waiting APC, Sandra emerged from the council house which was her home. She was seventeen years old, but already a woman. Gillespie had braced himself for another earful of the richly inventive abuse no briefing could ever describe, but she'd simply touched him lightly on the arm, and made him falter for a moment, hesitating, one foot in the road.

'Be careful, soldier,' she'd said. 'Because the wee boy didn't do it.'

She'd looked at him, squarely in the eyes, one of those moments that restored a brief sense of reality, of real people, working-class people, his own sort of people, trying to make a life for themselves. Except that here he was, a foreigner on her streets, a helmet and a snarl, part of the occupation force that simply compounded the problems they were battling to solve. Lousy housing. No jobs. And the incessant, implacable hostility of the surrounding Proddies.

The moment had come and gone, the big steel doors slamming shut on the armoured car, the boy calling out for his mother. Gillespie had watched through a slit in the side of the wagon, watched the girl stepping back towards the house, watched her glance over her shoulder, seen the expression on her face. She'd been stoical even then, her own person, but she was contemptuous too, and it showed.

He'd met her next a week later. The boy had been released from detention. Gillespie was part of a four-man patrol, on foot, back in Turf Lodge. He'd been standing by a hedge, across from the Post Office. He had a loaded SLR, and a short-wave radio, and a section leader who was convinced they'd been set up for an ambush.

The girl had crossed the road to talk to him, direct, quite fearless, oblivious of the knot of women watching from the boarded-up supermarket opposite. Gillespie had watched her narrowly, only too aware that his section leader might, for once, be right. Only when she was standing on the pavement in front of him, did he recognize who she was.

'Soldier,' she said.

Gillespie scanned the houses across the street. The gunmen preferred upstairs bedrooms, end-of-terrace houses. There'd be a car out back for the getaway. Someone to grab the Armalite. A couple of screaming women in the parlour to make things even more awkward. Gillespie eased his own SLR up, his index finger sliding inside the trigger guard. The girl looked at him.

'Thank you,' she said simply. 'Thank you for what you did.'

Gillespie frowned. For some reason, the girl seemed to think that he had been instrumental in the boy's release. Sure, he'd dissuaded a particularly zealous RUC man from opening the interrogation in the back of the wagon. And sure, he'd had a quiet word with the receiving Sergeant at the barracks at Ballykelly. But that had been all. Nothing else. He eyed the girl. Nodded.

'Pleasure,' he said drily, still watching the windows across the street.

The girl had gone. Not a smile. Not another word. But two years later, when he was back on those same streets, and the tensions had eased a little, they'd met again. The meeting had been by accident, a chance encounter, a smile of recognition, a word or two at a street corner. But after that, they'd met socially, at considerable risk, knowing that any real relationship would have to be conducted on the mainland, a hundred miles and a century or two away from the community she called home.

Gillespie's tour had ended in November that year. Three weeks before Christmas, Sandra had packed her bags, and hugged her mother, and kissed the framed photo of her father on the mantelpiece, and taken the ferry from Larne. Gillespie had met her on the quayside at Stranraer, two coach tickets in his pocket for the journey south. They'd spent a night in London, blowing twenty quid on two tickets for a Queen concert, and then travelled south again, camping out in his step-father's council flat. He'd been as happy as he could ever remember, happier than he'd thought possible, and when the nurse at the Health Centre confirmed that Sandra was five months pregnant, he went out and bought her a ring. They were married on New Year's Day. Sean arrived in time for Easter.

In truth, deep down, Sandra had known that life with Gillespie would never be easy. Already, she'd sensed how alone he was. He had no brothers, no sisters, and his father had been killed at Suez when he was still a kid. Nevertheless, juggling her life between her new husband and her new son, she did her best, trying to enfold him into the kind of warm, noisy chaos she knew so well from the tiny front parlour on the Andersonstown Road.

For a while, just, it had worked. But as the years passed, and Sean began to grow up, she realized that Gillespie was immutable, that there were parts of him that were simply beyond reach. He was never hostile towards her. He never hit her, or cursed her. They seldom even rowed. Instead, he'd simply withdraw, and if he showed any kind of emotion towards her at all then it was a hint of faint resentment that he'd ever let her get that close in the first place.

The divorce had come as no surprise. He'd been away for a while. An exercise in Norway. He'd returned with a head cold and a bag full of washing. The following evening, she'd left Sean with a friend and they'd gone to a pub and they'd sat for an hour without saying a word, and then agreed that it would be best to split up. The actual suggestion had been hers. He'd simply shrugged his agreement, and swallowed the remains of his pint, and headed for the door. It was six months before she saw him again, and by that time they were formally divorced, the papers returned to her by post, his signature scrawled at the bottom of the last form. The marriage over, they'd become friends again, and since then – oddly – she'd had more real support from him than she could ever remember.

Now, she put the kettle on and cleared a space amongst the pile of shopping which still cluttered the small kitchen table. Gillespie looked at it all. Bags of sugar. Loaves of bread. A dozen or so packets of soup. Two cartons of salt. And a small mountain of tins: sardines, pilchards, peaches, and the small mandarin oranges Sean still liked in jelly for treats. No doubt about it. Sandra was stocking up for something serious.

Sandra turned from the gas stove and followed Gillespie's eyeline to the table.

'You think it's funny?'

There was still a hint of Belfast in her voice, vowel sounds that fifteen years on the mainland had failed to flatten.

'You hate sardines.' He tossed the bag of fresh fish onto the table. 'Stick to the real thing.'

She looked at the white polythene bag. Something brown was oozing from one corner.

'That's disgusting,' she said. 'They gutted?'

'Of course.'

'Yuk.' She pulled a face. 'Thanks Dave.'

'Pleasure,' he said.

There was a silence. Sean slid out of the room. Used to quite separate relationships with each parent, he rarely hung around when they were together. Gillespie heard his footsteps on the stairs, the sound of his bedroom door shutting. Then music. Sandra decanted boiling water into the teapot.

'There's an old boy across the road,' she said, 'been sticking strips of paper on his windows. Shocking job he's made of it, too.'

Gillespie nodded. He'd seen the house as he stepped out of the car, each window clumsily latticed with brown paper tape.

'I know,' he said.

'But why's that'? Sandra asked. 'Why's he doing it?'

Gillespie didn't answer for a moment, looking again at the pile of food on the table.

'Same reason you've been shopping,' he said at last.

'I went shopping because they're running out,' she said. 'That's why I went shopping.'

'Ah. . .' Gillespie nodded. 'I see.'

He reached into his back pocket and pulled out his wallet. From the wallet he removed a twenty-pound note. He leaned forward and left it on the table, next to the bag of fish. Sandra gazed at it.

'What's that for?'

'The shopping.'

'You can't afford twenty quid.'

'Can't I?'

'No.'

She picked up the note and tried to give it back. Gillespie waved it away.

'I'm seeing Jenner later,' he said. 'He's bound to have something for me. Time like this.'

'Think so?'

'Bound to.'

Sandra shrugged and left the note on the table.

'You still haven't told me about the old boy across the road,' she said. 'What he's doing with all that tape.'

Gillespie nodded. Upstairs, for a moment, the music had stopped.

'Same reason the shops are empty,' he said. 'There's a war on the way.'

Sandra paused, the old smile, amused, slightly sardonic, rich with her knowledge of the man.

'Wonderful,' she said. 'Just what you've been waiting for.'

It wasn't until Mick Rendall ordered his third pint of Stella that the idea began to acquire real shape in his mind. For over an hour, he'd been pushing around the various bits and pieces of evidence, Cartwright lecturing him about States of Emergency, the scene at the petrol station, the little vignette they'd driven past en route to the pub: a middle-aged man in a suit jig-sawing suitcases into the back of a Granada Estate while a woman fussed around him, trying to make room for a budgerigar in a cage. Albie had given them both a sour look, and a derisive blast on the two-tone, but there was little ambiguity about the scene. It meant they were going. Leaving town. Today. Because times had evidently become too dodgy to stay.

From the pub, Mick had phoned the number about his garage. He'd asked for Mr Prior. Mr Prior had evidently been busy, but when he explained who he was, the voice in his ear confirmed that his garage had been demolished under Section VII of the Emergency Powers Act. There was a polite expression of regret that there'd been no time for consultation and an assurance that compensation would be discussed 'in due course', but when Mick began to hassle about the figures, and protest his rights as a taxpayer, the phone went dead.

Back at the bar, Mick shared the bad news with Albie, gazing morosely into his lager, and trying to calculate exactly where they'd lay hands on the fifty thousand pounds it would take to keep the bailiffs out of his house. Although he had his doubts about Cartwright in other respects, he knew enough about the man to recognize that his threat was probably kosher. Cartwright had some powerful friends. And some of these friends, he knew, rarely took prisoners.

For the next hour, Mick put together every combination he knew to try and float the business out of trouble. He thought about a cut price, one-off sale of his lingerie stock. Any three items for a fiver. Any eight for ten. The idea sounded great in theory, cheques flooding in from everywhere as a tidal wave of scarlet G-strings and assorted leatherware broke upon a grateful nation. But it had been Albie, as ever, who'd reminded him of the organization required, the postal delays, and the growing likelihood that people might have other things on their minds.

Next, he'd thought of a drugs hit. He scored his own cocaine from an ex-croupier who'd abandoned the gaming tables for a full-time career in the narcotics trade. He packaged his deals in a big house out on the mainland, and transacted his business from the driving seat of an 'F' reg Mercedes, and although he never said a word about his sources of supply, Mick knew for a fact that he drove up to London twice a week, buying in bulk from someone in Notting Hill. His one weakness was for black ladies, whom he consumed in great numbers, and the journeys back from London were often made in the middle of the night. Child's play, Mick told Albie, to lay on a modest ambush, and liberate the coke, and thus get Harry off their backs. Albie, once again, had been unimpressed, sipping his pineapple juice with the air of a man bored with fairy tales.

'You're off your head,' he said, when Mick had finished. 'You'll end up in tins of dog food.'

After drugs, Mick had wandered disconsolately up one or two other alleys – the property business, a gambling scam, or something really tacky like doing a sub-Post Office – but whatever he came up with, wherever he turned, the same brutal deadline hung over their heads. Fifty grand. Forty-eight hours. Or else.

Finally, with Albie in a corner feeding small change into a fruit machine, he'd stumbled on the Big One. A small, bronzed Frenchman, very obviously a yachtie, was standing beside him at the bar. He wanted change for a hundred-pound note, five tens and a fifty. Mick, mellowed by the Stella, had attracted the barman and organized the exchange. The Frenchman had extended his hand, a formal gesture of thanks. Mick had beamed at him. Playing the affable Englishman, he hoped he was enjoying his stay. The Frenchman had nodded vigorously, and said that England was a fine place, but that he and his family must keep heading west. He'd stopped only for water, and fresh vegetables. He would now resume his journey before they closed this city too.

Mick's smile froze for a moment. He blinked at the Frenchman. He asked him to repeat what he'd just said. The Frenchman, glancing at his watch, obliged. The French ports, he explained, were closing down. The military had taken over and all private boats had been requisitioned. No questions permitted. No exceptions made. Soon, it would happen here. Tomorrow, perhaps, or the next day. The British, after all, were always a little . . . he frowned, searching for the right word.

'Slow on the uptake?' said Mick thoughtfully.

'*Oui*,' nodded the Frenchman, heading for the phone. '*Exactement*.'

Mick turned slowly back to the bar, reaching for his third pint. Albie joined him, with a handful of pound coins. He let them fall on the counter.

'Twenty quid,' he said. 'Forty-nine thousand to go. Give or take.'

Mick glanced up at him.

'Careful,' he said, 'you nearly made a joke.'

Albie played deaf, ordering another pineapple juice and a cheese sandwich. Mick bent towards him, highly confidential.

'Listen,' he said, 'I've cracked it.'

Albie leaned across the bar, catching the barman by the lapel of his new cotton jacket.

'Remember,' he said. '*White* bread. No pickle.'

The barman nodded, repeated the order, and disappeared. Albie resumed his seat. Mick waited for him to settle.

'I've cracked it,' he said again.

'Cracked what?'

'The problem. The fifty grand.'

Albie looked at him, amused.

'Arms dealing?' he said.

'No.'

'A kidnap?'

'No.'

'What then? Surprise me.'

Mick crossed one leg over another, enjoying the tension, taking his time.

'Tell me. . .' he said, nodding around at no one in particular, 'what happens to this lot when there's no more petrol?'

'They take the bus.'

'And what happens when there's no more buses?' He smiled. 'Or trains, or anything? And when the roads are so jammed no one move anyway?'

Albie frowned.

'What do you mean?'

Mick leaned forward.

'People are talking about a war, Albie. The real thing. This place is Ground Zero. Target Number One. Numero Uno.' He nodded at the window. 'Naval port. Repair facilities. Ammo dumps. You name it. So. . .' he moistened the end of his finger in a pool of spilled beer and began to trace the outline of the island on the bar, 'loads of punters. . .all wanting out. . .before the Russians arrive and drop the big one.' His eyes rose skywards 'With me so far?'

Albie nodded, still sceptical.

'Yeah. . .'

'So. . .' Mick's finger tracked towards the landward side of the island, 'what happens when there's no petrol and no transport and no trains and no anything, and they're making if difficult to get onto the mainland because they don't want us all slopping around the countryside, and everybody's going to bed shit scared they're going to wake up as pork kebabs? Eh, Alb? What happens then?' He paused, intense, dramatic, the peddler of doom. 'Remember, Alb, a lot of these people have wives, kids, families. Nothing's moving any more so they've got fuck all to do except sit on their fannies and wait to be blown away. So think about it. Go on. Think. What are they gonna want most in life? Eh?'

'Out,' said Albie.

'Exactly.'

'But you say they can't get out.'

'No. Not by road they can't.' He paused again, leaning forward, inviting Albie to share his secret. 'So what do they do?'

Mick looked at him, waiting for an answer, waiting for the penny to drop. Albie caught sight of his cheese sandwich, returning in the hands of the barman. He examined it closely, lifting the top slice to make sure they'd left out the pickle. Mick reached over, tapped him on the knee.

'Boats, Alb. We need to get into boats.'

He glanced across at the phone. The Frenchman was pocketing his change from the refund slot and heading for the door. Mick got off his stool.

'Listen,' he said, 'it's brilliant. Let's try it on Cartwright.'

The Conference at the Civic Centre broke up at 2 p.m. The meeting had ended with an agreement to create a number of sub-committees, each charged with trouble-shooting a particular aspect of the problems posed by Davidson's brisk announcement: how best to curtail the train schedule, what to do about the postal service, how to maintain food supplies into the city, whether or not to suspend the parking regulations, what provisions to make for DHSS benefits when the banks and Post Offices were no longer open. The main committee, with a handful of unavoidable absentees, would reconvene the following morning.

As the meeting broke up, Goodman found himself cornered by Nigel Quinn. The policeman had a pale, set expression on his face, and it took Goodman a moment or two to realize that he was very angry indeed.

'It's lunacy,' he said at once, 'madness.'

Goodman smiled, trying not to look too resigned. In truth, he shared Quinn's feelings, but that was hardly the point.

'It's what they want,' he said simply. 'Our Master's voice.'

'But have they thought the thing through?' Quinn said. 'Have you? Has anyone?' He shook his head at once, answering his own question. 'No,' he said, 'because they can't. Because the whole thing's bloody impossible.'

'Lipscombe seems quite sanguine,' Goodman pointed out. The Brigadier had accepted Davidson's announcement without a murmur. He seemed to have prior knowledge of the plan, and saw no real problem. Quinn was scornful.

'Lipscombe?' he said. 'The Army? Do you know how many men they're proposing to send in?'

Goodman shook his head.

'Four hundred or so?' he guessed. 'Five?'

'Fifty.' Quinn was contemptuous. 'Reservists to a man.'

'Perhaps he's found some more.'

'Where from?' He paused. 'There are no more troops. They've all gone to Germany. The cupboard's bare.'

'I see.'

Goodman hesitated, feeling less than adequate. These were numbers he should have known for himself. Had Eric not been in hospital, had he had time to read the briefings, he'd have been up to speed. As it was, he was trailing badly. Perhaps tonight he'd find time to wade through the file. Perhaps early tomorrow morning. He looked Quinn in the face. The two men had never got on. He considered Quinn a time server, one of yesterday's breed of policemen, cautious, and bureaucratic, and slow on his feet. Quinn, in turn, regarded the young acting Chief Executive as hopelessly out of his depth, a lightweight with a flashy management degree, a great deal of ambition, and far too much charm for his own good. The fact that he was now in overall charge, Controller-Designate, capable of turning the entire city into a personal fiefdom, he found difficult to believe. Now, having sat through the Conference, he was practically certain that Goodman was simply a cipher for Whitehall control, someone who'd make the right noises, and let Davidson get on with it.

He tucked his papers into his briefcase, and snapped the lock shut.

'I'll phone you later,' he said to Goodman, and turned on his heel, and left.

Goodman watched him go, letting his own anger subside. He was perfectly aware of the other man's contempt, but he saw no point in giving him the satisfaction of a public row. There'd undoubtedly come a confrontation, but he'd make sure it happened on his own terms, and on his own territory. A figure appeared at his side. Dark suit. Rimless glasses. Watery smile. Davidson.

'Oliver,' he said pleasantly. 'You certainly chose your moment.'

Davidson acknowledged the comment with a small, neat dip of his head.

'Had to be done,' he said. 'I hope it wasn't too much of a shock.'

'Not at all. I'm sure we'll all cope.'

The room began to empty, figures hurrying away down the corridor towards the lifts, one or two in conversation, the rest preoccupied, deep in thought. Each of these men would spend the next eighteen hours standing their jobs on their heads – how *not* to run the trains on time, how *not* to keep the schools open – and each one would have to battle the instincts of a lifetime to come up with some sort of realistic plan. Goodman's job would then be to jigsaw their proposals together, to shape a strategy that would withstand the stresses of the next few days, and ease the city into the No Man's Land between peace and war.

Joanna Goodman arrived at school a minute or so earlier than usual, parking her Metro in a cul-de-sac across from the school gates. She checked that Charlie was still asleep in his carrycot on the back seat before joining the gaggle of mothers waiting for their kids to emerge at the end of the school day.

Joanna crossed the road, nodding a greeting to faces she barely knew, looking for someone to talk to. Standing to one side was Molly Quinn, the policeman's wife. Joanna had spoken to her several times before, and had liked her on sight. She was an older woman, in her mid-forties, with a big, slightly masculine face, and a warm smile. She wore long cotton skirts and very old pullovers, and exuded an air of cheerful disorganization. She had four boys, and her youngest son, Gary, was the star of the school's football team. Thus the bag of sports gear at her feet.

Joanna joined Molly, nodding at the bag.

'Forgotten his things again?' she said.

'As ever.' Molly pulled a face. 'Mind like a sieve.'

'Incredible, aren't they, James would forget his name if he had half a chance.'

They shared the joke together, keeping the conversation going, discussing their kids, their idiosyncrasies. Joanna knew that her husband had no time for Nigel Quinn, and she suspected that the antipathy was mutual. Not that Molly would care less. She was far too independent for that. The older woman abruptly changed the subject.

'Have you heard the rumour?' she said.

'What rumour?'

'About the school.'

'No.'

'They say it's going to close.'

'What?' Joanna frowned. 'For ever?'

'No. Just for a bit. While this wretched business sorts itself out.'

'Oh?'

'Yes.' Molly looked at her, as direct as ever. 'I wondered whether that clever husband of yours might have said anything. He'd know. Bound to.'

Joanna shook her head and peered over the hedge towards the low brick buildings that housed the classrooms.

'No,' she said, 'he hasn't said a word. Not that I ever see him.'

Joanna felt the other woman smiling at her, another bond between them, another point of mutual contact, hard-pressed husbands, never home. She glanced back to return the grin, to share the joke, but when she did so, she saw something else in the smile, curiosity perhaps, a question mark, maybe even sympathy, and she knew at once that something was wrong, badly wrong, and that other people knew it too.

She tried to shake the thought loose, and shrug it all off, to talk about the kids again, or the weather, but instead she felt herself beginning to tremble uncontrollably, which only made the whole thing worse. Across the playground, the school bell began to ring, and she thanked God for the sound of chairs scraping back from desks, and children's voices, and the slamming of distant doors. She swallowed hard, and mumbled her excuses to Molly, and pushed forward into the onward rush of blue blazers.

On the way home, in the car, Caroline sat beside her with James in the back. They'd stopped at the corner shop for choc ices, a treat, and James was leaning forward between the front seats, trying to describe the latest member of his playground gang between mouthfuls of melting hazelnut. She half listened to him, the endless happy burble that was his world, unable to rid her mind of the scene at the school gates. Molly Quinn. The rumour about the school closure. And then that gently quizzical look, that moment of absolute truth between the two women. She slowed for a roundabout, automatically looking down to check that Caroline was properly belted in.

'Jo Jo. . .' she began, looking up at the face in the driving mirror.

The child frowned, concentrating on the last of his ice cream.

'Yes, Mummy?'

'How would you like to come to Granny's for a day or two?'

'Granny's?'

'Yes.'

'Can we?'

'If you want to, darling.'

Caroline looked up at her.

'All of us?' she said. 'Daddy too?'

Joanna said nothing for a moment. She wanted to stop and hug both her kids. Charlie, too. She wanted to tell them that everything would be OK. That their world was intact. For the second time that day, she felt the tears beginning to well up in her eyes. Absurd. Crazy. Pure imagination. She looked quickly away, masking her tears.

'I expect so, darling,' she said at last. 'If he's not too busy.'

Goodman studied the harbour master's face very carefully as he took them once again through the argument. Cut the city off from the landward side, he said, and you instantly create pressure elsewhere. People would still want to get away. Stood to reason. Couldn't blame them. Road-blocks on the major city exits. Armed guards. Barbed wire. God knows what else. Result? Chaos afloat. There'd be bodies everywhere, he assured them, damn-fool instant sailors without a day's experience to their name. The rescue services would be hopelessly overstretched. The whole thing appalled him, and the Navy wouldn't stand for it either. The harbour, and the coastal approaches, had become a Military Zone. The country had a war to fight. Everyone else must stay put.

Davidson began to reply, but Goodman held him back. It was time, he decided, to make his presence felt.

'So what do you suggest?' he said.

The harbour master pursed his lips, and Goodman knew at once that he'd thought the whole thing through, drawn up a mental agenda, a list of priorities, detailed measures to keep the thing good and tight.

'Number one,' he said, 'we need a register of all seaworthy boats. That means marinas. Club anchorages. Commercial fishermen. The lot. Even dinghies.'

'Done,' Davidson said quietly.

Goodman looked at him in surprise.

'Really?' he said.

Davidson nodded.

'Last two days. Naval Provost.'

Goodman made a note on his pad but said nothing. The harbour master extended a second finger, ticking off the measures one by one.

'Two. We need solid controls on diesel. No diesel, no go.'

Goodman nodded.

'No problem,' he said. 'The refineries are cutting off distribution tomorrow. Supplies will be exhausted within days. That applies to diesel as well.'

The harbour master shook his head.

'Not good enough,' he said. 'What about current stocks?'

'Prohibition on sales.'

'Can you enforce that?'

Goodman hesitated a moment, out of his depth. Davidson's voice again, softer than ever.

'Yes,' he said.

The harbour master shot him a glance, appraising, sceptical.

'You sure?'

'Yes.'

'Good.' The harbour master returned to his check-list but Goodman interrupted.

'What about yachtsmen?' he said. 'People with their own boats? Prepared to risk it without fuel? You can hardly stand in their way.'

The harbour master stared at him, impatient as ever.

'That's the whole point,' he said, 'that's what I'm talking about. We need controls, powers, authority. We need a Proclamation. A total ban on the movement of private craft. On the harbour and offshore. One or two special dispensations. But only in a handful of cases.' He looked at Goodman. 'Possible?'

'Certainly, if you think it's realistic.' He made another note on his pad, then glanced up. 'How will you police that?' he asked.

'Small flotilla. Men I can trust. There's plenty of them around. We'll base in the dockyard, and run twenty-four hour patrols.'

'And offenders? The people who won't play ball?'

'Jankers,' he said, 'in Haslar.' The harbour master named the Naval Hospital, comfortably within sight of the harbour. 'There's a secure wing on the western side. We'll use it if we must. It's for their own good, at the end of the day.'

He paused and blew his nose. Goodman, to his relief, sensed that they were coming to the end of the list, that the storm within him was beginning to blow itself out.

'Anything else?' he enquired.

The harbour master tucked his handkerchief back into his pocket and gazed out of the window, and for a moment Goodman had a glimpse of the empty, restless years that would await this man after retirement. He thrived on problems. He took life by the throat and shook it hard. He'd be lost without an office, and a uniform, and something to complain about. The harbour master sniffed, struck by a final thought.

'Yes,' he said. 'This dispensation business' – he looked around at them – 'needs to be rigorous. Very rigorous. We're – you're – creating a tricky situation here. Dispensations will be extremely valuable. I need hardly say *how* valuable.' He paused, arriving at the nub of it all. 'So who'll dispense the. . .ah. . . dispensations? Who'll be in charge of it all?'

'You will,' Goodman said at once. 'And you'll have sole control.'

'Good.' The harbour master stood up and extended a hand. 'Then I take it we have an agreement. Shall I minute this conversation? And send you a copy?'

'No need.'

'Are you quite sure?'

He frowned at them both. Clearly he wanted the exchange in print as soon as possible. Copies for the file. Copies for Home Command. Copies for the ferry companies. And copies for anyone else who needed to know how important he'd just become. Goodman retreated gracefully.

'By all means send me a minute,' he said, 'let's have it down in black and white.'

The harbour master grunted, as graceless as ever, and left the room. Davidson and Goodman strolled slowly after him, Davidson chuckling at the man's abrasive self-importance. The upper reaches of Whitehall had once been full of similar figures, he said, but the Thatcher administration had seen most of them off.

By the lift, Goodman looked at his watch. At six o'clock, he'd agreed to do a live interview on Wessex TV. Duggie Bullock had phoned at midday, and he'd accepted the invitation at once, a decision that Davidson had blessed with an approving nod of the head. There'd be nerves to calm, rumours to squash, tempers to soothe, hands to hold, and television was by far the best way of doing it. He hated the box himself, but there was no denying its power.

Now, by the lift, Davidson snapped open his briefcase and extracted a thin manila file. He'd be off for a couple of hours, he said, on a little private business. But in the meantime, there was yet more reading for Goodman to add to his file. Highly confidential. Goodman took the file, and opened it. He began to frown.

'What's this?' he said.

'Spot of background,' Davidson said easily. 'On your minder.'

'On what?'

'On your minder. Your bodyguard. We thought it prudent, once things warm up. Nice lad called Evans. Serving Marine on attachment. He'll double as your driver. Knows the city inside out.' He smiled. 'Discreet, too. In case you were wondering.'

Harry Cartwright arrived at the Ensign at half-past three, parking his black Jaguar beside the rows of articulated lorries waiting to load fresh produce from the Channel Isles. The container boats from St Helier and St Peter Port were still running, and the working area was thick with spillage from the busy fork-lift trucks.

Harry got out of his car, and began to walk towards the pub. Mick had seen him coming and met him by the door. On Albie's suggestion, he'd abandoned the Stella for tomato juice.

'Drink, Harry?'

Cartwright shook his head. He rarely drank, and never before six.

'I've got fifteen minutes,' he said pointedly. 'You'd better be serious.'

Mick nodded, unusually deferential. He'd spent the last hour refining the idea, pushing it downstream on a tide of enthusiastic spiel that had even begun to convince Albie. Turning his back on the pub, he took Cartwright by the arm, the cherished uncle, and began to walk him slowly along the quayside. Below them were the lines of fishing smacks, and seagoing yachts, and assorted other craft that used the dock as home.

The two men paused by a bollard, and Cartwright shook his head. Mick's theories about the city being cut off left him far from convinced. Why should the authorities give themselves so much aggravation? What would they stand to gain?

These objections Mick had anticipated, and he dismissed them at once. There were certain people, he said, friends of his, who were in the know. They'd passed on bits of information, tips, hints, guesses. They worked in the dockyard. They knew a thing or two. And they'd been kind enough to share their little secret.

Cartwright looked at him, still unconvinced.

'OK,' he said reluctantly, 'let's suppose you're right. The city's cut off. What then?'

Mick grinned at him, and nodded at the boats below.

'Two grand a berth,' he said, 'maybe even three.' Cartwright followed his pointing finger. The water was slack, the boats barely moving amongst the oily wrack. He frowned.

'For what? Precisely?'

'The works. The package deal.' He bent close to Harry, confidential, intimate. 'We dress the thing up. We market it properly. Small baggage allowance. Family valuables. 20 per cent discount for kids. Safe passage to the west coast of Ireland. Portugal. Some place like that. Fallout-free destination of your choice. Bunk in a cottage. Guaranteed fresh water supply. You name it.' He paused for breath. 'What do you think?'

'Three thousand? For that?'

'For survival? Sounds cheap to me.'

Cartwright looked at him, appraising, ever sceptical.

'How many people do you know in Portugal?' he said, 'or the west coast of Ireland for that matter?'

'None. But I can find some.'

'How?'

He shrugged. 'Dunno,' he said, 'but there'll be a way.'

Cartwright nodded. 'And how do they get there? These clients of yours?'

Mick drew Cartwright to the edge of the quay. The handful of fishermen still working on the smaller inshore boats looked curiously up at them. Mick returned their stares. Earlier, he'd counted more than a dozen boats that might, at a pinch, qualify for the scheme, from the tiny two-man twenty-footers, to the sturdy, deep-draught, broad-beamed ocean-going trawlers that disappeared to sea for days on end.

'Look around you, Harry,' he said. 'It's been a lousy year. Talk to any of these guys. They're on their uppers. Offer them cash, they'll take you anywhere. Especially now.' Mick paused. He could see that Cartwright, in spite of himself, was beginning to warm to the idea. But there was still the big question to come. Cartwright stepped back from the edge of the quay.

'And how do you propose to fund this little enterprise?' he said. 'Assuming they want cash up front?'

'Ah. . .' said Mick, '. . .now that's the point.' They began to walk again, Mick saying nothing, Cartwright waiting for some kind of answer.

'Well?' he said.

Mick stopped again, and looked Cartwright in the eye, partner to partner.

'Listen,' he said, 'it's simple arithmetic. We take, say, a hundred people. At three thousand a pop, that's three hundred grand. You can take your fifty grand off the top. Then there's another, say, fifty grand for exes. That still leaves two hundred grand. Give or take. That's nearly a quarter of a million quid. Easy, innit?' Cartwright conceded the point with the briefest smile. Then the frown, and the questions, returned.

'And what happens if the world blows up?'

'Then we won't be around to worry.'

'And if it doesn't?'

'Half each.'

Cartwright looked away, running the figures through his head, checking the sums. Then he lowered his gaze, down to the boats beginning to tug against their moorings on the first of the flood tide. Mick chuckled and squeezed his arm. Cartwright shook himself free. He hated being touched.

'OK,' he said at last, 'but why me? Why talk to me about it? Why not just do it?'

Mick smiled, nearly there.

'Three reasons, Harry,' he said easily. 'First, you're right. We need some money up front. Second, we need a certain class of punter. Your type of punter. All those fat cats you do business with. . .'

'And third?'

'Third, we might need a little official help.'

'What do you mean?'

Mick gestured around. The boats. The fishermen. Even the ferries.

'They might close the place down,' he said. 'The Navy might take over. Anything could happen.' He paused. 'The bad news, Harry, is that we might need one or two of those friends of yours. To get us out to sea. . .'

Cartwright nodded.

'And the good news?'

'We could double the price.'

'Why?'

'Because in that case nobody could move.' He smiled again. 'Except us.'

Gillespie found Jenner up a step-ladder in his office, detaching a large, framed print from a hook on the picture rail. Gillespie walked into the office, uninvited, and held out his hands, ready to take the picture. Jenner, unfamiliar with step-ladders, was starting to wobble.

'Mr Jenner,' Gillespie said. 'Here.'

Jenner looked back over his shoulder, recognizing Gillespie's voice.

'Thank you,' he said. 'How did you get in?'

'The door was open,' Gillespie said reasonably, 'and the bell still doesn't work.'

'No?'

'No.'

'Oh.' He paused, frowning. 'Must be the electrics again.'

He swung the big picture carefully around the steps, and let Gillespie take the weight. Gillespie put it carefully on the floor, beside a large tea-chest. There was another tea-chest in the corner, and a collection of cardboard boxes. A table and Jenner's desk were piled with books. Jenner clattered down the steps, and wiped his hands on the sides of his trousers, a big, rumpled man who'd never quite managed to throw off the habits of adolescence. Gillespie looked at him, then nodded at the tea-chests and the clutter around the office.

'Well,' he said, 'you're off.'

Jenner nodded. He looked tired.

''Fraid so,' he said.

'What are you calling it? Holiday?'

'Life insurance.' He pulled a face. 'I know it's terribly cowardly but I've a horrible feeling we're in for a bit of a pasting. Not the Russians necessarily. I don't suppose it'll get that far. But all the rest of it. Power to the people. *Aux barricades*. You know the way it goes.'

'No,' said Gillespie, 'I don't.'

'Demos. Punch-ups. Wild mobs.' Jenner rolled his eyes. 'There was a bit of a do this morning. At the War Memorial.'

'Really?'

'Yes. CND were at it with their placards, and our football friends arrived. I happened to be running the wife to the shops. We had a grandstand seat. Danced all over the car. Scared the wife witless. Poor love. Shaken rigid.' He paused, smiling to himself. 'Actually, it would have amused you. I counted four of our clients in the enemy. So much for gratitude.'

Gillespie grinned. Jenner's notions of social justice had reached deep into the city's toughest areas, and he'd recently defended a number of young thugs charged with riot and affray offences after the local football team had lost a fifth-round cup tie. Gillespie shook his head.

'Too bad,' he said. 'What about the rest of your clients?'

Jenner beamed at him, and indicated the contents of the nearest tea-chest.

'They're coming with me,' he said. Gillespie peered into the tea-chest. The chest was three-quarters full of files.

'What's in there?' he said.

Jenner frowned, trying to remember.

'House deeds,' he said, 'covenants, insurance agreements.' He paused. 'Wills.'

Gillespie nodded. 'Handy,' he said drily.

There was a silence between the two men. Jenner looked uncomfortable, and sniffed, and wiped his nose on the back of his hand.

'You came for a reason,' he said. 'You're a busy man.'

'Actually I'm not. Quite the reverse.'

'Ah. . .' he nodded, '. . .then you want work.'

'Afraid so.'

Jenner gazed around at the office.

'You any good with vans?' he said.

'Where are you going?'

'Scilly Isles. First thing tomorrow morning.'

Gillespie shook his head.

'Not that far,' he said.

'Staying put?'

'Yeah. For the time being.'

'Then I can't help you, my friend. People have a lot on their minds just now,' he said. 'They don't need solicitors.'

Gillespie looked at him, an expression close to disbelief.

'Nobody's been round?' he said. 'Nobody at all?'

'Nobody I can help.' He looked at the pile of papers on his desk. 'I had a couple of calls this morning,' he said, 'about that business at St Ursula's.'

Gillespie frowned. St Ursula's was a large, red-brick psychiatric hospital on the eastern fringes of the city, a big, cavernous Victorian institution, a dumping ground for the area's mentally ill.

'What happened at St Ursula's?' he said.

Jenner looked embarrassed.

'I'm not quite sure,' he said. 'They appear to have shipped some of the. . .ah. . .inmates out. Just released them.' He nodded at the telephone. 'It's the relatives who call me. What are we to do with Uncle Frank? Daft as a brush and nowhere to go?' He shook his head, another of life's little tragedies. 'You can imagine how I feel, poor souls. Still,' he shrugged, 'not very much I can do about it. Times like these.' He paused, then turned to Gillespie, struck by an idea. 'Why don't you enlist?'

'Enlist?'

'Yes. Special Constable. I understand the police are opening the books tonight. Background like yours. I'm sure they'll be delighted.'

Gillespie looked thoughtful. 'They pay well?'

'No idea, old friend. Go and ask.' He paused and wiped his hands on his trousers again. 'Otherwise you might try the removals business. Do you know how much they're charging now? Since it all started?'

'Yeah. I can imagine. Blood money.'

'Exactly.'

Jenner began to collaspe the step-ladder, trying to make sense of the sliders on the side. Gillespie watched him, marvelling that the man had managed to keep a business together for so long. He'd never met anyone so clumsy, so absent-minded, so totally uninterested in the smaller print of life.

'So you've got nothing?' he said.

''Fraid not.' He prodded his glasses back onto the bridge of his nose. 'Though if anything comes up in the next few hours, I'll let you know.'

'Thanks.'

Gillespie hesitated a moment, wondering if, after all, he shouldn't offer to go to the Scilly Isles. He shuddered to think what would happen once Jenner got behind the wheel of a loaded van.

'Listen. . .' he began.

Jenner gave him a small, bleak smile and shook his head. He was much shrewder than he looked.

'No,' he said, anticipating Gillespie's offer, 'you stay. You must stay. You should stay. We all should.' He extended a limp hand. 'Good luck.'

Gillespie shook his hand.

'You too,' he said. 'Drive carefully.'

Jenner nodded, and peered around, already at a loss to know quite what to do next. Gillespie paused by the door. For the first time, he realized that he might never see this man again. The thought saddened him, and he was about to say something else, something warm and direct, a thank-you for two good years, but Jenner turned away, thinking he'd already left, and so he didn't bother.

Martin Goodman stood at the window of his office on the fifth floor, and watched the rain falling on the flagstones below. At the kerbside stood his new official car, a black Rover. At the wheel, barely visible, the man called Evans. He had a newspaper propped on the steering wheel. He was eating a bar of chocolate. He didn't appear to be wearing uniform.

Goodman turned away from the window and walked slowly back to his desk. Fiona, his secretary, had typed out a schedule for him, a list of meetings that would occupy him for most of the following day. The first of the meetings was scheduled for eight o'clock. He had to create a Secretariat for the allotment of passes in and out of the city, some mechanism whereby individuals with a genuine need – food suppliers, key workers in the handful of firms still operational, GPs, inhabitants or relatives returning from away – could negotiate the roadblocks which Davidson's plan would inevitably require. Davidson had yet to announce a date for the implementation of the plan, but Goodman suspected that it would be sooner rather than later, perhaps even two or three days' time.

The roadblocks, he'd already concluded, would have to be sited on the southern side of the twenty-metre creek that separated the city from the mainland. There were only three roads off the island, plus a footbridge or two, and the operation seemed perfectly feasible, but thousands of people moved in and out of the city every working day, and he anticipated problem after problem in deciding who should qualify for a pass. What about the city's undertakers, for instance? The municipal Crematorium happened to be sited on the mainland. Was he really going to deny the bereaved the chance to incinerate their loved ones before the Russians obliged? Or should he say no, they must be buried, or embalmed, or stored in fridges pending developments, thus provoking more representations, more telephone calls, more wasted time? He shook his head. One of a million issues, none of them easily resolvable.

He put Fiona's schedule to one side, and turned to the rest of the material on the desk. On top of the pile, exhibit number one, was a plan of the city's bunker. The Bunker was buried under one of the nineteenth-century forts up on the hill overlooking the city. It had been constructed in the early days of 1938, a belated recognition that Hitler might mean business, and since the war it had been modernized and updated on a piecemeal basis – a reconditioned diesel generator, a new air-conditioning system, some modest provisions against gas attack. The current plans looked impressive enough – 3000 square feet of floor space and room for seventy-five souls – but the Civil Defence budget had always been pitifully small, and the yearly maintenance schedule had barely kept pace with the damp, and the mould, and the small army of field mice that had somehow made a home there.

Goodman leaned back from his desk and gazed out of the window. All day, he'd been aware of the sheer volume of decisions tightening around him, isolating him, exposing him, the man at the very top, and it made him realize just how out of condition he'd become. For more than a year, since meeting Suzanne, he'd allowed the job to look after itself. He'd coasted through, getting by with the minimum of effort, while he enjoyed a taste of the adolescence he suspected he'd never had. His times with Suzanne had been the richest adventure, an almost narcotic experience, utterly contrary to the quietly disciplined habits of a working lifetime, and he'd enjoyed it all, thrived on it, come to depend on it, the excitement, and the deceit, and the giddy surrender to something huge and dangerous, and utterly out of control.

Now, though, he knew that it was all under threat, that the fairy tale had been abruptly overtaken by real life. He was due to meet Suzanne at seven-thirty. It was time he knew he couldn't possibly spare. He'd already tried to phone her on the number at Gatwick. They said she'd left. He'd tried her office in the city. Her secretary said she assumed she was still at Gatwick. He'd even phoned her flat, in case she'd come back early, tired, alarmed, fed up, but there was no reply. He closed his eyes and lay back against the chair. He'd have to face her, to explain the realities of the situation, how dangerous it was, how important it might be for her to get away, abroad perhaps, while there was still a chance. They'd have to come to some kind of arrangement, while events ran their course, and the world decided whether or not to blow itself up.

There was Joanna, too, and the kids. So far, he'd managed to keep these two lives of his apart, not simply in practical terms – the one woman not finding out about the other – but also where it really mattered, in his head. He loved both women, one as a mother and friend, the other as a passionate soul mate, the keeper of his real self. So far, the arrangement had been ideal. But very soon, perhaps even now, there'd be a choice to make, another decision to add to the list, no less momentous for being personal, and infinitely more complicated than anything else on his desk.

He opened his eyes and ran a tired hand over his face, wondering whether it might not be time for a drink. Then he picked up the first of Fiona's files and opened it at random. 'Notes on the Payment of Contract Workers during the Transition to War Period.' He read a line or two of the opening paragraph, and then closed the file and leaned back once again in his chair. He had a good mind, he knew it, and soon he would read the rest of the material, scribbling notes to himself, highlighting key points in red, sorting out the facts from the fantasy, tabulating his decisions in a sane, sensible order. It wouldn't be perfect, far from it, but he'd do a good job, a better job than anyone else in the building, certainly better than Eric Moody, and at the end of it all, he'd know he'd done his best. The rest, all too probably, would be silence. A ruined city. Mountains of rubble. And a towering cloud of ash. He gazed out of the window, thinking again of Suzanne, where she was, what she was doing. The phone began to ring on his desk. He picked it up. Fiona's voice, as efficient as ever.

'A personal call,' she said, 'a Mr Harry Cartwright.'

Davidson sat on a bed in the big, bare ward. The place smelled of urine and carbolic soap. There were mattresses stacked against a door at the farther end. The light bulbs were underpowered, casting thin, pale shadows over the cracked green walls. The windows were barred on the inside. It was, as the Principal Secretary had promised, quite perfect.

Davidson shivered, pulling his coat around him. The place was cold.

'How many of these wards do they have?' he said. 'Remind me.'

The other man turned from the window. He was frowning at the dirt on his fingertip. He was tall, bulky, overweight. He was wearing a raincoat over baggy jeans and a rumpled sweater.

'Ten,' he said.

'That's how many beds?'

'Two hundred.' He paused. 'Double if we push them.' Davidson nodded, thoughtful.

'We'll need them all,' he said, 'every single one.'

Four

By 14.30 GMT, the key elements in the US Task Force racing north towards the *George F. Kennan* had reached lat. 45°N, broadly abeam the Bay of Biscay. At the heart of the Task Force, protected by her screen of missile cruisers, was the aircraft carrier USS *Dwight D. Eisenhower*. Nuclear-powered, she carried an operational complement of more than three thousand men, and a mixed bag of nearly ninety aircraft. The fully-equipped hospital on 'F' deck could deal with any of the survivable wounds sustained by the crew of the *Kennan*. The snub-nosed 'Phoenix' missiles, slung beneath the wings of the F-14s could, on the other hand, start the war that would make the option of medical treatment strictly academic.

The carrier's Captain, and the Rear-Admiral in charge of the battlegroup, convened a top-level meeting for 15.00 GMT. Scrambled satellite voice circuits were cleared to the Pentagon. Sea Knight helicopters ferried key officers from the escorting cruisers. And the carrier's senior Navigating Officer was tasked to prepare a brief address on the arrival options for what the Rear-Admiral was now calling the HMO, or Hour of Maximum Opportunity.

The meeting began three minutes late. There was a series of brief updates on correlative deployments in the north-eastern Atlantic, movements of other NATO naval units choreographed to keep the Soviets guessing, and to split their primary strike forces, should the shooting start. There was a flotilla of West German missile destroyers edging north along the Norwegian coast. The British had pushed three hunter-killer submarines into the area, and they were reporting dozens of sonar-contacts as Soviet submarines streamed west from the bases around Murmansk. A total of nine American hunter-killers were lurking under the Polar ice cap, awaiting orders, while a further seventeen hunter-killers were in rapid transit from naval bases on the US Eastern seaboard.

NATO C-in-C, Eastern Atlantic, in Northwood, Middlesex, had meantime thought it prudent to withdraw all missile boats, American and British, from their normal stations in mid-Atlantic, to waters rather closer to home. One of the mysteries of the current crisis was what the *Kennan* was doing off the Norwegian coast in the first place. The big 'boomers' were normally stationed well away from the principal Soviet transit routes. In theory, the crisis should never have happened.

The introductory updates over, the Rear-Admiral threw back the black drape on the big tactical display board, revealing a map of the western portion of the Barents Sea. The latest position of the *Kennan* was marked by a large blue arrow. Surrounding the blue arrow, were a cluster of other markers, some big, some small, all orange.

On the Rear-Admiral's invitation, the *Eisenhower*'s Intelligence Officer stepped up and began to detail the orange markers. On the basis of satellite reconnaissance, maritime overflights, and garbled reports from the *Kennan* herself, the London Fleet Ocean Surveillance Centre had positively ID'd one 'Kresta II' missile cruiser, four 'Kashin' destroyers, and one of the big 'Elbrus' class submarine rescue ships. In less than thirty-five hours, given the current weather in the area, the submarine would enter Soviet territorial waters. Until that moment, the US Navy had a perfect right to secure a line to the crippled submarine, to transfer the sick and injured, and to tow her away to a port of their choosing. But once the giant hull crossed the line into Soviet territorial waters, the rules changed. Technically, and actually, the US Task Force would be committing an act of international trespass. Their pursuit would be illegal. The rescue would become an invasion.

There was silence in the room. At a signal from the Rear-Admiral's EO, the Navigating Officer stepped forward. How long, asked the Rear-Admiral, did he anticipate before effecting a rendezvous with the *Kennan*? The Navigating Officer, a young high-flyer with the cool, crisp delivery of the Annapolis Command Course, looked briefly up at the map display, and then turned to a row of officers sitting before him.

'Forty hours,' he said. 'Minimum.'

Goodman met Cartwright in a small French restaurant tucked away behind the city's cathedral in mid-afternoon. Cartwright had an interest in the business, and had suggested the rendezvous as an alternative to his office. It would, he promised on the phone, provide them with a little privacy and perhaps a spot of late lunch as well. The place would be empty, but the chef would undoubtedly stay on. Their conversation need take no longer than half an hour.

Reluctant, but curious, Goodman had agreed to the meeting, all too aware that his diary would close that night: no more last-minute appointments, no more spare half-hours, no more time. Whatever Cartwright had to say would be important. Of that, he was quite certain.

He'd first met the accountant six years before. There'd been the makings of a financial scandal on one of the city's more powerful committees – Tory councillors involved in an elaborate scheme to tempt old ladies into private nursing homes in exchange for the freehold of their own properties – and he'd needed some shrewd financial analysis before the scandal had a chance to surface in the local press. Cartwright had been recommended by a trusted friend, himself a businessman, and he'd taken the worst of the evidence along to Cartwright's office. He'd closed the door, and sought and received an assurance about total confidentiality, and the little man had run a finger down the figures, and sipped at a glass of water, and asked a question or two, and confirmed what Goodman had suspected for weeks: that the figures were an elaborate fiction, and that the accounts were littered with false trails that had somehow foiled the city's own auditors. He'd offered the conclusion without surprise, or criticism, or even curiosity. Then, as now, he seemed utterly opaque, a man without personal opinion, or political preference, a small, neat, colourless figure who spent most of his working life behind a desk, and who had now acquired a reputation as one of the city's sharpest accountants.

Goodman had used Cartwright on a number of occasions since that first encounter, and had come to depend on him for advice, and the coldest of financial appraisals. Their meetings were always brief, uncluttered by sentiment or social ties. There'd never been any question of fees or favours, and from the start there had been a mutual respect, a tacit acceptance of two good minds coming together for the common good.

Now, Cartwright settled into the buttoned Dralon seat and reached for a bottle of Perrier. He poured two glassfuls and pushed one of them across the table towards Goodman. The gesture was an assumption. The wine list lay unopened beside the heavy crystal glasses. These were serious times.

'Your health,' Cartwright said drily.

Goodman nodded, raising his glass.

'And yours,' he said.

The two men sipped at the Perrier. The restaurant was quite empty, the tables already laid for dinner, the room in deep shadow behind the drawn curtain. The owner appeared from the kitchen, a tall, thin, rather bony man, immaculate in flannels and a striped blazer. He carefully placed a slender glass vase on the table between them. There were freesias in the vase, yellow, and purple, and a deep, deep red. The owner smiled a greeting to both men, but spoke first to Cartwright, the deference obvious in his voice.

'Will you be eating, Harry?'

Cartwright nodded. He didn't even glance at the menu.

'Dover sole,' he said, 'and mashed potatoes.'

The owner looked apologetic.

'We have a problem,' he said.

Cartwright frowned.

'No fish?'

'No chef.' The owner pulled a face. 'He's no longer with us I'm afraid. But I'll do what I can.'

'Where's he gone?'

'Canada. He managed to get a seat yesterday. His brother lives in Quebec.'

'I see.' Cartwright glanced at his watch. 'Are you any good with omelettes?'

The owner smiled and fluttered his hand.

'*Comme çi, comme ça . . .*' he said.

'Cheese omelette then.'

Cartwright looked enquiringly at Goodman. Goodman shook

his head. The owner disappeared into the kitchen, leaving the scent of freesias hanging in the air. The two men toyed with their glasses for a moment, then Goodman looked up.

'What can I do for you?' he said.

Cartwright gazed at him across the table, no trace of emotion, his face the usual mask. Anyone watching, any stranger, might assume they'd never met before.

'You're going underground soon,' he said. 'You must be.'

'We are. It's no secret.'

'How many of you?'

Goodman paused for a moment, wondering what was coming next. He'd shared a good deal of information with Cartwright over the years, but he'd never broken the Official Secrets Act.

'Seventy-eight,' he said.

'Married?'

'Most of them.'

'Kids?'

'Quite a few.'

Cartwright nodded.

'And what happens to them?' he said. 'When you all go underground?'

There was a silence. Goodman gazed at the tablecloth. White damask with a lace pattern around the edges.

'It's a tricky one,' he said. 'There are certain provisions for some of them. The possibility of . . . ah . . . selective evacuation.'

'Where to?'

'I'm not sure, to be truthful.'

Cartwright nodded.

'So some families go. And some stay,' he said. 'Is that wise?'

'No, it's not. Which is why I'll probably insist they all stay. When the time comes.'

Cartwright fingered his napkin, white starched linen folded into a fan shape on the plate beside his knife.

'I hear you're going to close the city,' he said.

There was another silence. Goodman looked Cartwright in the eye. No point, he thought. No point pretending otherwise. Not with this man.

'Yes,' he said, 'we are.'

'And will it work? Will it be . . .' he shrugged, 'watertight?'

'Yes. More or less. After a while, the country gums itself up.'

Cartwright leaned back, developing the analysis, remorseless, exact.

'Then your colleagues' families will be at risk,' he said. 'Pen people in. Fence them off. Give them no option but to sit and wait. They'll become desperate. They'll do anything.' He paused. 'Your colleagues' families will become sitting ducks.' He paused again. 'And your colleagues will know it.' Goodman nodded, conceding the logic of Cartwright's argument.

'Then they have to go.' Cartwright made a small, neat gesture with his knife. 'These wives. These children. For your sake. And your colleagues' sake.' He smiled, thinly. 'For all our sakes.'

Goodman gazed at him a moment, sensing at last the drift of the conversation, the shape of the deal.

'So what do you suggest?' he said carefully.

'I suggest we organize a charter. Out of the city.'

'The roads are impossible. And it'll get much worse. Even with fuel, there'll be nowhere to go.'

'We'll do it by sea,' Cartwright said, 'and we'll take them to a place of safety.'

'Who's we?'

'Myself . . .' he shrugged, 'and one or two associates. You'd supply a passenger list, and the appropriate dispensations. For fuel. Food. Plus permission to leave the harbour. The rest you should leave to us.'

'And who will pay?'

'It will be self-funding,' he smiled, 'as you can probably guess.'

Goodman nodded. Cartwright had a genius for identifying individual opportunities, and indicating ways they could be exploited; tiny, precise gestures with the carefully sharpened pencil he always kept on his desk. This philosophy tallied exactly with the revolution that had swept through Whitehall and had turned the city into a showcase local administration, quoted constantly in Ministerial memos, a model for the new Enterprise Culture. Goodman frowned.

'Can you be more specific?' he said.

Cartwright shook his head.

'No,' he said, 'not yet.'

'But it would work?'

'Certainly.'

Goodman hesitated a moment, knowing only too well that the broad plan made sense. He'd already been wondering what to do with Joanna and the kids. New bulletins all day had been reporting forty-mile traffic queues, and the log-jam on the nation's roads could only worsen once the petrol stations began to run out of fuel, forcing motorists to abandon their cars and walk. The prospect of consigning his own family to that kind of chaos was unthinkable. There had to be an alternative. Perhaps this was it.

'Where would they go?' he said.

'West.'

'But where?'

Cartwright shrugged.

'Ireland. Portugal. Somewhere non-NATO. Somewhere upwind.'

He measured out the facts, one by one, utterly logical, building the unanswerable case. Goodman paused again, letting the silence settle between them. Distantly, in the kitchen, he could hear the whisking of eggs.

'And you?' he said. 'Would you go with them?'

Cartwright, for the first time, permitted himself a genuine smile, a smile that touched his eyes.

'No,' he said.

'Why not?'

The little man looked away, out across the deserted restaurant. Then he shook the careful creases out of his napkin and tucked it into his collar, like a child.

'I've lived in this city all my life,' he said. 'Why should I stop now?'

Gillespie sat in front of the recruiting sergeant, waiting for the first question. He'd been at the police station for over an hour while the queue for registration slowly thinned. The sheer number of volunteers for the new Special Constabulary had taken the police by surprise. There'd been more bodies than chairs, and even now there were still a dozen men standing outside in the corridor.

The sergeant behind the desk glanced up. The office was tiny:

a single window, a desk, two filing cabinets.

'Name?' he said. He sounded weary.

'Gillespie.'

'Two "l"s is it?'

Gillespie nodded. 'Yeah,' he said, '"ie" at the end.'

The sergeant pulled a computer keyboard towards him.

'Date of birth, Mr Gillespie?'

'17 November 1951.'

The sergeant nodded and tapped in the name and the date. There was a brief pause. The sergeant loosened his tie and unbuttoned his collar. The central heating was on for some reason, and the room was uncomfortably hot. Lines of copy appeared on the screen. The sergeant began to check through it, methodically, one fact after another.

'David Arthur?'

'That's right.'

'20 Glengarry Road?'

'Yeah.'

'Clean licence,' he nodded, 'that sounds hopeful.' He paused, rubbed his eyes. 'You in the Marines once?'

'Yeah.'

'Sergeant? "B" Company? 43 Commando?'

'That's right.'

The sergeant made a note on the form and squinted at the screen again. Then he began to frown. Something was evidently out of order. Gillespie leaned forward, but the screen was invisible from his side of the desk.

'What's the matter?' he said.

The sergeant tinkered with the luminance control on the monitor screen. The lines of text brightened. The sergeant took a second look, and then a third.

'We've got a "K" reference,' he said, '211.'

He tapped the three digits into the computer and sat back a moment while fresh copy scrolled onto the screen. He scanned it quickly, then glanced across at Gillespie.

'Sergeant,' he said, 'I think we may have a problem.'

'What's that then?'

The policeman looked at him a moment, gauging what best to do, then glanced at the door, and gestured for Gillespie to join him. Gillespie did so, absorbing the lines of green print on the screen. When he'd finished, he looked down at the sergeant.

'Well?' he said. He was totally unperturbed.

The sergeant nodded at the screen.

'Is that lot right?'

Gillespie looked at him.

'Yeah,' he said. 'The date's wrong. It was the twelfth. Not the tenth. But the rest is OK. '85. Northern Ireland. Yeah . . .' He glanced at the screen again, and scanned quickly through the rest of the details, his mouth moving silently, intoning the names, the map references, the Army designation of the road, the name of the reporting pathologist. Finally he looked up. 'Yeah . . .' he said, 'spot on.' He returned to his seat on the other side of the desk and sat down. There was something new in the police sergeant's manner, and Gillespie recognized it at once. Respect.

'Unfortunately,' he began, 'there's a standing order about previous convictions.'

'It wasn't a conviction.'

'I know, but . . .' he shrugged, genuinely regretful, 'a court-martial's the next best thing.'

'I wasn't court-martialled, either.' He nodded at the back of the screen. 'That's the first time I've seen anything in print, you know, written down.'

The sergeant looked bewildered. 'K' references were obviously a rare event. He frowned at the screen again.

'But the bloke did die, didn't he?'

Gillespie nodded. 'Oh yeah,' he said, 'definitely.'

'And you were responsible?'

'I killed him,' he said, 'if that's what you mean.'

'So what happened?' He paused. 'Afterwards?'

'I resigned.' He shrugged. 'With a little gentle encouragement.'

'Well, then . . .' the sergeant sounded relieved, 'that's the same thing.'

'You serious?'

'Yes,' he nodded, and began to fold Gillespie's application form in half. 'A "K" reference rules you out.'

'Who says?'

'Standing orders, Sergeant. Rules and regulations. You know the drill.'

Gillespie looked at him a moment, wondering how far to take it, then changed his mind, and nodded goodbye, and left the room. Outside, in the corridor, the queue had lengthened again. The sergeant eyed the open door. 'Next!' he shouted. He sounded positively relieved.

Albie Curtis pulled the big old Bedford van off the main road and into the narrow cul-de-sac between the two rows of terrace houses. At the end was a pair of tall wooden gates topped with barbed wire. He parked the van outside the gates and hooted. When nothing happened, he hooted again. Then he got out of the van, and crossed the pavement, and kicked the gates, violently, twice. A dog began to bark inside. Albie rattled the gates, shaking them hard. There was the sound of footsteps, and the scrape of bolts, metal against metal. One of the gates opened. A face appeared, old and exhausted under an ancient flat cap. Albie nodded at him.

'Where's Jack?' he said.

The old man gestured inside, and Albie pushed past him without a word, ignoring the lunge of the big, black Alsatian, chained to a ring on the wall. Inside the gates was a builder's yard, piles of old bricks, breeze-blocks, timber, concrete, pipes. Beside the timber were four large drums. On the side, in black, they were stencilled MOD PROPERTY. DO NOT REMOVE.

A door opened in the low wooden shack at the back of the yard. A small compact man stepped out. He wore a lumberjack shirt and a pair of old jeans. He nodded at Albie and kicked the dog. The dog stopped barking.

'Mick's been on,' he said. 'He's trying to find you.'

'What did you tell him?'

'Nothing. I said I didn't know.'

'Good.'

Albie walked across to the big grey drums. There was a wrecking bar propped against the pile of timber. He picked up the wrecking bar and began to prise off one of the lids. The lid came off, clattering onto the ground at Albie's feet. Albie peered into the drum. The drum was full of white paint. He dipped a finger in, testing the consistency, watching it drip back into the drum. He smiled and turned to the other man.

'Bloke write the stuff OK?' he said.

The other man nodded.

'Fine.'

'Printer all right?'

'A thousand run. Like you said.'

'When's he ready?'

'Tonight.' He paused. 'I said you'd be round.'

'Good.'

Albie stooped to pick up the lid and fitted it back on the top of the drum, hammering it down at the edges with the wrecking bar. Then he tossed the bar to the other man. The other man caught it. Albie nodded at the drums.

'Forty quid,' he said. 'The lot.'

'Fifty.'

'Forty.'

The other man shrugged, turning away.

'Suit yourself,' he said. 'But take the stuff with you, eh?'

Martin Goodman and Oliver Davidson left the city at five o'clock, sitting together in the back of the big Rover while Corporal Evans, Goodman's new bodyguard and driver, eased the car through the beginnings of the evening rush hour.

Evans, Goodman had just met for the first time. He was tall, over six feet, with neatly cropped hair, and a wide, spare frame. His face – flat, neutral, guarded – gave nothing away, and he evidently had little inclination to talk. Davidson had handled the introductions at the kerbside, referring to Goodman as 'Mr Controller', a designation Evans had at once shortened to 'sir'. Now, with the Rover pushing eighty-five on the rise of the motorway flyover, Goodman was aware of the man watching them in the rear-view mirror, his eyes flickering up from the road ahead, noting their expressions, their mannerisms, their relationship to each other, stowing away his first impressions, making up his mind.

Goodman sat back against the contoured leather seat. Davidson had spent the afternoon away from the Civic Offices on something he referred to simply as 'business'. When he returned by taxi at half-past four, Goodman had wondered whether to enquire further, to try and establish some kind of stewardship over the man from Whitehall, but in the end he'd decided against it. He'd yet to mention his own excursion to meet Harry Cartwright, their conversation about getting the wives and kids away, and on reflection he decided to keep it to himself. His relationship with Harry didn't fit any official definitions and would be difficult to explain. Better, perhaps, to forget it.

Davidson pulled a small folded handkerchief from his breast pocket and mopped his brow. The rain had stopped by now, but it was warm for September. Goodman glanced at his watch. The Wessex TV nightly magazine started at six. He'd promised to be there with half an hour to spare. At this speed, they'd arrive slightly early. Davidson returned the handkerchief to his pocket.

'Tell me about Bullock,' he said. 'How well do you know him?'

'A little,' he said, 'on a social basis.'

Davidson nodded, gazing out at the flat expanse of the upper harbour as they crossed the bridge onto the mainland and began to filter into the traffic on the big east-west motorway.

'New, isn't he? Relatively speaking?'

'Yes. Been here a year or so. Since the station went on air.'

'Tell me,' Davidson inched down the electric windows, letting the rasp of the wind cloak their conversation, 'is he . . . ah . . . one of us?'

Goodman thought about the question for a moment or two. One brief, casual meeting at the grammar school play. A shared platform on a Rotary debate. A couple of halves in the pub across the road afterwards.

'No,' he said carefully, 'I don't think he is.' He paused. 'Does that matter?'

Davidson glanced at him, the eyes as pale as ever.

'Not really,' he said, 'not after tomorrow.'

Duggie Bullock and Annie McPhee sat in the tiny studio canteen. Annie was nursing a glass of fresh orange juice. Bullock was gazing into the remains of yet another coffee. He'd intended to chat about the Falklands project, but for the third time that day he found himself talking about events in the city.

'So what's going to happen?' he said simply.

'When?'

'Tonight. Tomorrow.'

'They'll take over. It's obvious.' She smiled at him, surprised at his naïvety. 'Where've you been, Duggie? All these years?'

He returned the smile, feeling far from amused.

'Simple as that?' he said.

She nodded. 'Simple as that,' she agreed. 'Give or take the odd detention camp. The political arrests. All the old guff they'll trot out about subversion and the defence of the realm.' She grinned, eyeing her Falklands notes. 'Same old garbage. Only slightly more obvious. The world being the way it is.'

'So should we be interested?'

'As human beings?'

'As programme makers.'

'Of course.'

He paused. 'Should *you* be interested?' he said.

Annie hesitated a moment, finally recognizing his drift, the purpose and point behind his near-obsession with what was happening down the road. Her problem was the Falklands. She'd invested a great deal in the project. She'd mastered the material, and developed a credible line of her own, and soon, once Gillespie had delivered, she'd be on her way. The thing looked very promising. Anything else would be a diversion. An irrelevance. Even the possibility of another war.

'I'm not sure,' she said. 'It depends.'

Bullock looked at her for a moment, understanding her preoccupation, but determined to prick the bubble she'd made her own.

'There's a man coming in for tonight's show,' he said finally, 'his name's Goodman. Martin Goodman. If we start anywhere, we start with him.' He paused and glanced at his watch. 'He's due any time,' he said, 'the interview's towards the end of the programme. Make sure you watch it.'

It was nearly half-past five before Evans pulled the big, black Rover through the gates of the Wessex TV studios and dropped Davidson and Goodman at the entrance to the main reception area. Goodman, who'd been to the studios before, led the way through the double glass doors. The receptionist recognized him at once, and phoned through to Bullock's secretary.

Seconds later, the secretary appeared. She thanked them for coming and led them towards the newsroom.

Annie, back at her borrowed desk by the window, looked up as the two men came in. She watched them carefully as they followed Bullock's secretary the length of the newsroom. She'd never seen either man before, but she suspected at once that Goodman was the younger of the two. He fitted the brief description that Bullock had given her as they returned from the canteen: the easy manner, the poise, the quick smile to the pretty girl on the copy desk, the way he very evidently felt immediately at home in the place. She'd seen the mannerisms before, in the better class of politician, the young high-flyers who made a name for themselves in some remote ministry or other, glad-handing their way through thickets of obstructive officials and difficult constituency meetings to a post downstage in the limelight.

The two men paused briefly outside Bullock's office while the secretary knocked on the glass partition door. Annie saw Bullock get up and gesture the two men into the office, advancing with his hand outstretched, and a small, tight smile on his face. Annie grinned, watching the ritual handshakes. She knew Bullock well enough by now to recognize that he didn't like Goodman at all, and she suspected that Goodman was far too acute not to know it.

Inside the office, there was a brief silence, while the secretary closed the door and the two men settled into their respective chairs. Goodman spoke first, his tone friendly, even intimate. It assumed at once a shared point of view, common values, joint membership of the same indefinable club.

Long time . . .' he said, 'no see. How's Wendy? The kids? I thought Tom was marvellous in the grammar play the other day. Racine's bloody hard for adults. Let alone kids.' Bullock accepted the compliment with a nod. He was already eyeing the clock over their heads.

'Thanks,' he said, 'I thought he was good, too. It's kind of you both to come along.'

He picked up the programme running order, finalized only minutes before, and ran his finger down the list of items.

'We've given you a decent spot at the end of the programme,' he said, 'live, of course. You should be away by seven at the latest.'

Goodman nodded. 'That sounds fine. What else have you got?' Bullock looked up. His voice was sharper than he intended.

'Beg pardon?' he said.

Goodman smiled, emollient, friendly, reassuring.

'Tonight's programme . . .' He paused. 'I was simply wondering how . . . exactly . . . you'll be treating today's . . . ah . . . events . . .'

'Oh,' Bullock shrugged, 'pretty straight. We're not short of stories, as you can imagine.' He glanced at the running order again. 'We're leading with the refugees. I had a very good girl down at the Ferryport. She did well. It's powerful stuff.'

'Refugees?' Goodman replied mildly. 'You mean tourists, surely?'

Bullock gazed at him for a moment, one finger still anchored on the running order. Then, abruptly, he leaned back in his chair, his hands clasped behind his head, looking at the ceiling, recognizing the conversation for what it was. Davidson stirred by the window.

'What else are you running?' he said.

'The motorway story. As you'd expect.'

'Ah . . .' Goodman took up the running again, the same smile, the same utterly reasonable tone. 'The repairs . . .'

'No. The midday closures. Our first taste of the Essential Service Routes.' Bullock let his chair tilt forward, bringing his eyeline level with Goodman's. 'We like to think of it as a service to viewers. Where to drive and where not to drive. How to avoid a nuclear depth charge convoy.'

Goodman looked regretful.

'Is that strictly necessary?' he said. 'Given the circumstances?'

'We think so.' Bullock picked up the running order again and slid it across the desk towards Goodman. 'And since we're talking about your city, there's item six. Today's little demo. The peace protest at the War Memorial. I'm afraid most of the pictures are far too explicit to run at this time of night, but I must say the NF boys made their point. Not that the police took much notice. Half a dozen people in hospital and not a whisper of a charge.'

'Oh,' Goodman frowned, 'surely not.'

Bullock nodded, determined to keep the anger out of his voice.

'Yeah,' he said, 'oh yeah.'

The two men looked at each other, a mutual acceptance of totally opposed interests. Then Bullock leaned back again, his voice softer, more accommodating.

'Listen, my friend,' he said, 'if what we hear is true, you've got a helluva job on your hands. In a minute we're going to stop playing these games, and you're going to ask me to make it easier for you. It's a reasonable request. If I was in your shoes, I'd probably be playing it exactly the same way. But I'm not in your shoes. And I might not quite see it the way you do.' He paused and retrieved the running order. 'You can't tell me what to transmit. Not yet, you can't.'

Goodman accepted the point with a smile.

'No,' he said, 'but we can ask. Politely.'

'Oh, sure. And you have. And tonight you've got six minutes to say your piece. I'm only sorry it can't be longer.' He got up and began to manoeuvre himself around the desk. Goodman stayed seated, looking up at him.

'There's one thing I thought I ought to mention . . .' he began.

'What's that?'

Goodman frowned, choosing the words with great care, the soul of discretion.

'If the full emergency powers are introduced . . .' he said, 'we'll be needing someone down in the Bunker to handle our information policy. Someone whose integrity and professional skills we admire . . .'

'If the Bill gets through or when?' enquired Bullock, fishing for confirmation of the afternoon's rumour on the AP tape.

'If,' said Goodman.

'Ah.' Bullock nodded and made a note on his blotter. Then he looked down at Goodman again. 'So you're after a tame journalist?'

'Yes.'

'Someone you can bend?'

'Someone we can trust.'

'Same thing, isn't it?'

Bullock smiled for the first time, a big spreading grin that Goodman recognized at once as a declaration of war. The conversation was over. There only remained the formality of the live interview. He got to his feet. Davidson did the same. There were more nods, more handshakes. The secretary was back at the door.

'Sandie will look after you,' he said. 'Good luck on the show.'

Goodman and Davidson took their cue and turned to leave. It was only when Goodman was nearly at the door that Bullock spoke again.

'Oh, by the way,' he said. 'My son's name is Adam, not Tom. And it was Corneille, not Racine . . .' he smiled, 'just for the record.'

When Albie Curtis got to the printers, the place was closed. There was a handwritten note on the door directing callers to a pub across the road called the Spanish Arms.

Albie found the printer in the saloon bar. He was sitting by himself at a table under the window, a pale, nervous man with a glass of brown ale and a facial twitch. The evening edition of the local paper lay open in front of him.

Albie stood over the man for a moment or two. There was a big photo in the paper – a row of young female faces pressed to the windows of a passing coach – and a headline which read HOSPITAL CHAOS – MUMS MOVE OUT. Albie nudged the table with his knee.

'That stuff of mine,' he said.

The printer looked up, recognizing Albie at once.

'It's in the shop,' he said.

'I need it now,' Albie nodded at the window, 'I've got the van.'

The printer hesitated for a moment, then swallowed the remains of his brown ale, folded the newspaper, and stood up. The bar was filling rapidly with stevedores and freight marshallers from the Ferry port as they headed for the door.

At the shop, the printer fumbled for his keys and unlocked the door. The place was dark inside, and smelled of ammonia. The printer walked through to the small store room at the back. The leaflets were on a table, neatly packaged. A small pile of rejects lay beside the packet. Albie picked one up. *Miracle Emulsion*, it read. *As developed by NASA. Guaranteed Blast Proof. Peace of Mind with the One-Coat Wonder.* There were further details, culled from the pages of a space fantasy magazine, and a phone number to ring for personal service. £10 a window, including VAT.

Albie held the leaflet at arm's length and nodded approvingly. Splashy red capitals on a yellow background. Big drawing of a mushroom cloud. Class production. Nice effect.

'Good,' he said. 'Thanks a lot.'

The printer grunted and turned to the photocopier. There was an invoice under the flap. He gave it to Albie. Albie glanced at it, then stuffed it into his back pocket and picked up the packet of leaflets.

'Usual terms?' he said, heading for the door.

The printer nodded gloomily, reaching for his keys.

'Suppose so,' he said. 'Twenty-eight days.'

Joanna Goodman carried Charlie's high chair in from the kitchen, and put it carefully on the carpet in front of the TV. Charlie crawled after her, hands and knees, leaving behind him a trail of crumbs from the bib around his neck. James was already on the sofa, balancing a plate of spaghetti on his lap, trying to peer round his mother's body at the screen. Caroline sat beside him, her plate already empty, neat and watchful as ever.

Martin had phoned from the TV studios only minutes before. Joanna had taken the call in the kitchen, one hand for the phone, one hand for Charlie. He'd told her he was due to be interviewed, and he wondered whether she and the kids might like to watch. He'd sounded amused, and warm, even a little excited, quite the old Martin, and she, in turn, had grinned at him down the phone, and said she'd have died of disappointment if he hadn't let them know. Her very own husband. A TV star. She'd wished him luck, and he'd said he'd need it, and she promised champagne on ice for when he got home, and he'd laughed at that, and said she was crazy. She'd smiled, treasuring the conversation, the laughter, the contact, the sudden flood of reassurance, and then Charlie had made a lunge for the cat, and she'd hung up.

Now, one minute to six, she settled Charlie into the high chair, and retrieved a loop of spaghetti from the carpet beneath James' plate, and plumped up the cushions, and settled back beside Caroline to wait for Martin to appear. James, his mouth full of spaghetti, turned towards her.

'What about Granny's,' he said, 'when do we go?'

'Ah,' she grinned at him, 'depends on Daddy.'

'What does he think?'

'I don't know,' she said, nodding at the TV. 'Let's wait and see.'

*

'Coastwise', the Wessex TV nightly news magazine, started on time at one minute past six. The bulk of the programme was on video, three- or four-minute reports from all over the area, and Martin Goodman, the only live guest, was on the interview set in the studio from the start. There were monitor screens suspended from the studio roof showing the programme as it was transmitted live, and he was able to watch the case building up against him. Interviews with anxious shoppers about food shortages. Interviews with worried mums about the rumoured closure of schools. Interviews with harassed businessmen about police roadblocks on the motorway entrances. Footage from the city's hospital, where one of the injured demonstrators had undergone exploratory brain surgery. And a colourful piece from a pensioner on his plans to raise a vigilante squad to patrol the city's more productive allotments. 'Couldn't have happened at a worse time,' he mused, 'nearly Harvest Festival.'

With five minutes to go to the start of his own contribution, Goodman was joined in the studio by Lawrence Prosser, an interviewer of national standing who'd abandoned the big time for a cottage beside the Solent, an ocean-going yacht, and occasional guest appearances on Wessex TV. Goodman knew that Bullock only wheeled him out for the big occasions, and he was flattered.

Prosser advanced across the studio, a bulky, cheerful man, one hand outstretched. Goodman knew him by sight, but had never met him personally.

'Martin,' he said, 'how nice to see you.'

Goodman began to get up, remembered he was tethered by a microphone, and abruptly sat down again. Prosser shook him by the hand, checked his appearance in the lens of a nearby camera, and sat down in the chair opposite. He waved away a make-up girl and propped a clipboard comfortably on his knee. Attached to the clipboard was a list of questions. Prosser nodded up at one of the monitor screens.

'You'll be wanting to watch this bit,' he said, 'I won't disturb you.'

He smiled briefly and bent to his notes. Goodman eyed the clipboard, untidy lines of scribble, certain words underlined, each question hand-written in red ink, impenetrable as code. He returned to the TV screen. A bearded man of about forty, a sociology lecturer at the city's polytechnic, was talking about the impact of events on the city's inhabitants. As the prospect of war became more and more real, he said he'd detected a deep unease. He said that some people were becoming depressed and fatalistic. He said others were becoming reckless and anti-social. He expected violence and apathy in about equal proportions. Today's demo, he said, was merely a symptom, a straw in the wind. Soon, certain sections of society would become scapegoats. Perhaps the French families, now flooding into the city. Perhaps the Asian community. Perhaps even the Jews. But whatever was happening now, and however scary that might seem, worse would inevitably follow because people were becoming progressively disoriented by events. They were losing their spiritual bearings. The man smiled. This interpretation of events was evidently his own. He called it the Hiroshima Syndrome. An off-screen voice asked him what he expected to happen next, and the man shrugged, and said that individuals were no more than the bricks in society's wall, and once the bricks crumbled then the wall would fall down. This image evidently appealed to him, and he smiled again, and the picture abruptly cut to a persuasive montage of the day's most haunting images – a French mother in tears at the Ferryport, ambulances loading casualties from the midday demo, a pensioner gazing at an air raid poster, Army sappers humping sandbags in the rubble-strewn no-go area around the dockyard wall. Finally, the reporter signed off and handed the programme back to Prosser in the studio.

Prosser, preoccupied with his clipboard only seconds before, looked abruptly grave, expressed his regrets about the day's body count, and turned the programme towards the one man who might throw a little light on it all.

Goodman blinked. In a second or two, it would be his face in the city's living rooms, his job to answer the impossible questions. Feeling curiously unreal, he listened to Prosser introducing him as 'the man in charge'. Goodman acknowledged his name with a nod. Prosser turned to him and asked at once how bad the situation really was. The question came at the end of nearly half an hour of bad news, a rising chord of alarm and disaster, and Goodman knew at once that he had, somehow, to stem this seamless flood of images and assumptions, to sound a different note, and to move the debate onto territory of his own choosing. He smiled apologetically at Prosser, only too aware of the importance of first impressions, offering himself as a man concerned to address the facts, to restore a little perspective, to somehow reassure a thoroughly frightened audience that all was far from lost.

'Well . . .' he said easily, 'can I first pick you up on one point. I'm not actually in charge.'

Prosser looked up from his clipboard, taken by surprise.

'But you are Acting Chief Executive? That is right, isn't it?'

Goodman nodded. 'That's perfectly correct, yes.'

'So you're in charge, are you not?'

Goodman smiled again, ever reasonable, ever polite.

'In charge is an emotive expression,' he said. 'I head the officers whose job it is to administer the affairs of the city. For everybody's benefit.'

Prosser looked at him for a moment, recognizing at once the path Goodman was trying to take. Democracy and the workings of local government were pure Nembutal. That kind of line would put any audience instantly to sleep. Sensibly, he changed the subject.

'But it is a city, Mr Goodman, that must be high on the Soviet hit list . . . must it not?'

Goodman smiled again, the easiest of openings.

'Well, I'm afraid I'm not a Soviet military planner,' he said. 'If I were I could probably answer that question.'

Davidson, standing in the shadows at the back of the darkened control room, permitted himself a smile. Goodman was doing well, better than he'd expected. He watched Prosser on one of the monitor screens, recognizing a new note of irritation in the interviewer's voice. Goodman wasn't obeying the script. His answers weren't at all in keeping with the thrust of the rest of the programme. He didn't look like a man on the edge of the abyss. On the contrary, he looked calm, and benign, the soul of reassurance. Prosser leaned forward, concerned, fearless, the people's tribune, the bringer of bad news, still convinced that the city lay under the Soviet cosh.

'But how else would you interpret what's been happening

around the dockyard?' he said. 'The no-go areas? The sandbags? The barbed wire?'

'Precautions,' said Goodman at once. 'The dockyard's an important national asset, and I'm sure you'd be even more concerned if we didn't protect it.'

'But isn't that precisely my point? Doesn't the naval link mean that the city is under direct threat? If and when the shooting starts?'

Goodman frowned, modifying his voice slightly, trying to strike the exact vocal balance between understanding and reassurance.

'Well . . .' he said, 'if you're implying that we all face extinction, which I suspect you are, then I have to say that's a very gloomy assumption. And one, I might add, that's very far from justified. Or justifiable.'

Prosser nodded, closing fast on the real meat of the interview.

'But tell me,' he said, 'do you have plans if things get worse?'

Goodman looked at him for a moment, trying not to sound defensive.

'Well . . .' he said, 'it's our job to make . . . ah . . . provision against certain eventualities. People would quite properly complain if we didn't.'

'And do these provisions, these plans, include the suspension of civil liberties?'

Goodman looked thoughtful, the expression of a man to whom such a possibility had not previously occurred.

'Good Lord, no,' he said. 'That's purely speculative. I don't think for a moment that we're in that kind of situation. Things are pretty serious, yes, but not *that* serious.'

'Nor likely to be?'

'Oh no . . .' Goodman shook his head. 'I don't think so.'

'Not even after today? Refugees? Arms convoys? Police recruiting Special Constables?'

Goodman smiled, patient again. Next door, Bullock stepped quietly into the control room, standing in the deep shadows by the door from where he could see both the screens and Davidson. The latter was still standing behind the seated row of technicians at the control desk, absolutely motionless, looking at Goodman on the monitor screens.

'These are purely precautionary moves,' Goodman was saying, 'any sensible government would make them. Take Special Constables. The Army and most of the Reserve have gone to Germany. The police have a lot on their plate, and they're simply back-filling. That's all. It's nothing sinister. It's a numbers game. Pure and simple.' He paused, trying to pre-empt further questions by bringing the discussion to a natural close. 'No . . .' he said, 'what we have is a serious international crisis abroad, and a sensible, responsible, measured reaction here at home. But, if I may say so, there's absolutely no cause for alarm.'

Prosser looked at him, waiting a moment for the director to change the shot. On screen at last, he leaned slightly forward.

'Do you have plans to ration petrol?'

'No. Absolutely not.'

'Food?'

'Well . . .' Goodman eased away from the firing line, 'you talk of food and fuel. But I must say the general point is more valid, and I'm afraid I can only repeat it. It's business as usual. Life, I'm afraid, goes on. Sorry to disappoint you, but that's the fact of the matter.'

In the control room, the PA was already counting Prosser out of the interview, and with nine seconds to go he had little choice but to accept Goodman's peroration with a sceptical nod, and to thank him for his time, and to make a final turn into his personal camera to wish the viewers good-night. Anyone who knew him well might sense the anger and frustration, but Bullock's eyes were still on Davidson. The man had allowed himself the quietest of smiles, the sorcerer applauding the clever young apprentice, and Bullock knew at once that things were far, far worse than they'd anticipated, worse even than Annie's cynical predictions, and that somehow they had to find a way of coming to terms with it all.

Davidson stepped towards him. The end credits were rolling on the screens behind his head. He smiled at Bullock and extended a hand.

'Fascinating,' he said. 'Quite fascinating.'

Bullock smiled grimly.

'Our pleasure,' he said. 'Do come again.'

*

Gillespie arrived back at Sandra's as dusk was beginning to fall. He got out of the car. Sean was visible through the window in the front room. He was re-whipping one of the rings onto his favourite sea rod, working under the dim spread of the overhead light, holding the rod section between his knees, the whipping twine in his teeth, one thumb pressed against the rod rings, the other maintaining the pressure on the twine. Gillespie hesitated for a moment on the pavement. What the boy needed was an extra hand, someone to help him. What he didn't have was a live-in father. He shrugged. The boy would find a way. Always had. Always would.

Sandra opened the door to his knock. She was wearing a long cotton skirt and a loose blouse, open at the neck. The lipstick was subtle, and the perfume he'd never smelled before. She looked tanned, and happy. He paused on the doorstep, all too aware of the intrusion.

'You're off out,' he said.

'That's right.' She smiled at him, enjoying his confusion. 'You after Sean?'

Gillespie frowned. 'No,' he said, 'you.'

'Oh?' She glanced at her watch. 'Better be quick.'

'Sure.'

Gillespie stepped past her into the house. Sandra began to say something, then stopped herself and followed him into the kitchen. A man in his early forties sat at the table. He was wearing a well-cut jacket and expensive shoes. He had a pleasant, open face, and his hair was flecked with grey at the temples. He looked distinguished, and faintly professional. A lawyer, perhaps, or a doctor. There was a glass of sherry on the table beside him, and a bunch of fresh flowers in the washing-up bowl. The man got up as Gillespie came in. He stopped. The other man extended his hand.

'Paul Millom,' he said. 'A friend of Sandra's.'

Gillespie nodded and shook his hand.

'Dave Gillespie,' he said, not bothering to qualify the introduction. He looked round. Sandra had picked up the bottle of sherry and was unscrewing the top.

'Drink?' she said.

He shook his head.

'No thanks,' he said.

There was an uneasy silence. Then Gillespie nodded towards the front room.

'You got a moment?' he said to Sandra. 'Won't take long.'

'Sean's in there.'

'I know. Doesn't matter.'

Sandra hesitated a moment, exchanged glances with the man in the jacket, then stepped down the tiny hall and into the front room. Gillespie followed her. Sean looked up, the roll of whipping twine still in his teeth. Gillespie shut the door behind him with his foot. Sandra turned on him. She was irritated, and it showed in her face.

'This better be important, Dave . . .' she began.

'Yeah, yeah . . .' Gillespie waved vaguely in the direction of the kitchen, 'sorry to barge in.'

'So what is it?'

Gillespie frowned. 'That twenty quid,' he said at last. 'I need it back.'

'*Now?*'

''Fraid so.'

'Oh . . .' she looked confused, 'cheers.'

'What's the matter?'

'I've spent most of it.'

Gillespie looked her up and down. The perfume. The skirt. The new blouse.

'Yeah,' he said, 'so I see.'

'No, you don't.'

Gillespie shrugged. There was a brief silence between them. Then Sean let the roll of whipping twine drop from his mouth. It rolled over the carpet, towards the skirting board.

'I've got a fiver, Dad,' he said, 'you can have that.'

'It's OK, son,' he said, 'we need twenty.'

Sandra frowned. 'We?' she said.

'Yes,' he said, 'we.'

'Who's we?'

'You and me,' he said carefully. 'And the boy.'

'Why's that then? Do we get to know?'

'Sure . . .' He hesitated, wondering whether to go into the details, to tell her about the rumours sweeping the city, the exodus already under way. Instead, he stuck to the meat of it all. 'We're heading west,' he said, 'and the boat needs more diesel.'

Joanna put James to bed at half-past seven. The child had sat through his father's interview on television, understanding very little of it but reaching forward time and time again, and tapping Charlie on the shoulder, and pointing at the screen, and shouting 'Daddy! Daddy!' insistently in his left ear. Charlie, who worshipped James and loved the attention, in turn chorused 'Daddy!' and pointed, like James, at the screen, kicking his feet and gurgling whenever Martin spoke. With these distractions, Joanna had found it difficult to follow the interview in detail, but she'd heard enough to know that the publicity and the news reports had been – as ever – overdone, and that there wouldn't be any need to drive to Wales. She'd also been impressed by her husband's performance, a warm, proud feeling that had surprised and delighted her. He wasn't, after all, remotely insane. Simply overworked, and overburdened. A clever man trying to do an impossible job.

With the interview over and the television off, Joanna had taken James on her lap, and given him a big, wet kiss, and told him that they wouldn't, after all, be going to Granny's. James, who was already old enough to hate being kissed, took the news badly, collapsing in a flood of tears. Joanna had quietened him for a minute or so, until the sobbing subsided, and then bent to his ear and whispered that he could wear his new Action Man pyjamas to bed, a special treat. The promise dried his tears at once, and he hopped off the sofa and ran out of the room. Joanna heard his footsteps up the stairs, and the squeak of the linen cupboard door as he rummaged around for his new pyjamas.

Downstairs, for half an hour or so, Joanna had hung on, preparing the meal, tidying the kitchen in the hope that Martin might drive straight back from the TV studios. But when there was no sign of him she supposed that he'd been delayed again, and decided to get the kids to sleep before he returned. That way, they could enjoy the peace and quiet alone. She thought briefly about the champagne, and smiled. There was a bottle in the cupboard under the stairs. She'd put it on ice.

An hour later, she closed James' book, and pulled back his curtains an inch or two, and kissed him softly before dousing the light and stepping quietly out of the room. Caroline, as usual, was still reading, but Charlie, when she checked the nursery, was already asleep with his thumb in his mouth, the impossibly blond hair splayed out against the fitted towelling sheet on the mattress. She kissed him, too, and gazed at him for a moment, before tip-toeing from the nursery and crossing the landing to her own bedroom.

On the big double bed, half full, were the two suitcases she'd readied in case they'd decided to head west. Now, humming to herself, she began to unpack them, returning her jeans and the odd dress to the wardrobe. She emptied one case and slid it into the space beside the wardrobe. Then she started on the other case, Martin's, carefully refolding his shirts and putting them back in his chest of drawers. At the bottom of the suitcase was a lightweight summer jacket she'd bought him three years back in Viareggio. He'd taken her there for a surprise holiday, leaving James and Caroline with friends while they celebrated his promotion to Deputy Chief Executive. It had been a wonderful week in a big, cool, cavernous hotel room, full of light and shadow, with a balcony and a view of the long curve of coastline down to Livorno. They'd lazed on the beaches, and idled through Florence, and taken long walks in the late afternoon, up in the forests that smudged the soft brown swell of the Tuscan hills. Martin had been loving, and attentive, and relaxed, hers entirely. Happiness, she remembered, smelled of pine needles.

She took the jacket out, and folded it carefully over her arm. As she did so, something fell from the inside pocket. Still humming, she stopped to retrieve it from the carpet. It was a postcard. It had landed face up. There was a black and white photo of a cat curled up on a bed. There were two pillows, one overlapping the other. The sheets were half drawn back, and rumpled. Very slowly, she turned the postcard over. Blue biro. Big, full, strong, rounded characters. She felt the chill begin, deep within her. She began to read, not wanting to go on, unable to stop.

'Darling. . .' it began, '. . .thanks for the weekend. And thanks for the pressies. And thanks most of all for the ring. The weekend I'll treasure. The pressies go into our bottom drawer.

And the ring will buy us champers when we're very, very poor. Love, and all the trimmings. S.'

Joanna took half a step backwards, a physical blow, and sat abruptly on the bed. She began to tremble. She wanted to cry. Nothing happened. Very distantly, in spite of herself, she began to understand.

Duggie Bullock sat in the empty newsroom, nursing a glass of whisky. His feet were propped on his secretary's desk, and he had one eye on the incoming news copy feed from London. The National Gallery was evacuating key pictures to an undisclosed destination. Greenpeace had draped a banner across the central span of Westminster Bridge. There was a seventy-mile traffic queue on the M4. Parts of the western suburbs were nearly empty. The Queen was expected to broadcast the next day.

Annie appeared at the other end of the newsroom. She'd been down in the editing suites, talking to the camera crews who'd spent the day in the city. Her weeks of Falklands research had closed her eyes to what was really happening. Only now, listening to their stories, did she realize that Bullock was right, that the secret state she'd spent most of her life trying to expose, that indefinable conceit that lay at the heart of her Falklands project, was about to give itself away. Not in London. Or on some distant battlefield. But here. Ten miles down the road. In the abstract, it was a fascinating thought. In reality, there was no longer any question what she should do.

She perched herself on the edge of Bullock's secretary's desk. Bullock pushed the bottle towards her. There was a weariness in him, a resignation, and she saw it at once. She eyed the bottle and shook her head. Bullock sighed and gazed out at the empty car park.

'You see him?' he said.

She nodded. 'Yes,' she said.

'Smooth bugger, isn't he?'

'Very.' She paused. 'They all are. It's a family trait.'

Bullock nodded, thinking of Prosser.

'Larry did well,' he said, 'and Goodman murdered him.'

'I know.'

Bullock shook his head, easing the top off the whisky bottle and refilling his glass. Under different circumstances, two years back, he'd have had the resources to pull in a team of researchers, to chase leads, identify themes, buy or bully his way to key interviews, build a case that might, after transmission, actually change things. Now though, with the big companies gone, and a hundred tiny operators squabbling over what was left of the audience, the costs of making that kind of programme were simply too high. He shook his head and reached for the glass. Watching Goodman's performance, meeting Davidson, pulling together the other bits of the jigsaw, he'd finally realized just how unequal the struggle had become. By deregulating television – by cutting audiences and slashing budgets – the Government, any government, had won. Real TV journalism, showpiece TV journalism, his kind of TV journalism, was dead and buried.

Annie looked at him.

'So what do we do?' she said.

He sipped at the whisky, letting it trickle slowly down his throat, a little warmth, a little reassurance.

'In theory?' he said. 'Or for real?'

'Both.'

He frowned, circling the rim of the glass with his finger.

'In theory there's not much we can do. Goodman will take charge. By tomorrow he'll be Controller. He'll have absolute power. He'll be able to do anything he wants.' He paused. 'It would make an interesting film.'

'Then let's do it.'

He smiled at her, the enthusiasm, the commitment, the belief.

'What with?'

'Me.'

'And?'

'A film crew.'

'And?'

Annie shrugged. Never short on self-belief, she saw no point in extending the list.

'Luck?' she suggested.

Bullock reached for the remote control for the copy feed, and blanked the screen.

'You realize what you're taking on?' he said.

'We're taking on.'

'You, love. There's only you. I'll back you all the way. You know that. But I'm here, behind this desk. Down there...' he nodded vaguely out into the darkness, 'you're on your own.'

'OK,' she said simply, 'no problem.'

He looked at her for a moment, trying to lay aside his preconceptions, trying to believe that this slight figure in jeans and T-shirt could really deliver what he knew was there. Maybe he was wrong about teams of researchers and fat production budgets. Maybe it really was simpler than that.

'So you'll have a go?' he said. 'Try and pull something together?'

'Sure.'

'Starting tomorrow?'

'Tonight.'

He nodded and reached in a drawer where his secretary kept the office contacts book. He opened it at 'M' and ran his finger down the page.

'You gave me a number,' he said, '862564.'

Annie hesitated a moment. The number belonged to Gillespie.

'Yes,' she said, 'I did.'

'Can I get you there?'

Annie frowned, thinking about it, the scene in the hall, the clatter of the last of the camera cases being loaded into the Volvo outside, Gillespie in his thick polo neck sweater and fishing gear. They'd parted friends, but only just.

'Not tonight,' she said finally, 'but later maybe.' She smiled at the thought. 'Fingers crossed.'

Jermyn's was a small, discreet, relatively new wine bar in an area of the city close to the seafront. It occupied the basement of a once-grand hotel, a place of shadows, and alcoves, and candlelight.

In the early evening, the wine bar was virtually empty, and Goodman and Suzanne had been meeting there for nearly a year: glasses of white wine, and the touch of hands, and the slow dissipation of yet another day spent apart. They'd invested the place with a sense of spiritual ownership and, with the exception of Suzanne's flat, it had remained one of the few rendezvous where they could feel safe. No one from the Civic Centre ever went near the place, and if any of the handful of girls Suzanne employed at the local office ever stopped by, they never bothered to enquire about her companion. He was simply an older man, probably married, definitely smitten. In this sense, and importantly, the wine bar had become somehow separate from real life, a world apart.

Evans dropped Goodman at the door and parked the Rover across the road. They'd already left Davidson at a hotel in the business area of the city, an enormous slab-fronted building, barely a year old, which offered him the services and the anonymity he evidently required. He'd decided to base himself there for the time being, scribbling Goodman a phone number and an extension. Goodman, in turn, had confirmed his own number but had asked him not to phone before ten. Davidson had nodded but said nothing, stepping quickly out of the car and hurrying away across the pavement without a backward glance.

Martin Goodman glanced at Suzanne's Golf GTI parked outside the wine bar, and hurried down the basement stairs. He'd agreed to meet Suzanne at half-past seven. It was now eight. He paused at the foot of the stairs, letting his eyes accustom themselves to the half darkness. Suzanne was sitting in the corner. Her glass of wine was untouched. She moved her bag, and a fold of her Burberry raincoat, and motioned him onto the bench seat beside her. He knew at once that something was wrong. Instead of kissing him, she touched him lightly on the cheek, a cursory gesture. He sat down and apologized for being late. She shrugged and made no comment. He looked at her, wondering quite where to start, how much to say, what to keep back. She saved him the trouble.

'I'm sorry I called,' she said, 'it was stupid.'

'Not at all.'

'Yes it was.' She reached forward and ground her cigarette into the heavy glass ashtray. There were three others in there, all half smoked. 'I was a silly cow.' She shrugged. 'The whole thing got the better of me. God knows what you think.'

'I don't think anything.'

'Yes, you do.' She corrected herself. 'Did. I could hear it in your voice.' She looked at him, direct, appraising, savouring the simple physical advantage the relationship had always given her. 'You were very busy and very remote, and I was. . .'

she shrugged again, 'a silly cow.' She paused and let the apology lie on the table between them, then she leaned quickly forward, and took his face in both hands, gentle, mischievous, assured, and kissed him on the lips. 'I love you,' she said, 'and I hate apologizing for it.'

Goodman blinked. Part of the intoxication of the relationship had always been Suzanne's ability to surprise him, to adopt a position, to stake out territory, and then to turn a series of deft somersaults that tore down the divisions between them, and confirmed yet again what they'd both known from the start. He felt for her hand, and began to tell her everything, nothing glossed, nothing withheld. He told her about Davidson, and the morning's key meetings. He told her exactly how bad things were in the city, and what was liable to happen next. He said it was time to leave, and he told her he'd found her a flight. He described the visit to the TV studios, Bullock, Prosser, and he ended by telling her about Evans, and his new official car.

'He's a nice lad,' he said, 'I'm lucky to have him.'

'I'm sure,' she said drily. 'Do bodyguards mind staying the night?'

Goodman smiled and squeezed her hand, but the chill was back again, the sense of threat, imperceptible but definitely there. Goodman reached up, and touched her lightly on the face.

'What do you say, then?'

'To what?' She paused. 'Exactly?'

'To the flight. Exxon are shipping their key people out tomorrow morning. They've chartered two Jumbos out of Heathrow. God knows how. . .' He toyed with the glass of wine the barman had brought over when he'd arrived. 'I can get you a seat. . .' he said, 'if you want. They're going to Boston.'

Suzanne said nothing for a moment, then looked away.

'What do you think?' she said.

Goodman studied her, choosing his words carefully.

'I think you should go.'

'And what do you think I think?'

'I've no idea.'

Suzanne's mouth curled into a smile. She turned back to him, soft, incredulous, forgiving.

'No,' she said, 'you haven't, have you?' She took his hand

and looked at him. 'Tell me. . .' she said, 'do you think I love you?'

Goodman nodded. 'Yes.'

'And if you think I love you, do you think I'm about to get on a plane and fly to America?'

'That's hardly the point.'

She looked at him again, that same expression.

'Isn't it?'

'No.' Goodman paused. 'You don't understand, my love. It's all going to get very difficult. Especially this part.'

'You mean it's been easy so far?'

'No. Of course not. But my time won't be my own. That's more than obvious.'

'Has it ever been?'

'No. But at least that was office hours. More or less.'

Suzanne looked away, out into the shadows. The barman was polishing glasses.

'I'm not talking about office hours,' she said quietly. 'As you well know.'

Goodman said nothing for a moment. He'd made his speech, done his duty, advised her to make the sensible decision, to bow to events beyond their control, and cut her losses, and get out while she still could. And yet she was right. The thing had never been sane. Never been sensible. Instead, it had been wild, and selfish, and totally beyond the laws of rational behaviour. It was a relationship that made no allowances for reality, or for other people. If the world was to end, so be it. He took her hand again, and felt her fingers tighten around his.

'So you'll stay. . .?' he said.

She looked at him, and then nestled her head against his shoulder, close, needful, complete.

'I'm afraid so,' she said. 'Finders, keepers.'

She paused, and he felt her fingers sliding the cuff of his shirt over his watch, a piece of private semaphore.

'I think we should celebrate,' she said. 'I'm sure an hour or two won't hurt.'

Inside the casino, the air was thick with cigar smoke. Mick and Albie sat perched on chrome stools by the bar, while the wealthier of the city's late night drinkers jostled around them. Mick was nursing a Pina Colada. Cartwright was already half an hour late, but he'd barely touched the drink. He'd spent most of the evening refining his idea, making preliminary enquiries amongst the fishermen at the dock, getting a handle on the kind of money they talked, sorting out deals on bulk food, studying maps of Southern Ireland, and the more he got to grips with the enterprise, the more attractive it became. At lunchtime, he'd viewed it as a reprieve from the bailiffs. Half a day later, it was a meal ticket for life.

Now, he nudged Albie and nodded across at the gaming tables, surrounded by Chinese waiters, newly arrived from the city's restaurants. They were betting with their usual fervour, heads bent over the green baize, chips piled up at elbows, faces impassive, eyes everywhere, hands moving fast, blurring the cards.

'Amazing, isn't it?' he said. 'The world's about to disappear up its arse, and these characters are still at it. Look at them. Could be any old night. What do they know that we don't?'

Albie examined his finger-nails. Most of the white paint had come off now, but there were still traces.

'Dunno,' he said.

Mick shook his head.

'Maybe it's because they're Chinkie,' he said, 'bound to be some of them left at the end. Bound to be. Then all they have to do is breed. Got it made, haven't they?'

A figure appeared at his elbow. Small. Neat. Suit and glasses. Cartwright. Mick grinned at him, the favourite uncle.

'Harry,' he said, 'my shout.'

He leaned across the bar and lobbed an ice cube at one of the barmaids. They were both dressed in low-cut black silk outfits. One of them came across. Cartwright ordered a Perrier, ignoring Mick's offer of something stronger. Albie looked hard at the little accountant.

'What happened?' he said, 'with your mate?'

Mick turned back from the bar with the drink, all smiles and banter, hastily interposing himself between Cartwright and Albie. Albie ignored him, refusing to be distracted, not taking his eyes off Cartwright. He looked like a boxer going through the preliminaries of a championship fight, ignoring the referee's recital of the rules, oblivious of the crowd. He didn't like Cartwright, didn't trust him, and no longer saw the point of disguising it.

'This mate of yours,' he said again, 'what did he say?'

Cartwright looked at him with obvious distaste.

'There won't be a problem,' he said simply.

'How much did you bung him?'

'How much did I what?'

'Bung him.' Albie rubbed two fingers together, about a millimetre from Cartwright's nose. 'Dosh, mate. Ackers. What did it take?'

Cartwright shook his head, a foreign language, and turned to Mick. He had the expression of a man in the wrong company, and the wrong place, far too late at night. Mick put his arm round his shoulders, friend for life.

'It's all right, Harry,' he said, 'Alb's got this little thing about corruption. All these books he reads. That and low company. Eh, Alb?'

He grinned across at Albie, trying to soften his hostility, trying to turn it into a joke. Albie had never liked Cartwright, he knew. But business, as he kept telling him, was business. Albie, his point made, returned to a study of his finger-nails. Cartwright freed himself from Mick's arm and accepted the glass of Perrier.

'You were right about the city,' he said quietly. 'They're cutting it off.'

Mick grinned, the man in the know.

'What did I tell you?'

Cartwright ignored him.

'We need two boats,' he said.

Mick frowned. 'Two?'

'Yes. One big. Say a hundred people. One small. No more than half a dozen. I'll take care of the small boat. You get the big one.' He looked out across the casino, the pale eyes taking in the crowd at the gaming tables, the heavies at the door, and the drunkards in between. He had contempt for these people, all of them, and it showed. He turned to Mick again. 'Phone me tomorrow morning,' he said, 'at the office.' He reached carefully through the jostle of drinkers at the bar, and left his glass on the counter. Then he produced a handkerchief, and blew his nose. Mick realized he was about to go. He frowned for a moment, wondering quickly what else he needed to agree, the terms of the deal, the small print, but by the time he'd got it in a coherent order, the way Cartwright liked it, the little man had nodded goodbye, and turned away, and was already heading for the door. Mick gazed after him, and raised his glass.

'Cheers, Harry,' he called. 'Here's to the end of the world.'

Joanna had been off the phone for nearly twenty minutes by the time she heard the crunch of wheels in the gravel drive, and the low murmur of conversation as Goodman arranged for Evans to return in the morning. She'd taken a long time to make the call, circling the kitchen, utterly preoccupied, quite unable to concentrate, to sort out sensibly the priorities in her own mind.

More and more clearly, she realized that she'd found the key to Martin's strange behaviour, to his detachment and incessant evasions, and yet she refused to believe that it could be that simple, that obvious. The man she knew so well simply wasn't the kind of man to cheat so totally on his wife, to hazard his kids, to shatter his family, to throw the whole precious thing away with such reckless abandon. Somehow, somewhere, there had to be an explanation.

Confronting him was the obvious solution, but she knew him well enough to shudder at the consequences. Faced with evidence as conclusive as the postcard, she suspected he'd simply turn on his heel, and disappear. The scene would leave him nowhere else to go, but back into the night, away from her, away from the kids, back to whoever it was who had written the wretched postcard in the first place. That was something she'd known at once, up there in the bedroom, and she didn't want it to happen. And so there had to be another way.

In the end, two gins later, utterly sober, she'd phoned Charles Jenner. What she needed, she realized, was information: a name, an address, some notion of what she had to cope with, what she had to beat, and Charles was the one person she could think of whom she could trust utterly. She'd known him for years. He'd sorted out her mother's chaotic estate, and done it with such tact, and such kindness, that she'd been close to him ever since. On the two occasions they'd moved house, he'd handled all the conveyancing. When a drunken youth had driven his Ford Escort into her ancient Metro outside the Oxfam shop, landing her with a £500 repair bill, it was Charles who'd established the liability. Socially, as it happened, they'd never got round to mixing, and Martin had only met him for long enough to sign the necessary forms on the house purchases. But that, in a sense, was ideal because it insulated their relationship from any conflict of interests. Charles Jenner was the only person, here and now, who could help her. It was as simple, and as complex, as that.

She'd found his home number in the book. He lived in a small village inland. She'd phoned him from the kitchen. A woman, perhaps his wife, had answered. Joanna could hear kids' voices in the background. She'd asked for Charles. He'd come at once. She'd told him who it was, and he'd laughed, and said she was lucky to find him in, he was just off for a while. She'd apologized at this point, realizing how late it was, half-past nine in the evening, but she did need his help, his advice. He'd asked why, and she'd explained, just enough detail to convince him she was serious. She wanted to hire someone to find out a few things, make a few enquiries, get her some information. Did he know anyone suitable?

There'd been a moment's silence, before he came back on the phone. He asked her whether he could help more directly. She understood at once what he meant, the offer of a personal chat, no fee, just sympathy and advice, but she said no as gracefully as she could. What she wanted most was a recommendation, a name and a phone number. Someone who knew their way round the city. Someone who'd do what she asked, return with the facts she needed, and maintain a discreet silence. There was another pause at the end of the phone, and more kids' voices. Then Jenner returned. He'd have to make a call, he said, then he'd phone her back. She thanked him and hung up. She was at the end of her third gin when her husband arrived.

She was back on the sofa by the time he let himself in through the front door, and folded his coat over the banister, and walked into the room. He was smiling. She blinked. It wasn't, somehow, what she'd been expecting.

'Darling,' he said. 'I'm late.'

She nodded. 'Yes.'

She couldn't think of anything else to say. He crossed the room towards her, and bent over the back of the sofa, and kissed her lightly on the forehead. He smelled faintly of soap. Something nasty. Camay.

'Drink?'

He turned back from the cabinet, decanter of gin already poised over the glass. She shook her head.

'No thanks,' she said, 'I've had one already.'

'Have another.'

He poured her a small measure of gin, and topped it up with plenty of tonic, the way she always liked it. Then he poured another for himself, the measures reversed. He crossed the room with both glasses, and gave her one.

'Here's to fame,' he said, raising his glass. 'Death to the media.'

She blinked again. She'd completely forgotten his television appearance. The promise of the champagne on ice. Already, all that felt like weeks ago, part of some previous life.

'You were very convincing,' she said. 'Was it all true?'

'No,' he said, 'not really.'

'Oh.' She looked blank for a moment. 'You were lying?'

'Yes,' he shrugged, sipping the gin, 'I suppose I was. White lies, though. Not the serious sort.'

'Oh,' she said again, running a finger round the rim of her glass. She wondered how recently he'd made love to her. Probably tonight. Probably an hour ago. Bloody fool. Bloody, bloody fool. She got up quickly, walking away from him, towards the drinks cabinet, anywhere to mask the tears she knew must come. She sliced a lemon in two, and wiped her eyes. She could feel him watching her, more cautious now, suddenly aware that something profound had happened between them.

'You're crying,' he said quietly.

'I know.'

'Why?'

She glanced round. He was still sitting there. He'd made no attempt to move.

'I'm frightened,' she said truthfully. 'I don't know what's going to happen.'

He sipped his drink and looked away.

'We're going to close the city,' he said. 'We're going to go underground.'

'When?'

'Tomorrow. The next day. The day after that.' He shrugged, 'There's a bunker. A command set-up. I'm in charge. That's why the man came this morning. Oliver . . .' He gestured vaguely at the chair where Davidson had been sitting, coaxing a little sense from last week's crossword. 'It . . .' He paused a moment. 'I'm afraid it's a twenty-four hour job. You and the kids.' He hesitated, not looking at her. 'You'll be safer away.'

'No,' she said.

'Wales. Your mother's. Seriously . . .'

'No,' she said again, shaking her head, meaning it. He looked at her, properly, for the first time. The puffiness round the eyes. The tell-tale glint of tears. He got up and walked towards her, very slowly, in obvious reluctance.

'I'm sorry,' he said, 'it's going to be hard. But you really must go. I'm afraid I'm going to insist.'

She looked at him, an inch or two away. She wanted to reach out to him, a child, to caress him, to smooth it all away, to make it all better, to cure him of this hideous affliction. But at the same time, she could feel him wanting to be apart from her, to take a step back, to preserve his distance, his freedom, his precious bloody options. She shook her head slowly.

'No,' she said for the third time, 'we're staying. All of us.'

There was a long silence. Miles away, down in the city, the sound of a police siren. He looked at her, toying with his glass, hesitant, and she sensed he wanted to say something. Then the phone began to ring, trilling in the kitchen. She remembered Jenner, the promised call, and she stepped back at once, mumbling an apology, and ran through to the kitchen. She picked up the phone.

'Charles,' she said at once, 'I'm in a terrible rush. Do you have a name?'

'Yes,' he said, 'do you have a pen?'

She nodded, reaching for a biro from the jam jar on the shelf. She could hear her husband's footsteps padding lightly down the hall, and she saw his shadow fall on the kitchen tiles as he stopped to listen at the door. She made a note of the name and the telephone number, muttered her thanks and hung up. Goodman stepped into the kitchen. The glass in his hand was empty. There was a silence. She looked down at the phone, and at the name on the back of the bill.

'Man called Gillespie,' she said blankly. 'Domestic repairs.'

Five

The first symptoms of radiation sickness began to appear amongst the crew of the *George F. Kennan* in the early hours of the next day. Given the severity of the initial fire – the searing heat, the narrow companionways thick with dense choking smoke – the medical Corpsman knew that they'd been fortunate to have taken such light casualties. There were burns, certainly, and some internal damage to the soft, delicate pulmonary tissues of the fire crews that had fought the blaze. But nobody had died, and there were no injuries amongst the handful of casualties still confined to the submarine's sick bay that he regarded as life-threatening. In this sense, at least, they'd been remarkably lucky.

But the radiation was another matter. In the immediate aftermath of the accident, the Geiger read-outs had been, if anything, on the low side. While the engineering officers isolated the reactor, and shut down all but the most essential systems, the medical Corpsman had organized monitoring teams to tour the boat, taking readings in the hundreds of compartments that honeycombed the hull.

For the first six hours the read-outs had been innocuous, no more than one would expect in a normal operational environment. But over the next six hours, the data began to suggest that the damage to the reactor was in fact more serious than the engineers had at first believed.

The whole-body radiation figures climbed higher and higher, and – one full day after the accident – the hull had become uncomfortably hot. If the radiation got any worse, the Corpsman told the Captain, they could expect physiological symptoms to appear amongst the crew. The Captain had accepted the news without comment. With his ultra short-wave communications out, and his back-up systems wrecked by the fire, there was little possibility of consulting the guys on the beach. For the time being, until the communications specialists patched something together, they'd simply have to cope with the situation as best they could, aware all the time of the gigantic prize the submarine and its crew represented to the surrounding Russians. War, he suspected, was only days away. Somehow, they had to hang on until help arrived.

Now, in the submarine's tiny medical suite, the Corpsman ran cursory checks on the two men who had reported sick. They were both complaining of diarrhoea and vomiting, and one of them had the beginnings of significant hair loss. Without even tabulating their temperatures, and blood pressures, and other vital signs, the Corpsman knew only too well that these symptoms registered the onset of radiation sickness. Soon, they could expect small haemorrhages in the skin and bleeding from the gums. After that, there would be weight loss and high fever. Within a month or so, they'd probably be dead.

He looked the older of the two men in the eye. He hadn't been feeling well himself. What he was offering was a group diagnosis, applicable to every man on the boat.

'You've taken a little heat,' he said easily. 'We ought to keep an eye on that.'

Davidson gave the order to seal off the city at midnight, sitting on his bed in the new Novotel. At the other end of the line, in the cavernous TA Centre which Brigadier Lipscombe had adopted as temporary headquarters, he could hear the sound of men running, the revving of distant engines. Lipscombe, he knew, would be on another line by now, passing the word, commissioning the dozens of other calls that would have to go out, actioning the master plan they'd spent the last eighteen months trying to refine. The troop supplements he'd bargained so hard for, those extra four hundred or so men, would, he knew, be vital, the real teeth behind the thin blue line of local police officers that Nigel Quinn would doubtless insist on retaining up front. A face-to-face with Quinn was next on his list. He anticipated the man would be difficult. But first he had one more call to make. He glanced at his watch. Seven minutes past twelve. His new Controller should be home by now, tucked up in bed with that poor bloody wife of his. A voice returned, abruptly, in his ear.

'Under way,' it said simply.

Annie McPhee picked up the howl of the APCs from a mile and a half away, and she recognized the sound at once. She was up in the north of the city, sitting in a darkened car, talking to a local radio reporter she'd phoned an hour earlier. The reporter, a recommended contact from the Wessex newsroom, was briefing her on the local power structures: who mattered, who had real clout, where the principal bodies were buried. When she'd called, the man had been in bed. She'd mentioned Duggie Bullock's name, and the man had said no problem, he'd get dressed and be with her in ten minutes. His reaction had surprised her. She'd expected an earful of abuse. Now, listening to him in the car, she realized why. Like her, he sensed that the game was nearly up.

They drove north, at speed, along the eastern edge of the harbour. The road was empty. Up ahead, where the road crossed the creek, and joined the east-west motorway, she could see activity: Land-Rovers parked up on the verge, a couple of three-ton trucks and an Armoured Personnel Carrier slewed across the tarmac. Sappers in Army fatigues were erecting a road-block in front of the trucks, wooden trestles supporting baulks of heavy timber, rolls of razor wire, oil drums, sandbags, and a thicket of powerful floodlights mounted on poles. She'd seen the technique in Northern Ireland: whole areas of West Belfast isolated in five minutes or less, the roadblocks cleverly echeloned to slow approaching traffic, and permit passage only through a sequence of sharp, right-angled turns. As an essay in control, it had a certain functional beauty. More to the point, it offered the marksmen in combat gear, already dug into firing positions on either side of the road, perfect targets.

Annie slowed the car, and stopped at the kerbside fifty yards short of the roadblock. The reporter looked across at her, and she saw the apprehension in his eyes. Maintaining his subscription to the *New Statesman* and a variety of left-wing pressure groups was one thing. This was quite another. Annie nodded at the tape recorder he'd dumped on the back seat, the standard Uher, shoulder-slung, broadcast quality.

'Now's your chance,' she said, 'death or glory.'

She got out of the car and opened the boot. At the bottom of her bag was the tiny Sony Handycam she used for scouting locations. It took 3-hour, 8-mm video cassettes, and could record half-decent pictures in virtual darkness. She checked the batteries, and removed the lens hood, in readiness.

The reporter was out of the car by now, threading a new roll of tape onto his Uher. As yet, there were no police in evidence, only the soldiers. Annie paused a minute, recording a long wide shot, the whole scene, then a tighter pan across the sappers, bent over the portable generator, a couple of officers conferring together, the squaddies manhandling the heavy sandbags across the road, and finally the point where the razor wire and the trestles ended, and the formless hump of the tussock at the road's edge gave way to the inky blackness of the harbour.

They began to walk forward again, approaching the roadblock. One of the two officers broke off from his conversation, and stepped towards them, into the pool of light from the overhead lamps. He looked, if anything, embarrassed.

'Can I help you?' he said.

The reporter introduced himself, and lifted his microphone. Annie saw the spools revolving on the tape recorder, and began to film. The officer frowned and took a pace back. The reporter followed him. He was murmuring a running commentary on what he could see around him: the sappers uncoiling the razor wire with their thick, heavy-duty gloves, the Corporal kneeling beside the radio, muttering co-ordinates into a lip mike, the flanking marksmen, up on their elbows, making final adjustments to the bulky night sights. The reporter extended the microphone towards the officer.

'What's happening?' he said. 'What's going on?'

The officer shook his head, refusing to comment. The reporter repeated the question. The officer glanced over his shoulder and barked an order. A soldier ran towards him, and saluted. Annie moved in with her camera, determined to catch the exchange between them.

The officer began to say something. The soldier's eyes flicked left, towards Annie, by now only feet away. The officer turned on her, angry at the intrusion, at his authority being so obviously ignored in the presence of one of his men. He held out his hand.

'Give me that,' he said nodding at the camera.

Annie continued to film, closing the shot a little, head and shoulders, rimlit by the lights behind. Nice. Dramatic. The real thing. The officer reached out for the camera, trying to sieze it. Annie stepped back. There were headlights down the road, moving at speed towards them. The officer was distracted, shielding his eyes, stepping back towards the kerb, motioning the soldier forward. Annie swung round with the camera in time to focus on the approaching car. A big, black Rover drew up. One of the rear windows purred down, and a hand extended a pass. She recognized the Home Office seal, embossed above the small colour photo. She zoomed on the face at the window: a blur at first, then more and more distinct as the automatic focus adjusted. Middle aged. Pale. Rimless glasses. Suit and tie. The face glanced up at the officer, said something she didn't quite catch, and then looked directly into the lens with what she instinctively recognized as the beginning of a smile. She never felt the blow, but remembered only the darkness, a thick black woolly blanket of nothing that took her by surprise, and stole the face away.

Martin Goodman sat at the long conference table that dominated the centre well of the city's Command Bunker. To his left, raised above floor level, the glassed-in two-man cubicle he'd be sharing with Davidson: a couple of desks, a big grey filing cabinet with a combination lock, and two telephones, one a direct line to County HQ, the other patched through to the bunker's main switchboard. To his right, behind a locked door, the Telex room with hardened lines to the Wiltshire quarry complex which would shortly serve as the UK's centre of government. At his feet, the hastily packed holdall in case, as Davidson put it, the main feature went on a little longer than originally advertised. By the big grey government issue clock on the wall over his head, it was still only half-past two. Except for a couple of technicians from Naval Support, the place was empty.

Goodman rubbed his eyes. Davidson had woken him an hour earlier, using the car phone in the official Rover parked outside his front door. He'd been half asleep, only too conscious of the body of his wife beside him, silent, barely breathing, her eyes wide open, staring up at the bedroom ceiling. He'd twice tried to talk to her, to reassure her, to tell her that it would, in the end, be all right. That they'd both survive. But the more he tried to soothe her, to find those precise words that would get to the heart of it, the deeper the ambiguities became. He knew what she was really talking about, they both did, but admitting it was far too complex and far too dangerous a risk for either of them to take. Their world was teetering on the edge of disintegration, and if anything saved it that night, it was probably Davidson's phone call.

Goodman had packed the holdall in the light from the landing. Socks, pullovers, shirts, items pulled at random from his chest of drawers. He'd collected the rest of the stuff, the bare essentials, from the bathroom. A toothbrush. A razor. A half-flattened tube of Mintyfresh. He'd stepped briefly into each of the children's bedrooms, stooping low over their sleeping bodies, kissing them softly on the cheek. Already, in his new pyjamas, James looked like a stranger, someone else's child. Caroline's eyes had briefly opened, gazing sightlessly up, her warm sweet breath on his face, before she'd rolled over again, sound asleep. Charlie was flat on his face, the sheet around his mouth moist. To each child, he murmured a phrase or two, told them how much he loved them. These, he knew, were farewells. He was leaving home.

Joanna came downstairs with him, to the door. He'd opened it, not wanting to prolong the scene, but she'd reached beyond him, pushing it back against the latch, a brief gesture, a screen between their world, and Davidson, waiting outside in the big black car. She'd looked up at him, grieving, and taken his face in her hands.

'I still love you,' she'd said. 'And we're still here.'

He'd tried to say something in return, some small crumb of comfort, some tiny down payment on a joint future, but all he'd managed in the end was an official pass which would get her back into the city if she needed to.

'Take it,' he said. 'It might come in handy.'

Now, in the Bunker, he tried to empty his mind of it all. Davidson was briefing him on the roadblocks, his hands moving quickly over the map of the city, unfolded on the table before them. The operation, he said half-apologetically, had been initiated on direct orders from Whitehall. Speed and surprise had been judged essential. Such a task had never before been attempted in mainland Britain, and there was significant anxiety in certain quarters about the outcome. The situation was thought to be volatile. Anything might happen.

Under the circumstances, though, the operation had gone remarkably well. The roadblocks were all in place. By dawn, the police would be in position on the mainland, diverting traffic away from the city, long before it got anywhere near the roadblocks. In the city itself, a similar operation, more police screening the approach roads, filtering traffic out into the maze of side-streets that criss-crossed the island, defusing situations before they became a problem. Local TV and radio editors were already being briefed for their morning broadcasts, what to say and what not to say. The official line was very clear – the national interest was paramount – and it would be the broadcaster's job to peddle the Government's various messages with as much flair and conviction as they sold any other commodity. Since midnight, and the hasty passage of the second Emergency Powers Act, editors no longer had the right to comment, or to raise questions of their own. Second guessing the official line had become an offence, punishable by summary arrest. Journalism, in any meaningful sense, no longer existed.

Goodman listened to Davidson's easy exposition, recognizing the planning that must have gone into it, but asking himself time and again what would really happen in the morning, when years of careful organization collided head on with reality. Amongst Davidson's careful phrases, there was no room for doubt, for anger, for fear, for panic. People, even hundreds of thousands of people, were simply walk-ons in an elegant script, masterminded from offices seventy miles away, choreographed by men in uniform who'd simply do what they were told. For the first time, Goodman truly understood the real power of Government, the enormous reach of the animal that lurked in the recesses of Whitehall, and it frightened him.

A door slammed. A figure burst into the room. Goodman looked up. It was Nigel Quinn. The policeman strode across the room. He was white with anger. He stood in front of Goodman. There was another man with him, younger, sandy hair and watchful eyes, the uniform of a Chief Inspector. Quinn looked at the map for a second or two, getting his breath back, regaining his composure. Whatever was wrong, it was plainly Goodman's fault.

'For God's sake,' he said at last, 'what on earth is going on? The place is thick with troops. No warning. No consultation. Nothing. We can't even access their command net. What sort of war is this? Who are we fighting?'

Goodman looked at him, and then at Davidson, deflecting the question. Quinn turned his anger on Davidson, putting his hands on his hips, no nonsense, man to man.

'Well? Do I get any answers?'

Davidson, imperturbable, picked up a phone and dialled a number. Quinn gazed at him, momentarily nonplussed. A voice answered, female. Davidson murmured a name. There was a pause, then another voice, male, deep. Even a couple of feet away, Goodman recognized the blunt Yorkshire tones of the county's Chief Constable. Davidson murmured something else and offered the phone to Quinn. Quinn had recognized the voice, too. Goodman could see his face beginning to sag, his self-righteousness and indignation draining away. He took the phone.

'Quinn, sir,' he said.

The voice at other end spoke for perhaps a minute. Quinn nodded several times, deflated, compliant, his master's servant. Then he put the phone down, and glanced at his watch.

'We ought to talk,' he said gruffly, 'there's a hell of a lot to do.'

Gillespie re-cued his ansaphone and listened to the message for the second time. A woman's voice. Middle-aged. Middle-class. Slightly breathless. Slightly anxious. No name. No return number. Just the beginnings of an enquiry, a request for help, before the second sentence ran out of steam, and there was a pause, and the sound of a child crying, and the click of the receiver as the phone went dead.

He frowned, and glanced at his watch. Eight o'clock. He'd woken, as usual, at six, aware at once that something was wrong. Instead of the news on his radio alarm, there'd been a religious address from some tame vicar or other. The man had spoken of the gravity of the situation, and of the need for prayer, and of the benevolence of Our Lord. He'd urged listeners to recall, once again, the days of their youth, their dependence on their mothers and their fathers, the sanctity of the family unit in times of dire emergency. And he'd ended by proclaiming the beauty of God's works, and the warm assurance of the life to come.

For a moment or two, lying in bed, Gillespie wondered whether the war had actually started, whether the T-80s were even now rumbling into the heartland of the Bundesrepublik, but then the broadcast had cut to the familiar voice of the BBC's early morning announcer who apologized for the reorganization of programmes, added a word or two about the day's expected weather, and introduced a concert of lesser-known Viennese waltzes. At that point, with Gillespie, the penny began to drop. They've taken over, he thought approvingly, they're going to sort the whole thing out.

On a whim, minutes later, he'd abandoned his usual morning route, and run inland, away from the beach and the promenade, through street after street of terraced houses, towards the Guildhall Square and the civic offices. If he wanted hard evidence, incontestable proof that his hunch was right, then he knew he'd find it here, in the city's administrative nerve-centre. Sure enough, as he rounded the corner by the new insurance block that had replaced the city's Victorian theatre, he ran into the first of the clues. Nothing elaborate, nothing obvious, just a couple of squaddies with a local policeman. They were standing on the blind side of the corner, in front of a pub, conferring over a map, their conversation punctuated by the ceaseless chatter of voices from the policeman's lapel-mounted radio. Gillespie hesitated for a moment, pausing for breath, wondering whether to approach them. But then he caught sight of the removal vans parked beyond them, in the shadow of the Civic Centre. Men in overalls were humping plastic crates full of paperwork out of the building, and down the steps, and into the vans. The vans were blue, a commercial firm, Freeman & Co. There were more squaddies, armed, on the pavement, and a small command post had been established in the shadows to the left of the main door. Gillespie smiled, wiping the sweat from his brow, recognizing the tall whiplash aerial and the backpacked radio. He'd been right, after all. The administration was leaving town.

Now, back at home, he picked up the remote TV control box

and fingered his way through the channels. The national morning chat shows were evidently intact – familiar faces on the same old studio sofas – but when he paused to listen for a minute or two, he knew at once that something profound had indeed happened. The endless hours of review and analysis had disappeared completely. No more studio pundits dancing round maps of the Barents Sea. No more retired admirals pontificating on inherent flaws in nuclear submarine technology. No more tasteless interviews with pretty young US Naval wives in Savannah or King's Bay, with their tacky assumption of imminent widowhood. Instead, there were figures from showbiz talking about their latest exercise fads, over-long gardening items, lengthy profiles of popular sporting heroes, and ceaseless promotions for re-runs of evergreen sit-coms and favourite game shows. Someone had been at the broadcasters. Someone had barged into all those studio centres, and torn up their transmission schedules, and told them what to do. The result, on the evidence of five minutes' viewing, was bizarre. The world was very evidently on the point of blowing itself up. And yet life, at the nod of a Ministerial head, had become one long Saturday night: a feast of game shows, and sit-coms, and gales of canned laughter. Gillespie shook his head, amazed, and blanked the screen. Not with a bang, he thought. Not even with a whimper. But with drawn curtains, and a six-pack or two, and a whole evening of Game For A Laugh. Pathetic.

He looked again at the ansaphone. Maybe the woman would phone back. She might have work, something quick and easy, and he could certainly do with the money. He'd give her until ten, at the latest. Then he'd get himself organized. Sort out Sandra and the boy. Look for fuel. And head west.

By nine o'clock, Annie had got over the worst. When she first came round, flat on her back in a strange room, she hadn't a clue where she was. A pocket inside her head was heavy with pain, a constant pulsing hammerblow that made her want to vomit, and when she groaned, and reached out into the darkness, there was a hand there at once, a voice she recognized only dimly, a man's voice, the young radio reporter. He'd guided her head over a bowl, and she'd thrown up, retching with the pain, and then collapsed back onto the bed, her face covered with sweat. Sleep, said the voice, take it easy, and she'd muttered her gratitude, and complied at once, not because she'd wanted to, but because her body left her no other choice. Consciousness hurt too much. Better, for now, to sign off.

Now, daylight spilling round the curtains, she felt a little better. She looked around, let the room swim into focus, looking for clues, half remembering the voice, an hour or two earlier, the young reporter. The room was small, cluttered with furniture, a bookcase, pictures on the wall, something Parisian, a woman's touch in the hanging basket by the window.

Annie rolled slowly over, trying to stifle the groan. The door opened. The reporter stooped over the bed. Annie looked up at him, not knowing quite what to say. He had ash blond hair, cut fashionably short. His face was bruised over his left eye, and there was swelling around his mouth. He smiled at her.

'OK?' he said needlessly.

Annie pulled a face. Pain flooded up over her skull. She felt sick again, shutting her eyes.

'What happened?' she said.

The young reporter sat down on the bed. He was wearing a dressing gown over tracksuit bottoms. Distantly, elsewhere in the house, Annie could hear the whistle of a boiling kettle. The whistling stopped.

'We were taken aside,' he said, 'at least, I was.'

'And me?'

The reporter looked at her.

'I don't know,' he said, 'I didn't see. Not exactly . . .' He hesitated, apologizing more than necessary. 'It all happened very quickly. It was all over like that.' He snapped his fingers. Annie winced.

'What was?'

'Whatever happened to you.' He gestured at her face, the blood stains on the pillow.

Annie's hands went up to her face for the first time. High on her forehead, just below the hairline, she could feel a thin crust of blood. It seemed superficial, like a graze or a gravel scrape. She explored further. The back of her head was swollen, and there was more blood matted in the tight curls of hair.

'Someone hit me,' she said reasonably. 'Quite hard.' She

frowned, remembering the camera, and the face in the back of the car. She had the evidence. She could press her case.

'Where's the camera?' she said.

The young reporter shook his head, regretful.

'They took it,' he said. 'My Uher, too.'

'Took it?'

'Yeah.'

'Who took it?'

'They did. The military.'

'Oh.' She nodded. 'So why didn't they take us, too? Do the job properly?'

The young reporter shrugged. 'No idea,' he said. 'They just told me to bugger off. A couple of them put you in the back of your car, and I drove it home. They . . .' He shrugged again, letting the sentence trail away. Annie looked at him. The more he talked, the more she pressed him, the more evasive he became, and Annie began to recognize what must have happened while she was lying there, unconscious, in the road, the threats they'd made, the pressures they'd applied, the brisk promise of violence in support of civil power. She'd seen the technique before, during the miners' strike in '84 . . . except that this time it had been the Army, without a police uniform in sight, though the face in the car, she was positive, had been a civilian.

She struggled upright in bed and swung her legs over the side of the divan. The inside of her head began to throb again, and she swallowed the hot gusts of nausea that bubbled up from her stomach. She tried to stand on the threadbare old carpet. The reporter caught her.

'Who were they?' she said.

He looked wary. 'Army,' he said.

'Names?'

He looked away and shook his head, and she knew at once that she'd been right. He'd been badly frightened. He'd say no more.

'This your place?' she said, looking round.

He nodded. He looked uncomfortable. He knew what she wanted, names, numbers, units, details, some sort of handle on the experience she'd been through, some sort of toehold on the near-impossible climb she'd set herself, but he'd been there too, understood plain English, and whatever they'd told him, however they'd put it, they'd done a very good job. He helped her towards the tiny basin in the corner of the room, and began to fill it with water. Annie looked at herself in the mirror on the wall. She'd been right about the forehead. The skin was grazed, the blood black against her sallow skin. There was another abrasion on her nose, more blood, and her face looked doughy and misshapen. The reporter tested the temperature of the water with his elbow, and began to soap a flannel. He was a kind man, she thought, caring, and for the first time she realized how young he was.

The door opened behind them and a woman stepped in. She was carrying a very small baby in the crook of one arm, and a cup of tea in her other hand. She looked anxious and strained. She offered the tea to her husband, nodding at Annie, a gesture of helplessness. Annie studied them both for a moment in the mirror, understanding it all, the reluctance to become involved, the sudden absence of memory. On reflection, she realized it had been brave of him to come with her in the first place. But that had been before he knew what they were up against, the scale of the thing, the odds stacked against them. She took the flannel from him. He gestured, half embarrassed, at the woman with the baby.

'Evie,' he said. 'My wife.'

The woman did her best to smile, but it didn't work. Annie answered the question she wanted so badly to voice, but couldn't.

'Hi,' she said. 'I'm off in a minute. Don't worry.'

The reporter frowned, genuine concern.

'Where will you go?' he said. 'The city's closed.'

Annie smiled at the lumpy face in the mirror, a private joke.

'There's a friend of mine,' she said. 'Lives locally.'

Albie Curtis had known since dawn that the city was finally on its own. His younger brother, who had a half-share in a fruit and veg stall in the market, had driven north to pick up produce from a market garden on the mainland. He'd been turned back by police well short of the roadblock, though he'd seen enough movies to recognize the oil drums and barbed wire and sandbag clearly visible half a mile up the road. When he told the police he had work to do, spuds to collect, a living to make, they'd simply shrugged and indicated the lay-by on the left where he could start the U-turn that would take him back into the city. He'd given them a good mouthful, but he'd done their bidding, and by the time he'd got to Albie's tiny bedsit down by the seafront, what was left of his anger was strictly philosophical.

'Pissing in the wind,' he told Albie, as his brother decanted hot water onto a tea bag. 'Fuckers never listen. Not now. Not ever.'

Albie, who hadn't got to bed until three in the morning, had asked him about the petrol in the van. His brother had told him he had a half a tank, maybe a bit less. Albie had nodded, indicating the pile of leaflets on the floor. He tried to treat his brother the way Mick treated him. It never worked, and he never really understood why.

'OK,' he'd said, 'deliver that lot.'

His brother had frowned. After the tea, he'd other plans. First a visit to the market to elbow the stall for the day. Then an early call on a bird he was shafting. Her husband was in the Navy and away for the duration. Any time, day or night, she couldn't get enough of it. Albie had looked pained.

'There's a war on,' he said. 'We might all be dead by lunchtime.'

His brother, who had neither the taste nor the time for international crises, had simply grinned.

'Exactly,' he'd said, throwing Albie the keys. 'You do it. I'm off.'

Now, a couple of hours later, Albie had personally delivered about half of the leaflets, and given a couple of local kids five quid each to get rid of the rest. He'd chosen the poorer areas of the city, tightly packed, back-to-back houses, old people with long memories, and modest savings, and perfect recall of the cold January nights when the Luftwaffe had levelled street after street. Then, during the war, white paint on the windows had been highly prized, the official antidote to the heat and the blast of exploding bombs. Now, fifty years later, there was no obvious reason why it shouldn't work again. Unless of course, you happened to know anything about the terrible chemistry of nuclear fission, about blast rings and overpressure, about lung haemorrhage and third degree burns. And even then you might still pop a tenner or so on the offer, one last fatuous gesture in the face of oblivion.

That, at least, was Albie's theory, a totally individual piece of free enterprise that had nothing to do with Mick Rendall and his fancy ideas. The telephone number on the leaflet belonged to a hairdressing salon in the city's commercial precinct. His sister's best friend worked there. Evidently trade was on the thin side, and he'd promised her five per cent for taking firm orders. These orders he'd pick up later in the day, and service as best he could, cash on the nail. He'd done the sums several times, but whichever buttons he pressed on the borrowed calculator, it still came out on the right side. If he was unlucky, if he'd got it all wrong, he'd still make a quid or two. But if it worked the way he knew it could, he'd make a fortune. 50 per cent take up at ten quid a window? He smiled, swinging the van out of the last of the streets he'd targeted, and heading for the docks. Last night, outside the casino, he'd fixed to meet Mick at eight. It was already half past nine.

Oliver Davidson brought his borrowed car to a halt, stifled a yawn, and stepped out into the sunshine. The main block at St Ursula's was away to his left: a big, four-storeyed Victorian pile with tall, shadowed windows, and an imposing flight of steps leading to a heavy revolving door. The building housed all the hospital's administrative offices, the principal out-patient clinics, and a handful of specialist wards for drug addicts, alcoholics, and sundry other rogue groups which now qualified for psychiatric care.

Elsewhere, dotted amongst the shrubs, and gardens, and dusty copses of trees, were the half-dozen or so villas which served as regular psychiatric wards, smaller, two-storeyed buildings, self-contained, each with beds for up to forty patients. Over the past three days, the less severely afflicted had been discharged, returned to relatives, or friends, or the uncertain mercies of the DHSS bed and breakfast hotels that littered the city. In their place, overnight, a convoy of coaches had arrived, each with its separate escort of police cars, shipping in a new category of inmate. Many of them were young, most of them were politically active, and all of them had been roused from their beds in a series of 2.00 a.m. raids across the south of England. The small print of the operation had been organized by Special Branch and an offshoot of MI5 known as 'Waste Disposal'. But the broad strategy had been framed by a working group at the Home Office. Davidson had served on this officially non-existent committee for eighteen months, and it was he who'd coined the expression 'Out Takes' or 'OTs' to designate this new category of citizens who found themselves suddenly qualifying for a bed in a psychiatric ward in one of the country's high-risk target areas. By 'OTs', he'd confided to a colleague, he'd actually meant Political Detainees, but the latter phrase had a slightly South African ring to it, and on balance he felt happier with the new formula. Words, he was constantly reminding the Committee, were democracy's favourite camouflage. With words, he assured them, you could get away with anything

By and large, so far, the thing had worked remarkably well. The city, he knew, had a reputation in Whitehall for mute compliance, bred from generations of dependence on the Naval Dockyard. Lately, according to private soundings amongst people who should know, there'd been an upsurge in drunkenness and after-hours street brawling, but this violence was no different from anywhere else in the country: a sullen mix of adolescence, money, and high octane lager. It certainly had nothing to do with political discontent or any discernible undertow of left-wing sentiment. On the contrary, Tory councils had governed the city since the war, and their stranglehold on the committees that mattered was complete. Nevertheless, it was wise to be cautious. No one, no city, had ever been in this situation before. It was virgin territory, and in the absence of maps, one could only do one's best to apply the lessons of the past, to divide and rule, to keep apart the combustible elements of any successful opposition: the students and the intellectuals on the one hand, and what now passed for the working class on the other. It was all pretty orthodox stuff, but the city had a large polytechnic, and a vigorous working population, and he felt a little easier to know that the local OTs included forty or so of the likelier subversives on the Special Branch arrest list. It was these individuals, articulate, passionate, well-read, who must be silenced.

He smiled, pocketing the car keys, and remembering the

curious little incident at the roadblock in the early hours, the girl sprawling in the gravel, her boyfriend standing aghast to one side, the officer pulling the soldier away, the camera lying under the front wheel of the big, black Rover. Evans had accelerated away immediately, scenting danger. Davidson had heard the camera disintegrate beneath them.

A figure stepped out of the villa and walked across the grass towards him: tall, bulky, rumpled, the enormous face curtained by the black, lank, shoulder-length hair. Davidson had only known Ingle for a month or so, but he'd already developed an enormous respect for the man. He'd never met a more unlikely policeman, but he'd read the files, and made his enquiries, and now he saw a perfectly logical path from the neat, cropped unsmiling face in the Hendon class photo, to the figure standing before him in the sunshine.

A decade of undercover work had left its mark on the man. Unusually, he'd emerged from the Drugs Squad without a whisper of gossip. No rumours of graft or free holidays in Miami. No expense account lunches in the Dorchester or the Inn on the Park. No funny bank accounts in Zurich or Dubai. Just the big, flat, slightly Slavic face, and the coal black eyes, and the first hints of grey in the eternally unwashed hair. Ingle had a reputation for cunning and endless patience. He was said to get results not by any of the usual methods, not by closing the door, and pulling the curtains, and rolling up his sleeves, or by plea bargaining, or verballing, or dropping fat hints about insurance rewards, but by something infinitely more subtle. He could, said the handful of people who knew him well, have been a psychiatrist or an actor. He had an uncanny talent for empathy, for getting behind the denials and the anguish and the endless protestations of innocence, for taking a good look round, for sussing what really made a man tick, and for easing him towards the confession they'd both, finally, agree was inevitable.

Enemies of Ingle, and he had many, said he was slow and difficult, a bit of a liability. By the latter, they normally meant that he was unduly exercised by the truth, by the record of what had actually happened to a man, and Davidson now knew enough about justice to recognize that this could indeed be counter-productive. Nevertheless, he valued Ingle highly, and he'd brought him south to take charge. Ingle was a one-off man for a one-off situation. And Davidson was glad to have him.

The two men shook hands, and Davidson took Ingle by the arm and steered him away from the villa, out into the grounds where they could talk more freely. He wanted to know how the transfers had gone, how the OTs had settled in, whether there'd been any nonsense about solicitors or civil rights. Ingle told him that there'd been an incident or two, but nothing they couldn't handle, and that the guards supplied by the local security firm were, if anything, over-zealous. He suspected they'd been watching too many Clint Eastwood movies. Some of them, he said, wanted to be issued with firearms, a request he'd turned down flat.

Davidson asked about the surveillance teams, shipped down from London over the past few days, men and women hand picked by Ingle after the Queen's Gate decision to make the city the principal OT reception centre for the south. Ingle nodded, confirming they were already deployed, already out there, haunting the pubs, queueing for bread and milk, ears to the ground, alert for gossip and rumour. So far, he said, it had been remarkably quiet. People, if anything, were bewildered, unable to distinguish between the real threat – their home, their kids – and the international soap opera transmitting hourly on the nation's screens. Now, of course, all that had changed. No more news. No more comment.

The two men paused by a bench. One of the long-stay patients sat back against the warm woodwork, a man in his early sixties, gaunt, hollow-eyed, with big bony hands, and thin wisps of white hair. He had a handbag on his lap, and kept removing the contents: a pension book, a box of crayons, and a single dirty woollen glove. His body rocked back and forth as he mumbled to himself, packing and re-packing the bag, itemizing the objects, an endless private mantra.

Ingle gazed at him thoughtfully. Davidson sensed an instant kinship, uncluttered by embarrassment, or pity, or any of the usual social defences. He glanced over at Ingle, an enquiry, an unvoiced question. Ingle blinked, momentarily off-guard, and then started to walk again.

'Ex-copper?' he mused after a while, 'or civil servant?' He

smiled at Davidson. 'What do you think?'

Gillespie arrived at the rendezvous a couple of minutes early. The woman had rung again shortly after nine, the same voice, the same slightly brittle defensiveness. She said that she wanted to talk, and that she would meet him on the old fortification walls overlooking the harbour mouth. She'd be wearing a dark blue dress, and a light tan coat, and a red silk scarf. She left no name and no number. Gillespie had made a note of the rendezvous, shaken the creases out of a newly laundered pair of jeans, fed the cat, and walked the mile and a half to the harbour mouth.

Now, five minutes past the rendezvous time, he sat on the big stone wall overlooking the sea trying to guess the woman's age and what kind of car she might drive. He'd nearly settled for a Volvo estate when a voice interrupted him.

'Mr Gillespie?'

He swung round, squinting in the sunshine. The light tan coat was unbelted, and the woman had a small leather bag slung over one shoulder. The red scarf was loosely knotted at the side of her neck. She looked cool, and thoughtful, and not at all the way he'd imagined. An attractive intelligent woman, coping with a difficult situation.

Gillespie levered himself off the wall and wiped the dust from his hands. For September, it was very warm. He nodded at her.

'Mrs . . .?'

She looked at him a moment, frank, appraising.

'Goodman,' she said, 'Joanna Goodman. Charles Jenner put me onto you. He said you . . .' she frowned, looking for the right phrase, 'did jobs.' She smiled for the first time, a chill rearrangement of the lower half of her face. 'I hope I didn't wake you up,' she said, 'the first time I phoned.' Gillespie shook his head, remembering the message on the ansaphone, the sentences trailing away into silence.

'Not at all,' he said, 'I was out.'

'Out?'

'Running.'

'Oh,' she nodded, still looking at him, 'I see.'

There was a brief silence, then Gillespie fell into step beside her.

'How can I help you?' he said.

The woman said nothing for a moment or two, then looked at him again. They both stopped.

'It's my husband,' she said. 'He's having an affair.'

She paused, frowning, hating the expression, its theatricality, its cheapness. Gillespie nodded, saying nothing. He felt curiously flattered by her candour. Normally, it took an age to coax out this initial admission, this statement of the facts, and by that time the relationship between them, client and customer, would already have been distorted, an open pocket for the woman's feelings of shame, and neglect, and failure. In this sense, Gillespie himself became tainted, part of the betrayal, a feeling which no fee on earth could recompense. This was one of the reasons he'd recently decided to abandon matrimonial work, preferring to pass the jobs onto other men in the city, more thick skinned, less choosy. But this woman was different, with her composure, and her icy poise. She'd obviously done the thinking. She knew what she wanted, and it would simply be Gillespie's job to help her get it.

She produced an envelope from her shoulder bag. The envelope was light blue, Basildon Bond. She began to open it.

'My husband's name is Martin,' she said. 'He's the city's Chief Executive. He works at the Civic Centre for the time being, but I understand that might all change.' She paused. 'Am I making sense?'

Gillespie nodded, remembering the removal vans at the kerbside in the Guildhall Square, the watchful squaddies looking on. The woman handed him a photograph, colour, postcard size. He glanced at it. A man in an open white shirt was sitting on a swing. A child of about seven was sitting in his lap. The child had purple lolly-stains around his mouth. The man had his hands around the child's stomach, holding him still for the camera. He looked relaxed and cheerful. He wore glasses.

'Last Easter.' The woman hesitated a moment. '. . . It's the most recent I could find.'

'It's fine,' said Gillespie. 'What do you want from me?'

The woman stiffened imperceptibly, a question she'd obviously been expecting.

'I want to know who he's seeing,' she said. 'I want her name.

And her address. And a phone number . . . if that's possible.'

Gillespie nodded.

'That's possible,' he said.

The woman looked at him again, the same candour, the same determination.

'And then I want the photo back . . .' she tapped the print in his hand, 'and I want you to have no more to do with it.'

'Sure.'

The woman opened her bag again.

'How much do you charge?' she said.

'Fifteen pounds an hour,' Gillespie said, 'plus expenses.'

'Do you want something in advance?'

'It would help.'

She nodded and produced another envelope, small and brown. She offered it to him.

'Here,' she said. 'That's forty pounds to be going on with.'

Gillespie fingered the envelope, decided against opening it, and slipped it into his back pocket.

'How do I contact you?' he said.

'There's a telephone number in the envelope. You can phone me.'

'Any time?'

She hesitated a moment, and blinked, and Gillespie had a glimpse of the real woman behind it all, behind the mask, angry, and hurt, and bitter, but no less determined.

'Any time,' she confirmed.

He nodded, extended a hand. She touched it lightly, no more than politeness demanded, and began to turn away. Gillespie glanced at the photo again.

'One thing . . .' he said.

She hesitated, not wanting to talk any more.

'Yes?'

'Do you want photos?'

The woman's eyes narrowed a moment while she thought about the proposition.

'Is it usual?' she said.

'Sometimes.'

'I see.' She thought about it some more, and looked inland, towards the high rise blocks that rose from the city centre.

She began to belt the coat. She didn't voice the thought, but the implication was clear enough in her face. Men, it said. Men and their silly, silly games. She sniffed.

'Yes,' she said, 'send me the photos too.'

She gave him a thin parting smile and turned on her heel. Gillespie watched her walking away, firm, neat steps, in charge of herself again, her own person. He leaned back against the warm stonework, glancing down at the photograph, memorizing the face. On closer inspection, he wasn't sure about the smile. It might have been genuine, or it might not. It was that kind of expression, practised, opaque, designed to impress, or amuse, or reassure, or baffle, wholly synthetic.

He looked to the east. The woman was already a dot in the distance. He turned away, and walked in the opposite direction, towards the Round Tower, one of the twin fortifications that guarded the entrance to the harbour.

Suddenly he caught the harsh metallic tones of a megaphone. He crossed to the wall again, and looked down at the water. Two powerboats, one big and one small, were converging on a yacht. The yacht was about forty foot, big, edging slowly out against the flood tide. He counted eight people in the cockpit. One of the powerboats, the larger of the two, nudged alongside. An officer in naval uniform boarded the yacht, hopping nimbly from one deck onto the other. Even from a hundred yards, Gillespie could see the sidearm strapped to his hip. An argument began, voices raised, fingers pointing, heads shaking. Two other men emerged from the cabin, big men. One of them shouldered his way through the crowded cockpit, dwarfing the man in the naval uniform. He picked him up bodily, and threw him overboard. Gillespie heard the splash of the falling body, and the cheers and claps from the yacht.

A sailor on the powerboat ran forward with a boathook, but the officer had already floated past on the flood tide, back in towards the harbour mouth. He was swimming slowly, keeping his head above water, letting the current do the work. Another figure appeared on the powerboat. He carried a gun of some sort, snub barrel, stubby magazine, wooden stock. He knelt carefully on the foredeck and took aim at the bow of the yacht. A moment later, Gillespie recognized the sharp bark of the Uzi sub-machine-gun as the bullets stitched a line of holes in the yacht's hull, inches above the water line. A woman screamed. The yacht hove to, broadside across the current, already beginning to settle in the water, and the naval officer, still holding his hat, drifted slowly out of sight.

Gillespie let the tableau settle in his mind, the powerboat closing again on the yacht, the woman cowering against the men, a new voice on the megaphone telling everyone to keep calm, and he realized, rather late in the day, what it all meant. They were closing the city down, by road, and by sea. And they meant the blockade to stick.

Mick Rendall heard the gunshots and ran to the end of the dock. A Royal Navy Land-Rover had been there since dawn, the three matelots from the Naval Provost taking a leisurely inventory of the boats moored alongside, preparing the Requisition Forms for each of the owners, checking names against a master list, ignoring the sour jokes from the fishermen lounging outside the pub at the dock entrance.

Now, breathless, Mick stood beside the Land-Rover, peering out towards the harbour mouth. The shooting had stopped, but he could hear the roar of a powerful outboard. Seconds later, a big inflatable appeared, circling a figure in the water. A lifebelt was thrown. A man knelt at the waterline, extending a helping hand, and a figure in naval uniform wriggled aboard. Mick blinked, not understanding it, and began to walk back towards the eighty-foot trawler he'd finally managed to charter.

The *Timothy Lee* was an old boat, the oldest in the dock's commercial fleet, and twenty years at sea had taken their toll. The hull was chipped and rusting, the woodwork around the wheelhouse was beginning to rot, and the accommodation aft was cramped and airless. The narrow companionways stank of fish, engine oil, and old chip fat, and most of the boat's navigation aids were unserviceable.

By choice, Mick would have preferred one of the modern boats, the big beam trawlers that fished out in the south-west approaches, but the skippers of these, though willing enough to take his money, were wary of their boss, a self-made man called Neville Price. Price, who'd begun life as a navvy in the dockyard, had a very short fuse and a legendary impatience with paperwork. He settled most company disputes the only way he knew how, and most of his skippers carried the scars to prove it.

And so Mick, in the end, had been obliged to return to Arthur McNaught, the one deep-sea fisherman in the dock with a boat of his own. McNaught, a slight, tanned, thin-faced, canny little man in his late fifties, had taken a good living from the *Timothy Lee* over the years, though lately the fishing had been poor. He now spent more time in the pub than he should do, and he'd listened to Mick's pitch over his morning brandy, making no comment until Mick got to the meat of it all. Then he'd laughed at Mick's first offer, and scratched the tattoos on the back of his hand, and told him to double it, and double it again. Mick, who'd seen this kind of arithmetic coming, doubled it once and left it on the table between them.

'Forty quid a head,' he said.

'Up front?'

'Half.'

'*How* many people?'

'A hundred,' Mick said, 'give or take.'

They'd put the price on one side for a while, sorting through the practical problems. Victualling - food and drink - was obviously down to Mick. Likewise the sleeping arrangements. A hundred bodies, said McNaught thoughtfully, would fit nice in the big fish hold. The floor was pretty flat and there was plenty of room for a layer of mattresses. They'd be sleeping side by side, head to toe, packed in like sardines, but it was a fishing boat, after all, and any kind of berth was presumably preferable to staying put.

Mick had agreed with this, acknowledging the logic but nonplussed at the vision of a hundred punters jigsawed into a fish hold. He wasn't sure it was exactly what Cartwright had in mind, but the fisherman was right. Beggars couldn't be choosers.

The question of the destination had come up next. In principle, McNaught was prepared to go anywhere. The boat was solid, he assured Mick, and he wasn't to be too bothered by the dodgy navigational aids. He never went to sea without a sextant, and if needs must, he'd use it.

'Ireland?' Mick had enquired cautiously, 'Portugal?' The

little man had shrugged.

'Your shout,' he said, 'we'll go wherever you want.'

The other details – like fuel – were again down to Mick. There was evidently plenty of diesel around, but the supplies were now under the Government cosh, and Mick would need some kind of official permission to get at the pumps. Quite how he'd acquire this, McNaught didn't know, but he assumed that Mick had connections and he advised him to overbid on the capacity of the trawler's tanks. The black market in diesel, he said, had quadrupled the price. Anything spare would be more than welcome.

With McNaught studying yet another empty glass, they were finally left with only one problem. Since dawn, said McNaught, the Navy had taken control of the harbour. All movements were banned. Anyone casting off, and making any kind of way in the harbour, was liable to summary arrest and forfeit of the boat. At the time, eight o'clock, Mick hadn't believed him. It was, he'd told himself, a wind-up, an obvious device to screw the charter fee even higher. Since eight, though, he'd heard of a number of incidents which confirmed McNaught's information, and now, walking back along the dock, it was all too clear that the Navy meant business. He didn't know exactly what the shots had signified, but gunfire was very definitely something to avoid.

Mick clambered aboard the *Timothy Lee*. McNaught had disappeared for the time being but Albie was hard at work, stacking mattresses beside the gaping mouth of the fish hold. Mick paused, one foot on the gangway, one foot on the deck.

'Harry turned up yet?' he said.

Albie barely looked at him, humping the heavy mattresses across the deck, and dropping them one by one into the fish hold below. He'd picked them up from a friend of a friend who ran a DHSS bed and breakfast place on the seafront. He'd taken thirty-two at a quid each, with the promise of another couple of dozen to come. The place was a right doss-house, and a lot of the mattresses were falling apart, others soaked in urine or worse. It was disgusting. It offended him. The way people lived. Mick repeated the question. 'Where's Harry?'

'Dunno,' he said, 'you tell me.'

'He mention anything about this other boat he wants?'

'No.'

'Oh.'

Mick frowned, remembering Harry's brief description. Small. Fast. Seaworthy. He looked around the dock, wondering why two boats, why the need. Harry was a sharp man. Did everything for a reason. Problem was, he rarely shared his little secrets.

Martin Goodman returned to the city mid-morning, sitting in the back of the official Rover as Evans inched the car carefully out between the small mountains of sandbags and barbed wire that now flanked the Bunker's entrance. This addition to his personal safety had appeared, quite literally, overnight. When he'd arrived with Davidson, at one in the morning, they'd been waved through by a couple of soldiers and a dog. Now, only hours later, it looked like a Hollywood set: layer after layer of sandbags, thickets of barbed wire, floodlights cabled to the Bunker's mains supply, and a large sign declaring the area a Prohibited Zone. There was an obvious reassurance in it all, a commitment to enfold and protect the administrative heart of the city, but there was something else as well, infinitely more personal. He'd begun to be aware of a growing sense of claustrophobia, of circumstances closing around him. It gave him a feeling of tightness in the chest. It made him anxious and fretful, uncertain where to turn next. In this sense, the sandbags and the barbed wire heightened the walls around him. He hated the Bunker. He was glad they were getting out.

The car telephone began to bleep. Goodman watched Evans reach forward, and pick up the phone, and put it to his ear. He nodded several times and eyed Goodman in the rear-view mirror. Goodman leaned forward, anticipating the call: more problems, more decisions, another colleague utterly bewildered by it all.

'Young lady, sir. A Miss Wallace.' He paused. 'She's phoned already, sir. She sounded quite upset.'

Goodman reached forward and took the phone.

'Hi,' he said, 'how are you?'

Suzanne reacted at once, a mixture of anger and something she tried to pass off as bonhomie. Just another day. Just another phone call.

'I'm fine,' she said, 'Just wonderful.' She paused. 'I suppose you've heard the news?'

'There isn't any news.'

'Precisely.' There was another pause. When she spoke again, the anger had gone. Instead, she sounded vulnerable, and frightened, and utterly alone.

'Martin . . .' she said, 'I have to see you.'

'You do?' he said mechanically, watching the back of Evans' head, wondering what he must make of it all. The speedometer was touching 100. The harbour was flashing by. Suzanne's voice again, lower.

'Soon.'

'Of course.'

'This morning.'

'I . . .' He hesitated, looking at his watch, knowing how impossible it had already become. Suzanne returned, in his ear, pleading, no games, no clever dialogue.

'Martin . . .' she said again, 'please.'

Goodman leaned back and shut his eyes, feeling the big car slowing for the roundabout at the end of the motorway.

'Half-past twelve,' he said, 'on the bench.' He handed the phone back to Evans without saying goodbye. The Marine clipped it back into its cradle on the central console.

'Still the harbour master, sir?' he said drily.

Goodman nodded. 'Yes,' he said, 'still the harbour master.'

'And then?' He nodded at the fuel gauge. 'Only I'll need petrol.'

'The Civic Centre,' he said, 'for twelve-thirty.' He leaned back against the warm leather. The sandbags, he thought again, the barbed wire.

Gillespie sat on his bed, loading film into his faithful old Olympus OM-1. The huge zoom lens lay beside him on the duvet. The last time he'd done a photographic job, he'd closed the case in less than a day and a half. But this one would be different. Already, it had the makings of a combat situation – a complicated stalk, a heavily protected target – and the exercise might, for a day or two, return him to the world he thought he'd left for ever. He grinned. After too many years of civilian life, flabby, torpid, dull, things were at last looking up again.

He stepped across the tiny landing, and took the stairs two at a time. He found the number in the book within seconds. A receptionist answered. He asked for Martin Goodman. There was a pause, then another woman's voice.

'Freeman & Co,' Gillespie said gruffly, 'want to know whether Mr Goodman'll be needing another wagon.'

There was a pause at the other end. The girl was evidently puzzled. Finally she said she didn't know. Mr Goodman was out at the moment. She'd check as soon as he returned.

'When's that, love?' said Gillespie.

'Half-past twelve,' said the girl.

Goodman stood in the window of the harbour master's office and repeated his request.

'Two boats,' he said, 'leaving tonight.'

The harbour master frowned, considering the application, enjoying the authority the situation had given him.

'Why?' he said.

Goodman looked at him, the small bright eyes, the thin bony nose, the crisp white shirt with the gold epaulettes. He hadn't come to argue, or pick a fight, but he was suddenly sick of the emptiness of his authority, the helpings other men were taking from his plate.

'Because I say so,' he countered briskly. 'Because I think it's the right thing to do.'

'What sort of boats?'

Goodman hesitated, determined not to be wrong-footed, remembering Cartwright's terse description.

'One big, one small,' he said, 'don't ask me for details because I haven't got them. Yet.'

'I see.' The man pursed his lips. 'And where are these . . . ah . . . craft going? Exactly?'

'Ireland,' said Goodman blindly.

'South? North?'

'South.' Goodman frowned, recalling the shapes on the map, the long fingers of land extending out into the Atlantic. 'West.'

'I see.' The harbour master paused, fingering the binoculars on the desk, his badge of office. 'And the passenger list?'

'About thirty people.'

The harbour master nodded, suddenly businesslike, pulling a pad towards him. 'Names?'

Goodman began to lose his temper, a hot, gusting anger that he tried, briefly, to contain.

'Forgive me . . .' he said evenly, 'but I'm a busy man. We're all busy men. I want you to know what we're doing. I'm offering you the courtesy of telling you in advance. I have a team of men. The city depends on them. It's vital I give them what little peace of mind I can. I intend to ship their loved ones out. Tonight . . .' he did his best to smile, 'with your permission.'

The harbour master looked at him, too thick-skinned to heed the warning signals, to note the tell-tale flicker of nervous strain beginning to appear beneath Goodman's left eye. He tapped at the pad.

'Women and children . . .' he said speculatively. 'Have you thought this thing through? Properly? Are you aware of the risks involved?'

'The boats are perfectly seaworthy. I'm assured of that.'

'I'm not talking about the boats. Though naturally we'll require an inspection.'

Goodman looked briefly nonplussed, trying to out-guess this tiresome old bureaucrat, trying to beat him at his own game. Cartwright had made it sound utterly feasible, a question – as ever – of supply and demand. No hitches. No drawbacks. Simply a matter of casting off and heading west. The harbour master got up from his desk and turned his back on Goodman, gazing out of the big picture window. The harbour was virtually empty, a tribute to the zealous efforts of his private flotilla, recruited overnight, and already assured of a modest line or two in the history of the place. So far, in six brief hours, they'd turned back more than a hundred boats, from six-foot yacht tenders risking the five miles to the island, to fifty-foot ocean-going sloops, victualled for months at sea, equipped with satellite navigation aids, and jam-packed with instant sailors. Most of the skippers had conceded to the blockade without a fight, sour, sullen, resigned. A handful, especially some of the city's lawyers, had tried to argue their way to the open sea, disputing the authority of the harbour master, and citing obscure constitutional precedents in support of the citizens' rights of passage. Arguments like these were simply ignored. Boats were either taken in tow and confiscated, their crews dumped in the shallows on one of the city's beaches, or turned around at gunpoint, and left to drift back inland, up-harbour, towards the muddy creeks and saltings that led, quite literally, nowhere.

The harbour master turned slowly back into the room.

'These passengers of yours . . .' he began. 'These dependants. Where will they go aboard?'

'The Camber Dock,' he said. 'As I understand it.' The harbour master nodded.

'And have you thought about the security implications? All those lucky people, with their children, and the odd chattel or two? Getting away? With our blessing?'

'What do you mean?'

The harbour master shrugged, the gesture of a man weary of dealing with fools and *ingénues*.

'The Camber is an open area,' he said. 'You'll have a riot on your hands.'

'I'll seal it off,' Goodman said automatically, feeling the anger again.

'With what?'

Goodman was aware of something snapping inside him, something almost palpable. He pushed his chair back and stood up. The exchange between them was over.

'The boats will leave tonight,' he said coldly. 'They'll be under my direct jurisdiction. You will be notified of their names, their tonnage, and their intended destination. You will not receive a passenger list, and you will not impede them in any way.' He looked the harbour master in the eye. 'Is that clear?'

The harbour master nodded, pale with outrage, and Goodman knew at once that he'd made an enemy for life.

'Perfectly,' he said. 'Though the responsibility is entirely yours.'

It was nearly midday before Annie risked the stairs, and the garden path, and the drive back to Gillespie's place. The worst of the nausea had gone, and her head had stopped hurting quite so much, but there was something else, deeper, an insecurity so physical that once or twice she had to sit down, and force her knees together, and hug herself tightly to stop the trembling that threatened to engulf her. She'd never been assaulted before, and she'd always been mildly curious to know what it felt like, what it did to you, the difference it made. Now, she knew. And the countless interviewees she'd filmed all over the world, the men and women who'd been beaten and humiliated in the name of some political creed or other, had been right. It hurt like nothing else. Not a physical hurt. Nothing a casualty nurse could enter on an admission form. Nothing a swab, and a bandage and a couple of days' rest could put right. But something far deeper, a profound sense of unease, a feeling that the world wasn't quite the place she'd assumed it to be, but somewhere infinitely colder, more alien, more dangerous.

The young reporter felt it too, she knew, and when she paused by her car, and he gave her the keys back, she reached forward and touched him on the cheek, a fellow member of this curious brotherhood to which they now both belonged.

'Don't worry,' she told him, 'I won't be back.' She smiled. 'And I don't blame you.'

He pretended confusion, and shrugged, and said it was all beyond him, all too much, which was a kinder form of capitulation. They'd both been listening to the radio all morning, waiting for word from London, from abroad, some hint of exactly where events might be leading, but the news channels had closed down, and the normal hourly bulletins had been condensed into a brisk two-minute address on the importance of obeying local directives, and the folly of trying to plan any kind of journey. The nation's road network was evidently clogged solid, hundreds of miles of stationary cars, most of them without fuel. Quite what the occupants of these vehicles were now doing was never discussed, though Annie had her doubts about the truth of the story in the first place. Visions of starving families foraging for food in a bleak and hostile countryside was a great way of keeping the punters at home. And this Government, like any other, would pull any stroke to maintain control. Of that, she was quite certain.

She got in the car, and headed back through the warren of streets towards Gillespie's house. Her knowledge of the city was far from perfect, and twice she had to stop and ask for directions. On both occasions she was struck by how friendly people had become, how approachable. As well as answering her question – second left, first right, right again at the burned-out cornershop – they wanted her to pause a while, to share the gossip, to listen to the latest rumour, to agree that things were tough, yes, but would undoubtedly get much worse. In the latter expectation, she sensed a certain grim delight, a feeling that this final cataclysm was somehow inevitable, that the world had been living beyond its means for far too long, and deserved what was coming to it. 'It's been on the cards since the last one . . .' an old man told her three streets from Gillespie's, 'and about time too.' She'd smiled at the comment. Maybe the film was a simpler proposition than she'd thought. A blitz movie, scored for wagging heads, and brave smiles, and the usual chorus of sentimental tosh.

Annie parked outside Gillespie's house, retrieved her bag from the back seat, and got out. She peered up the street, looking for the rusty old Marina, but it had gone. She wondered for a moment whether he'd already shipped out – Sean, Sandra maybe, a crate or two of Guinness, and the big sheaf of Admiralty charts he kept under his bed. The more she thought about it, the more likely it became, and to her surprise she realized she'd be disappointed if it was true. It had been difficult the last time they'd met. She'd bullied him into doing the interview, and, she'd offended him with her final impatient volley of questions. Yet beyond it all – his war, her series, her precious bloody career – she realized that she missed this strange reticent man, with his gruffness, and his gaucheness, and his old-fashioned ideas. When they laid aside all the clutter about making films, all the arguments about patriotism and the hidden hand of Government, it had been remarkably simple. They'd had a good time, a few laughs, and they'd touched each other in close, important ways. Annie had a deep mistrust of phrases like falling in love, regarding them as a cop-out, but her months with Gillespie had been as good as it ever got, and it saddened her to think that the relationship might be over. Especially now. Especially the way she was.

She rang the front door bell a final time, and then searched her bag for the key he'd given her way back. She found it and let herself in. The house smelled, as ever, of bleach and fresh air. Gillespie was meticulous about the way he kept the place. He hated dirt. She walked down the hall.

'Dave?' she called.

She paused for a moment, then went into the living room. The curtains were still half-closed, the room in semi-darkness. She put her bag on the floor and gazed around. There was a towel draped over a radiator under the window. An open book lay face up on the armchair by the fireplace. *Montgomery: Master of the Battlefield.* She smiled, and walked across to the telephone, meaning at last to talk to Bullock, to find out what was going on, to tell him about last night, to bring him up to date. Beside the telephone was a photo. She picked it up. The photo showed a man on a swing, his arm around a small boy. He was smiling at the camera. She picked the photo up and walked slowly across to the window, where the light was better. Her head was beginning to throb again, the pressure and the pain returning. She gazed down at the photo, remembering the man in the newsroom, the man in Bullock's office, the man in the interviewee's chair, deftly fielding Prosser's questions, turning them to his own advantage, rewriting the script. No doubt about it. Martin Goodman. The city's new Controller.

Gillespie had been in the Guildhall Square for more than forty minutes by the time the big black Rover returned from the dockyard. During the morning, since his last visit, the security had been tightened. There were crowd control barriers barring the steps to the Civic Offices, and armed troops knelt in the shadows flanking the entrance to the building. Police were everywhere, in twos and threes, and there was a modest demonstration taking place which gave Gillespie all the cover he needed.

The Rover pulled to a halt at the kerbside, and one of the policemen opened the back door. His salute alerted Gillespie at once to the passenger, a tall, slim figure in an expensive suit and glasses. The man acknowledged the salute with a nod, and turned briefly back to the car to talk to the driver. As he did so, Gillespie recognized the face on the swing: good, even features, signs of strain around the mouth and eyes.

Gillespie folded his paper and returned it to his shoulder bag. The big Rover slid away from the kerb and disappeared. Goodman, his target, hesitated, one foot on the first of the steps up to the Civic Offices, checking that the Rover had, in fact, left. Then he turned abruptly on his heel, and walked away across the Square, hurrying towards the exit that led to the station and the city's Botanical Gardens. Gillespie watched him carefully, and then began to follow.

From Martin Goodman's fifth-floor office, Oliver Davidson monitored the scene below. He'd been waiting for Goodman since noon, impatient to confirm the details of his first official broadcast, booked for transmission at ten past nine, after the Queen had addressed the nation on the national networks. Davidson had already drafted the speech, a deft blend of regulation and reassurance, and he'd arranged for Goodman to record both television and radio versions in mid-afternoon, leaving the evening clear for the detailed conferences he'd itemized in another long memorandum.

Now, though, looking down on the square below, the city's new Controller was nearly out of sight, picking his way amongst the handful of protesters who'd broken off from the main demo and were arguing with a shirt-sleeved police inspector. More to the point, there was another figure, thirty or forty metres behind, moving in the same direction, not taking his eyes off Goodman.

Davidson had noticed the man earlier, away in a remote corner of the square, his head buried in a newspaper, his back against the wall. At first, there'd been nothing remarkable about the man, but every time Davidson had looked out of the window, waiting for Goodman, the man had still been there, and when Davidson looked more closely, he began to realize that the man was plainly there for a purpose. He appeared to be watching someone. Davidson, after a while, had drawn the obvious conclusion, but when he'd picked up the phone and called Ingle at St Ursula's, Ingle had disclaimed any knowledge of a surveillance operation. He had no men in the square, he said, though he had plenty available should they be required. Davidson had told him no, not for the time being, but now he lifted the phone again, and dialled the same number, only to find that Ingle had, as usual, beaten him to it.

'Jeans?' he said. 'Leather jacket? About thirty-five? Forty?'

Davidson turned towards the window, watching Gillespie disappear after Goodman.

'That's him,' he said, looking for Ingle's man but picking up nobody obvious. 'Under control?'

He heard Ingle chuckling at the other end.

'Ours,' he said. 'And thanks for the introduction.'

Martin Goodman found Suzanne on a bench in the shadow of the big glass hot-house that dominated the Botanical Gardens. The Gardens, three acres of shrubs, and trees, and neatly trimmed flower beds, was one of the few areas of open ground in the city's centre. Normally, at lunchtime, it was full of secretaries and office workers enjoying a sandwich and a brief hour in the sunshine. Today, though, with most of the city's offices closed, it was nearly empty.

Goodman walked across the grass, and joined Suzanne on the bench. Suzanne glanced across at him. She looked wooden, and cold. Her face was drawn, and she'd taken less care than usual with her make-up.

'I'm sorry,' she said. 'Again.'

Goodman didn't answer at once, staring out across the gardens. Suzanne had no parents. They'd both died when she was barely ten, killed in a motorway pile-up on the M6. She had no brothers and sisters, either, and this isolation of hers, a human being with no relatives – quite literally – to turn to, had always made her somehow even more attractive. She very rarely talked about it, hiding the aloneness and the vulnerability beneath a busy life and a successful career. But it was there, none the less, and now he felt it acutely. His responsibility. Someone who had come to depend on him.

'Suzanne . . .' he said, 'Suzy . . . this isn't easy. None of this is easy.'

Suzanne reached for his hand.

'My love, it never was.'

Goodman nodded.

'No,' he said. He looked at her for the first time, seeing how gaunt she'd become, the shadows under her eyes, the obvious strain. 'You *mustn't* use the car phone,' he said.

She looked at him, a curious blank look, almost autistic in its emptiness.

'So I gather,' she said. 'I've told you. I'm sorry. I apologize.'

Goodman withdrew his hand and sealed the subject with a shrug.

A chill silence descended on the conversation. Goodman felt suddenly exhausted, wondering what he really wanted, what he really felt strongly about, and realizing that it was sleep, the simplest release of all. Suzanne shifted beside him, a small uncomfortable motion of her body. Her voice had lowered. Flat. Dead.

'There's something you ought to know,' she said.

'What?'

She looked at him. Then away again.

'I wasn't going to tell you,' she said, 'but under the circumstances . . .' She shrugged. 'I thought it merited a phone call.'

'What is it?'

'I'm pregnant.' She looked at him again. 'With our baby.'

Goodman nodded, numbed. Flesh and blood. His. Theirs.

'I see,' he said. 'How pregnant?'

'Nearly four months.'

'I see,' he said again.

They both stared out, across the grass, towards the row of trees that usually softened the roar of the traffic. Today, there was no traffic, and the silence made it somehow worse. Suzanne felt for his hand again, and turned towards him. There was a warmth in her voice, and something else that took Goodman a moment or two to recognize. Finally, he was able to put a name to it. It was pity. Suzanne smiled at him.

'My poor love,' she said. 'You don't know what to say, do you?'

She leaned over him, solicitous, caring, and kissed him gently on the cheek. Goodman, in spite of himself, stiffened, wanting it to stop, wanting everything to stop, to go away, to leave him alone. Suzanne left her hand in his for a moment or two, reading his mind, his expression, his half-hearted attempt to mask what he really felt. She stood up.

'It's all right, Martin,' she said, cold again, 'playtime's over. You can go back to the office now. I just wanted you to know. That's all.'

She looked at him a moment longer, and then turned on her

heel and left. Thirty metres away, between the leaves of a rhododendron bush, Gillespie had time to get three more good shots, head and shoulders, before the focus began to drift. While she was still walking away, he snapped two more studies of the man on the bench, his face beginning to sag, his chin slumping imperceptibly towards his chest, a tiny twitch under his left eye. The roll of film finished, he stowed the camera in the bag, looped the strap over his shoulder, and walked away, keeping track of the girl as she hurried towards the gate that led to the car park.

In the car park, she got into a grey VW Golf GTI. Gillespie noted the registration while she dabbed at her eyes with a corner of Kleenex. Then she gunned the engine, and accelerated away. The squeal of tyres masked the motordrive on the Nikon in the hands of the man on the pavement across the road. Still watching the car, Gillespie didn't notice the gleam of sunlight on the lens, or the face behind the camera, or the swirl of black raincoat as the man turned quietly away and began to saunter east, towards the sea.

By the time Goodman returned to his office, Davidson had gone. A curt note on his desk reminded him of the afternoon's recording session, and drew his attention to the copy of the speech lying beside the telephone. Goodman scanned the speech, altered a phrase or two, tore up the note, and reached for the telephone. Harry Cartwright answered on the second ring.

'Harry,' he said shortly, 'it's Martin. About tonight.'

'Yes?'

'You're to leave after dark. I'll arrange for fuel to be available. You have a dispensation to leave harbour. I'll fax you a list of passengers this afternoon.' He paused. 'One other thing.'

'Yes?'

'There's a woman called Suzanne Wallace. She's in the travel business. She has contacts. She'll make the arrangements the other end.'

'I see . . .' There was a thoughful pause. 'And will this Miss . . . ah . . . Wallace be coming too?'

Goodman hesitated, staring out of the window.

'Yes,' he said at last, 'she will.'

Six

In the air-conditioned cool of the big office in Little Creek, Virginia, the man behind the desk was waiting, once again, for the phone call. Twice already in the last twenty-four hours, he'd conferenced on the secure hook-up with the NSA Liaison Officer at Fort Meade, Maryland, and the Captain in charge of the SEAL teams at Machrihanish, in Scotland. For a day and a half now, the SEAL teams had been standing by at optimum readiness, the big Hercules C-130s preloaded on the tarmac, the men themselves on fifteen minutes' notice to move, checking and rechecking equipment, studying plans and models of the huge 'Ohio'-class submarine, conferring with the weather men on the conditions they'd meet as they parachuted down into the Barents Sea.

They'd rehearsed the operation a number of times, using an old 'Ethan Allen'-class submarine fifty miles off the coast of Northern Ireland. The drops had gone well, the men scaling the sides of the enormous hull, hauling inboard their special flotation packs, stowing away the various devices, defensive and otherwise, they needed to fulfil their mission, should the Russians move in and try and seize the crippled sub. In theory, now, they should already be airborne, somewhere over the Norwegian Sea, counting the minutes until the rear cargo door hinged down, and they filed aft, the usual sticks of four, and the Drop Master signalled readiness, and then swept them out into the thin cold air, and the slipstream smacked them in the face as they plummeted the first 7,000 feet in free-fall towards the chill grey waters below. Except that something had happened, some curious late development, something for which the master plan had made no allowances.

The man behind the desk, a Commander, leaned back in his chair. The clock on his office wall said seven-thirty. He'd been up since dawn. Today, his wife had predicted, would be Go-Day.

The phone rang. He reached forward, taking his time. It was

Fort Meade. The man from Intelligence again, the guy he'd talked to twice already, careful, precise, non-committal. These conversations had given him no clue about the reason for the delay. Only, de facto, that it had been Intelligence-related. The Commander fed a new stick of chewing gum into his mouth.

'Hi,' he said cheerfully. 'We goin'?'

The man at the other end of the line began to talk. Short-wave communications problems with the *Kennan*, intermittent contact, evidence of Soviet sampling operations, suspicions finally confirmed. There was a pause. The Commander, none the wiser, tucked the gum into a corner of his cheek.

'So are we goin'?' he said again. 'Do we move?'

'Negative.'

'Later today?'

'That's a negative, too.'

The Commander frowned.

'God damn,' he said. 'These guys of mine . . .'

The Intelligence man broke in. Time was obviously precious. Motivation wasn't his concern.

'The sub's hot,' he said. 'So hot she'd burn most of DC right now.'

The Commander paused, robbed of the end of his sentence. He looked abruptly thoughtful.

'Well now . . .' he said. 'That's a little different . . .'

Gillespie arrived back home at half-past one. He'd stopped off at a call box en route, dialling a number from memory and asking for a Detective Constable by his first name. The man was away from his desk for a moment, a call of nature, but Gillespie hung on until he returned. He'd read him the woman's car registration number on the phone, open line, and waited a minute or so while the Detective Constable left the room for a second time. Back again, the Detective Constable dictated an address from the printout linked to the National Police Computer at Swansea. The address Gillespie recognized. A smart block of flats on the seafront, ninth floor, near the top. He'd thanked the Detective Constable, and made the usual joke about 'elevenses', a mutual euphemism for the £20 note that Gillespie would add to Joanna Goodman's bill.

'Cheers,' said the voice at the other end. 'Let's hope I get the chance to spend it.'

From the phone box, Gillespie had detoured via the seafront. The Marina was getting low on fuel by now, but he'd laid his plans carefully, and he knew that he had enough to risk the extra three miles or so it would take to check the information out. On the seafront, outside the block of flats, he recognized the woman's grey VW Golf. He parked the Marina round the corner, and walked slowly past, noting the ABTA sticker in the back window, and the hand stitched cushions on the rear seat. On the passenger seat were two discarded envelopes from the morning's mail. He confirmed the name and the address from his conversation with the Detective Constable. Ms Suzanne Wallace. Flat 913. Ocean Towers.

He glanced up at the flats. Big picture windows and sliding doors opening onto generous balconies, each balcony cleverly echeloned to preserve a little private sunshine. The balconies on the ninth floor faced in two directions. South-west, above him, towards the Common and the harbour, and south-east, round the corner, towards the island and the sea. Glancing at the address, he suspected that 913 was on the south-easterly quadrant, but unless he actually went up there and checked the orientations, he couldn't be sure. He wondered for a moment whether he should, but then he dismissed the idea. His client wanted a name, an address, a phone number, and a photo. The phone number would come from directory enquiries. The rest he'd cracked. The view from the balcony was irrelevant.

Now, back home, he coasted the Marina to a halt, recognizing Annie's borrowed Escort outside the house. He'd thought about her a good deal in the last twenty-four hours, irritation at first, at her pushiness, and her lack of respect, but all that had gone and he'd discovered in its place a curious hole. Nothing silly. Not a longing, or a sadness, but a hole. Until she'd overstepped the mark, she'd fitted nicely into his life. She'd been her own person. She'd matched him pint for pint, dig for dig, and as long as they stayed off politics, she was very good company. She had a slightly male attitude to life – few illusions, no nonsense – yet she was wholly a woman when it mattered most, and in that department, as in the rest, they'd shared the best of times. Now, for some reason, she was back. And he realized he was glad.

He got out of the car, picked up his bag from the boot, and went indoors. Annie was in the living room, curled up on the tiny sofa. He knew at once there was something wrong. She looked as though she'd been in a traffic accident. Her face was misshapen, and there was blood on her forehead. Gillespie put the bag carefully on the ottoman under the window.

'What's up?' he said. 'What happened?'

Annie looked up, more pleased to see him than she knew how to say. She tried to get up, then thought better of it and sank back onto the sofa.

'Battle wounds,' she said. 'I've been in the wars.'

'So tell me,' he said again. 'What happened?'

Annie shrugged, abandoning the banter, and told him exactly what had happened. In her own mind, it still wasn't completely clear. But she assumed she'd been hit from behind, and fallen forward onto her face in the gravel. Interpreting the young reporter's silences, that had probably been the full extent of the violence. She'd looked hard for other injuries but found none.

She finished the story and looked up at Gillespie again. He drew the curtains back. Light flooded the room. He bent over her, and turned her face up towards the window. He peered closely at each eye, ran his fingers through her hair, felt his way round the swelling at the back of her skull. When he'd finished, he looked down at her.

'How am I?' she said.

'Bloody lucky.'

'Meaning?'

'They could have meant it.'

She caught his tone at once. Disapproval. Mixed with a little concern.

'Could?' she said, 'or should?'

'Could,' he said briefly. 'Your head ache?'

'Yes.'

'Vision OK? Seeing double?'

'No,' she shook her head, 'only one of you.'

'Yeah?' he stepped back towards the telephone table under the far window, unconvinced. 'How many fingers?' he said, holding one closed fist in the air.

'None.'

'OK,' he nodded slowly. 'You're out of the game, love. And you should stay out. They might hurt you next time.'

'They did hurt me.'

'You got a tap.' He shrugged. 'Rifle butt. Night stick. Something to show your friends.'

'That's all?'

'Yeah.' He nodded. 'For now. They take your name?'

'Not that I know . . .' She frowned, remembering the reporter, his shyness, his silences, his evident embarrassment. 'But yes, let's say they did. So what?'

'So they might be back. So you ought to . . .' he shrugged, 'I dunno.'

'Show a little respect?'

'Something like that.'

She looked at him, marvelling at his composure, his matter of factness, the lack of indignation, of outrage at what was happening, at what she'd caught them doing to the city. One hundred and fifty thousand people. Cut off. Corralled. Consigned, for all they cared, to oblivion.

'You know what's going on?' she asked him. 'What they're up to?'

He nodded. 'Yeah,' he said. 'They've taken charge. As they should.'

'You say.'

'I say.'

She glanced at him, the old argument.

'You're not bothered? All this . . .' she gestured vaguely at the street, the city, the blood still caked on her forehead, 'doesn't bother you?'

'Not at all,' he said. 'You'd be bitching even more if they'd all gone off and left us.' He shrugged again, rearranging a photo of Sean on the mantelpiece, the tiniest movement, irritated with having to argue with her so soon. 'No,' he said again, 'they're doing a job. New rules. New situation. Stands to reason.'

She looked up at him, her head beginning to throb.

'Doesn't matter that there's no more news? No more radio? TV?'

'Best thing.'

'Don't care about summary arrests? Imprisonment without trial?'

'I don't know about that,' he said.

'Neither do I. But I'm sure it's happening.'

'Ah . . .' he smiled at her for the first time, 'but that makes you lucky, doesn't it? Them letting you get away with it?'

He grinned at her, breaking her arguments one by one and tossing them aside, a litter of socialist gobbledegook, wholly irrelevant.

'Tea?' he said, heading for the door.

She shook her head and struggled to her feet. She walked unsteadily towards him, feeling the blood emptying from her head. He waited for her, not quite certain, unsure what she meant to happen next. She paused by the telephone. She picked up the photograph of Goodman.

'One question, Dave. Just one. What are you doing with this?'

Gillespie looked at her, still grinning, refusing her the satisfaction of an answer. She turned the photo over. There was nothing on the back. She returned it to the table by the phone.

'You know who he is?' she said.

Gillespie nodded. 'Yes,' he said.

'You know he's Controller?'

'Yes.'

'Our Lord and Master? Second only to God?'

'So I gather.'

Annie paused, and picked up the photo again.

'Unelected? Absolute authority? Life or death? You or me?'

'Yes,' he said again.

She stared at him, trying to provoke a reaction, getting nothing in return.

'So tell me,' she said, 'why a photo?' She tried to smile, but winced instead. 'Business?' she said. 'Or personal?'

Gillespie looked at her for a long moment. For the second time in twenty-four hours, she was chancing her arm, breaking the rules, sticking her nose into forbidden territory, other people's business. Even after a belt across the head, and a dose of concussion, she still didn't understand, still couldn't help herself, still couldn't resist one last question. He grinned.

'Two spoons or one?' he said. 'I can't remember.'

He didn't wait for an answer, but left the room. In the kitchen she could hear him filling the kettle, turning off the tap, lighting the gas. She looked down at the holdall he'd left on the ottoman. The holdall was partly unzipped, and she recognized the shape of the camera inside. She stared at the photograph again, at Goodman, not beginning to understand.

Ingle stood at the desk, studying the first of the big colour blow-ups. The processing laboratory had been installed overnight in what had once been the dispensary, and these were the first prints off. He turned to the man who stood beside him, the man who'd taken the shots in the first place. His name was Reese, a small, dark, anonymous-looking Welshman from the hills behind Swansea. He'd returned to the hospital with the film at half-past one. He'd stood behind the technician in the darkroom while he rinsed the fixer from the strip of negatives, and he'd selected the blow-ups without bothering to go to the contact stage. Now, barely an hour later, he indicated another of the prints. It showed a crop-haired man of about thirty-five with a bag slung over one shoulder, looking at a woman in a grey Volkswagen. The rest of the car park was empty. The man was evidently unaware of being watched. Ingle peered at the photo, recognizing the face from the first print.

'What happened next?' he said.

Reese nodded at the rest of the blow-ups.

'He picked up his car. Old Marina. Local registration.'

'What's his name?'

'Gillespie.'

'Form?'

'Nothing criminal. Lives in the city. Glengarry Road. Used to be a Marine.' He paused. 'Earned himself a "K".'

Ingle looked up.

'Really?' he said, interested.

Reese nodded, 'Yes,' he said, 'alleged to have shot a Mick in Northern Ireland. 1985. Funny little incident.'

Ingle frowned, remembering something, a name, a detail.

'Ballycombe?' he said finally. 'Bloke called McMullen?'

Reese looked at him, surprised.

'Yes,' he said, 'Dessie McMullen.' He paused. 'You know

the incident?'

'Yes,' Ingle said, 'I do.' He tapped another of Reese's photos, Gillespie peering at a patch of rust on the sill of his old Marina. 'So what's his game now then? Any idea?'

Reese shook his head. 'None,' he said.

'You mentioned a woman.'

'Yes. Goodman met a woman in the park there.'

'Do we know her?'

'A Miss Wallace.' He tapped the blow-up that featured the VW. 'That's her car.' He sniffed. 'I gather he's over the side.'

Ingle nodded, ignoring Reese's obvious disapproval, the Welshman's prissy little moral scruples.

'Yeah,' he said, 'he is.'

He glanced again at the photos, and then turned away, deep in thought. Reese stirred uncomfortably. Working for Ingle was an acquired taste, and he didn't have it.

'What next?' he said. 'Shall I pull him in?'

Ingle considered the proposition for a moment or two, standing at the window watching an old lady feeding handfuls of bread rolls to a stone pigeon in a small ornamental bird bath.

'No,' he said at last, 'I don't think so.'

'We leave him alone?'

Ingle turned back from the window.

'Oh no, no,' he said, 'stay in touch. By all means.'

Goodman let himself into Suzanne's flat, using the key he'd had since Christmas. Standing on the landing outside the door, he could see Evans in the Rover outside, head back, window down, enjoying the early autumn sunshine on his face. Goodman had told him fifteen minutes. With luck, he could be out in ten.

He turned the key in the lock and stepped into the flat. He walked straight through to the lounge, with its fitted carpet and shag rugs and big french windows onto the balcony outside, but the room was empty. He frowned, retracing his steps down the hall. The bedroom door opened. Suzanne stood there, long T-shirt, bare feet, hair tousled. She looked briefly frightened, then relieved, then something else. Perhaps curious. Perhaps wary. Perhaps both.

'Oh,' she said, 'it's you.'

Goodman nodded, determined not to lose the momentum of the decision he'd taken, not to lose his way.

'I'm sorry,' he said, 'I should have rung.'

'No . . .' she shook her head, 'it's OK. I was . . . asleep.'

'Ah.'

They looked at each other for a moment. Then she smiled at him, and kissed him briefly, on the cheek, and walked past him into the kitchen.

'Coffee?' she said, over her shoulder.

Goodman shook his head, aware of the initiative slipping away from him.

'No thanks,' he said, 'I haven't got much time.'

He heard her lighting the gas, filling the kettle, hunting for coffee and the cups. He remained in the hall, uncertain, like a travelling salesman. The place smelled of *Calèche*, the ripe, heavy scent of deceit, of stolen evenings. For the first time in nearly a year, he felt uncomfortable, out of place. Suzanne reappeared in the kitchen doorway.

'You can come in,' she said, 'I won't embarrass you.'

'Embarrass,' he queried uneasily, 'why embarrass?'

She looked at him, knowing him inside out, recognizing the weakness and the uncertainty. Her smile held a certain wary affection. The doctor at the clinic had been right. It was trickier thinking in threes.

'What's the news?' she said. 'I imagine you must know.'

Goodman seized the question gratefully, neutral territory, all too welcome. At the same time, he realized he couldn't give her an answer. Not because he didn't trust her, but because – like everyone else in the city – he simply didn't know.

'I'm not sure,' he said, 'to tell you the truth.'

Suzanne nodded, spooning coffee granules into the waiting cups.

'You're busy,' she said, 'I can tell.'

'I am,' he said, 'you're right.'

She smiled at the cups, screwed the lid back onto the coffee jar, and turned into him, a simple fluid movement, unsignalled, entirely spontaneous. She put her arms around his neck and looked at him.

'You're worried about the baby,' she said. 'You shouldn't be.

Everything will be fine. I promise you.'

Goodman closed his eyes for a moment, trying to keep the darkness at bay, trying to shut out a world he could no longer control. Her simple phrases could mean anything. Or nothing. He no longer knew. Or even cared. Just another problem. He felt her fingertips on his face. She kissed him lightly, on the forehead, on the eyelids, his mistress, his best friend, his nurse.

'I love you,' she said softly, 'I want you to know that.'

'I know,' he said hopelessly, 'I know.'

The kettle began to whistle, and she turned away. By the time he was back in charge of himself, she was decanting hot water into the cups. They walked through to the bedroom, the place where they'd always talked, always settled things. The bed was unmade.

He sat down, balancing the coffee cup carefully on his knee. She made a space amongst the pillows, and sat beside him, her shoulders flat against the quilted bedhead, her knees drawn up to her chin.

'You came for a reason,' she reminded him. 'You don't need me dripping on.'

He smiled, wondering how to start. He was quite empty now, all the resolution gone, the strain and the tension put aside for a moment or two in this dark little cave of a room, their very own foxhole.

'I'm organizing a little trip . . .' he began, 'a voyage . . .'

He outlined the plan, the need to get the wives and kids away, his responsibility to his colleagues, his feeling that they'd all perform better with one less problem to worry about. He mentioned Harry Cartwright, and the agreement he'd reached with him. He said there were still knots and bows to tie, loose ends to arrange. He needed to be sure about the destination. He needed to know what lay in store for these women and children when they finally arrived at journey's end. He needed to know they'd be safe.

'And?' she said, when he'd finished.

He smiled at her, touching the warm flesh, the easiest thing in the world.

'And I want you to take care of it.'

'Me?'

'Yes. Harry will give you an office. Best if you work there. You'll need to find accommodations. Places these people can stay. Food. Lodging.' He smiled again. 'Your stock in trade.'

'Where, though?'

'Southern Ireland. Or Portugal. Somewhere west. Somewhere out of the way. Your choice.' He paused. 'But I need to know they'll be safe. We have to be certain.'

She frowned for a moment, turning the plan over in her mind, suddenly the businesswoman, the bright young travel executive, multi-lingual, charming, ruthless, hotly tipped by the trade papers for stardom.

'Ireland,' she said at last. 'It's closer.'

'You've got contacts?'

'Some. But I know where else to look.' She paused. 'When does the boat go?'

'Tonight,' he said, 'about ten.'

'*Tonight*,' she looked at her watch, 'it's half-past one already.'

He put his coffee on the side table, beside the book, and reached across for her.

'I know,' he said, 'I know.'

'Business ends at five.' She paused. 'Four in Ireland.'

Goodman squeezed her arm.

'Harry's there now,' he said, 'he's expecting you. You've got a good two hours.' He hesitated. 'In any case, the phones go off tonight. Or most of them do, anyway.'

'Off?' she said blankly.

He nodded, remembering Davidson's curt reminder. The Telephone Preference System, a mechanism for disconnecting 95 per cent of the nation's telephones, would be actioned at dusk, yet another little incentive to keep fifty million people in place.

'Yes,' he said, 'off.' He paused, reluctant to clutter the conversation with any further details. 'So . . .' he began, 'what do you say?'

'To what?'

'To my proposal. My little scheme.' He paused. 'Sorting out the Irish end.'

She hesitated, stirring her coffee, not looking at him.

'Tell me something,' she said at last. 'Is your wife on this list?'

He looked at her, the long firm line of her thigh, the swell of her breasts under the T-shirt, the warm animal scent of the bed she slept in, and he knew, deep down, that there was no longer any hope.

'Yes,' he said, 'she will be.'

'And me?'

'You . . .' he smiled, and reached out for her, '. . . you stay.'

By the time Harry Cartwright closed his personal passenger list, it was early afternoon. He'd been on the phone since eight o'clock, working carefully through a list of clients he'd culled from the business files he held on a new IBM PC computer he reserved for his personal use in the office. After some thought, he'd decided to limit the offer to a relative handful of premium clients from the hundred or so he serviced, men and women with serious money to their names, individuals with the necessary clout and confidence to make an instant decision about a largish sum.

He knew most of these people well, knew how he'd put it to them, knew the calculations they'd make in their own minds, knew that even now, even with their lives on the line, it would be a strictly business decision, balancing outlay against return, measuring the up-front fee against the risks of staying put.

The exact size of the fee, Cartwright had pondered overnight. Mick's first suggestion – £3,000 – had sounded far too high, but the more he thought about it, and the more aware he became of the city's predicament, the more he realized that Mick's fee was probably too low, that the latest security measures had created a commodity it was almost impossible to quantify in simple figures. What they were selling, after all, was the prospect of survival. And that required a pricing mechanism infinitely more subtle than a crude flat rate. It was a question, as ever, of presentation. Handled properly, the right mix of persuasion, and advice, and plain common sense, some of these clients would part with a great deal more than £3,000.

At this point, early hours of the morning, Cartwright had returned to his files, displaying the spread sheets of his chosen clients one after the other, last audited sets of accounts, profits and losses, accumulated funds, capital charges, and that key figure at the end of it all which indicated the pre-tax profit at the year's end. Within this figure, he drew an arbitrary line. Only clients reporting pre-tax profits of one hundred thousand pounds or more would qualify for an introductory call. He wrote a simple program and fed the figures into the computer. A list of clients appeared on the screen. He counted them. They numbered thirty-four. A man who'd made a small fortune manufacturing hosepipes for washing machines. Another, a design consultant, who'd patented a number of hi-tech gizmos for the defence industry. A husband and wife partnership who'd made a success of a string of small hotels. An Asian who'd started the city's first oriental wholesale food operation. A young ex-builder who'd gone into cut-price funerals. A middle-aged woman whose aerobics studios had given her the money to expand into more exotic services. The list went on and on, names and phone numbers. He began to list them carefully on one of the yellow legal pads he always kept to hand.

The list complete, he gazed down at the pad, preparing the pitch in his mind, casual, a word or two on the telephone, an enquiry about their plans, an agreement that things looked pretty bleak, and an invitation to participate with him in a very special piece of life insurance. Put that way, he could preserve the fiction that this was strictly business as usual, just another investment, an utterly logical financial decision totally in keeping with the relationship he'd so carefully built up with these people. That, he knew, was essential. There might, after all, be a city left to come back to, a career to resume, and looking at the list of names on his desk, the cream of his clientele, he could think of nothing tackier than a simple bald demand for a certain number of pound notes, to be delivered on the dockside, cash on the nail. He'd obviously have to charge something nominal – say a hundred pounds – to take care of his own expenses. But an up-front fee on the scale suggested by Mick Rendall would destroy him utterly, an exercise in simple extortion that would shred his reputation and leave him totally exposed. Far better to dress it up, to disguise it. Just another piece of business. Just another of Harry's little winners.

He'd lifted the phone at eight in the morning, dropping the tiny pellets of Sweetex in his coffee, glad of the silence in his empty office. The first call had gone to an old client, a man he'd admired, an ex-restaurateur who'd abandoned pretentious menus and French cuisine and made a small fortune from a modest chain of licensed pizza bars. The man, he knew, applied the same sense of stern realism to every department of a complicated life, and the conversation would provide Cartwright with the clues he'd need to refine the offer.

The man was interested at once. He'd already tried to leave the city by road, packing his latest wife and sundry children into the back of his Mercedes estate, and arguing the toss at the big roadblock that sealed off the motorway to the north. His arguments had got nowhere, cut short by an officious young captain who'd simply waved him back into the city, back along the line of cars awaiting a similar fate. Back home, he'd tried phoning, pulling strings, calling in old favours, but whoever he talked to the answer was always the same. City closed for business. City under siege. Everybody stays put. *No can do.* Cartwright's opening line, therefore, was all the more persuasive.

'Peter . . .' he said, 'I'm organizing a little excursion. Might you spare the time?'

The client hooked, Cartwright then explained the deal in detail. He'd acquired certain rights of passage. He had access to a boat. He'd secured a supply of fuel. There were a limited number of berths available. They'd be leaving tonight. The pizza man short-circuited Cartwright's prospectus with a brisk question of his own.

'How much?' he said.

'A hundred pounds a berth.'

'A hundred quid?'

Cartwright smiled to himself, letting the surprise die in the man's voice, the lowness of the figure. Then he outlined the rest of the deal, an arrangement which would, he believed, serve their mutual interests. It involved the eventual transfer of certain assets out of the country, to a designated account in St Helier, Jersey. He and the client would be co-signatories on the account, and in the event of peace breaking out, Cartwright would oversee the future investment of these assets for the benefit of both parties. The pizza man, who had an acute sense of the obvious, butted in again.

'These transfers,' he said. 'You mean cash?'

Cartwright shrugged. 'Or a bond,' he said. 'Against securities.'

'But how much?' he said again.

Cartwright paused. '50 per cent,' he said, 'of last year's audited profit.'

'Pre-tax?'

'Correct.'

'*Half?*'

'Yes.' He paused, before sugaring the pill. 'I invest these moneys thereafter.'

'And?'

'We split the profit.' He smiled. 'After subtraction of a service charge.'

'What's the split?'

'Fifty-fifty.'

There was a pause at the other end of the line. Cartwright could imagine the man running the sums through his head, making the odd note, scribbling down the figures, trying to compute a price for another couple of weeks on planet earth. Or perhaps he was doing none of that. Perhaps he was simply staring out of the window, watching the flowers grow. The voice came back. Cartwright had been right first time. The man had the deal word perfect.

'So you want half my last year's profit, to invest on your own account?'

'On our account.'

'At your discretion?'

'With you retaining half the profits.'

'Yes, I understand that.' The man paused. 'For how long?'

'Five years.'

'Then what?'

'The capital reverts to you.'

'All of it?'

'Yes.'

'I see.' There was another pause. 'We sign an agreement?'

'I'll fax you a draft.'

There was a silence, and Cartwright wondered for a moment whether the arrangement wasn't *too* complicated. Protecting himself by laundering his fee through joint accounts and offshore banks was one thing. Trying to sell it in the time available was quite another. His earlier calculations had suggested a potential capital take of nearly two million pounds. Even at building society rates, should they all survive, he'd be looking at an annual yield of nearly £200,000. Split two ways, that gave a £100,000 annual income. Good money for a night's work, and easily defensible should questions be asked afterwards.

The pizza man picked up the conversation again. He'd evidently been sharing the same thoughts, doing the same thinking, reaching the same conclusion.

'It's a good deal,' he said briskly. 'Send me the fax.'

Now, more than six hours later, Cartwright was exhausted. He'd contacted twenty-five of the thirty-four clients, adding nine more to the list from other client files. He'd explained the deal to them all, adding the odd refinement, varying the percentages according to the temperature of the conversation and his knowledge of their financial commitments. A handful had refused point blank, preferring to take their chances in the city rather than mortgage a hefty chunk of whatever was left of the next five years. Others took an opposite view, interpreting the deal as an opportunity to share in Cartwright's undoubted investment flair. The percentages, and his service charge, were incontestably high - one client used the word 'penal' - but these were extraordinary times, and there was a general feeling that Harry, their little Harry, had once again stood the impossible on its head and somehow conjured up a means of escape. If it amused him to play financial games on the side, then so be it. He wasn't asking for much cash up front. He wasn't milking them dry. He was simply asking them to sign a form, and take a risk or two, and trust him with their money. In that sense, quite literally, it was business as usual.

The cathedral clock was still chiming two when Cartwright finally put the papers to one side, and sat back in his big leather seat, and let the tension ease from his body. His assistant was already faxing out the contracts and sealing the legal loopholes. To the best of his belief, the agreement was legally binding, but his assistant had an excellent analytical brain, and it was best to be sure. Cartwright opened his eyes and gazed down at the final calculations he'd made on the yellow foolscap pad. After deductions for expenses – food, fuel, money for the skipper – he'd be looking at a post-war bounty of £2.1 million, a little more than he'd first anticipated. From this, he could expect an annual yield of at least a quarter of a million, half of which would remain with the clients. That left him with around £125,000 a year for a personal investment fund which he knew could produce a million within five years. He'd yet to decide quite where Mick Rendall belonged in this scheme, but he was no longer impressed by the bravado and the bluster, and he knew there'd be no problem.

He picked up the telephone and dialled a number from memory. The phone was answered at once, a cultured voice, male, languid, slightly amused.

'Tristan,' he said, 'it's Harry.'

The man at the other end of the line gazed out of the window, at the few yachts left in the harbour. St Helier, and the anchorages on the east of the island, had virtually emptied over the past few days, their owners heading west, out towards the Atlantic, and the farthest reaches of southern Ireland. Cartwright briefly explained his morning's work, the deals he'd struck, the boatload of clients he expected to arrive late the next day. The other man's smile widened. He'd been right about Harry. The little man never lost his nerve.

'Excellent,' he said, 'quite excellent.'

'Any problems with berths?'

'None.'

'Hotels?'

'Virtually empty.' He smiled again. 'The season's dead . . . if you forgive the phrase.'

Cartwright nodding, risking one of his few words of French.

'*Demain*,' he said.

'*Demain*,' the other man agreed, '*et bon voyage*.'

Cartwright replaced the telephone, aware of a figure at the door, a young woman, neatly dressed, businesslike, attaché case, dark glasses. She smiled at him, a brisk professional smile.

'My name's Wallace,' she said. 'I've come to talk to you about Ireland.'

Mick Rendall sat on a crate of potatoes aboard the *Timothy Lee*, gazing at his solar-powered calculator, trying to turn his wilder fantasies into a set of real figures. He'd still heard nothing from Harry, and Albie had disappeared yet again with the van, mumbling about unfinished business and promising to return within the hour. Intrigued by Albie's evident affection for white paint, Mick had by now concluded that he was into a spot of decorating. Quite why he should bother at this point in history, he didn't know, but there were parts of Albie that had always remained a mystery, and he suspected it was wise not to push it any further. If Albie wanted to swap notes on décor and the virtues of Dulux Silthane, he'd gladly oblige. Otherwise, he'd give the whole thing a miss.

He punched a final set of figures into the calculator, lost track of the running total, and gave up. McNaught, the skipper, had completed the refuelling, and was now trying to coax a little life from the main engines. Mick could hear the big diesels coughing down below, setting up vibrations all over the hull, making the wheelhouse rattle where the glass was loose in the window frames. Finally, they began to turn, and Mick watched the thick black smoke bubbling up from the stubby funnel aft of the bridge, and the rust chips dancing on the forward deck. As yet, he still had no idea where they were going, though McNaught appeared to be uninterested. Full tanks, he'd told Mick, would keep them at sea for two weeks. South-west Ireland was four days away. Portugal, eight. Piece of piss.

Mick eased himself upright, and picked tiny splinters of wood off his new Chinos. Getting hold of supplies had been easier than he'd thought. An assistant of Harry's had turned up mid-morning with a letter of credit from a local wholesaler. He and Albie had taken it along to the address provided, a modest cash and carry operation on one of the city's seedier trading estates. There'd been armed guards, with dogs, outside the big fold-back doors, and a surly-looking crowd of locals up the road. A couple of kids had begun to stone the van as it turned the corner towards the estate, and Albie had been on the point of running them over when Mick persuaded him to stick to the business in hand. Survival, he pointed out, was the better part of valour. Albie gave him a wooden look, but left the kids alone, easing the old van through the gates of the trading estate, and parking round the side of the building, out of sight of the locals.

Only when they were safe inside the big warehouse did Mick realize that the place stocked only Asian food, but curries were back in fashion after the vogue for Italian cuisine, and he filled a convoy of shopping trolleys with sacks of Basmati rice, and boxes of onions, and big drums of ghee, and case after case of exotic tinned vegetables. Albie, who hated curries, organized two trolleys of his own, and found a cache of marmalade jars in a far corner that went nicely with the six dozen loaves of sliced white bread he'd lifted from a deep freeze near the main door. Elsewhere in the warehouse, they stored up on what Mick called 'the Biz': toothpaste, soap, washing powder, disinfectant, and twelve dozen rolls of toilet tissue. The latter came in a choice of colours, but Mick settled in the end for pink. It would, he told Albie, add a little class to McNaught's single working toilet.

The bill, at the end of it all, came to more than £500, small change, Mick thought, to the take they could expect by the night's end, and en route back to the dock they detoured via another address where Cartwright's Asian friend ran a discreet off-licence operation for the city's less devout Muslims. There, they blew another £600 on cases of beer and lager, boxes of Liebfraumilch and French red *vin de table*, and – Mick's idea again – three cases of Bacardi to cheer up the gallons of Coke Albie had already lifted from the big warehouse down the road.

Their final purchase, an afterthought, had been five empty jerrycans they'd spotted at an Army surplus place near the dock. Mick paid cash for the items, and now they stood in a line beneath the bridge housing, chained together, secured to a ringbolt in the forward deck, brimming with diesel. Before they left, Mick agreed, it might be nice to transact a little private business. Strictly petty cash. The price for black-market diesel had already quadrupled, and would probably go even higher. He grinned to himself, reaching for the calculator again.

By mid-afternoon, Goodman and Davidson were back together again, riding north, out of the city, towards another rendezvous at the Wessex TV Studios. Davidson said nothing about the morning's incident in the Guildhall Square, Goodman making off towards the Botanical Gardens, the tail in his wake. Davidson had by now received Ingle's laconic report on the incident, and had agreed his recommendation. Let it develop. See where it leads. Keep it tight around the man Gillespie.

The big car slowed for the roadblock that corked the entrance to the motorway and began to zig-zag past the watchful young men in their close fitting combat helmets, and camouflaged battle tops. Already, the sandbags and the razor wire had become part of the landscape, an established fact. Goodman glanced across at Davidson, detecting the faintest hint of pride, something almost proprietorial; his own work, an entire city, cut off. Davidson stifled a yawn, as the car began to pick up speed again.

'Remarkable,' he said, 'quite remarkable.'

'What is?'

'All this.' He gestured vaguely out of the window. 'When we game-planned this operation, we anticipated problems from the start. Civil discontent. Problems with food. Problems with the DHSS. Vagrants. Students. The Left. You name it. And yet,' he turned to Goodman, 'nothing. Not a whisper. The odd demonstration. Mothers for Peace.' He smiled, the contempt evident in his face. 'I'm astonished.'

'Relieved?'

'Yes, of course.' He sniffed, passing judgement for the second time. 'But astonished, too.'

Goodman nodded, wondering for a moment how far the contempt stretched, what this urbane civil servant from Whitehall really made of the city, and of the people he was obliged to work alongside. People like Quinn and the harbour master. People like himself.

'It's early days,' he said mildly. 'I don't think people really understand the implications. They think it's a game. They think it'll all stop soon.'

'And well it might,' said Davidson, ever reasonable, ever keen to admit another point of view.

Goodman glanced across at him, trying to assess how much this man knew about what was happening out there, in London, in Oslo, in the Barents Sea, and whether or not he was prepared to share the information. It was odd being so totally in the dark. It made everything so remote. So unreal.

'Really?' he said. 'You think it might be over soon?'

Davidson toyed with the question for a moment or two. Then he shook his head.

'No,' he said, 'I don't think it will.'

They arrived at the Wessex Studios ten minutes later, coming to a halt in the near-empty car park. As they headed for reception, Goodman could see Duggie Bullock working alone in the newsroom. He glanced out of the window at them. He didn't get up.

The girl behind the desk in reception recognized them both from the previous day and asked them to wait for a moment. They sat on a couch by the window. A television in the corner was showing an ancient episode of 'Blind Date'. Three eager young contestants in tuxedos were competing for a Blackpool waitress with a huge bosom and a lifetime's desire to roll naked in a bath of ripe strawberries. The audience loved it.

The door to the newsroom opened, and Bullock appeared. Goodman got up at once and extended a hand. Bullock complied with the gesture, the reluctance obvious in his face. He nodded for them to follow him back into the newsroom. He seemed physically diminished from the previous evening, smaller, a shadow amongst the now empty desks. They walked the length of the room, back into his office. Goodman noticed that his in-tray was quite clear, except for a small packet of Anadin. Bullock sat on the corner of his desk and nodded them into chairs.

'Well?' he said.

Goodman said nothing for a moment, wondering what would sound most appropriate. An apology? An expression of regret? A solicitous enquiry about the welfare of his unemployed journalists? Instead, he chose another tack.

'If you're asking me what's happening, what's going on, I'm afraid I don't know.'

'You don't?'

Goodman shook his head.

'No,' he said, 'I don't.'

Bullock looked at him, testing the strength of the denial. Since last night, he'd lost all faith in Goodman's integrity. On air, the face in thousands of city living rooms, the man had promised that things were normal. He'd denied accusations, killed rumours, counselled good sense, and moderation, and the merits of a peaceful night's sleep. Yet within hours, the city had been closed down. And when Bullock had finally got to work himself, next morning, picking his way through jam after jam as the mainland roads seized up, it was only to find the station off the air, the transmission staff under Government orders to relay soap operas and game shows from some central source in London. All this, Goodman must have known. Regardless of the greater good, regardless of Queen and Country, the man had lied. It was as simple as that. Bullock nodded at the rolls of copy from the telex machine, reports from AP and Reuters, no further use to the broadcasters, but still available. He tossed the latest reports across to Goodman.

'There,' he said, 'you can take them home with you. Read them at your leisure.'

Goodman glanced down at the dense lines of typescript. The talks in Oslo had finally come to an end. The Russians had got what they'd come for. Norway was formally pulling out of NATO. The Royal Marines, in common with certain other units, were being asked to leave. The battle for the Northern Flank was over, lost without a shot being fired. Bullock watched him, the way his eyes scanned the copy, marvelling that even now, even here, when it didn't matter any more, the man should still pretend ignorance.

'Go on,' he said, 'tell me you didn't know.'

Goodman looked up.

'I didn't know.'

'And last night? The roadblocks?'

Goodman studied him carefully, aware of the yawning gap between total absence of trust, the mute but obvious assumption that he was a liar.

'I didn't know that, either,' he said quietly.

Davidson coughed and looked pointedly out of the window. Bullock was frowning, eyes still riveted on Goodman, hamstrung by his own question.

'You didn't?' he said.

'No.'

'That all happened without your say-so?'

'You mean the roadblocks?'

'Yes.'

Goodman hesitated a moment, then shook his head.

'No,' he said, 'I didn't know.'

Bullock gazed at him, encouraging him to say more, then let the air out of his body in a long, slightly plaintive whistle.

'Good story,' he said. 'Bloody good story.'

Davidson was still looking out of the window.

'Pity you can't use it,' he said drily.

Bullock glanced across at him, the motionless silhouette by the window, beginning to recognize for the first time the real battle, local authority usurped, *diktats* from Whitehall, the city versus Big Brother.

'You're right,' Bullock said carefully, 'I can't use it now. But later,' he shrugged, 'who knows?'

Davidson turned back into the room, a thin mirthless smile on his lips.

'Later,' he said, 'we'll either be dead or back to normal. In the latter case I suggest you consult the Official Secrets Act.'

'Information liable to damage the national interest?'

'Exactly.'

'Oh' – Bullock slid off the desk and began to roll his sleeves up – 'come now,' he said, 'that's a bit thin, isn't it?'

Davidson didn't answer, but stood up, and looked at his watch.

'I understand you have a studio standing by,' he said. 'I'd be grateful if we could use it.'

Bullock nodded. 'Of course,' he said, 'it's ready and waiting. Be my guest.' He smiled. 'I understand you want us to transmit your piece between Donald Duck and The Best of Bugs Bunny. I just wonder whether anyone will spot the difference.'

Davidson ignored the dig. Goodman did his best to suppress a smile, but failed. Then, abruptly, a car door slammed outside, and there was the sound of running feet. All three men glanced towards the window. Evans was already in reception. Seconds later, he burst in through the newsroom doors, moving quickly down the room, bodychecking between rows of desks. Goodman got to his feet and stepped out of Bullock's office.

'What is it?' he said.

Evans glanced beyond him, at Davidson, and Bullock, hesitating a moment, but Goodman signalled for him to continue. He bent close, his voice low.

'There's been an incident, sir. Young lad.'

'Oh?'

'Shot. In the Creek. They're dealing with it on the Army net. It's getting a bit out of hand.'

Goodman was suddenly aware of Davidson at his elbow. The man had heard every word.

'How bad?' he said crisply.

Evans looked at him.

'The boy's dead, sir. There's a big crowd.'

'And?'

He shook his head. 'I dunno, sir. That's all I picked up. They're handling it from TAC HQ. Battalion level.'

Davidson hesitated a moment, then looked at Goodman.

'Mr Controller?' he said.

Goodman began to walk towards the door, aware of Bullock watching him from his office, studying the interaction between them, drawing the obvious conclusions. Davidson and Evans followed behind, picking their way between the desks.

'I'll do the recording later,' Goodman said. 'There may be a little more to say.'

They hurried through the big swing doors at the end of the room, back towards the car, and Bullock hesitated for a moment before sinking back into his chair behind the desk. A phrase of Annie's had stuck in his mind. She'd phoned only minutes before, from the number she'd given him in the city, telling him about the roadblock, and her efforts with the camera before it all went black. 'Big white face,' she'd said, 'rimless glasses. And a really nasty smile.'

Bullock stood in his office, watching Davidson climbing into the back of the Rover, beginning to wonder.

Gillespie heard the gunfire, afloat in *Harriet*, pushing up-harbour against the last of the ebb tide. Two bursts of automatic fire. One long, one short. Sean emerged from the cuddy, alarmed, looking away, inland. His face furrowed into a frown, denied a simple explanation for the noise.

'What was that?'

'Gunfire,' Gillespie said.

'Where?'

'Dunno.'

The boy didn't pursue the subject, but it was a minute or two before he ducked back into the little cuddy and carried on sorting out the tangle of mackerel lines left over from the expedition before last.

Gillespie eased the wheel to starboard, following the buoyed channel in towards the saltings. He'd decided to move the boat at midday, a precaution in case another party from the Naval Provost descended on the anchorage and decided to requisition the craft they'd already registered. His name was on the log, he knew, and he'd been around the other boats in the anchorage long enough to recognize that his was better than most, a tidy addition to the nation's resources. He was as patriotic as the next man, but the last thing he intended to contribute to the war effort was his sole means of escape.

He sat on the transom for a moment or two, riding easy with the motion of the boat, enjoying the sun on his face, and the trickle of wind that feathered the water around them. He'd left Annie back home with a pot of tea and an aspirin. She'd asked him about Goodman again, approaching it from a different direction, setting him traps, trying to catch him offguard, unawares, but he'd seen the questions coming a mile away, and he'd simply ignored them. He was keen to see the job off, to get it tidied up and parcelled away and he'd rung Joanna Goodman from the phone extension upstairs. The woman had been brisk, a busy housewife dealing with a tradesman. She'd meet him on the seafront, same place as before, but it would have to be late afternoon. They'd agreed a time, and she'd rung off. Now, on the harbour he could see the little inlet where he planned to leave the boat. It was barely ten metres wide, but it never dried out at low water, and there were the remains of a small wooden landing stage from way back when the inlet must have been in regular use. The spot was surrounded by reeds, almost invisible from the main road, and was ideal for his purposes.

He nosed the boat in towards it, keeping an eye on the depth sounder. *Harriet* drew barely two feet of water, and even at this stage of the tide, he still had four-and-a-half feet beneath the keel. He pulled the engine into neutral and tucked the boat in beside the landing stage. The planks were rotten and green with mildew. He called to Sean, warning him to be careful, and the boy stepped gingerly ashore, testing the woodwork, stepping over the gaps, feeling his way. He half-hitched the forward warp to a post, and Gillespie threw him the rope for the stern. It was a trickier operation than it looked, and it took them half an hour or so to make sure that the boat was properly secure.

They worked in silence, a familiar routine. When they'd finished, the boat secure, Gillespie picked up the empty fuel can and stepped ashore. The sun was already dipping towards the Western horizon. He glanced at his watch. In half an hour he was due to meet his client, hand over the information, get paid.

'Where's best for diesel?' he asked Sean, absently. 'Time like this?'

A quarter of a mile away, hidden by the tall, coarse grass, Reese lowered his binoculars, and reached for the two-way radio. He'd already marked the location on the map of the city by his side.

'Privett's Stage,' he confirmed quietly, 'up near the bird sanctuary.'

Goodman and Davidson got to the Brigadier's tactical headquarters at four o'clock. The Brigadier had established his command set-up at the local TA Centre, a cavernous red brick building on the mainland side of the creek. Army sappers had strengthened the defences overnight, and there were rolls of barbed wire at the foot of the chain link fences. Evans eased the Rover through the sandbagged emplacements at the gate, and parked on the apron of tarmac that doubled as a parade ground.

The Brigadier met them in his office. He waved them into chairs and barked an order down the corridor for tea. Goodman sat down. Davidson remained on his feet.

'What happened?' he said.

The Brigadier looked across at him. He'd never had much time for civil servants, though he'd worked with Davidson for more than a year now, and he was wary of the man. He pulled down a map on a roller on the wall. Goodman had the impression it was a movement he practised regularly. It gave him certain rights of ownership. His city. His men. His problem.

'One of the local kids,' he said briskly, 'tried to get across the creek.' The Brigadier turned towards the map and tapped a section of the creek towards the east of the city. 'Here.' He paused, the ruler moved west, no more than an inch or two. 'I had patrols here . . .' the ruler moved west again, 'and here. Full daylight. Perfectly visible.'

'And?'

The Brigadier frowned, not used to direct questions.

'Yellow card procedures,' he said. 'You know the drill.'

'Were your men in danger?'

The Brigadier hesitated, reluctant to commit himself, the old conflict, loyalty versus the truth. Goodman wondered when he'd start using the term 'enemy'.

'Yes,' he said at last, 'in their judgement, yes.'

'How?'

'The boy was armed.'

'What with?'

'This.'

The Brigadier lifted a fold of newspaper on his desk, revealing a small, black pistol. There was mud on the barrel. He offered it to Davidson. Davidson looked at it, but didn't pick it up.

'It's a starting pistol,' he said, 'fires blanks.'

'My men didn't know that.'

'Ah . . .' Davidson nodded. 'Live by the gun . . .'

'Exactly.'

Goodman walked across to the window and gazed out, listening to the Brigadier. The boy had come from a tower block of council flats in the very middle of the city. His mother, and her common-law husband, had already held an impromptu press conference. There had not been many journalists there, but the activists were out in force. For days they'd been looking for a handle on the situation, a stick to beat the authorities with, and now they'd found it. Jason Duffy. Fifteen years old. Killed in action. The city's first martyr. The rioting was still sporadic but the Brigadier's men were thin on the ground, and the situation was fast getting out of control. Goodman smiled grimly, remembering Davidson's earlier comments about the lack of public reaction, how easy it had all been. He walked to the desk and picked up the gun. He looked at it a moment, thoughtful, and then turned to the Brigadier.

'If I wanted to talk to the boy's parents,' he said, 'how many men could you spare?'

The Brigadier stared at him.

'What?' he said.

Goodman repeated the question, glancing across at Davidson for support. Davidson remained impassive. The Brigadier shrugged.

'Seven,' he said, 'eight at the most.' He paused. 'Are you serious?'

'Perfectly.'

'Is that an order?'

Goodman looked at him, at Davidson.

'Yes,' he said. 'It is.'

Annie was woken up by the telephone. She rubbed her eyes and hinged upright on the sofa, and got to her feet. She was nearly at the telephone when she realized that her head didn't hurt any more, just ached, a dull, muted, background feeling, like an underscored bass note in a symphony. She picked up the telephone, wondering how to announce herself. She recognized Bullock's voice at once.

'Annie?' he said.

'Me,' she agreed.

'How are you?'

'Much better.'

'Listen. There's been a shooting. Somewhere along the creek. Army job. I'm getting phone calls. Have you got a pen?'

Annie nodded, reaching for a biro from the bookcase.

'OK,' she said.

'The kid's name's Jason Duffy. His mother lives at 1804 Hudson House. That's a big tower block near the library. She's not on the phone.'

Annie frowned.

'Jason Duffy,' she confirmed, writing down the name. Her hand was shaking. '1804 Hudson House.' She paused. 'That all?'

There was silence on the other end of the phone. Then Bullock came back.

'No,' he said, 'your friend Goodman.'

'Yeah?'

'Keep an eye open. He and the bloke from Whitehall have been up here again. I don't think it's as simple as it looks.'

'What isn't?'

'The relationship between them.' He paused. 'The command set-up.'

'No?'

'No.'

There was another pause. Annie gazed down at the photo of the man on the swing, wondering whether to mention it, but Bullock didn't give her the chance. She could hear the other phones ringing in the background.

'Get what you can,' he said briskly, 'but be careful.' The line went dead and Annie stood there for a moment or two wondering what, precisely, he'd meant about Goodman and Davidson. Not as simple as it looked?

She put the phone down and glanced at her watch. Nearly five o'clock. She ran quickly up to the bathroom, and soaped her face. Then she retrieved her leather jacket from the banister and made for the door. Only when she was on the pavement outside did she think about Gillespie's camera. She hesitated for a moment, still searching for her car keys, then she went back into the house.

The Olympus with the big zoom lens was still in the holdall. She took it out, very carefully. It was evidently loaded with film, but the frame counter told her that the roll was fully exposed. She rewound the film, and opened the back of the camera, taking out the film and putting it to one side. There was more film in the holdall, and she loaded a roll of 400 ASA, fast enough to let her shoot interiors. Then she checked the light meter, adjusted the ASA ring, and slipped the camera over her shoulder.

The exposed roll of film lay on the bookcase where she'd left it. She looked at it for a long moment, knowing it probably contained the answer to the questions Gillespie refused to even acknowledge, questions about Goodman, the new Controller, the master of the little white lie. She wondered whether to take it, to put it in her pocket and simply walk away, but she knew that would stretch their relationship to breaking point, and she realized to her own surprise that she didn't want that. She made for the door, then paused again, annoyed with herself, another hideous compromise, putting sentiment before principle, her feelings for Gillespie before the demands of the situation. She stood there, not knowing what to do, which way to turn, then she stepped back into the room, and cursed herself, picking up the exposed roll of film, and slipping it into her pocket. Her head was beginning to throb again, and she recognized the churning in her stomach. The fear had come back.

She drove north, towards the city centre, and the tallest of the council blocks. About a mile from Gillespie's place, at the point where the new road system swept around the shopping area, she met the first of the police patrols, a stick of half a dozen men, helmets, visors, short wooden truncheons, and the big Perspex shields she recognized from Saltley and Brixton. Riot control, she thought, engaging gear again and pressing forward.

Hudson House lay a couple of hundred yards from the Civic Centre, an enormous Sixties tower block, an up-ended shoe box, slab-fronted and system built. Annie pulled into a lay-by, and walked the hundred yards across wasteland and builders' rubble to the path that circled the estate. A largish crowd had gathered at the foot of the flats, and a man was haranguing them from a balcony four floors up.

Annie slipped the camera off her shoulder, and wound on the film to the first exposure. The man in the balcony was in full flood now, plenty of movement, both arms, one finger stabbing the air, driving home point after point. Once or twice the crowd cheered, but for the most part they were dour and sullen. One or two of the women were obviously drunk, screaming obscenities.

Annie lifted the camera and took a couple of shots of the man on the balcony. It was difficult to hear exactly what he was saying but it obviously related to the shooting, an incident he twice described as 'plain fucking murder'. This phrase drew spontaneous applause from the crowd, and Annie began to realize that events were rapidly getting out of control. Of the police, there was so far no sign.

She pushed forward through the crowd. What she needed, she knew, was five minutes alone with the parents. Only then would she start to put together the case she needed, start to assemble facts, make friends, forge relationships, earn herself a tight secure niche in their affections, ready for the day when it might suddenly all be over, and she could make the film that Bullock wanted. When that happened, scenes like these would already have become legendary, the stuff of public bar tirades, distorted beyond recognition. It was then, as a film maker, that she'd need the hard evidence, that precious handful of shots that would say it all, the faces, the grief, the hatred, expressions that no re-enactment could ever recapture.

She emerged at the front of the crowd. Three large men blocked the door to the flats, young, ugly, local. Annie fumbled in her jacket and produced a press pass. She showed it to one of them. He had tattoos on his knuckles, and smelled of stale tobacco.

'What's that?' he said.

'Press pass.'

'What do you want?'

'A word.' She nodded up at the flats. 'With Mrs Duffy.'

He looked at her narrowly. He obviously hated the press.

'You know they killed her nipper, don't you?'

'Who did?'

'The Bill. The fucking Army. How do I know?'

She nodded. 'Yeah,' she said, 'I'd heard. That's why I'm here.'

'She's in a right state.'

'I'm sure.'

There was a pause. Some of the youths at the back of the crowd had drifted across to the patch of wasteland and were picking up bits of rubble and were stoning passing cars. Totally random. Totally meaningless. Annie glanced up at the balcony, where the man was developing a nice line in incitement. 'Fascists,' he was saying, 'deserve every fucking thing they get.'

Annie looked at the man with the tattoos.

'Who's he?' she said, nodding up at the balcony.

'That's his brother,' he said. 'Young Billy.' He sniffed. 'He's upset too. We're all upset. Fucking upset.'

There was a sudden movement in the crowd, and the deep two-tone of a pair of powerful air horns. Over to the left, towards the city centre, was a car park. Into the car park drove a pair of Army Land-Rovers. Seven or eight troops jumped out. They carried rifles. They formed the tight end of a flying wedge. Behind them, in a dark suit, strode a figure that Annie recognized at once. Martin Goodman.

Annie lifted the camera and racked the image into focus. Martin Goodman was looking left and right, not stopping, still coming forward, committed to the protection of the troops up ahead. She tightened the shot on his face, seeing the surprise, and the shock, and the beginnings of fear, as the first chunks of rubble began to sail over the crowd and shatter on the concrete at his feet. The soldiers hesitated a moment, looking round, checking each other, Goodman, their line of retreat back to the Land-Rovers, but already the path was closing as the crowd surged around them.

Overhead, from the balcony, Billy Duffy was roaring now, urging them on, leaving the faces below in no doubt that here was their chance to get their own back, to redress the balance, to do the decent thing by little Jason and teach the pigs a lesson they'd never forget. Annie's fingers trembled on the shutter release, shot after shot, as the first of the soldiers went down, blood pouring from an open wound in his face. She briefly glimpsed Goodman, hair flying, glasses smashed, trying to get to the soldier's side, trying to calm things, pleading with the crowd to take a pace back, to show a little respect. But it was hopeless, and he knew it, the big empty face in the viewfinder, still struggling towards the fallen soldier, still trying to make amends. Annie took more shots, an instinctive admiration for the man, his folly, his blind courage, and suddenly there were bodies falling, as the first of the shots rang out, and women were screaming, men cursing, turning left and right, pack animals, trapped, not knowing where to run, not understanding how this carnival of violence, their due and proper revenge, had turned so suddenly into a nightmare.

The crowd began to stampede, away from the flats, away from the Land-Rovers, and as they flooded out across the open ground behind the flats, Annie glimpsed the helmeted line of police, squatting beside the path, amongst the clumps of tired shrubs, reloading their riot guns, and sending the long plastic baton rounds skeetering across the tarmac behind the fleeing mob.

Annie took more shots, the film nearly exhausted, then swung around again to the Land-Rovers. The injured soldier was lying on his face. Blood was pooling around his head. Goodman knelt beside him, staring down, utterly immobile. There was a wail of a siren, and a squeal of tyres, and a police Transit van drew up. The passenger door opened and an officer stepped out. Annie recognized the insignia of a Chief Superintendent on the shoulder of his jacket. He glanced around, hands on hips. The rubble. The broken glass. The injured soldier. Goodman. He shook his head, a sudden movement, raw anger. He walked quickly across to the soldier and knelt beside him, checking his pulse. He said something terse to Goodman, and then got up again, signalling to the driver of the van. The van began to move slowly forward. Goodman got to his feet, unsteady, and Annie watched, fascinated, as the police officer walked away. Annie began to raise the camera, one last shot, Goodman back on his knees, looking for his glasses, then she felt a pressure on her arm, the lightest of touches, polite, almost regretful. She lowered the camera slowly and looked around. A man stood beside her. Suit. Glasses. And that same faint smile. The face in the car. Davidson.

Seven

The briefing took barely half an hour. The Squadron Leader sat on the table at the front, taking them through the blow-ups, one after the other. The blow-ups were projected onto the wall behind him, the best of the line-scans from the afternoon's radar recce flights. Black and white with a tinge of blue. Barely four hours old, they showed that nothing had changed: the same tank parks, hidden deep in the foothills of the Harz Mountains, the same tell-tale traces of field hospitals, and refuelling bowsers, and hastily camouflaged SAM-7 sites that circled the forward air bases the other side of the border. After the false dawn of Glasnost, the Russians were back in force, and it was a tribute to years of RAF training that none of the young men in the room was the least bit intimidated.

They'd seen the grey silhouettes a million times before, and they knew exactly what do about them: on which runways to plant the big deep-penetration cratering bombs, when to deploy the smaller anti-personnel cluster bombs, and exactly what circumstances should call for release of the nuclear-tipped WE177 free-fall bombs that would move the war into an entirely new phase. The job of these young pilots, should it come to it, would be to cause havoc behind the Soviet front line, halting the second wave of armour, and turning an invasion of NATO territory into a fifty-kilometre traffic-jam, a prime target for the short-range tactical nukes the British had so successfully kept out of the SNF talks. That they could achieve this end, none of them doubted. That they'd survive intact, was far less certain.

The Squadron Leader finished with the last of the blow-ups. The adjutant snapped on the lights. The two dozen or so men in the audience, G-suits wedged behind tight little desks, flying helmets on the floor beside their chairs, blinked in the harsh neon. Most of them had already flown two sorties that day, taking the sleek Jaguars, heavy with ordnance, to within kilometres of the border, probing the Soviet defences, helping to plot the major radar emissions, flying fast and low over the fields that lapped the barbed wire, and the watch towers that once again divided East from West. 450 knots at 500 feet converted most features into a blur, but sometimes, in one of the tight 4G turns, it was just possible to pick out the shirt-sleeved figure of a farmer below, cupping his hands over his ears, staring up at the plane, wondering whether it was really worth harvesting the crops around him.

The Squadron Leader called for a weather update, and while the Met. Officer chinagraphed fresh lines on his map, and traced the progress of the latest front, he studied the rows of watching faces. By and large, he was pleased with the way they'd coped, but there were one or two individuals who were beginning to look tired.

One in particular, a lad from the north called Craddock, was a real worry, and the Squadron Leader had begun to wonder about standing him down for a day or so. The boy flew number two to one of the squadron's best pilots, and he knew that he was finding it increasingly difficult to match the other men in the air. The work load on Jaguar pilots was enormous, and ever since Craddock's wife and baby had departed for the UK on one of the Gütersloh emergency trooping flights, the lad had been on edge. Only that morning, he'd been spotted alone on the airfield, head down, hands in pockets, walking slowly away from the Mess. The Adjutant had stopped his car, and offered him a lift, but the lad had shaken his head and said no thanks, and simply walked on. There'd been egg stains on his trousers, and his shoes needed a clean. Bad signs.

Now the Met. man finished his update, and the Squadron Leader brought the briefing to an end. The pilots pushed back their chairs, stretched, yawned, turning to each other, comparing notes. The squadron would shortly return to instant readiness. The men would be back in their cockpits within half an hour, lined up at the end of the runway, fully armed, fully fuelled, ready to go. Once airborne, each of them would listen out for the special code that would wheel the squadron east, towards the border. At that point, they'd be three-and-a-half minutes away from the thick red line that always ended every NATO exercise, the thick red line beyond which the world, so far, had chosen not to go.

The room began to empty, the pilots drifting away in twos and threes. Craddock was one of the last to leave. The Squadron Leader stopped him by the door.

'OK, Barry?' he said.

The young pilot looked up, surprised. The strain showed in his eyes. He'd not slept for three nights. He talked to his wife twice a day on the phone. And he couldn't stop thinking about his tiny baby daughter, Emma-Louise.

'Fine, sir,' he said, his voice quite dead, 'fine, thanks.'

Evans drove Goodman home. Goodman sat in the back, quite alone. His suit was torn, one shoulder ripped along the line of the stitching. His tie was askew, and there was blood on the front of his shirt. It was Davidson, in the end, who'd helped him away from the scene of the riot, found the remains of his glasses for him, assured him that the situation was, after all, totally under control. The crowd had dispersed, leaving a litter of rocks, and empty baton rounds. Billy Duffy, the man on the balcony, had been arrested, but Quinn was retaining a presence in the area in case trouble should flare up again. Of Quinn, after the first few minutes, Goodman had seen nothing, but he remembered the policeman's terse comment as he stood over him amongst the rubble and the broken glass.

'Your own fault,' he'd said. 'Your own bloody fault.'

Now, as Evans hauled the big Rover off the motorway and up the hill, Goodman felt a cold, hard anger knotting inside him. Events had at last found a focus, and he'd been there, in the middle of it. He'd seen the bitterness, the grief, the implacable hatred for any form of authority, and he understood only too well what he, as Controller, would have to do. He'd already instructed Davidson to meet him at the Wessex TV Studios in an hour's time. There, a little later than planned, he'd record the first of his messages for the city, Public Communiqué Number One. After two days of confusion, of indecision, of events getting the better of him, it was suddenly very clear. Of his own life, and of the city, he'd now take charge. The time for compromise was over.

The car swung in through the gates of the house, and stopped outside the big Georgian front door. He glanced out for a moment, the neatly trimmed lawn, the sandpit, the swing, the oblong of pale grass where he'd recently spent the night in a tent with James. His life. His kids. His responsibilities. Evans eyed him in the mirror.

'Time's getting on, sir,' he said, 'I told Mr Davidson six o'clock.'

Goodman got out of the car and let himself into the house. Caroline heard the key turn in the lock and ran out of the lounge to meet him. She was half-way across the hall before she saw the torn suit, the blood on her father's shirt, and she stopped at once.

'Daddy!' she said, in genuine alarm, 'Daddy!'

He reached out for her, and patted her cheek. The kitchen door opened, and Joanna appeared at the far end of the hall. She was wearing a coat, dressed to go out. She stood there, taking him in, the state of him. She ran across the hall towards him. She reached out, hands on his face, exploring, finding out, making sure. Then she kissed him, pulling his body into hers, folding her arms around him.

'What happened?' she said. 'What have they done to you?'

He led her upstairs by the hand, explaining, leaving out the details, minimizing the dangers, but talking far too fast, and admitting that, yes, there'd been a spot of bother, a minor local upset. He paused on the upstairs landing, looking down at her, his wife, his Joanna, the mother of his children. He felt the tears rolling down his face, the shock of it all, the tension, the realization of what might have happened, and he counted the seconds before Joanna was back again, from the bathroom, with a wet flannel and a towel. She wiped his nose, and dried his tears, and pressed the cold flannel to the back of his neck, the way he'd seen her attend to James, sprawled on the gravel, his millionth accident on the bike. She looked up at him, forgiveness as well as compassion. He reached out for her, folding his arms around her small, slight body. Joanna squeezed his hand.

'My love,' he said, beginning to sob again, 'my love.'

Gillespie parked the Marina outside his house, and checked his watch. Nearly half-past five. In ten minutes, he was due to meet Goodman's wife. After that he'd drive round to Sandra's to sort out about the boat and the boy, who was going, who wasn't. Then he'd find some diesel, wait for darkness, and ship out. Annie would come too. Of that, he was quite sure.

He stepped out of the car, and hurried across the pavement. The curtains downstairs had been pulled. Annie must have woken up again, drunk the tea, swallowed the aspirin, and felt OK enough to risk a little daylight. Maybe she'd even had enough time to reflect on the lessons of it all, to draw the odd conclusion, pull in her horns, take a back seat for a change.

Gillespie let himself into the house and closed the front door with the back of his foot. The cat came sideways down the hall, arched back, mewing and tipping up its nose, the old accusation.

'You never fed the mog,' Gillespie called, stopping to pick the cat up. 'Bloody thing's starving.'

Hearing no answer, he walked into the living room. The room was empty. He frowned, trying the kitchen. The kitchen too, was empty.

'Annie!' he called, 'Annie!'

He returned to the living room. The blanket lay in a heap on the floor at the foot of the sofa. It suggested haste, a summons, or perhaps worse. He walked slowly across to the telephone and picked up the pad, inspecting it closely under the light from the window. He traced the faint line where the biro had tracked across the pad. Hudson House. Some kind of number. One . . . two. Then two digits he couldn't decipher. He looked around, frowning again, suddenly aware of something missing, and then he had it, the holdall, with his camera, and lenses, and film. He turned on his heel and sprinted upstairs. Annie's bag lay where he'd left it, beside the bed. Of the holdall, there was no sign.

He swore to himself, softly, under his breath, not, as yet, able to piece it all together, not able to coax the clues into any real pattern, but knowing all too well the exposed film, his morning's work, had gone. And that Annie, once again, was to blame.

Suzanne Wallace sat in the tiny windowless office, staring at a map of southern Ireland. Upstairs, she could hear Cartwright on the telephone again, nothing distinct, nothing intelligible, just the soft murmur of his voice between long silences. He'd been making calls all afternoon, getting up occasionally from his desk, footsteps on the floorboards overhead, the metallic rattle of drawers in a filing cabinet. She'd been far too busy on the phone herself to take much notice, but now she was nearly through, and she'd begun to wonder. For a business that had apparently closed, the man was still remarkably active.

She consulted the list at her elbow, and transferred more details onto the map. She'd worked from the contact book she always carried in her attaché case, the distillation of five years in the travel trade, and the first calls had been to the obvious sources: the Tourist Board in Regent Street, the big hotel groups in Dublin, the South-west Accommodation Bureau headquarters in a quaint little street in Killarney. She had contacts in each of these offices, men and women with whom she'd done business over the years, but the more calls she made, the more obvious it became that Ireland was rapidly filling up, and that the tourist and hotel organizations were swamped with bookings. None of her contacts was blunt or tactless enough to talk about refugees, but this assumption hovered at the edges of their conversations, and Suzanne knew enough about Irish history to appreciate the sweet ironies implicit in the situation. The Irish were once again on the receiving end. But the terms were at last their own.

Finally, after an hour and a half on the phone, Suzanne had abandoned the usual channels and struck out on a new tack. Three years back she'd had a brief affair with an Aer Lingus pilot. The man had been big, red-faced, eternally cheerful, with a warm sense of humour and the most expressive hands she'd ever seen. She'd met him at a Folk Festival in Tralee, part of a special Bord Failte promotion, and she'd stayed on for a week afterwards, driving south with him to a huge draughty house overlooking the Kenmare River. He'd inherited the house from his parents, but since the death of his wife he'd spent very little time there.

Recently, though, he'd begun to tire of the twice-weekly milk run to JFK, and decided to convert the place into a country hotel. He had the grandest plans, and they'd spent five wet days pacing the big old house, trying to decide which of the ten bedrooms offered the best view, and whether or not rich Americans could survive without central heating. The week in Kerry had been marvellous, and she'd seen the man a couple of times over the next year or so, weekends in the Tara Hotel in Kensington, one wild night in Boston. The relationship had never threatened to go anywhere serious – they laughed too much for that – but they'd parted firm friends, and she knew she could call him any time. Whether or not he'd actually abandoned Aer Lingus for the big house in Kerry, she didn't know. But the rest of Ireland was full, and she was now desperate to give it a try.

By some miracle, he answered her call in person, his voice hollowed by the big empty hall where he kept the phone. She could almost feel the rain on the windows, and the wind lashing the tall stand of conifers at the back of the house.

'Hi,' she said, the usual greeting, 'it's me. Your little English tart.'

He recognized her voice at once with a roar of approval, and they compared notes for a minute or two before she got round to explaining why she'd called. He'd understood at once. Kenmare was full of the infidel, he said, but there'd be no problem putting folk up. The house was, he warned, a little bare, but he'd do what he could in the interim, to make preparations for her arrival. She hesitated at this, wondering whether to tell him she herself wouldn't be coming, but decided against it. When she mentioned forty people, he simply laughed. Forty. Four hundred. Made no difference at all. They were to steer for the south-west corner of Ireland, turn north, take the third river to the right, and head inland. Unless it was raining, he'd hang white sheets out of the top windows. When they got to Kenmare, they'd have gone too far. He rang off, still roaring with laughter.

Relieved, her job done, Suzanne had transferred the important details to a tourist map of Ireland, a souvenir of one of her many trips. She'd already phoned a chandlery down near the dock, and tried to reserve an Admiralty chart of the area. The man at the shop had been apologetic. He said they'd run out of charts of the south-west approaches, the demand had been unbelievable, but when she pressed him hard, explaining exactly what she was trying to organize, mentioning Martin's name, he promised to ask around and phone her back before six.

Suzanne put a last heavy ring around the location of the house, added a name and a phone number, and began to tidy her papers back into her attaché case. As she did so, a light on the fax machine in the big office outside began to blink. She looked at it through the open door, remembering Cartwright's promise that a detailed passenger list was expected from Goodman at any time.

She got up and walked out, into the big office. The fax was rolling slowly out of the machine, line by line, the print slightly smudged, the paper still warm. The line at the top, in capitals, read 'Agreement'. There was a space, then the first paragraph. She began to read it, idly, realizing at once that it wasn't the list she'd been expecting. The language was formal, dense legal prose. One party was making certain undertakings to another. There was a question of assets and percentages. Dates were mentioned. A bank. An account number. An address in St Helier, Jersey. Suzanne smiled to herself. Maybe news travelled slowly in the Channel Islands. Maybe it was some client who hadn't picked up a paper for a week, never listened to the radio, never watched the TV news, didn't know that business had been suspended for a while, pending the end of the world.

The machine paused for a moment or two, some interference on the telephone line, and she turned away, wondering whether to phone Martin and confirm the numbers herself, tell him that it was OK, that she'd done her job, his personal travel agent, worthy of his trust, worthy of a corner in his heart, and that his wife and kids would be safe, away from it all, away from them, in deepest, farthest Kerry.

A door opened across the room, and Cartwright appeared, this strange little man, with his shiny suit, and his tiny moustache, and his long white hands. She'd never met him before, but she'd heard a good deal about his reputation, surprised that he should be such a close friend of Martin's. He looked across at the fax machine, at her, and she knew at once from the expression on his face that something was wrong. He looked irritated, slightly embarrassed, like a conjuror caught in some private rehearsal.

'Finished?' he said abruptly.

She nodded. 'Yes,' she said.

'Found somewhere?'

'Yes.' She nodded at the open door into the office where she'd spent the afternoon. 'It's all waiting for you.'

'Good.'

He crossed the room towards the fax machine, carefully circling her, giving her the widest berth. She knew he wanted her gone, out of it, away. She walked back into the tiny office, still waiting for the phone call from the chandlery. She picked up the map, checked her annotations one final time, then turned round. She frowned. The big office was empty. Cartwright had disappeared again. The fax had gone.

Annie McPhee lay on the iron bed, staring at the ceiling. The ward was big, two dozen or so other beds, all occupied. The windows were barred on the inside, and there was a guard in a blue uniform on the door, a large man with a day's growth of beard. Annie recognized the silver insignia on the epaulette of his jacket, the badge of a private security firm she normally associated with bank deliveries and the guarding of building sites. Privatization rules, she thought. Even now. Even here. She smiled grimly. Especially now. Especially here.

She yawned, trying to fight the instinct to doze, to drift away, to lose track of it all. She'd recognized the place as a hospital at once, peering out through the mesh windows in the sides of the Land-Rover. A big, red-brick pile, sister institution to all the other psychiatric hospitals she knew around London. They'd driven past the main building, and out into the grounds, bumping over the potholes in the tarmac. She'd been taken from the Land-Rover into a small building, put in a room by herself, then searched by a brisk, efficient woman in jeans and a tennis shirt who'd stripped her naked with the skill of a trained nurse. The search had probed the usual nooks and crannies, but the woman had been nice enough to warm her hands first, under the tap, murmuring an apology at the length of her nails. The body search had produced nothing to add to the small pile of possessions on the table, stuff from her jacket and her jeans, and afterwards she'd been allowed to dress again. Minutes later, another woman had come in for the booty, picking up Gillespie's roll of exposed film with great care, thumb and one finger. Annie had already parted company with Gillespie's camera, slipped gently from her shoulder by the big man with the long black hair who'd met the Land-Rover when it finally rolled to a halt. Annie had noticed him at once, head and shoulders above the rest of the small reception committee. She'd noticed his eyes, coal black, and the way he absorbed things, the long appraising look he gave each of the figures that stumbled out of the back of the Land-Rover.

Now, nearly an hour later, she wondered again what had happened to Gillespie, and what he'd make of his absent camera and missing roll of film. Yesterday's interview, the questions about Northern Ireland, already seemed a month ago, but the man had a very long memory, and she suspected her credit was almost exhausted. Pity, she thought.

Three rooms away, down a corridor and round a corner, Davidson and Ingle sat on opposite sides of a small wooden table. Gillespie's camera lay between them. Beside it was the single exposed roll of film, already tagged with a buff label by the woman who'd retrieved it from Annie's jacket pocket. Davidson was still wearing his coat. Any moment now, he'd have to leave and return to the TV studios. Goodman was due to record his broadcast in half an hour.

Ingle rubbed his nose. Davidson had already told him about the girl, using the military net after the riot. Ingle had told him to bring her in. Now he gazed at the camera.

'Journalist, isn't she?' he said at last.

Davidson nodded. 'Yes. Freelance. Working locally at the moment. Based in London.'

'Ah . . .' Ingle smiled. 'The real thing.'

He picked up the exposed roll of film, looking at it speculatively, dispensing for a moment with the formalities of developing fluids and fixer baths and all the other clutter. The newly installed darkroom had been working non-stop since coming on line before dawn. It would be hours before they got round to this one.

'Any ideas?' he said.

Davidson shook his head. 'No.'

'She make a fuss?'

Davidson smiled briefly, remembering the scene at the road-block in the middle of the night, her body stretched full length in the middle of the road.

'No,' he said again, 'none.'

'You think she might be a problem?'

'I don't know.'

'But you think there's a chance?'

Davidson considered the proposition for a moment. For most journalists he knew, work amounted to little more than a visit to the cuttings library, and a handful of precautionary receipts in case the expenses were ever questioned. This girl, though, was different. For one thing, the soldier at the roadblock had hit her pretty hard. Yet back she'd come, twelve hours later. Different camera. But same motivation. Same instinct. Same fascination for the noise, and the swirl, and the danger at the centre of it all. It could, of course, be something pathological, some private nerve she liked reality to touch, some affection for raw violence from which she got her kicks. On the other hand, it could be something else, something infinitely more dangerous, a putting together of the symptoms, a diagnosis of the underlying disease. Until they had time to access her Special Branch file, to give the girl a history, friends, contacts, political affiliations, they couldn't be sure. But in the meantime, it was wise to be cautious. The riot at the flats was a nasty portent. There might be worse to come. He asked himself Ingle's question again, and nodded.

'Yes,' he said, 'I think she might be a problem.'

Gillespie had almost given up waiting by the time the woman finally arrived. He'd been sitting up on the sea wall, overlooking the water for nearly an hour, watching the patrol boats blockading the harbour approaches. They worked in pairs, idling on the edges of the swept channel, one either side of the tidal stream. Inside the harbour itself, there were more of them, criss-crossing the broad, flat expanse of slack water, obviously in radio contact, probably controlled from the big observation tower that dominated the entrance itself. Some of the boats had radar. Others were simply too small, no more than speedboats, manned by government trusties on God knows what sort of deal. Maybe they got paid by results, commission, so many quid a head. Or maybe they were doing it for the love of their Queen and the sake of their Country, two concepts that Gillespie, for the first time in his life, was beginning to suspect might not be entirely identical. Annie's story about the road-block, despite his bluff dismissals, had made him uneasy. He'd never let a man of his club a woman to the ground. Not under any circumstances.

He glanced inland again, looking for the tan raincoat and the red scarf, but the promenade that topped the sea wall was quite empty. He glanced at his watch. Fifteen more minutes. Then he'd go.

A small beige Metro slowed in the main road that fed traffic into the nearby dock, signalled left and pulled onto an area of wasteland beneath the big sea wall. The dust settled and a woman got out. Gillespie recognized her at once, more casual than last time, slacks and a pink sweater, loose stitch, low neck. He got off the wall and wiped his hands on his jeans. The woman was climbing the stone steps towards him. She looked pale, but determined, somehow thinner, slighter, than before, and he wondered what had happened to her since they'd last met. He extended a hand. She barely touched it. She was out of breath.

'I'm sorry I'm late,' she said, 'it's been difficult.'

Gillespie nodded at the car.

'How did you get in?'

'In from where?'

'Your house? Into the city?'

She looked at him.

'How do you know where we live?' she said. 'It's ex-directory.'

Gillespie reached into the top pocket of his jacket and produced the photo of her husband.

'This,' he said, 'the view behind.'

She glanced at the photograph a moment. Her husband on the swing. The city, slightly out of focus, in the haze below.

'Of course,' she said, 'how clever.'

Gillespie shrugged, letting her keep the photograph. He produced an envelope, sealed.

'Here,' he said, holding it out, 'it's all in here. Name. Address. Phone number.'

She looked at the envelope, making no attempt to accept it. Perhaps she'd decided that ignorance was kinder than the truth. Perhaps she'd decided that one last night and a salvo or two of Soviet ICBMs were preferable to a name and a face and hours of bitter fantasy.

'Tell me,' she said, 'where does she live?'

Gillespie frowned a moment, then squinted east. Ocean Towers was clearly visible about a mile away, on the other side of the common, a big twelve-storey block, head and shoulders above the rest of the parade.

'There. Ocean Towers. Number 913.'

She nodded, the secret out, bricks and mortar, just another address.

'I see,' she said. 'And what does she look like?'

'You really want to know?'

'Yes, please.'

Gillespie shrugged, remembering the face in the viewfinder, wondering whether to break the news about the missing film.

'She's young,' he said.

'Very young?'

'No . . .' he glanced across at her, wondering how best to phrase it, 'but, you know . . .'

'Younger than me.'

It was a statement rather than a question. Gillespie nodded. 'Yes,' he said.

She looked unsurprised.

'Pretty?'

Gillespie shrugged again.

'OK,' he said, 'quite nice.'

'Tasty?' She paused. 'Isn't that the phrase?'

'Depends . . .' He looked at her, recognizing the tone of voice, the old temptation to blame the messenger. He'd been here before, often, but now he was past all that. Fifteen quid an hour didn't run to abuse. She looked him in the eye, not giving up.

'Depends on what, Mr Gillespie?'

'Depends on what you like.'

'Did *you* think she was tasty?'

'Me?' He laughed at her, a short low grunt of laughter. 'I just hoped she was in focus.'

'Just another job?'

'Yeah,' he nodded, giving her what she wanted, yet another macho response, corroboration of her case. All men are pigs.

'Yeah,' he said again, 'just another job.'

She looked at him a little longer, then opened her shoulder bag and produced a small leather purse.

'How much do I owe you?'

'Another forty pounds,' Gillespie said. 'Eighty all up.'

She counted out the money, new ten-pound notes, and gave them to him without comment, accepting the envelope in return. Gillespie folded the notes and stowed them in his back pocket. The woman glanced down at the envelope. Gillespie's careful capitals. Her husband's name. Her appellation. Her label. Mrs Goodman.

'Tell me something, Mr Gillespie . . .' she looked up, the tone of her voice quite different, softer, more philosophical. 'Are you married?'

Gillespie glanced at her, taken by surprise.

'Was,' he said finally, 'once.'

'Children?'

'One.'

'Boy? Girl?'

'Boy.'

'You see him still? Now?'

Gillespie nodded. 'Yes,' he said, 'a lot.'

'Ah . . .' She nodded, turning over the information in her mind, laying it out, inspecting it, looking again for easy parallels. She glanced up at him again, very direct. 'And how did your wife feel,' she tapped the envelope, 'when she got one of these?'

Gillespie eyed her.

'She didn't,' he said coldly. 'It wasn't like that.'

The woman looked away, quickly, and began to redden. She swallowed hard.

'I'm sorry,' she said, 'it's none of my business.'

'You're right,' Gillespie said. 'It's not.'

'I'm sorry,' she said again, 'truly sorry.'

Gillespie shrugged, embarrassed by the conversation.

'It's OK,' he said. 'No offence.'

She looked at him again, and he saw the uncertainty, and the grief, nothing in focus, everything out of control. He felt vaguely sorry for the woman, just another victim of a lifetime's misconceptions. Someone who'd got it wrong but had spared herself the news until it was far too late. He glanced at her, expecting her to do what they all did, to sniff a little, and to dab at her eyes, and wonder very plaintively whether she couldn't ask his advice. But he was wrong. There wasn't a shred of bitterness left in her voice.

Just a bald, comfortless recognition of the facts.

'Do you know what's so sad, Mr Gillespie?' she said.

'No.'

She began to stow the envelope away in her bag.

'It's men. They never grow up. They never learn. All this . . .' She gestured round, the patrol boats in the harbour, the distant thunder of a jet fighter climbing under full power. She snapped the bag shut and looked at him. 'My husband's a child. Just like the rest of them. He's never grown up. Ever. He wants what he can't have, and he'll destroy everything before he gets it.' She smiled at him, a cold mirthless smile. 'Ironic, don't you think? Now that he's got the whole city to play with?'

Duggie Bullock met Martin Goodman at the door of the studios. Goodman had changed in the hour or so since they'd last met. Different suit, different shirt, and a pair of Seventies glasses that gave his face a curiously wooden look.

The two men nodded to each other but said nothing. Davidson followed them both into a studio where a technical crew were ready to shoot Goodman's piece to camera. Goodman settled behind the presentation desk, very still, very contained, very sure of himself, not looking at anybody, not risking a smile, or a greeting, or anything that might break his concentration. Davidson retired to the adjacent control room. Bullock stood in the shadows, waiting and watching. The floor manager called the studio to readiness and counted Goodman down. At zero, he looked up and began to talk.

Public Communiqué Number One lasted four minutes. Goodman did it in a single take, without notes, without autocue, without once having to reach for a phrase or remember a detail. When he'd finished, and the studio lights had been dimmed again, he asked for the recording to be played back, watching it on the little black and white monitor sunk into the presentation desk. He bent to the screen, listening intently, finding no ambiguity in the crisp, clear phrases, recognizing with a strange and growing detachment the expression in his eyes, something never there before, a glint, a gleam, establishing beyond doubt that, at last, he meant what he said. Here was a man who'd tired of irresolution and half measures. Here was someone who wouldn't be frightened of facing up to the hard decisions. They were right, he thought grimly as he heard himself wish the city goodnight. The camera never lied.

The review over, he got up from behind the presentation desk and stepped out onto the studio floor. The floor manager motioned him to hang on for a moment while he bent his head and listened to a message from the Control Room in his headphones. The message came from Davidson. The floor manager looked up.

'One more take, please, sir,' he said. 'A little less stern.'

Goodman shook his head.

'Sorry,' he said, 'you'll have to make do with that.'

He patted the floor manager on the shoulder, and walked across to meet Davidson by the door. Davidson was looking, if anything, amused.

'Dear me,' he said, 'Nigel won't be at all pleased.'

The two men disappeared into the Control Room, and Bullock stirred in the shadows in the far corner of the studio. He'd seen the beginnings of mental breakdown before, and he recognized the symptoms. The floor manager walked across to him, still confused about who was in charge.

'OK, boss?' he said, nodding at the empty presentation desk.

Bullock shrugged. 'Who knows?' he said. 'I'd stay tuned, if I were you.'

It took Albie Curtis exactly forty-seven minutes to realize he wasn't going to make a fortune from miracle emulsion. He'd rung his sister's best friend from a pay phone in the pub at the dock gate. She was in the middle of a perm – her first for a day and a half – but she had time to read him a list of names and addresses, punters who'd phoned in, impressed by Albie's claims for the anti-blast paint, wanting the treatment for their own windows. Albie had noted the details on the wall beside the phone, memorized the first address, and driven straight round in the van.

His first clients had been an elderly retired couple, three streets back from the seafront. They occupied the top floor of a big Victorian five-storey house, sub-divided into flats. They had two windows at the front, and the windows were at least fifty feet above ground level. Albie, who hated heights, stood by his van and gazed up. His only ladder had three rungs missing and would barely reach the window boxes on the second floor. He was on the point of returning to the pub for another address, when the couple appeared at the top window, shocks of white hair, beckoning fingers. Against his better judgement, Albie lifted a brush, and a tin of white emulsion, and headed for the front door.

The flat was spotless, a time warp from the early fifties: squirly carpet, and heavy chairs, and a big old standard lamp in one corner. The old man had obviously spent most of his life in the Navy. There were photographs of warships everywhere, lovingly framed, good quality hardwood, and shots of a younger face, gap-toothed, permanently grinning. Albie looked around. He fingered a 4.5″ shell casing, solid brass, knee high, one of a pair flanking the tiny gas fire. There were places in the city that would pay good money for this kind of gear.

The old man buried his roll-up in a big glass ashtray and introduced his wife, a small bird-like woman with crossed legs and a nervous smile. Albie gave her a nod, noticing more brass on the bookcase behind her head. Neat little ornaments, oriental stuff, souvenirs from runs ashore in the Far East, Hong Kong, Singapore.

'The windows . . .' the old man was saying, 'that paint of yours . . .'

'Yeah?' Albie said absently, picking up a heavy junk-shaped paperweight, and examining the Chinese characters on the bottom. Brass was hard to come by. Blokes in the market would part with serious dosh. He turned round. The woman was reading the leaflet he'd stuffed through the door. Blast-proof wonder paint. NASA-approved. She looked up at him. She was much tougher than she seemed.

'Arthur swears by this,' she said, nodding at her husband. 'Says it's just what we need.'

'He's right.'

'I've told him we'll try it on the front ones first. See how it goes. If it works, you can come back and do the windows at the back.'

Albie stared at her. 'There won't be any windows at the back,' he said. 'That's the whole point.'

'Just those two,' she said again, nodding at the front

windows, ignoring him.

The old man was looking at the paint Albie had left on the carpet.

'What's the score, then?' he said.

'Ten quid a window,' Albie said. He walked across the room and glanced down at the street. It was even higher than he'd thought. He turned back into the room. 'Half price if you do it yourself.'

The old man's wife shook her head at once.

'Arthur's not doing it,' she said, 'you are.'

Albie looked at them both, at the bric-à-brac, at the paint pot, wondering whether the times justified simple robbery. Maybe he should just pocket the stuff and leave. He'd be away in seconds. They'd never even know. Then he remembered the leaflet, and the phone number, and decided against it. He was far from convinced the world was about to end, and rash decisions had always returned to haunt him. He walked across to the window again and looked out. The street was no closer. He picked up the brush.

'Got any newspaper?' he said.

The woman frowned. 'What do you want newspaper for?' she said.

'Save your carpet,' he said. 'We always paint the inside of the window.'

Three-quarters of an hour later, Albie was back in the street. The job had taken for ever, the woman watching his every move, hovering at his elbow, warning him against drips, making him sponge the carpet where the paint had splashed beyond the newspaper. At the end of it all, in what was left of the daylight, he'd tried to hassle them for the non-ferrous, the shell cases and the Chinese paperweight, but they'd hung onto them, carefully counting out the twenty pounds, coins mostly, from a jam jar hidden in a sliding cupboard. Afterwards, the jam jar half emptied, the old man had asked about a written guarantee.

'What happens if it doesn't work?' he said, 'where do we get hold of you?'

Thoroughly depressed, Albie had bent to the carpet and retrieved the leaflet.

'Here,' he said, handing the old man the leaflet. 'Give us a ring when the war's over. If the stuff's no good, I'll come round and do it again.'

Now, driving the van back into the dock, Albie brooded about the prospects for the rest of the paint. Twenty quid for an hour's work was pathetic. At this rate, he wouldn't even cover his costs. He turned the van into the dock and brought it to a halt beside the *Timothy Lee*. Mick was standing on the quay, looking down at another boat moored alongside. It was about the same length, sixty foot or so, but it was a motor yacht, brand new, gleaming paintwork, flared bow, scrubbed teak deck, tinted glass. Albie got out of the van and stared down at it. It belonged in a movie, or one of those slick TV commercials. It looked unreal.

'What's that?' he said.

Mick shook his head, thoughtful. 'Dunno . . .' he said slowly, 'something to do with Harry.'

Gillespie drove towards Sandra's, eyeing the fuel gauge. Twenty miles, he thought. Just enough.

He parked outside Sandra's house. The road was emptier than he'd ever seen it. He rang the doorbell. Sean opened the door. He nodded at the boy, seeing the rucksack and an old Service issue suitcase of his standing by the door, already packed.

'Yours?' he said.

The boy nodded. 'Yeah.'

'Your mum?'

'She's in the kitchen.'

Gillespie nodded and stepped into the house. Sandra was sitting on a stool in the kitchen, slicing onions. There was a bowl of stewing steak on the table, and a pile of potatoes, and some carrots, and celery, and a couple of Oxo cubes. A bottle of red wine stood on the fridge. A Burgundy. Good year. She definitely wasn't making sandwiches.

Gillespie closed the door behind him.

'Settling in?' he said, nodding at the food on the table.

Sandra glanced up, and wiped her eye with the back of her hand. Gillespie could smell the onions.

'Little something to eat,' she said.

'When?'

'Tonight.' She raised one eyebrow. 'That allowed?'

Gillespie frowned. 'I thought I said we were off.' He paused. 'Out of it.'

'You did.'

'So why . . .' he nodded at the table again, 'all this?'

There was a silence. Sandra finished chopping the onions and tipped the board over a big glass oven-proof dish. Gillespie had no taste for casseroles, but he knew enough about cooking to recognise the meal couldn't possibly be ready for at least a couple of hours. Sandra crumbled the Oxo cubes over the onions in the bottom of the dish. Gillespie glanced at his watch. Six o'clock. Time was moving on.

'I'll be back,' he said, 'in an hour.'

'Oh?' She looked up. 'Why's that?'

'To pick you up. Get your stuff ready. The boy's already packed.'

He began to turn for the door. She called him back.

'Dave . . .' she said.

He hesitated. 'Yeah?'

'I'm not coming.'

'What?'

'I said I'm not coming.'

He looked at her, the hands still dusted with Oxo, the food on the table, the bottle of wine, her own private mortgage on a different future, not his. He had no right to the obvious question, but he raised it none the less.

'Why not?' he said.

She reached for the celery and the knife, and began to chop the sticks, one by one. Within their marriage this would have been a crisis already, days of silence. Now, years later, it was simply an exchange of information.

'Because I prefer to stay,' she said, 'OK?'

Gillespie nodded. Her right. Her call.

'That bloke the other night, is it?' he said.

She stopped chopping for a moment and looked him in the eye. She knew she owed him nothing, but it didn't really matter any more.

'Yes,' she said.

Gillespie shrugged.

'He can come too if he wants,' he said, 'plenty of room.'

'Thanks, but . . .' she smiled and laid the knife aside for a moment, 'he can't come.'

'Why not?'

'He works at the hospital. He's an anaesthetist. He thinks he ought to stay.'

'The hospital's closed.'

'Yeah,' she nodded, 'for now.'

'Ah . . .' Gillespie smiled. Inside information. 'I see.' He paused. 'Have you thought about the boy at all? How he might feel?'

'Sean's seventeen. He's like me. He copes.'

'I know.'

'Well then . . .' she shrugged again. Gillespie resisted the temptation to leave, to obey the instincts of a lifetime and simply abandon it all, closing the door behind him, cutting his losses, getting out. But he knew he might never see her again, this woman with whom he'd shared more than half his life, off and on, and he wanted to get one or two things straight, if only in his own mind.

'Do you love him?' he said. 'This bloke of yours?'

She nodded. 'Yes.'

'Why?' he said.

'Because he's kind . . .' she hesitated, hating the corner the conversation had opened up, 'and because he cares about me.'

Gillespie nodded, recognizing what she was really saying, the hidden reef beneath the simple phrases.

'You think I never cared about you?'

'No. I don't think that.'

'What, then?'

She put the knife down. There was a tiny curl of carrot peel on her wrist. Gillespie wanted, absurdly, to reach out and pick it off, to tidy up the scene, make it comprehensible.

'What, then?' he said again.

Sandra got up and stepped towards him. She came very close. He smelled the onions on her. Her eyes were a deeper green than he could ever remember. She put her hands on his face, holding it lightly.

'I think you cared as much as you could,' she said, 'and I think you tried your hardest.'

'But not hard enough?'

She looked at him for a long time, thinking about the question, making up her mind, not about the truth, but about whether or not to voice it.

'You did what you could,' she said again, 'you did your best.'

'But not enough?'

'No. Not enough.'

Gillespie nodded, feeling his stomach describe that long slow somersault he recognized from way back. His body telling him to brace. To get ready. To expect the worst. Sandra was back behind the table. She smiled at him, softening the blow.

'Don't get me wrong, Dave . . .' she said, 'lots of it was bloody good.'

'But not good enough.'

She looked at him for a moment.

'It was your decision, Dave. You went. Not me.' She paused. 'Where are you off to this time?'

'Ventnor,' he said, 'John's place.'

'Ventnor?' She stared at him. 'Why would you be any safer in Ventnor?'

Gillespie shrugged. He'd done the thinking, drawn out the blast circles, calculated the overpressures, made allowances for the weather and the wind and a less than perfect trajectory. Ventnor lay beneath a big shoulder of chalk downland, protected from the heat and the blast, and John's place, he knew, had a deep basement. They'd be as safe there as anywhere. He looked at her and shrugged.

'It's complicated,' he said. 'But it'll be OK.'

She smiled at him.

'You should have said Marbella,' she said lightly. 'I might have come if it was somewhere nice.'

Gillespie shrugged again, and stepped back towards the door.

'Yeah . . . well . . .' he said, 'beggars can't be choosers . . .'

She glanced up at him and smiled, a wry, affectionate grin, the left-overs from twenty years of friendship,

'Yeah . . .' she said, 'I know. Same old story, eh Dave?'

The Bunker was nearly full by the time Davidson and Goodman

returned from the TV studios. The individual desks that flanked the long central well were all manned, Civic Centre executives trying to make sense of electronic typewriters, other heads bent to telephones, hands racing across lined foolscap pads. There was a series of alcoves that ran the length of the room, bays between the big concrete pillars that supported the blast-proof ceiling. Each of the bays housed a different secretariat – transport, medical services, Royal Observer Corps, food supplies – and there was also a small four-cubicle switchboard to handle incoming and outgoing calls. At the far end of the Bunker, raised above the central working area, was the glassed-in office from which Goodman and Davidson would direct operations. The office was sound-proofed behind thick double-glazing which, under the circumstances, was just as well.

Goodman opened the door and stepped in. Nigel Quinn turned from the big wall map. Small red circles ringed the evening's major trouble spots. Goodman counted them. There were seven. He looked at Quinn.

'Make yourself at home,' he said drily. 'Be my guest.'

Quinn ignored the sarcasm.

'There are three of my men in hospital,' he said, 'and you put them there.'

Goodman looked at him, unmoved by the directness of the accusation. Since the riot, he'd begun to feel a strange sense of detachment, of immunity from the pressures building up around him. Briefly, in front of his wife, the pain and the shock had come flooding in, but she'd sealed this one gap in his defences, dammed it up with her compassion, and her good sense, and her limitless forgiveness. His life, where it mattered, was whole again. The rest of it, all this, was simply a series of decisions, the application of cold logic, the kind of exercise that had put him where he was today. Goodman glanced at the map again. He knew about Quinn's casualties. Davidson had told him in the car.

'They were doing their job,' he said, 'and I'm duly grateful.'

'That's hardly the point. You put their lives at risk. It was quite needless. Pure whim.'

Goodman looked at him.

'I don't agree,' he said. 'As you might expect.'

He sat down, and gestured for Quinn to do the same. The big policeman stared at him for a moment or two, finding it as difficult as ever to submit to the younger man's authority. Successful policing, he knew, depended above all on consent, on preserving the fiction that the forces of law and order were really the paid servants of the public at large. Destroy that illusion, and the whole damn thing would come tumbling down.

Already, since the riot, he'd lost two police cars, ambushed, overturned, and set on fire by marauding gangs of youths, fuelled on rumour and copious supplies of looted lager. In both of these incidents, men of his had been injured, and one of the drivers had been lucky to escape with his life. Areas of the city were beginning to resemble west Belfast, and only the shortage of fuel supplies was preventing the mass manufacture of Molotov cocktails, though soon someone was bound to discover that certain other substances worked just as well. For the time being, the situation was still in hand, but nightfall would bring out the real loonies, and then the city might go critical. It was a terrifying thought and he had no intention of keeping it to himself. He finally sat down in the chair opposite Goodman.

'You've got about an hour,' he said, 'to think of something to do.' He leaned forward. 'Otherwise, there'll be chaos.'

Goodman looked at him, that same dead look, the look of a man apart, on his own, utterly beyond reach.

'I've done it,' he said bleakly.

'Done what?'

'Recorded the broadcast.' He glanced at his watch. 'They're transmitting at ten past nine. After the Queen.'

'And what have you said?'

Goodman hesitated a moment, fighting the sudden urge to yawn. Or laugh. Or cry. Anything to lighten the darkness around him. Two grown-up men. Behaving like three-year-olds. He leaned back in the chair, letting the moments pass.

'I've imposed a curfew,' he said. 'Anyone on the streets after ten will face the consequences.'

Quinn stared at him, pure disbelief.

'You've done what?' he said.

'Imposed a curfew.' He smiled. 'Stay at home or else.' He glanced across at Davidson. 'That *is* the national policy, isn't it?'

Davidson nodded. 'In essence,' he said, 'yes, it is.'

Quinn's eyes travelled between them, trying to measure the collusion, trying to guess the weight of the alliance. At first, he'd assumed that Davidson was in control. Now, he wasn't so sure. He looked at Goodman again.

'Or else what?' he said.

Goodman gazed out through the thick plate glass. Fiona, his secretary, was making tea. He wondered idly whether the milk was OK. They'd been having trouble with the fridge. The coolant pipes were corroded, and the thing wouldn't work properly. He sighed, another problem, and quickly looked back at Quinn again. The man was staring at him very oddly. He frowned, remembering his question. The curfew. The big stick. How to deal with miscreants. He yawned.

'I'm not entirely sure,' he said, 'but I suggest we shoot them.'

Gillespie was several streets away from Sandra's house when he first spotted the car on his tail. He was driving fast, taking care with the gear changes, choosing his line through the corners, checking and rechecking the mirror, trying to swamp the anger he felt inside himself. It was an old Service trick, total concentration on the task in hand, and if it didn't work entirely, then it certainly drew his attention to the car, always there, the shape in his rear-view mirror, a hundred yards or so behind him.

Something about the car, its colour, snagged in his mind. It was an old Ford Cortina, with a 'T' registration plate and a broken-off aerial on one of the front wings. The driver, at a distance, was totally anonymous, a small, hunched figure at the wheel. Glancing at his fuel gauge, Gillespie applied the simplest of tests, turning left, and left again, and then completing the square through a grid of streets he'd known since his youth. After the third turn left, he stopped and reversed quickly into a tiny cut between two rows of terraced houses. Parked in the cut, engine off, he was invisible from both directions.

He waited for about a minute, winding down his window, smelling rain in the air. He heard the Cortina before he saw it, the familiar rattle of loose tappets, the hoarse wheeze of an off-tune carburettor. He stared out at the road. The Cortina crept past.

The man at the wheel was talking into a hand-held microphone.

Gillespie let the Cortina go past. His feelings about Sandra, the anger and the jealousy, had disappeared completely. In its place was a small, hard determination to find out exactly who, or what, had been sent to keep tabs on him. He was a private man. He paid his taxes. Knew his place. He neither sought nor wanted attention. The shape in his mirror, the man in the buff Cortina, was an intrusion, an affront, an act of the grossest trespass. He felt threatened. Worse still, he felt insulted. You've got the wrong man, he thought, reaching for the ignition key. You've made a big mistake. A big, big mistake.

Suzanne Wallace was still waiting for the phone call about the chart when Cartwright appeared again. She'd already heard him locking his office above. Now he stood in the open door of her own tiny cubby hole. He was wearing a knee-length raincoat and carried a small black briefcase. He was evidently going out.

'Finished?' he enquired.

She shook her head.

'One last call,' she said. 'Still waiting.'

'Important?'

'Afraid so,' she said, not bothering to explain any further.

He hesitated a moment, as awkward as ever, then glanced at his watch. She knew it was already gone six, but she wouldn't leave the office until she was certain she could lay hands on the chart. Sending Martin's wife and kids blind into the Atlantic would be unforgivable. She smiled at Cartwright.

'Don't worry,' she said, 'I'll lock up.'

He nodded, clearly far from happy, and told her to put the lights out and pull the front door shut behind her. The alarms would automatically engage. She need worry about nothing else.

'What about the fax?' Suzanne enquired, as he turned to leave. 'Shall I turn that off too?'

Cartwright hesitated a moment, recognizing the mischief in her voice. Since he'd disappeared with the mysterious Agreement, she'd heard him overhead, back on the phone, his voice as quiet and toneless as before, the calls incessant, never incoming, always at his own instigation. Once or twice, she'd been tempted to creep up the stairs, and listen through the keyhole, curious to know what could possibly occupy so much of his time, but there was a dimension to this man that she found creepy, and the last thing she wanted was any kind of confrontation. Far better he leave her to it. Far better she work alone. Cartwright pulled the raincoat around him, the long white fingers fumbling with the bottom button.

'The fax is off,' he said. 'You needn't touch it.'

He sealed the conversation with a nod, a busy man bidding good-night to his secretary, and walked across the office, and out into the hall. She heard the front door open, and close, and the low purr of his Jaguar outside.

She got up and switched on the overhead light. The weather had been dull since midday, big banks of heavy grey cloud rolling in from the west, and now she could hear rain on the windows of the big office outside. She gazed at the map of Ireland she'd been using all afternoon, and checked the arrangements she'd made. Her airline chum had been garrulous and cheerful as ever, a man unbothered by the prospect of Armageddon, but she trusted him implicitly and she knew he'd deliver what he'd promised. In a way, she was sorry she couldn't be there. If there was anyone who could see the lighter side of World War Three it would surely be him, and there'd be worse ways of spending one's final weeks on planet earth. Whether a chilly bed in County Kerry would provide any permanent security in the event of war, she didn't know. But she assumed that Martin had done his homework, and she was glad above all that this hasty evacuation had finally obliged him to make up his mind.

She loved the man more than she'd ever thought possible, and she'd never been in any real doubt that he felt the same way. They were simply too close, too well matched, too similar, for there to have been any possibility of mistake. She never played games with people. Never had. Never would. She always spoke her mind, and expected the same in return. Martin had seen it, and understood it, and taken up the challenge. That was why it was so strong between them, and so durable. And that was why it was right to keep the baby.

She smiled, fingering the ring he'd given her only a couple of weeks back, a plain gold ring to be worn, he'd said, on the finger of her choice. She wore it now, on the third finger of her right hand, continental style. It was, she told herself, a modest and entirely personal piece of symbolism. One day, they'd get away from it all. Far, far away. Somewhere warmer. Somewhere south. Somewhere exclusively their own. In the meantime, as ever, they'd cope.

The phone began to ring, out in the big office. It rang three times, and then the recorded message engaged on the ansaphone. Suzanne got up and walked through. The ansaphone was on a small desk under the window. She reached down and turned the volume control to full. A woman's voice was telling the caller to leave a message after the tone. There were three beeps. Then a rich, dark brown voice on a bad line, but perfectly audible.

'Harry?' said the voice. 'It's Tristan. I've had some thoughts about your evacuees. I'm faxing back the list in a moment or two. You'll find the account numbers beside each name. And some contractual queries at the end. The sums look good. Oh . . .' the voice chuckled, 'I've found a berth for your boats. Even the *Timothy* bloody *Lee*. Hotels, too. Bye for now.'

The phone went dead, and in the silence that followed, Suzanne could hear the click and whirr of the ansaphone as the tape re-cued. She walked slowly across to the fax machine and switched it on. The stand-by light glowed red. Another phone began to ring, back in the office where she'd been working. She ran back across the room. It was the man from the chandlery. Her chart was ready. She'd need to pick it up at once. The shop was closing in fifteen minutes.

'Yes,' she said, eyeing the fax machine, 'of course.'

She put the phone down and gazed out into the big office. Whatever was happening had something to do with Martin's plan. Of that, she was certain. The voice on the phone, Tristan, had talked of evacuees. Of a list. Of hotels. That meant the boat plan. Had to. Yet her understanding was a handful of people, thirty at the most, to go to Ireland. Official approval. Safe passage out of harbour. She frowned. All afternoon, something had been bothering her about Cartwright, and she now realized what it was. The man didn't want her around. She was supernumerary. Irrelevant. Deadweight. That was why he'd barely listened when she'd told him her arrangements. That was why he'd been reluctant to leave her alone in the office.

She heard the fax machine engage, and she watched the leading edge of the paper roll begin to appear. She wondered whether it was a long document, whether she could afford to stay, or whether she should just forget it, put out the lights, shut the door on it all, and do only what she'd been asked.

She walked slowly across to the fax machine. Four lines of type were already visible. Names. Sums of money. Tens of thousands. She twisted her head sideways. Hundreds of thousands. She squinted in the dim light. A Jersey address at the top, and a phone number. Abruptly, the machine stopped and a yellow light on the side began to blink. She looked at the instruction symbols printed on top of the machine. 'Call discontinued,' it read, 'pending re-connection.' She glanced at her watch. The chandlery would be closing any minute. Already she'd kept them waiting. She must go now, return later.

She collected her attaché case and keys from the desk where she'd been working, and ran quickly out of the office. At the front door, she hesitated, remembering Cartwright's instructions. Pull the door shut, and she'd never get back in. She looked at the door, heavy oak. She opened her attaché case and sorted quickly through it, finding what she wanted at the bottom, a thick leaflet from a company pushing Aegean sailing holidays. She folded it twice and wedged it carefully between the tongue of the lock and the door itself. She tested the door a couple of times, the lightest of pressures, making sure it wouldn't swing open, and then ran to the car.

The chandlery was barely a minute away. The man behind the counter gave her the chart and accepted a cheque in payment. She thanked the man and ran back to her car. Then she hesitated, wondering for the first time whether she wasn't being a little hasty. Cartwright, after all, was an accountant of some standing. It was highly likely he'd still have business to attend to, deals to close, clients to service, even at this late hour. Perhaps she'd got it wrong about Jersey. Perhaps she'd simply confused one scheme with another. Perhaps it was some obscure code, two clever businessmen conferring in a private language of their own. She looked down at the chart on the passenger seat beside her. Perhaps, after all, she'd pay a precautionary visit to the dock, meet the skipper, hand over the chart, do what she was told, secure the office afterwards, confident – after all – that everything was OK. She smiled to herself. Martin's baby, she thought. Our very own child.

Davidson and Quinn stood together on a small hummock on the very crest of the Hill. Fifty feet beneath them, buried under the chalk, the Bunker was at last fully operational. They could hear the faint hum of the generator, transmitted up the ventilating shaft which emerged beside them, squat concrete louvres, hardened against blast.

Davidson glanced across at Quinn. The invitation to a discreet talk had been his own idea, broached in a lull between conferences. He'd led the way out of the Bunker, using a small rear staircase, then a series of iron ladders up to the ventilation shaft. Now, they stood together, gazing down at the city. Faintly, in the far distance, he could hear the wail of a police siren, one of Quinn's patrol cars. He thought of Goodman again, kneeling amongst the rubble in the shadow of the flats, looking for his glasses. Then, he'd seemed shaken, but not visibly hurt. Now, only hours later, it was a very different story.

'I think he's going mad,' he said quietly, 'nervous collapse.'

Quinn said nothing for a moment or two. In a year and a half of intermittent contact, it was the first time Davidson had seen the policeman smoke. Small filter-tips, the smoke drawn deep down into the lungs. Davidson watched him, thinking of Goodman again. His detachment. The cave into which he'd retreated.

'I tried to stop the broadcast,' he told Quinn. 'You should know that.' Quinn turned away from the view.

'How?'

Davidson smiled. 'I suggested a retake.'

'And?'

'He refused.'

'And?'

'I phoned our friend Bullock. About half an hour ago.' He paused. 'I wondered whether it was strictly necessary to . . . ah . . . transmit the wretched thing . . .'

He let the sentence trail away. The call had been a mistake, the first he'd made since arriving in the city. Bullock had been curious at once, wanting to know why the sudden request, why the volte-face. He'd picked up far more than Davidson had realized about what was happening to Goodman, the tell-tale facial twitches, the strange gleam in his eye, his public refusal to toe the Whitehall line. Quite what the editor made of it all wasn't clear, but he'd played the conversation very cleverly, fishing for more information, baiting traps, tempting Davidson to compound his original error and reveal exactly why he'd made the call in the first place. This, of course, Davidson declined to do, but Bullock had closed the conversation by confirming that he would gladly withhold the broadcast, providing the order came directly from Goodman himself, a condition that Davidson couldn't possibly meet. Now, he watched Quinn take a final pull on the cigarette, and flick the glowing end out into the darkness, down towards the sandbags below.

'Constitutionally . . .' he mused, 'it's very tricky.'

'So I gather.'

'If he's really mad, we'll need to get him certified . . .' He paused, hands in pockets, thinking the thing through. 'But if he's really mad, that in itself would be an appalling admission.' He turned to Quinn again. 'Can you imagine? Powers of the kind we've conferred on him? Life and death? A hundred and fifty thousand people? And we choose a lunatic?' He winced. 'Have you thought about what the Bullocks of this world would make of that . . .?' He paused again. 'Afterwards?'

Quinn nodded. 'Tricky,' he said.

'Quite.'

There was another silence. The police siren, abruptly, had stopped. Davidson stirred. It was nearly dark now.

'This curfew . . .' he began.

The uneasiness was obvious in his voice. Quinn shook his head, dismissive, quite sure of his ground.

'No one will get shot,' he said.

'Thank God for that.'

'My pleasure.'

Davidison laughed, genuine appreciation. It was the first time he'd heard Quinn make anything approaching a joke, and he didn't want the occasion to go unmarked.

'There's another spot of bother . . .' he began, 'you may have heard.'

Quinn looked across at him. 'The boat?'

'Yes. I came across his manifest. He's been playing it rather close to his chest. I only hope he knows what he's doing. There are lots of kids on that boat.'

'Including mine,' Quinn said grimly.

'Quite.' He paused. Goodman had kept the evacuation plan remarkably quiet, only approaching a handful of key personnel, discreet conversations on the internal phone system, the assurance of a berth down Channel, and a bed in southern Ireland. At first he'd put a mental tick against the idea, sensible initiative, but now he wasn't so sure. He looked at Quinn again.

'Who's organizing it all?' he said.

'Man called Cartwright.'

'Do we know Cartwright?'

Quinn smiled. 'Oh yes,' he said, 'everyone knows Harry.'

'So should we be worried?'

The policeman looked at him for a moment or two. Then shook his head.

'No,' he said, 'it's all under control.'

Ingle sat on a stool in the dark-room, eating a plate of corned beef sandwiches. The laboratory technician had rung him, as instructed, the moment the first prints were expected from the bath of fixer. Now, the negatives hung in strips in the deep red glow of the tiny overhead bulb, clothes-pegged to a line he'd hung across the sink. The negs had already been through the developer, and in a minute or two he'd ease the first prints from the fixer bath, sluice them under the tap, and offer them to Ingle for formal inspection. Ingle peered up at the negatives, making enough sense of the shapes in the frame to recognize a park bench, two figures, a man and a woman.

The lab technician swirled the fixer in the sink, grunted approval, and reached for a pair of plastic tongs. He lifted out the first of the prints, and let it drip for a moment or two before pegging it to the clothes line. Ingle leaned forward on the stool, frowning with concentration. He recognized the faces from Reese's earlier shots. The man on the bench was Goodman. The figure beside him was his girlfriend. Of Reese, he was glad to note, there was no sign.

He patted the technician on the back, and murmured his thanks. Outside, in the corridor, he paused for a moment, looking out into the gathering darkness. The photographs had been taken by the man Gillespie. The photographs had been lifted from the reporter, McPhee. Logic suggested that they were, at the very least, friends. Goodman was the man in charge, the man whose authority he'd been sent to protect. Time, therefore, to talk to Gillespie.

Ingle walked slowly down the corridor, and into the consulting room that now served as a communications base. A man in plain clothes sat at a small console, reading a very old copy of the *Sun*. There was a microphone in front of him, and a half-finished packet of chocolate biscuits. The man glanced up, folded the paper, and pushed the biscuits towards Ingle. Ingle took two of the biscuits, and leaned back against the door, closing it.

'This fella Gillespie,' he said. 'Tell Reese I want a word.'

Gillespie finally found Reese in a lay-by near the dock. For nearly half an hour, he'd cruised slowly up and down, trailing his coat, offering himself as a target, as obvious as possible, trying to tempt the other man out. But wherever he looked, wherever he drove, he drew the same blank.

Now though, nearly out of petrol, he'd found him. He drove slowly past, watching the man in the rear-view mirror, the slow unhurried movements, the tell-tale puff of blue exhaust smoke, the careful signal indicating left, the Cortina easing out, resuming the chase. At the end of the road, he pulled a U-turn, making absolutely certain, not wanting to end up the victim of his own paranoia. Sure enough, after a discreet pause, a glance up and down the street, the Cortina turned with him, heading back into the city.

Gillespie eyed the fuel gauge. It was three miles to the area of wasteland he'd mentally earmarked at the south-eastern tip of the island on which the city was built. He might just make it.

He dropped the Marina into top gear as early as he dared, squeezing out every last spoonful of fuel, crawling along the empty seafront at barely 30 mph. Both cars had their lights on now, but the Cortina was silhouetted against what little was left of the daylight, and Gillespie could see the driver quite clearly. A smallish man, he thought, the most difficult kind.

At the end of the seafront, the road swung briefly inland, and then seaward again, along a bumpy tarmac track that led to the anchorage. He knew the area by heart, every yard of it. Off to the right, between the track and the sea, was a big expanse of waste ground, baked hard by the summer. Couples came here a lot to screw, and he knew at least two marriages that had finally come to grief in the bitter privacy of a parked car. It was a place for intimacies, and secrets, and confessions. Rather appropriate, he thought grimly, as he pulled the old Marina off the road and onto the first of the rutted tracks that led across the wasteland to the sea.

It was quite dark now, and he drove for fifty yards or so at walking pace before he dropped the car into neutral, and opened the door, and rolled out into the darkness, letting the car coast on, away, lights still on. The impact with the damp grass knocked the breath out of his body, and he lay still for a moment or two, listening for the wheeze of the Cortina behind. For a while there was nothing, just the odd bump as his own car slowed to a halt. Then he heard the Cortina. He got up on one knee, saw it turning in from the road. The man was driving on sidelights only, feeling his way.

Gillespie got up, crouching, cautious at first, then bolder. Staying low, he ran to the left, careful where his feet went, remembering the clumps of tussock and the deep ruts where the kids spun their old bangers. The Cortina was moving slowly forward, the driver uncertain of his bearings. Gillespie closed on the car from the side, eyes fixed on the shadowy profile of the figure behind the wheel. The lights from the dashboard gave his face the slightest tinge of green. He looked older than Gillespie had expected, perhaps forty, forty-five.

The car stopped. The driver seemed to have sensed danger. He looked around, began to get out. Gillespie let him put one foot on the ground before he stepped out of the darkness, driving hard at the door, slamming it shut against the man's body, hearing him grunt with pain as the metal bit into his arm and shin. Gillespie took his arm, and pulled the man towards him, spinning his body as he did so. The man's arm came nicely up behind his back, high up, inches from the point where the first ligaments in his shoulder would start to tear. The man lashed out backwards with his feet, more pride than anything else, and Gillespie took a handful of his hair, and drove his face hard against the car roof. The man gasped, his nose broken, and Gillespie did it twice more before the body went slack in his arms, and he let it fall to the ground, sacklike, spent. The encounter had taken no more than ten seconds, faster than he normally worked, and he found the gun almost immediately, a short-barrelled Smith and Wesson, good in a tight corner, dodgy beyond twenty yards. He checked the chambers in the headlights. Six bullets. Double action trigger. He stuffed the gun into his jeans pocket and quickly examined the contents of the man's wallet. A mug shot on the Scotland Yard pass showed a face that had never learned to smile. The man's name was Reese. He worked for Special Branch. Gillespie gazed at the pass a moment longer before putting it in his pocket. He'd got the man's age wrong by five years. He was younger than he looked.

He bent to the body by the car, and rolled the man over onto his back. Blood was beginning to cake on his face, but his breathing was OK. His nose would recover in time, and a good dentist would rise to the challenge of what was left of his mouth. Gillespie stepped over the body and got into the car. The fuel gauge was half-full, and the engine was still running. He eased it into gear and slipped the clutch, bumping over the wasteland towards his own car. In the back of the Marina was the empty fuel can. Now, at last, he could buy diesel.

He stopped by the Marina and threw the can into the back of the Cortina. On the way back towards the road, he paused briefly by Reese's body. The man was beginning to stir, his eyes half open, his brain trying to cope with the pain, and the lights, and the shadow that fell across his face. As Gillespie got back into the Cortina, he could hear a voice from Reese's personal radio. The voice was indistinct, muffled by several layers of nylon anorak, but the irritation was obvious.

'Reese, you clown,' the voice was saying, 'where the fuck are you?'

Suzanne drove carefully round the dock, looking for some sign of Cartwright. His Jaguar she'd already spotted, parked outside the pub, but he wasn't at the bar and when she asked a fisherman whether he'd seen a small guy in a suit, he'd just shrugged and turned away.

Now, on her second circuit, she spotted the *Timothy Lee* under the floodlights, recognizing the name from the message on Cartwright's ansaphone. She pulled up on the quayside and got out. The boat was smaller than she'd expected, and a lot shabbier. Cardboard boxes were piled up beneath the wheelhouse, and there were a couple of shadows, cats probably, sniffing around a sack of onions. The only access to the boat was via an iron ladder. She ran back to the car, and retrieved the chart. Then she began to clamber down the ladder, one hand for the pitted old ironwork, one for the precious roll of cardboard, with its bearings and its depths, and its curt reminders to beware of this maritime hazard or that.

She got to the foot of the ladder and stepped onto the deck. The fish hold was open, a huge rusty mouth, and she dimly recognized the shapes of the mattresses below. The smell was appalling, a mix of engine oil, and fish, and urine. She shook her head, amazed, and walked aft, to an open door of the bridge. It was dark inside, and she paused to let her eyes make sense of the deep shadows.

Slowly, she began to distinguish shapes, more doors, a narrow companionway. She moved slowly aft, towards the trawler's stern and came to a door. The door opened. She stood there, beginning to regret her curiosity, her diligence. She could hear a man breathing, slow, shallow breaths, someone asleep. She backed away deciding to leave, to abandon it all, to get back to the ladder, and into her car, and away, but as she turned, her foot slipped on the greasy deck, and she fell heavily on one knee, hearing her own small yelp, surprise rather than pain.

The breathing paused. A man grunted. A hand fumbled in the darkness. A light came on. Suzanne got up, embarrassed, feeling foolish. She brushed herself down. Her skirt was black with grease and oil. A man of about fifty-five blinked up at her from an ancient armchair. His skin was tanned, the texture of old leather, an outdoor face. He wore an ancient blue sweater, holes at the elbows, and there was a bottle of whisky on the table by his side. The bottle was a third full. The glass on the floor by his foot was empty.

'Who are you?' the man said. A Scots accent, thickened by age and alcohol.

Suzanne blinked at him, introduced herself, told him she'd come to give the skipper a chart, the directions he'd need, a destination.

'Destination?' The man frowned. There were charts already spread on the table baside the bottle. She glanced at them. Central Channel. Wight to Cap de la Hague. There was a heavily pencilled line slanting south. It ended in Jersey. East coast. St Helier. She blinked.

'You're the Skipper?' she asked.

'Aye.'

'Mr Cartwright's?' She paused. 'Small man? Suit? Moustache?'

The man nodded again, reaching slowly for the bottle, beginning to frown.

'Aye,' he said again.

'I see,' Suzanne nodded, offering him her own chart, totally out of her depth.

Behind her, in the darkness, she could hear footsteps on the iron ladder, voices. The boat shuddered a little as someone jumped the last few feet. The footsteps got nearer. Someone tripped and cursed. Someone else laughed. She picked up the chart again, and straightened her skirt, precautionary, instinctive movements. She turned towards the door. A tall man came in first, with a big Afro perm, and a wide smile. He stopped and gazed at her. Another man pushed in behind him, smaller, somehow meaner, a narrow face, short hair. Last of all was Cartwright. He waved the other two into the cabin, terse flaps of his hand. The man with the Afro looked at Suzanne, and then at the Skipper, and laughed. The cabin smelled suddenly of beer, a hot, yeasty smell that made her want to retch. She turned towards the door, towards the fresh air, but Cartwright stood in her way. He was looking beyond her. At the table. At the map.

'Well . . .' he said, 'you've found us.' He smiled. 'How clever of you . . .'

Eight

The *George F. Kennan* was barely thirty-five kilometres away from Soviet territorial waters when the first man died. The Captain, who'd spent most of the last twenty-four hours vomiting over the small stainless steel basin in his cabin, absorbed the news without comment. The dead man, a young ensign in one of the damage limitation crews, had avoided even light injuries at the time of the fire, but had obviously taken a lot of radiation. Or so the captain assumed.

The Captain had known the man moderately well. They both came from the same part of the country, way out in Montana, high up in the Rocky Mountains. They'd talked sometimes, end of watches, wilderness talk, horse talk, fishing talk. The boy had worked out every day, pumping iron in the crowded recreation space aft, between the missile tubes, proud of his physique, determined to preserve it. The last couple of days though, he'd been almost continually sick. Then came the diarrhoea, and the sweats, and an exhaustion that barely left him the strength to climb back into his bunk. They'd found him only minutes ago, a note to his wife tucked under his pillow. The pillow was soaked in blood. He'd slashed his wrists, a quiet, private death, administered in the full knowledge of what the radiation was doing to his gut, and the deep recesses of his bone marrow.

The Captain toyed for a moment with the small white envelope, Navy issue, the Ensign's careful scrawl across the front. Against the odds, he'd managed to re-establish contact with Washington, using open circuits easily accessed by the growing Soviet Task Force upwind. He'd told them the worst, the radiation levels, the symptoms amongst the crew, and they'd confirmed that plans for an air drop were off. *Counter-productive* was the phrase they'd used. He'd asked them for further orders, but the circuit had gone down in a storm of static, and now, four hours later, he was still pondering whether or not to scuttle the boat. In a thousand metres of water, the radiation hazards would be lessened. His men would be picked up by the surrounding Soviets. With good hospital care, some of them might even survive, though each man would then represent an astonishing Intelligence windfall. Years of specialist training. An intimate knowledge of the latest Trident boomers. And a clue to why the sub had ever ventured so close to Northern Europe in the first place.

The Captain closed his eyes and passed a tired hand over his face, feeling the nausea gusting up from his belly again. The Lieutenant in his cabin, the man who'd brought him the news, stifled a polite cough. The Captain opened his eyes again, and put the envelope carefully to one side. It was addressed to the dead Ensign's wife. It was none of his damn business. He looked at the Lieutenant.

'Yes?' he said.

'I was wondering about burial, sir.' He paused. 'Given the circumstances.'

The Captain looked at him and nodded slowly, another decision. The Ensign's body would be radioactive, a pollution hazard, like the rest of them. He thought about it a little more. Ensign Seymour Schwarz. Barely 23. World War Three's first victim.

'Tomorrow morning,' he said briskly, 'lead coffin. First light.'

After an hour's search in the Bunker, the keys were still missing. Soon now, they were to exercise the standard fire and contamination drills, part of a three-page directive that had been telexed that afternoon from the Regional Commissariat to City Bunkers throughout the Central South. The drills required that all Bunker personnel wear the regulation NBC suits, a specially designed garment that would help them against gas attack, germ warfare, and light radiation. There were forty suits, enough for every member of the Bunker staff, and they were stored in a double-locked room next to the tiny galley.

At 7 p.m. one of the secretaries had gone to collect the keys to the store room. The keys were kept on a large board beside the telephone cubicles, rows of hooks, each hook carefully labelled, each key carefully tagged. On the second row, half-way along, there were two empty hooks. The keys had gone.

Goodman, deep in conversation with the transport chief over a distribution problem, had ordered an immediate search. Desks had been moved. Drawers emptied. Waste bins shaken out. Even the big filing cabinets, full of microfilmed copies of the city's records, had been wrestled away from the wall, in case – as one tired secretary put it – the keys had jumped off the hook, walked across the room, and hidden themselves underneath. The sarcasm was well-founded. After nearly an hour's search, they were still missing.

Now, it was Quinn who once again tried to force the issue. He knocked twice on Goodman's door and walked in. Goodman looked up. He was alone now, and there were doodles on his blotter. Imperfect circles, interlinked. A sun in a cloudless sky. Seagulls. Triangular shapes, endlessly repeated. Quinn stood over the desk, physically dominant.

'We'll have to break the door down,' he said. 'We have no alternative.'

Goodman looked up at him, pained. The suggestion offended him. The noise. The needless damage.

'No,' he said, 'we won't do that.'

'We have no choice.'

Goodman gazed out at the well of the Bunker. Everyone had returned to their desks. The ROC Co-ordinator was chalking careful symbols on one of the maps of the area. The search was plainly over.

'How are things in the city?' Goodman said.

Quinn frowned, not wanting to change the subject.

'Quiet,' he said, 'thank God.'

'No more riots?'

'Nothing we can't handle.'

'People out and about?'

'Very few.'

Goodman nodded, imagining the empty streets, the pubs closed, the tiny terraced houses curtained against the world outside. Quinn tapped the desk, one thick forefinger, a peremptory gesture, calling Goodman to order.

'We should use the fire axe,' he said.

Goodman gazed at him, startled.

'What?' he said.

'The fire axe. On the cupboard door.'

'Oh,' he nodded, 'I see.'

Quinn stood there, waiting for an answer.

'Well?' he said at last, 'shall I organize it?'

Goodman sighed, leaning back in the big leather chair he'd had specially transferred from his office in the Civic Centre. A trusty friend. Familiar contours. Nice smell. He looked up at Quinn.

'No,' he said slowly, 'I don't think so.'

Quinn gazed at him for a moment, wondering how far to take it, wondering whether it might not be best, for everybody's sake, to break Goodman now, before it was too late. The man was plainly on the edge. He'd seen it before, in his CID days, the lengthier interrogations. Deprive a man of sleep. Set him impossible choices. Trap him this way and that. Whittle down his options. Narrow his breathing space, his territory, until the direct physical sense of threat was nearly unendurable. Then blow in his ear. Often no more than a single simple phrase. The right choice of words, the right inflection. The knowing smile. The bare knuckles exposed. He looked down at Goodman, biding his time, awaiting his opportunity.

Goodman reached for a file in the wire basket beside his blotter. He opened the file and glanced at a list of names inside.

'The boat's leaving before midnight,' he said, turning over the page, changing the subject yet again.

'So I understand.'

'She should be well clear by daybreak.' He looked up. 'If you're worried about Molly.'

Quinn shook his head. 'She'll be fine,' he said, 'fine.' He paused. He'd seen the list an hour earlier. One name hadn't made sense.

'Who's Suzanne Wallace?' he said.

Goodman looked up. 'A friend of mine.' He smiled, amused at the small truth of his answer. Quinn frowned.

'I thought it was relatives only? Wives and kids?'

Goodman ignored the innuendo, the hidden accusation.

'She's in the travel business,' he said, 'she's taking care of the arrangements the other end.' He shrugged. 'She's a courier of sorts.'

'Southern Ireland, I understand.'

'Yes.'

'Where, exactly?'

'I don't know. She's organizing it at the moment.' He glanced at the big clock on the wall. 'I'll be phoning her later. Before they pull the plugs. In fact I'll be going down there myself.'

Quinn looked at him sharply, remembering the results of his last excursion. A major riot. Lives in danger.

'Oh?' he said.

Goodman nodded. 'About nine,' he said, 'just to make sure.'

'Make sure what?'

Goodman looked at the blotter, the thickets of doodles, making no attempt to answer. Fiona had packed a framed photograph of Joanna and the kids. Now it stood on his desk, beside the wire basket. He moved it an inch to the left. Then back again. He'd always been fascinated by the shot, the way the photographer had shadowed the wall behind Joanna's head, the artful naturalness of it all. He'd tried to duplicate the effect himself since, and failed. It was inexplicably clever, a trick – he supposed – of the trade. Quinn was still waiting for an answer, his patience clearly running out. Goodman glanced up at him.

'To make sure they leave in one piece,' he said. 'Does that sound reasonable?'

Gillespie turned slowly into the dock and coasted the Cortina to a halt. The engine was clapped out, and the radio didn't work. He got out of the car and walked the ten yards across the slippery cobbles to the pub. It had stopped raining by now but it was still wet underfoot. He pushed the door open and went in. The pub was nearly deserted, two fishermen playing cribbage over pints of lager, and a man in the corner reading a book. There was no one behind the bar. Gillespie stood over the fishermen. One was about to toss a couple of cards into the box. He had a good hand. Two fives and a jack. The fisherman looked up.

'I'm after fuel,' Gillespie said.

'I bet,' said the fisherman. He threw away a seven and a one. Cautious play. Gillespie tapped him on the shoulder.

'I said I'm after fuel,' he said again, 'and I want to know

who's selling.'

The fisherman didn't look up.

'No one's selling,' he said, 'there is no fuel.'

The other man glanced up at Gillespie and winked. Gillespie didn't wink back. There was a silence. Gillespie sighed, a faintly sad whistle of escaping air. The fisherman laid down a low card, a three. The other man was still watching Gillespie, more cautious now, watchful.

'There's a boat called the *Timothy Lee*,' he said quietly. 'You'll find her along the quay.'

Gillespie nodded. 'The *Timothy Lee*,' he said, 'thanks.'

Gillespie left the pub and walked along the quayside, past the line of moored yachts, and the rows of fishing smacks, three deep against the harbour wall. At the end of the quay, close to the dock entrance, lay the *Timothy Lee*. He read the faded white lettering on the stern, noticed the battered cork fenders and the low rumble of engines. There was smoke bubbling from the squat funnel aft. He could smell it before he saw it. Diesel.

He stood over the boat for a moment or two, up on the quayside, gazing down. There were bare bulbs jury-rigged in the open fish hold, and he could see someone working down there, piling mattresses, shifting cardboard boxes, making ready. Up on the bridge, there was another light under the binnacle, the soft green glow of the radar display. Aft of the bridge, there was movement in the cabins, and he could hear voices occasionally raised in argument. The boat was tatty beyond belief, offensive to his own high standards, but it held a certain promise. No doubt about it. These men would soon be going to sea.

He swung down the iron ladder and stepped softly onto the deck. He'd already spotted the fuel cans from the quayside. He bent to them, unscrewing the top of the nearest can, inserting his finger, smelling the sour heavy smell of the diesel. He screwed the top back on, and traced the chain that secured the cans to a big ringbolt on the deck. Pity, he thought. Might have saved a lot of time.

He padded across to the lip of the fish hold, and looked down. Something about the cut of the leather jacket stooped over the pile of mattresses, the shape of the shoulders, the line of the hair at the back of the neck. He tried the name that came to mind, the name that cropped up in so many of the carefully typed reports he left on Jenner's desk. Old ladies winkled out of tenanted properties. Young couples scared into the street, preferring homelessness to yet another brick through the window.

'Albie,' he called softly, 'Albie Curtis.'

Albie looked up, over his shoulder, not recognizing the voice, not able to make sense of the face against the glare of the overhead floodlights on the quay.

'Who the fuck are you?' he said.

Gillespie glanced round at the empty dock and then vaulted over the lip of the fish hold, landing on his feet on a mattress beside Albie. He smiled, wiping the rust from his hands.

'Well, well . . .' he said. 'Long time, no see . . .'

Albie peered at him, recognizing the voice at last, and the haircut.

'Gillespie,' he said without enthusiasm. 'What do you want?'

'Fuel.'

'Oh.' He paused, and Gillespie sensed the interest in his voice, the instinctive anticipation of hard cash.

'You've got diesel,' Gillespie smiled, 'I've seen it.'

'Yeah.'

'It's in cans. Up on the deck.'

'Yeah.' Albie nodded. 'Fucking locked up.'

'How much?'

Albie looked at him. He'd given up with the white paint, and he badly needed something to restore his morale, his self-respect.

'Fifty quid,' he said. 'A can.'

Gillespie shook his head.

'That's their price,' he said.

'Whose price?'

'The blokes who own it,' he said reasonably. 'Yours is lower.'

Albie shook his head.

'Wrong,' he said, 'fifty quid. You want it, you fucking pay for it.' He paused. 'Cash.'

Gillespie thought about it for a moment, then shrugged and put his hand in his back pocket. Albie looked briefly smug, the bargain struck. He kicked a mattress with his foot, and prepared to climb back out of the fish hold. When he looked up, he was ready to count the money. Instead, he found himself looking at

Reese's revolver.

'What's that?' he said.

Gillespie smiled, motioning him up, out of the fish hold, onto the deck.

'That's a gun,' he said. 'That's why you're going to give me one of those cans.'

Albie looked at him, the harsh shadows across his face, the crooked smile, the hand rock-steady, the gun inches from his chest. He shook his head.

'They're right about you, Gillespie,' he said, 'you're off your fucking trolley. What do you think this is? War?'

At his desk in the Bunker, Goodman looked up as Fiona knocked twice and walked in. Her face spoke louder than her voice. Behind the calm, orderly phrases, she was clearly anxious.

'I've tried those numbers again,' she said, 'Mr Cartwright's, and the other one you gave me.'

'No go?'

She shook her head. 'Nothing,' she said, 'there's no one there.'

'I see,' Goodman nodded.

He'd been trying to raise Suzanne for more than an hour. She needed to pack her bags, to ready herself for the voyage. It wouldn't be a simple conversation but times had changed, and this particular issue, the decision to be taken in this corner of his life, was as clear as the rest of it. She had to go. It was as simple as that. There was no alternative. As Controller, he had sole authority in the matter. Fiona gave him a sheaf of memos, directives for the Bunker staff, meal rotas, rest schedules, the small print of life underground. He glanced at them, scrawling a signature above his name.

'Keep trying,' he said, without looking up.

In the small, airless cabin aft, Cartwright sat at the table, the Skipper's pencil in his hand, ever the accountant. McNaught was still in the armchair, one leg tucked under the other, the glass half-full again, the bottle empty. Mick Rendall stood by the door, trying to keep the grease off his new oilskins, trying to place this latest addition to the passenger list, not beginning to understand Cartwright's hostility.

'So how will you reach him?' Cartwright said again. 'How will you get in touch?'

'I have a number,' Suzanne said.

'Is he expecting a call?'

'Of course.'

'And what will you say?'

There was a pause. Suzanne shrugged, seeing no alternative to the truth.

'I shall say you're going to Jersey.' She turned to McNaught. 'That's right, isn't it?'

McNaught was looking at the map, deep in thought, trying to remember where, in fact, the voyage was supposed to end. Mick Rendall, he recalled, had been uncertain. Only the little bloke in the suit had mentioned Jersey.

'Jersey,' he said thickly, to no one in particular. 'We're going to Jersey.'

Cartwright ignored him, still looking at Suzanne.

'Suppose I told you there were two boats,' he said slowly, 'and suppose the other one was going to Ireland?'

'Then that would explain it,' she said.

'Would it?'

'Yes.'

'Are you sure?'

Suzanne thought about the question, the afternoon in his office, the list of names waiting for her on the fax machine. None of that was relevant just now. Not in this conversation. Not in this company.

'Yes,' she said, 'I'm perfectly sure.'

Cartwright nodded. 'And under these circumstances . . . two boats . . . you'd be able to assure your . . . ah . . . friend . . .' he smiled at her, the merest flicker of warmth, 'that we are all . . . ah . . . on course?'

Suzanne looked at him. Her knee was beginning to throb and she knew, at all costs, that she had to get off the boat.

'Yes,' she said again.

There was a long silence. Then Cartwright got up.

'Then I suggest we make the call,' he said. 'All of us.'

Mick recognized his cue and stood aside. Suzanne stepped out of the cabin and walked carefully along the companionway, steadying herself with one hand. The rail felt cold and greasy to the touch. Mick Rendall was a step or two behind her. She could hear the mutter of conversation back in the cabin. Cartwright talking to the Skipper.

'When does everybody turn up?' she said, over her shoulder.

'Dunno,' Mick said, ever friendly, making amends, 'no one's said.'

Suzanne nodded and stepped out onto the deck. As she did so, she saw a movement up ahead, in the shadows beneath the quayside. Two men were climbing the iron ladder. One of them she recognized, the smallest of the threesome who'd surprised her in the cabin. He was carrying a large can. Something was slopping around inside. The other man was beneath him on the ladder, taller, also climbing with one hand. Mick saw them, too.

'Albie,' he called, 'what's up?'

Albie paused. The other man on the ladder gestured, a brisk, impatient movement of the right hand. Albie began to climb again, got to the top, put the can down on the quayside. Suzanne glanced round at Mick. Mick was staring at the other man, puzzled, sensing danger, the unexpected, not knowing quite what to do.

Suzanne stepped quickly down the slippery deck, towards the foot of the ladder, avoiding the coils of rope, and litter of abandoned fishing gear. She was half-way up the ladder, fighting to catch her breath, before she heard Mick in pursuit.

'Here,' he was saying, 'steady on, girl.'

She carried on climbing, ignoring the pain in her knee, tearing her hands on the rusty iron rungs, knowing only that she had to get to the top of the ladder, away from the boat, away from this strange collection of men, and their mattresses, and their empty bottles of Scotch, and their mystery destinations. She reached the top of the ladder and looked up. A tall, lean man stood watching her. He was wearing a leather jacket and jeans. He cast a long shadow. The gun in his right hand was pointing at the man with the can. She smiled at him, feeling faintly absurd, a stranger in someone else's script, uninvited, eager to leave.

'Help me,' she said, 'please.'

The man nodded.

'Sure,' he said. 'Pleasure.'

He motioned the other man forward.

'Leave the fuel,' he said. 'Just walk.'

Albie did what he was told. When he'd walked ten yards or so, clearing the stern of the trawler, Gillespie told him to stop. He stopped. Cartwright appeared below, a silhouette in the lit doorway. He looked up. Saw Gillespie. Saw the gun. He glanced sideways, at Mick. Mick was still at the foot of the ladder.

'Get up there,' he said to Mick.

Mick began to climb, one rung at a time, in no obvious hurry. Gillespie motioned Suzanne aside. Mick's head appeared at the top of the ladder. Gillespie smiled at him, white teeth in the shadowed face. Then he kicked him, once, under his left ear. Mick disappeared with a grunt of surprise. There was a thud and a groan as he hit the deck. Gillespie picked up the fuel can and began to walk back, along the quay, towards the car. Suzanne followed him, limping, a yard behind. Beside Albie, Gillespie paused. The gun was inches from Albie's neck. He waved him forward, to the edge of the quay, and smiled, regretful, extending his arm, the lightest of pressure, but enough to send Albie toppling off the quayside, and down into the darkness. Suzanne heard the splash, and then the sound of Albie surfacing, spitting water, cursing this strange man, with his revolver, and his can of fuel, and his crooked smile.

'Gillespie,' he kept shouting, 'fucking Gillespie.'

Annie saw Ingle the moment he entered the ward, a big untidy man in a dirty brown pullover and a pair of baggy cords. He paused for a moment, looking down at the long row of empty beds, taking in the feel of the place, the smell of disinfectant and cheap tobacco, the drab greens and thin yellows of the paint work.

Annie watched him carefully. For a big man, he moved lightly, on the balls of his feet. He might have been an athlete, Annie thought, a runner or a footballer, years back, before the belly and the folds of flesh around his chin began to appear. He stopped at the foot of the bed, and looked at her speculatively, not bothering with the usual formalities, the minor detail of a name or a handshake, but bump-starting the conversation at once, as if he'd known her for years.

'We've got some photographs,' he said. 'It's a bit of a puzzle.'

Annie didn't answer. She'd had a full hour to work out her relationship to this place, what she was doing here, what rights she had, what kind of line to draw. She looked up at him, this big man at her bedside, saw that she needed some help of her own, the odd clue, and that he seemed the best place to start.

'Who are you?' she said.

'My name's Ingle.'

'And what's this place?'

'The nuthouse,' he said cheerfully, 'I'm afraid it's the best we could do.'

She looked at him a moment. The voice was slightly hoarse, the accent flat, East London, or maybe south of the river, Southwark or Rotherhithe, somewhere like that. She guessed he was Intelligence or Special Branch, had to be; yet he was the reverse of what she'd expected. He was close-in, candid. His whole manner invited instant intimacy. She should talk to this man. She should trust him.

Clever, she thought, pulling the sheet towards her. Ingle smiled, following her every step of the way, knowing exactly the conclusions she'd come to, knowing he'd been right all along, knowing it wouldn't be easy.

'Photos,' he said again.

She nodded. 'Photos,' she agreed, wondering exactly what he meant.

Ingle let the conversation lapse. The first set of prints from Gillespie's camera, the shots featuring Goodman and the girl on the bench, were now lying on his desk. They confirmed what Reese had already established, that Gillespie had been in the park with a camera. The detail of the shots, the framing, the choice of angle, had favoured the girl, and Ingle had already tucked away in his mind the possibility that Gillespie had been on some kind of job. He did, after all, work for a solicitor. Solicitors dealt in evidence. The photographs would be admissible in court. Perhaps a divorce case. Perhaps a tussle over a matrimonial settlement. But all that was minor detail. What was really important was Annie McPhee. How much did she know about the grainy black and white images on his desk? Why was she carrying the film in the first place? How well did she know

Gillespie? What, exactly, was the relationship between them? As soon as Reese got back in touch, he'd pull the man in, tackle it from both ends, but in the meantime this was all he had, a girl in an empty psychiatric ward, very canny, very smart.

The Special Branch file had impressed him. Her address book, photographed one lunchtime after she'd been lured away on a hoax call, read like a directory of the radical left. She had all the right contacts, all the right political connections, and her professional record suggested that she was determined to secure a far wider audience for all the twaddle about freedom of information and the workings of the Secret State. Here, in the city, she'd found herself in the dress circle, the one place in the country where the curtains had been truly parted. A command performance. Everything out front, down stage, perfectly lit, perfectly choreographed. She was sitting on the career opportunity of a lifetime. Problem was: did she know it?

Now, from the bed, she smiled at him.

'Done something wrong, have I? Taking snaps?'

He shook his head. 'No,' he said, 'oh, no.'

'Then why all this?'

She nodded round the ward. Ingle looked faintly apologetic, the accommodation not quite up to scratch.

'A precaution,' he said. 'In case you get into trouble.'

'Ah . . .' Annie nodded, duly grateful. 'Saving me from myself.'

'Something like that.'

'An act of charity?'

She smiled at him, and folded back the sheet, and began to get out of bed. The movement was a gesture, a declaration. She'd had enough. She was leaving. Ingle leaned forward and restrained her. His strength surprised her. Beneath the banter and bonhomie, there was no ambiguity about their private rules of engagement. She'd been ordered into bed. And there she'd stay. The big man leaned back and folded his arms.

'It's a lousy night,' he said briefly. 'You're better off where you are.'

She nodded.

'Tell me . . .' she said, 'am I under arrest?'

'No.'

'Just detained?'

'Yes.'

'For the duration?'

He nodded at her, speculatively.

'Depends . . .' he said.

'On what?'

'On how well we get on . . .' He paused. 'There's someone we ought to talk about.'

'Oh yes?'

Annie picked up a small thread of cotton from the sheet. The hems were falling apart. She looked up.

'And who would that be?'

Ingle grinned. A big, wide grin.

'Mate of yours,' he said. 'Bloke called Gillespie.'

Gillespie drove fast out of the dock, putting distance between himself and the chaos aboard the trawler. The fuel can lay on the back seat. The girl sat beside him. Her perfume got the better of the diesel, but only just.

He glanced sideways at her, her face shadowed by the passing street lights. She'd got her breath back now, but she was obviously shocked, her eyes fixed on the road ahead, one hand still massaging her knee. She was younger than he'd first suspected, photographing her in the park, 120 mm at 30 metres. Late twenties, he thought, maybe even younger. He swerved briefly to avoid a baulk of timber in the road. Her other hand reached forward, instinctively, for the dashboard.

The old Cortina settled down again. A car appeared in the road in front of them, driving fast, lights on full beam. The car flashed past, a big estate. Gillespie glimpsed kids' faces in the back, pressed up against the window, and wondered briefly where they were off to, what they were up to, on a road that led nowhere but the dock. He glanced at the girl again, Suzanne Wallace. 913 Ocean Towers.

'Those blokes back there,' he said, 'you know them?'

She shook her head.

'Only the older one,' she said, 'in the suit.'

'Harry Cartwright?'

She looked across at him. 'That's right,' she said, surprised.

'Accountant?'

'Yes.'

Gillespie nodded.

'Dodgy reputation,' he said.

'I wouldn't know.' She paused and fingered a tiny mole on her face. 'But yes, I expect so.'

Gillespie dropped the car down through the gear box, gliding to a halt in a tiny lay-by in the shadow of the city's cathedral. He turned off the engine and wound the window down. There was a rustle of wet leaves from the trees overhead. The darkness smelled of autumn. The girl had stiffened again, wooden, braced for the next shock, the next hideous twist in the story. Gillespie stared ahead, out through the greasy windscreen.

'The rest of them,' he said. 'The young bloke. And the one I put in the water.' He looked across. 'Rough trade, love. You should be careful, company like that.'

Suzanne nodded, a small token movement of her head. She was fast losing track of events. She wanted to go home. She wanted to be back in the flat, with the door locked, and Martin making cocoa in the kitchen, and the rest of it irrelevant, someone else's business. Gillespie hesitated for a moment before pushing the conversation on.

'So tell me,' he said at last, 'what were you doing there?'

She closed her eyes and took a deep breath, knowing there was no longer any point in avoiding the issue, in keeping anything back. She hadn't a clue who this man was, with his beaten-up old car and his gun and his precious can of fuel, but there was something about him that she trusted, a curious stillness, some kind of strange integrity. She cleared her throat, and told him about the plan to get the wives and families out of the city, about the existence of a list, officially approved, about her own role, finding a destination, a landfall at journey's end, and about her afternoon on the telephone at Cartwright's office. She ended by telling him about the call she'd overheard in the office, about the fax she'd so nearly intercepted, and about her suspicions that the official evacuation was merely a front for something else. Gillespie followed the story carefully, stage by stage, making mental notes, the way he did for Jenner, steady, methodical, listing the details in his mind. When she'd finished, he nodded, patting the thing into shape, committing it all to memory.

'So two lists . . .' he said. 'One official. And one . . .' he shrugged, 'freelance.'

'That's right.'

He smiled. It was very Harry Cartwright.

'Neat,' he said, 'clever.'

He glanced across at her. The obvious question.

'Your boyfriend know about this?'

She stared at him, eyes wide.

'What?' she said.

'Your boyfriend. Goodman,' Gillespie hesitated. 'He know about this?'

She paused, the breath gone from her body. How did he know about Martin? How did anyone? Their relationship? Their careful secrets? She swallowed hard, wondering whether to deny it, or to challenge the man, demanding an explanation. Gillespie, reading her mind, waved it all away, irrelevant.

'No games,' he said, 'just tell me.'

She shrugged, robbed even of indignation, her privacy so blatantly ignored.

'He organized it,' she said, 'if that's what you mean. The official part. But the rest . . .' she frowned, 'no, I'm sure he doesn't. In fact they wanted me to phone him. Tell him everything was OK. That's where we were going. Just now. Back there . . .' She lapsed into silence.

Gillespie glanced across at her. She was thinking of Goodman. It showed on her face.

'How well do you know him?' he said.

'Very well.'

'You trust him?'

She looked at him. Her eyes were beginning to moisten.

'Yes,' she said, 'completely.' She paused. 'They can't leave without his permission.' She added, 'He's the one in charge.'

'So I gather,' Gillespie said drily, reaching for the ignition keys.

She followed his movements, frightened again, thinking she'd gone too far, said too much, that they were going back to the dock. Gillespie put his hand briefly on her arm, reading her mind, one step ahead.

'Harry's place,' he said 'We need the fax.'

Nigel Quinn sat at his desk in the Bunker, looking at the fire axe. By the big clock on the wall, it was nearly eight. In an hour or so, after the Queen's and Goodman's broadcasts, they were due to rehearse the fire and contamination drills, break out the NBC suits, each member of the Bunker with a buddy, working as a team, checking that the wretched things fitted properly, checking the over-boots and thick rubber gloves, checking the seals around the tight-fitting rubber face masks, tidying each other into the bulky dark green suits that should – in theory – preserve them from gas or chemical attack.

It was a manoeuvre that most of them had practised on the two-day Civil Defence exercises and everybody hated it. The suits were hot. They made you sweat. They were claustrophobic. They sealed you into a world of your own, and cut you off from all the normal clues. You no longer knew who was who. You addressed people by the names on the ID tags they wore on their chests, and you took it on trust that the names were correct. Voices were barely audible, muffled by the thick rubber masks. Expressions were impossible to gauge, totally invisible. You no longer knew whether people were smiling, or frowning, or looking apprehensive. They were simply a pair of eyes in a mask, faces from a nightmare. It was like living underwater, and even for a man like Quinn, who viewed complaint as a form of moral weakness, the bloody things were hateful.

But that wasn't the point. The point was that the plan called for NBC suits. It was his job to administer the plan, to make sure that the system continued to function as effectively as it could, for as long as it could. And if that meant Noddy Suits and rubber gloves, and the sour taste of your own sweat, then so be it. Except that the keys were still missing. And that Goodman was still refusing to authorize the obvious alternative.

He studied the fire axe. The storeroom was double-locked, with a heavy metal door. It wouldn't be easy smashing it down, but it would have to be done. He pushed his chair back from the desk and began to get up. As he did so, the door to the Telex room opened, and Davidson stepped out. He'd already made it clear to both Quinn and Goodman that access to the Telex room was restricted to himself. Anything incoming for the city would be circulated at once. Anything else was strictly at his discretion.

Davidson hurried the length of the Bunker, a roll of telex paper in his hand. He knocked once on Goodman's door and went in. Through the thick glass panel, Quinn watched Goodman looking up from the paperwork on his desk, accepting the telex, scanning it quickly, glancing up at Davidson, some comment, some question, then reaching for the white internal telephone on his desk. Quinn's own phone began to trill, and it took him a second or two to associate the two events. He picked up the phone. It was Goodman.

'Nigel,' he said, 'a word.'

Quinn got up and hurried over to Goodman's office. Davidson was still standing by the desk. He was beginning to look grey with fatigue. Goodman glanced up and handed Quinn the telex. He read it quickly, then again. The telex quoted from a GCHQ intercept. The Russians were preparing to board the crippled submarine. The President was reported to have left Washington, by helicopter, for an undisclosed destination. SAC bombers were on two minutes' readiness to move. War was expected to break out before midnight. Quinn looked up, chilled.

'Well?' he said.

Goodman shrugged, helpless, thinking quite suddenly of Suzanne. He realized he missed her badly. He pushed the thought to the back of his mind.

'Go ahead,' he said. 'Use the fire axe.'

Suzanne led the way across the road to Harry Cartwright's offices. Gillespie had parked the Cortina under the shadows of the buildings opposite, lights off. They ran across the road. The door was still unlocked, wedged by the folded leaflet. Suzanne pulled it out. The door opened. She stepped in, switching on the light in the narrow hall, Gillespie behind her. He gazed round. The tasteful regency stripes. The framed prints of the city a hundred years back.

Suzanne was in the main office by now, standing over the fax machine, quickly checking the roll of paper, the dense lines of type, the names, the addresses. She looked up and he nodded.

'Take it,' he said.

She hesitated for a second or two, then tore off the list, and folded it quickly, before rejoining him by the door. They were back at the car in seconds, the engine coughing into life, the dim headlights disturbing yet another cat.

Gillespie glanced in the rear-view mirror. No sign, so far, of Cartwright. Or Mick. Or Albie. Nothing but the leaves, and the rain, and the windy darkness. He pulled the car into a tight U-turn, and set off, back towards the seafront. Suzanne ran a hand through her hair.

'Where next?' she said.

'Your place.'

'My place?' She glanced across at him. 'You want the address?'

He shook his head. 'No thanks,' he said.

She gazed at him, wanting an answer, information, some clue to this puzzle, this strange man beside her, the big hands on the wheel, his knowledge of her, culled from God knows where, for God knows what reason. Questions queued in her head. Why this? Why you? Why me? But she kept her peace, sat quietly, clutching the list from Cartwright's fax machine, saying nothing. There was something forbidding about this man, and she knew instinctively that it was best to let him make the running, take charge. She thought of Martin, in his Bunker, at his command post, trying to keep chaos at bay, trying to cope. She must phone him, she realized, she must tell him what was really happening.

Gillespie parked the Cortina outside Ocean Towers, and waited a moment longer before getting out. The roads were quite empty. He opened the door and motioned the girl out. They took the lift to the ninth floor, saying nothing. At the door of the flat, the girl fumbled for her keys, and opened it. They walked in. He closed the door behind him. The place was warm. Yards of fitted carpet. The smell of fresh flowers. He hesitated a moment. He could hear the ticking of the central heating, and fainter, miles away, the heavy thwack-thwack of one of the big Sea King helicopters. Suzanne had disappeared into a room at the end of the hall. She stood by the big picture window in the lounge, staring out at the darkness.

'Who are you,' she said. 'What's your name?'

'Gillespie,' he said.

He looked round, recognizing the framed photo of Goodman

on the television. He was leaning against a low wall, his jacket off, his sleeves rolled up, a wide smile on his face. There was water behind him, a riverbank, and the familiar buttresses of the Houses of Parliament. Westminster Bridge, Gillespie thought, a summer excursion, a stolen hour or two aboard one of the pleasure boats that cruised up and down the Thames. Suzanne turned round. She was still holding the list. She saw Gillespie, followed his eyeline.

'London,' she said, 'July. I expect you know all about that, too.'

Gillespie shook his head. 'No,' he said, not bothering to explain any further.

He wondered briefly what he'd find in the flat. Goodman's favourite aftershave in the bathroom. A couple of his old sweaters in the wardrobe. Keepsakes. Smells. Her tenuous grip on this busy life of his, some small comfort during the long hours when he was half a generation and a wife away. He glanced back at Suzanne. She'd shaken off one shoe, and she was rubbing her knee, not daring to take her eyes off Gillespie. She looked bewildered, frightened, utterly lost in it all. Poor bitch, he thought. Poor, bloody bitch.

He held out his hand. He wanted the fax. She gave it to him, without comment. He opened it. There was a brief greeting, a cheerful line and a half, someone who obviously knew Cartwright well. Then a list of names and addresses, a figure beside each. He glanced quickly through them, recognizing the odd name here and there, putting faces to the dense, smudged lines of type. The sums of money were large – one or two in six figures – and it wasn't immediately clear what role they played in the scheme the girl had outlined, but the fax closed with a brisk paragraph about mooring berths, and tide times, and there was no doubt whatsoever that the message directly related to the trawler they'd left at the quayside. '*Timothy Lee* also booked,' ran the final sentence, 'please inform overall length.'

Gillespie folded the fax again and put it in his pocket. He motioned the girl into the big armchair. Hand stitched cushions. The same pattern he'd noticed in the car.

'Sit down,' he said, 'take the weight off that knee.'

Suzanne did what she was told. Gillespie glanced at his watch.

Nearly half-past eight.

'What time are they due to load?' he asked. 'When do you expect passengers?'

She blinked. 'Ten o'clock,' she said, 'Martin said ten. He wanted them to sail before midnight.'

Gillespie nodded. 'Are you in touch with him?'

'I've got a number.'

He nodded, and held out his hand again.

'Give me your keys,' he said.

She frowned. 'Keys?'

'Car keys.'

'Why?'

'I need to borrow your car.'

She looked blank. 'You do?'

'Yes.'

'Oh.' She hesitated. 'Am I allowed to say no?'

Gillespie shrugged. 'Say what you like,' he said, 'I still need the keys.'

'Do I get the car back?'

He nodded. 'Of course, I'll be back for you later.'

'Why?'

'Because you shouldn't stay here.' He nodded at the door. 'Anyone comes looking for you, don't answer the door.'

He walked quickly across to the picture windows, and opened the sliding glass door that opened onto the balcony. Outside the wind whipped round the edges of the building, cold, from the sea. He glanced over the parapet. There was a clear drop to the concrete path below. He stepped back into the room again, glad of the warmth, and locked the door behind him. Suzanne watched his every movement, one leg tucked up beneath her.

'You've done this before,' she said drily. 'Are you some kind of policeman?'

Gillespie shook his head. 'No,' he said.

He bent quickly to her shoulder bag, tan leather with brass buckles. He'd seen her slip the keys inside the moment they'd entered the flat. He found them at the bottom of the bag. He took them out. Car keys and door keys. She watched him, quite helpless, quite resigned.

'That's robbery,' she said, 'I should phone someone.'

'Do,' he said. 'I'll be back later.'

'Why?' she said again.

He paused, half-way through the door.

'To get you out,' he said, 'before they get really nasty.'

He smiled at her for the first time, and she fought the temptation to smile back, a battle she lost. He had a nice smile.

'OK,' she said, 'whatever you say.'

He nodded, a brusque farewell, and left the flat. She heard him pull the door behind him, test it once or twice to make sure it was secure, then footsteps, quickly receding, down the concrete stairs. She sat quite still in the chair for a full minute, her face a mask, not looking right or left, scarcely daring to breathe. Then she shivered, a deep, involuntary spasm of movement, and reached for the phone. Martin, she thought. Please, please, Martin.

It took almost a quarter of an hour to smash the locks on the security store in the Bunker. Two men worked at it, Quinn with the fire axe, and Bob Spiller, the housing Chief, with a crowbar. Spiller claimed some working knowledge of demolition but even he had to admit that the job was far from easy. Finally, Quinn saw the gap widening between the door and the splintered jamb. One lock was already smashed, tumblers and springs scattered on the floor at his feet, and the other one was hanging on by a single screw. He raised the axe, and drove it down against the tongue of the lock. There was a harsh sound, metal against metal, and the thick lozenge of hardened steel sprang back. He put the axe down and pulled the door open. Faces turned towards him. In a confined space, the noise had been nearly unbearable, and in the last hour or two something had gone wrong with the air-conditioning, pushing the temperature into the seventies. Several of the heavier men were sweating, their faces gleaming under the harsh neon strip lights. Others had simply gone quiet, withdrawing into themselves, taking occasional sips of water from the clear plastic beakers, not looking at each other, not risking conversation.

Quinn stepped into the storeroom, and began tossing out the NBC suits, each in its clear polythene bag. Spiller stacked them in a pile, sorting them for size. They were working fast. Fiona,

Goodman's secretary, watched them from her desk across the room. She saw the urgency, the quick, impatient movements, the deep 'V' of sweat on the back of Quinn's shirt. And when Spiller glanced round suddenly, her phone beginning to trill, she saw something else in his face, and recognized it at once. It was fear. Everyone had seen Davidson hurrying through with the telex. And everyone knew what it probably meant.

She reached forward and lifted the phone. She placed the voice in seconds, from the dozen of other calls, discreet, personal, over the past year.

'Controller's line,' she said automatically, 'may I help you?'

'It's Suzanne.'

'I'm sorry?'

'Suzanne. Suzanne Wallace . . .' The voice paused. 'A friend of Martin's . . .'

Fiona hesitated a moment, catching Goodman's eye, semaphoring Suzanne's name, the usual code. The girl sounded frightened. Goodman shook his head and resumed a conversation with Davidson. Fiona bent once again to the phone.

'I'm afraid he's busy just at the moment,' she said. 'But I have a message for you.'

'Oh?'

'He says he wants you to be on the boat. He says he'll come down at ten to collect you.' She peered at the pad, making sure of her shorthand. 'Does that make any sense?'

There was total silence at the other end of the line. Fiona frowned, quite sure she'd got the message word perfect.

'Hello?' she said. 'Are you still there?'

The girl's voice came back again, very faint, barely audible.

'I need to talk to him,' she said. '*Please.*'

Fiona glanced up at Goodman again. He was watching her closely. He shook his head at once. Very firm. Very positive.

'I'm afraid not,' she said. 'He's in conference.'

'But . . . please . . .'

Fiona glanced up. Quinn stood by her desk. He had a handful of NBC suits. One was clearly for her. She blinked at it. She'd missed the Civil Defence course, and she'd never seen one before. It looked horrible. Dark green. Folded in the bag. Two big perspex eyes in the black rubber mask. It reminded her of

Hallowe'en. She swallowed hard.

'I'm sorry,' she said quickly, 'I have to go.'

She put the phone down and looked at Quinn again. He nodded at a small curtained area at the end of the room.

'Change in there,' he said briskly. 'If you're modest.'

Joanna stirred Marge's cocoa, and put it carefully on the floor beside her chair. Her neighbour had volunteered to babysit for another hour or so while Joanna went out. All the children were asleep, and she had a pile of old copies of *Vogue* to keep her company. Joanna promised she'd be back by ten at the latest. Just a silly errand, she said. A piece of business she should have seen to long ago.

She checked her make-up in the hall mirror, pulled her coat around her, and stepped out into the night. Before she got into the car, she felt in her pocket for Gillespie's card. It was still there. She read the address once more. Suzanne Wallace. 913 Ocean Towers. She hesitated a moment, wondering whether she really had the strength to go through with it. Then she realized, once again, that she had no choice. One way or another, the thing had to be done.

Ingle finally got the call from Reese at 8.32 p.m., a strange, old, gummy voice at the other end of the telephone. Ingle was sitting in his office, feet on the desk, reading a French novel about Oran. The last thing he expected was a call from Reese on the public telephone system.

'Where are you?' he said. 'What's happened to your radio?'

Reese explained as much as he knew, trailing Gillespie to the eastern edge of the city, watching his car bumping away into the darkness, beginning to follow, having second thoughts.

'I was jumped,' he said. 'Set up.'

'By?'

'Gillespie.'

'And?'

Reese skipped the rest of it, his face smashing down on the edge of the car roof, the blacks and the reds swirling together, the sheer speed and strength of the man, his efficiency, years of steady practice. He'd come to in pitch darkness, his car gone, his pass gone, his body holster empty, bits of his teeth in the wet grass. He'd half crawled, half limped the four hundred yards to a phone box, and even then he'd had trouble getting the hospital switchboard to accept a transfer charge call.

'Not your night,' Ingle commented tartly.

'No,' Reese agreed.

Ingle glanced at the big street map of the city his assistant had pinned up on the wall opposite. Green crosses tallied arrests to date. Gillespie's name had yet to join the list.

'Where does he live?' he said.

'Glengarry Road,' Reese muttered, 'number 20.'

Ingle made a note on the fly leaf of the novel.

'Thanks,' he said. 'Give us a ring later.'

Reese put the phone down without saying goodbye, and Ingle hesitated a moment before dialling another number. The number answered at once. Ingle smiled, fingering the address.

'Rambo?' he said, making the usual joke. 'Got a little job for you.'

The first of Cartwright's passengers arrived at the dock an hour and a half early, a prosperous estate agent with a Volvo, three kids, and a wife called Sarah-Jane. He parked the Volvo and gazed down at the rusty trawler. The boat stank. He looked round for signs of life. There was no one on the dock, only a light in the cabin aft and the low murmur of voices. He frowned, wondering what to do. His wife was still in the car, trying to persuade the youngest child to go to sleep. Fat chance, he thought, eyeing the mattresses jigsawed into the hold below. There had to be some mistake. Had to be.

In McNaught's cabin, aft, Cartwright stood beside the tiny basin, looking thoughtfully at the Channel chart still open on the table. McNaught sat in his armchair, glass in hand, a new bottle of Scotch on the floor at his feet. Mick was sprawled on the bunk. Albie dripped slowly onto a small square of threadbare rug. He'd done what he could with McNaught's one towel, but his clothes were soaking, and his hair was still wet.

'What about the dosh?' he said again.

Cartwright hesitated. He'd already spotted the lights of the Volvo up on the quayside. Soon there'd be more cars arriving, more hands to shake, more explanations to be made, the mattresses, the single working toilet, the smell, the times we live in.

'Dosh?' he said.

'Money.'

'Ah . . .' he nodded. 'A hundred pounds a berth.' He paused. 'Cash.'

Albie frowned. 'A *hundred*?' he said. He turned to Mick. 'You said thousands.'

'I did,' Mick admitted, 'you're right.'

'So what's all this then? A poxy ton?'

Harry looked at him with obvious distaste. The man with the Volvo had made it to the deck. Footsteps suggested he was picking his way aft.

'There may be more...' he said, 'under certain circumstances.'

'You're fucking right,' Albie said. 'How much more?'

'I don't know.'

Albie stepped towards him, a trail of drips across the cabin floor. Mick closed his eyes. He'd seen this happen before. It was never less than ugly.

'Albie . . .' he hissed, a man talking to his pet alsatian, impatience and caution in about equal measure. Albie hesitated, his head about six inches from Cartwright's face, measuring him up, all the frustration and contempt focused in one swift butt, the plain man's answer to all the fancy talk about profits and losses and tens of thousands of pounds. A shadow fell over the cabin. The Volvo owner. Nice new blazer. Crisp white shirt.

'Harry . . .' he said, beaming, 'I thought for one moment we were sailing on this shit heap.'

Cartwright extended a limp hand and gave him a watery smile.

'We are,' he said. He turned to Mick. 'This is Michael,' he added. 'He's in charge of accommodation.'

Suzanne Wallace sat alone in her flat, gazing at the wallpaper, trying not to think of anything in particular, trying to forget it all. The brief phone conversation with Martin's secretary had left her numbed. The message had been quite unambiguous. There'd been no room for mistakes, or misunderstandings. She was to go on the boat. She was to ship out, to head off into the darkness, down Channel, away from him. There'd been no apologies, no attempt to soften or explain it, just a curt message, passed on by a third party. Do as you're told. Pack your bags. Get out of my life.

She poured herself another drink, a double measure of gin from a bottle she hadn't touched since Christmas. She added orange juice from a carton on the floor but didn't bother with ice. The fridge was in the kitchen. Going to the kitchen felt like crossing the Atlantic. After the phone calls, and the business with the fax machine, and the encounters on the trawler, and Gillespie, her body had given up. She was exhausted. She sipped at the drink, her mind quite blank.

The front door bell rang about five minutes later. She stiffened at once, remembering Gillespie and his parting advice. Let nobody in. Nobody. She closed her eyes. The bell rang again. She swallowed hard and eyed the clock on the mantelpiece. Twenty to nine. In half an hour, she knew, Martin was due to broadcast. They'd said so on the radio. The Controller speaks, they'd said, at ten past nine tonight. Public Communiqué Number One. The broadcast, she assumed, had been pre-recorded. Maybe he'd come down to see her, to be with her when the thing went out. It was the kind of careful surprise he liked to spring, bringing home his trophies, her clever, clever man.

The door bell rang for a third time, and she got up, unsteady on her feet, but determined to be proved right. Martin. Her Martin. Back at the door. Without the key. Full of apology. Full or remorse. Full of love. She walked through to the hall, bare feet. She felt slightly woolly, but not at all afraid. She hesitated for a moment at the door, then peered through the tiny glass peephole. A woman stood outside. She was middle aged. She wore a tan raincoat, well cut. She had a scarf round her neck, red silk. Her face was quite expressionless. Suzanne closed her eyes for a moment, knowing at once who it was. The ring of the bell, much closer, made her jump. She opened her eyes and reached for the chain on the door. Better this, she thought, than Cartwright.

She opened the door. The woman in the tan coat looked at her coldly.

'My name's Joanna Goodman,' she said, 'I'm his wife.'

'I know,' said Suzanne.

The two women stood there for a moment, then Joanna

nodded beyond her, up the hall.

'May I come in?' she said briskly, 'this won't take very long.'

Suzanne nodded, holding the door open, standing to one side.

'Of course,' she said.

Joanna walked past her, up the hall. Her perfume reminded her of Martin. His suits. His cuffs. The collar of the big cashmere coat she must adjust for him, every morning, before he left for work. Little, wifely gestures, eighteen years in the making.

Confused again, unsure of her bearings, Suzanne closed the door. Joanna had already walked through to the big lounge. She seemed to know her way around. Perhaps they've talked about it, Suzanne thought, maybe they've discussed the lay-out of the place, the make of the carpets, the colour of the sheets. She shut her eyes and leaned briefly back against the wall. The gin was beginning to envelop her again, waves of it, lapping at her brain. She steadied herself and walked into the lounge. Joanna was standing by the window, staring out. She turned back into the room, loosening the scarf at her neck.

'Must be an interesting view,' she said, 'in daylight.'

Suzanne nodded. 'It is,' she said. 'Would you like a drink?'

Joanna glanced round, surprised at the invitation.

'Yes, please,' she said, 'I would.'

'Gin OK? Orange?'

'Fine.'

There was a silence. Suzanne bent to the drinks cabinet and felt for a glass, pouring a measure of gin while Joanna circled the room, hands deep in the pockets of her coat, inspecting this and that, touching nothing. Suzanne recognized what she was doing, taking charge, the older, wiser, woman. She stopped by the framed photo of her husband, the smile in the sunshine, Parliament behind. She picked it up, reflective. Suzanne heard herself talking, and listened wonderingly to her own voice, so sure of itself, so suddenly bold.

'I'm pregnant,' she said. 'Did he tell you that?'

Joanna glanced round. She tried to keep her voice as neutral as possible, total self-control, but the contempt was all too obvious.

'No,' she said, 'but I suppose I should have expected it.' She paused. 'He got the last one pregnant, too.' She put the photo down, carefully, and inspected a line of books on a shelf over the television. 'You'd be surprised,' she said, 'he's careless like that. Dirty shirts. Socks. Babies. . .' She shrugged, turning round again. 'Do you want to know the rest?'

Suzanne stared at her, holding out the drink. She felt dizzy. Joanna took the glass and sipped thoughtfully at the gin and orange. Suzanne sat down.

'Rest?' she said.

'Yes,' Joanna smiled, 'about the other one.'

There was a long silence. Suzanne began to reach down for her drink but then thought better of it. No amount of gin and orange could possibly halt this woman, her hideous lies. She shrugged.

'Say what you like,' she said, 'if it makes you feel better.'

Joanna nodded, accepting the invitation.

'Her name was Sheila. He had an affair with her. Years ago. He was passionately in love, of course. They meant the world to each other. It was . . .' she frowned, remembering her husband the day he confessed, tears on the sofa, the words he used, trying to justify it all, 'very warm . . . very tender . . . very real . . .' She smiled again. 'Sound familiar?'

Suzanne said nothing for a moment, fighting the urge to reach down for the heavy crystal glass, and throw it in the woman's face, bringing the whole charade to an end. Instead, she tried to keep up, tried to argue the conversation to a standstill.

'So why did you stay with him? If he put you through all that?'

'Because he was the father of my child.'

'And now? Me?'

'Because he's the father of my three children.' She paused. 'Our three children.' She glanced at the photo a moment. 'Does he ever talk about them at all? As a matter of interest? In between trips to London?'

Suzanne nodded. 'Oh yes,' she said. 'Yes, he does. We both do.'

'Do you?' Joanna looked at her. 'How sweet.'

'Yes, he's devoted to them. And he thinks there'll be no problem, you know, afterwards . . .'

'After what?'

'The divorce.'

Joanna checked a moment, a body blow, and for the first time Suzanne began to think there might, after all, be some hope, that she might have got it all wrong, the message from Fiona, the visit from this terrible woman. Maybe Martin really meant what he said. Maybe he did love her. Maybe. Suzanne picked up her glass, bolder.

'Tell me something,' she said. 'Do you still love him?'

Joanna nodded. 'Yes,' she said, 'I do. Funnily enough.'

'He thinks you don't.'

'Is that what he says?'

'Yes. He says you're cold.'

'Does he?' Joanna smiled, totally at ease again, totally in charge. 'He said that to the last one, too. Before she got pregnant, and he came crawling back.'

She put her glass carefully on the mantelpiece and started to button her coat. Suzanne gazed at her, beginning to question her sanity, her grasp on what she'd always mistaken for reality. Martin loved her. He'd told her so. A million ways. There was to be a divorce. A remarriage. And now, a baby. Yet here was this icy woman, this wife of his, contradicting it all, telling her lies about a previous affair, lies about a woman called Sheila, lies, lies, lies. She remembered the phone call again, Fiona, and she decided on one last test. Do or die, she thought, looking at Joanna. You or me.

'Enjoy the trip,' she said carefully.

'Trip?'

'The boat,' she said, 'the boat that's going tonight.'

'Ah . . .' Joanna nodded, 'you think we're leaving? Me? The kids? Leaving you to it? Is that what he told you?'

Suzanne stared at her, refusing her the satisfaction of an immediate answer, all hope gone.

'Yes,' she said at last, 'that's what he told me.'

Joanna looked at her for a long moment. She'd been thinking of the postcard all day, the big loopy characters, the teenage prose. It was a crazy thought, but she almost felt sorry for the girl. She'd signed herself Suzy. That's the word they probably used together. Fond. Close. The adolescence he'd never had.

'Suzy . . .' she said, 'my husband's a child. A creature of whim. Very charming. And very plausible. And quite inadequate. He's a very bright man. But he knows not what he does.' She smiled. 'Good luck,' she said, 'you'll need it. Both of you. Assuming we all survive.'

Suzanne nodded, her eyes drifting back to the photo on the television.

'Thank you,' she said, 'I'm sure we'll cope.'

Joanna smiled again.

'I meant you and the baby, dear. Goodbye. I'll find my own way out.'

She turned on her heel and left the room. Suzanne heard her footsteps down the hall, the turn of the latch, the door shutting softly behind her. She lay back in the chair, numbed again, quite dead, the hot tears falling down her face. Joanna's glass lay on the mantelpiece where she'd left it, barely touched.

Gillespie parked Suzanne's Golf two streets away from the photo shop. He pocketed the keys, and jogged along the pavement, towards the corner. The windows in the tiny bay-fronted houses were curtained against the world outside. From room after room came the opening bars of the National Anthem. The Queen, Gillespie thought. Nine o'clock.

The camera shop lay on the main road. He used the place a lot, and he knew the owner well. The shop was fully alarmed, a sophisticated system on which Gillespie himself had offered advice. The alarms were triggered by a combination of touch-pads and photoelectric cells, and Gillespie knew there was no way he could short-circuit them. The alarms were wired direct to the city's Central Police Station, but he also suspected that no squad car would arrive for at least five minutes. Ample time to lay hands on the gear he needed.

On the main road, Gillespie checked right before climbing the wall beside the camera shop. The road was quite empty. On the other side of the wall was a small yard. The back door of the shop was double bolted, and the ground floor windows were barred on the inside. Upstairs, was a rented flat. There was a light on in one of the rooms, the ceiling purpled with the glow from a TV set. The other window was dark, a kitchen perhaps, or a bedroom. A drainpipe ran up the wall. Gillespie shook it, testing how firmly it was bedded in the brickwork. He began to climb, one foot on either side of the pipe, body well out, taking the strain on his arms and thighs. At window level, on the first floor, he stepped sideways onto the narrow wooden sill, and reached in to release the catch. The window swung open. He stepped in, onto a draining board. He froze a moment, recognizing the smell of stale chip fat, and the steady drip of water in the sink.

Next door, he could hear the Queen counselling resolution and good neighbourliness. Sticking together, she was saying, was the best possible antidote to the fear and anxiety she was sure everyone was feeling. High technology, she said, has broken down the barriers between classes. The missile and the H-Bomb have turned us into a single nation, all equally vulnerable, all equally at risk. Gillespie smiled grimly, one foot on the draining board, one foot on the window-sill, remembering the list in his pocket, the names, the money, the men and women determined to buy their way out at all costs. Equality, bollocks, he thought. It's power, and money, and the same old network of favours. Just like always.

He levered himself slowly onto the floor, and padded across to the door. Outside, in the hall, he headed downstairs, away from the blare of the television. On the ground floor, there was a connecting door through to the shop. The door was locked, but it was old technology, wonderfully responsive to a Smith and Wesson .38. He drew the revolver, stood carefully to one side, and shot obliquely at the door. He fired twice. The sound of the shots was deafening. The hall stank of cordite. He pushed the door. The door opened.

Upstairs he heard a chair moving. Then footsteps in the hall overhead. A figure appeared at the top of the stairs. A man. Medium height. Less than eager. Gillespie stood at the foot of the stairs. Take charge, they'd always told him. Be firm. Call the shots from the start.

'Put the light on,' he said evenly, 'and don't be frightened.'

The man did what he was told. Gillespie let him see the gun. He motioned the man downstairs. The man was pale with fear. First the Queen, and her list of cheerless homilies. Now this.

'Go in there.' Gillespie waved him into the shop. The man did what he was told. He was about 45, with a cardigan and slippers. His mouth was smudged with chocolate. Gillespie followed him into the shop. In the flat above, Gillespie could hear the National Anthem again. The Queen must have finished. Gillespie pushed the door half-closed behind him with his foot. He spoke very quietly, but slowly, too, risking not the slightest ambiguity.

'Lie down on the floor . . .' he said, 'and don't move. Otherwise I'll shoot you.'

The man got to his knees and lay full length on the brown tiles. The light from the hall through the half-open door was enough. Gillespie circled the shop, as quickly as he could, choosing the equipment he needed. A Pentax camera body. A Vivitar zoom lens. He crossed to the big white fridge in the corner and opened it. Two rolls of the new 1000 ASA colour stock. He closed the fridge again and motioned the man to his feet. They walked into the hall, Gillespie behind, the gun steady in his right hand. Upstairs, from the television, he could hear a voice announcing a series of measures for the city. A curfew was to be imposed, effective immediately. Anyone on the streets after ten faced summary arrest. Shops would open tomorrow for one hour only. Demonstrations of any kind were banned. Looters risked being shot. Gillespie told the man to open the back door. The man did so. Gillespie pushed past him, still carrying the camera and the lens. The owner, he knew, would be down within an hour, summoned by the police.

'Tell Paul I owe him,' he said. 'Tell him not to worry.'

He stepped out into the dark, hearing the click of the door behind him, and the footsteps up the stairs as the man with the cardigan raced for the phone.

By half-past nine there were at least twenty cars drawn up at the quayside at the dock, Jaguars, and Mercedes, and a couple of the big new Audi estates. Husbands and wives ferried provisions to and fro, cardboard boxes full of heirlooms, favourite knick-knacks, oil paintings, family pets. Children stood in groups, clutching teddy bears and comics, not saying very much. Some of them were wearing pyjamas, or light tracksuits, dressed by mothers with visions of en suite cabins and cocktails with the Captain. The reality, an ancient over-loaded trawler with all the charm of a public lavatory, had come as a profound shock. One or two of the women had simply turned away, shaking their heads, and driven back home, telling their husbands it was a hideous con, totally unacceptable, but the majority – more than fifty individuals – had simply accepted it, just another twist to the nightmare that had so swiftly engulfed the city.

Many of the families, having lowered their possessions on board, had chosen to remain on the quayside until the very last minute, preferring the relative comfort of their cars to the chilly squalor of the fish hold. They sat in silence, windows up, engines on, the car heaters keeping the darkness and cold at bay. After listening to the Queen, and to Goodman on the radio, they knew they were lucky, the chosen few, and under these circumstances the *Timothy Lee* seemed no longer quite so bad. Indeed, the very state of the boat seemed to mirror the world they'd found themselves suddenly part of. Everything was crazy. Everything was upside down. Too bad the boat stank. Too bad it cost the earth. Needs must, they told each other. Grin and bear it.

Mick Rendall, who'd decided to have as good a war as possible, had detected this mood early on, and had made the most of it. When one mother reproached him about the state of the lavatory – no toilet seat, the floor thick with grease – he shook his head, and took the woman to one side.

'My grandad was at Dunkirk,' he told her, 'and he had to do it in the sand dunes.'

The woman nodded, none the wiser.

'Did he?' she said politely. 'How ghastly.'

And so it went on, the big cars arriving, pulling onto the dock, spilling out wives and children, joining the mêlée around the boat. Cartwright watched it all from the bridge, keeping track of the money, storing the bundles of notes in a biscuit tin McNaught had produced from the tiny galley. Some of the money, £30 a head, would go to McNaught himself, the agreed charter fee. The rest, he now decided, would go to Mick Rendall to be split with Albie. The latter had buried his reservations for the time being, and was doing what he could to impose some kind of order on the chaos around him, finding stowage space for the endless suitcases, allotting mattresses in the big hold, and keeping the stroppier kids quiet with handouts of chewing gum. The gum had come from Mick, who'd lifted a large supply from the Oriental cash and carry. He'd tried some himself, at first, but decided it didn't fit the nautical image and so Albie now had the lot. Mick sauntered towards him, hands in pockets, looking for the phrase that would finally bring a smile to Albie's face. A big Ford Granada had just arrived on the quayside above. Four kids and three adults. Mick tapped Albie on the shoulder. Nodded up to the car. Grinned.

'Seven hundred quid, mate,' he said. 'Think positive.'

The fire and contamination drills in the Bunker went better than Quinn had expected. At nine o'clock, all work stopped while the staff gathered round the three TV sets. The reception, for some reason, was appalling, but most of the sound got through, and by the end of Goodman's broadcast, the mood was sombre. The fire and contamination drills had ceased to be rehearsals, make-believe for the day when it might all come true. On the contrary, after the curt phrases about district Dressing Stations, and the wisdom of keeping a bath full of cold water, it was all too real.

It began with Quinn blowing a whistle. This was the signal to robe up, to shake the Noddy suits out of their plastic bags, the long baggy trousers with the Velcro fastenings, the anorak-like jacket with its drawstring hood. Quinn insisted on the buddy system, everyone working in pairs, checking each other for mistakes, uncovered areas where the poison gas, or the thin mist of air-dropped germs might penetrate. One moment's carelessness, he kept telling everyone, moving from group to group, one square inch of exposed flesh, and the whole exercise would be pointless.

After five minutes or so, everyone was suited up, standing in small groups, self-conscious and sheepish. The face masks, a separate operation, had yet to go on. People hated them. They were the ultimate state of readiness. In theory, said the text books, you could wear them comfortably for days. In practice, those who'd ever worn them knew different. Within an hour, you were claustrophobic to the point of panic. Within a day, you'd probably go mad.

Quinn blew the whistle again. Two short blasts. Goodman was buddied with Davidson. He'd never worn a Noddy suit before, but Davidson talked him through it, and he was pleasantly surprised at the trousers and jacket. They were hot, certainly, but by no means unbearable. The face mask, though, was very different. He'd had a horror of rubber masks since early adolescence. He'd nearly drowned one hot day off a beach in southern Crete snorkelling with a friend. His face mask had filled with water, and he'd been lucky to get to the surface before blacking out. As a direct consequence, he'd never touched one since.

Now, half a lifetime later, he looked at the object on the desk. Outside, in the Bunker, his staff were pulling the straps over the backs of their heads, unfolding the masks over their faces, keeping their hair from spoiling the air seal, taking their first exploratory breaths through the big round filter on the side. Davidson handed him the mask. He swallowed hard.

'What about my glasses?' he said. 'Can I still wear them?'

Davidson shook his head.

'Afraid not,' he said. 'Wrecks the air seal.'

'Then what do I do?'

Davidson paused, frowning, an oversight in the Master Plan.

'We normally have special glasses made,' he said. 'They fit in here. Like mine.'

He showed Goodman his own mask, the lenses held in place by a special clip across the rubber bridge between the perspex eyes. Goodman nodded.

'I have no special glasses,' he confirmed. 'So what shall I do?'

Davidson smiled, genuinely amused.

'You've got a choice,' he said. 'Blind or dead?'

Goodman looked at him for a moment, not even wanting to pick the mask up. The thing repelled him, the big empty eyes, a skull in the making. He glanced at his watch. In ten minutes or so, Evans would be driving him back down to the city, to call for Suzanne, and take her to the dock. He gazed up at Davidson, weighing up the choice, glad of the excuse.

'Dead,' he said, 'thanks all the same.'

Gillespie drove fast through the city towards the dock. He'd stopped briefly at a call-box, dialling his own number and waiting for the phone to be picked up. Sure enough, someone had answered. He'd heard a shallow breath or two.

'Annie?' he said, 'Annie?'

There'd been no answer. Just the silence, and then a ticking on the line, the tell-tale signature of the cheap equipment they were having to use, recording all calls. He'd put the phone down, his own house a prohibited zone, occupied territory, and got back in the car.

It had taken him a minute or two to break out the camera from its polystyrene mouldings, and fit the batteries, and load the film and the long zoom lens. Then he'd resumed his journey to the dock, using back roads, but knowing they'd be looking for the wrong car anyway, and that he was moderately safe.

He parked several streets from the dock, stepping lightly into the shadows, the camera in his hand. It was half-past nine. In half an hour, it would be curfew. But by that time, he'd be in place, a niche in the dock, a perfect view of Cartwright's scam, officially blessed, figures in the viewfinder, faces on film. One nation, he thought bitterly. One bloody nation.

Evans drove Goodman away from the Bunker, down the slip road, out towards the motorway. The guards in the sandbagged emplacements at the foot of the slip road saluted as they went through. Like Goodman, and like Evans, they too were wearing the bulky Noddy suits, the hoods thrown back, their faces clear.

As the big car settled on the motorway, a steady eighty-five, Goodman felt some of the tension begin to ease. Twice in the last three hours or so, he knew he'd come close to cracking up. It was an instinctive recognition, an almost physical awareness that his mind might soon split open, fracture, like an over-ripe fruit. In some ways, he suspected it might be a release. Deep inside, he almost welcomed the prospect.

Evans slowed for the roundabout, and Goodman eyed him in the mirror. He'd known the man for two days now, forty-eight busy hours, maximum stress, maximum demand. Circumstances like these were meant to bring men together, to bridge gaps, yet the quiet Marine was no less of a stranger now than when they'd first met, at the kerbside, with Davidson's careful introductions. Evans had rebuffed Goodman's attempts to open conversations, to start a dialogue. Instead, he'd remained sternly apart: cold, watchful, somehow disapproving. Goodman couldn't pin it down, couldn't cite a particular incident, an exchange of words that he could quote verbatim, but he knew the man had drawn his own conclusions, made his own judgements. Evans didn't like him. It was as simple as that.

Up ahead now, he could see the lights of Suzanne's flats. The next few minutes he knew would be difficult, perhaps even painful. But he was certain, at last, that it had to be done. He could no longer lead two lives. Otherwise he would go mad.

The car stopped. Evans glanced over his shoulder. They'd been here already today. He knew the drill.

'Fifteen minutes, sir?'

The question had the faintest edge of insolence. Or perhaps contempt. Goodman ignored it.

'Five,' he said briskly, getting out.

He took the lift to the ninth floor, fumbling inside the NBC suit for his keys. The material of the suit had already left a greasy black deposit on his hands, and he'd become aware of a faint smell, like charcoal. He let himself into the flat, and closed the door behind him. There was music coming from the lounge, a CD he'd given her in the early days, the Fauré *Requiem*. His step faltered for a moment. This was going to be worse than he'd anticipated. He shook his head, dismissing the thought, walking through to the big lounge.

Suzanne looked up, startled. She was sitting in the armchair by the picture window. The doors to the balcony were open. She'd obviously been outside. The room was cold. Goodman stood by the mantelpiece, looking round for the bags she should have packed.

'You're not ready,' he said.

She got up, unsteady, and then he saw the gin bottle beside the chair. It was nearly empty. She looked at him and laughed, a strange slow laugh.

'You look ridiculous,' she said, 'quite ridiculous.'

He began to walk towards her, but she turned away, keeping him at arm's length.

'No,' she said, 'oh, no . . .'

He frowned again, and looked at his watch.

'Darling, the boat leaves –'

'Darling?' She let the word hang in the air. 'Whose darling?'

Goodman hesitated. 'You've been drinking,' he said shortly. 'You're drunk.'

Suzanne nodded, a big extravagant nod.

'You're right,' she said.

'Why?'

'Because I've been listening to your wife. Poor bloody cow.'

Goodman stared at her. 'My wife?' he said. 'Jo? Here?'

Suzanne nodded again, coming closer. He could smell the gin on her breath.

'Yes, my love. Your wife. Your precious Jo-Jo. Here. In my flat. Telling me the odd home truth.' She paused, a terrible concentration in her eyes, measuring every word, utterly sober. 'Listen . . .' she said, 'I have no idea whether or not you ever fell in love with a woman called Sheila. And I don't even care any more whether you lied about putting your wife and kids on that bloody boat of yours. But just tell me one thing. One thing. Will you . . . ?' She was very close to him now, the accusation softening into a plea. 'Will you . . .?'

Goodman nodded, swallowing hard, losing touch, watching it all disappear, the whole thing.

'Yes,' he said, 'yes.'

She reached out and touched him lightly on the hand, his arm, this strange cloth, his face.

'Just tell whether one word . . .' she said, 'one sentence, one single thought, was ever bloody true.' She paused. 'Well?'

Goodman closed his eyes. He felt dizzy. He felt physically sick.

'Suzy . . .' he began.

'Yes?'

'Suzy . . .'

He started to cry. She watched him, cold, not helping, no comfort, no sanctuary, no place to hide.

'Suzy . . .' he said for the third time.

She turned away from him, walked to the window, gazed out through the open door. Then she came back. Her face had hardened. Her hands were flat across her belly. She was close to him again, inches away.

'You cowardly, callous bastard,' she said slowly, 'you've lied to me. And you've cheated. And you've taken what you want. And now you'd quite like it to end.' Her voice began to rise. 'But even now you can't tell me. Even now you haven't got the guts. Even now it's me who has to say it. Just like it's your poor bloody wife has to come to take you home.' She took him by the shoulders and began to shake him. 'Look at me, for Chrissakes. Do something honest in your life.' She paused. 'Can you do that small thing? Can you open your eyes? Dare you?' She stared at him. '*Well?*'

Goodman opened his eyes. There was something very strange there, remote, almost autistic, but she was too far gone to see it. She hit him twice, as hard as she could, across the face, her right hand. He felt the ring on her finger scoring his flesh. He lashed out, catching her high, across the temple, sending her crashing into the armchair. The armchair tipped over. She looked up at him, sprawled on the carpet.

'You bastard,' she said. 'You bastard.'

She got up and reached quickly for the heavy glass ashtray on the table. It caught him high on the forehead, cutting him badly. He wiped the blood from his face, and shook his head, grunting, a hideous, primitive noise from way, way down. He turned towards her, the room closing in on him, a narrow tunnel, directing him remorselessly onwards. She backed away, seeing the expression on his face, a stranger in green, knowing quite suddenly that this was life and death, that she'd gone too far.

'No,' she said softly, 'no.'

He closed with her, hands around her throat, her neck, and she tried to fight him off, kicking and biting and clawing at his face. He wrestled her backwards, towards the big plate-glass windows, towards the open door. She tried to wriggle free, to throw herself sideways, but it was hopeless, he was too strong, and they were out on the balcony, the music distant, shredded by the wind. She felt the chill on her body, the hands around her waist. She felt her whole body rise, her feet part company with the concrete, and she smelled the sea. She had time, a second perhaps, to whisper a name, to say goodbye, and then, quite suddenly, there was nothing.

Gillespie had been at the dock for nearly an hour and a half by the time the *Timothy Lee* sailed. He'd found a tiny recess behind one of the smaller warehouses, the perfect hide. There was a pile of sturdy wooden boxes that gave him the height he needed, and the angle of the two buildings cast a deep shadow. From a range of fifty metres, he could acquire all the detail he needed.

For an hour, he took shot after shot, men mostly, fathers, husbands, fat cats from the city's world of business, men who'd cashed in their assets and their influence to save their own skins. A lot of the faces he recognized, well-known figures in certain city circles. Others were less familiar. But each shot, he knew, told the same story. Bags. Chattels. Kids. Pets. All outward bound. Courtesy of their bank accounts. And blessed by the city's Controller. The same old story. What you're worth. And who you know. The scene disgusted him.

By eleven-thirty, the trawler was preparing to leave. A minibus had arrived, only minutes earlier, another thirty or so people, more faces, more shots, but these evacuees evidently qualified for another boat, moored alongside. The tide was too low for Gillespie to be sure, but what he could see of the hull and upperworks looked much smarter, some kind of motor yacht. The party from the minibus filed aboard, down a steep gangplank, each of the women carrying a suitcase, or a child, sometimes both. In this party, there were no men, and Gillespie remembered Suzanne telling him the original plan, a discreet evacuation, Bunker personnel only, strictly women and children. Gillespie took a handful of extra shots, beginning to understand. The one boat providing cover for the other. The official mercy mission disguising a multitude of other sins.

He glanced down at the camera. He had ten shots left. He looked at his watch. At this rate, the boats would soon be out on the harbour, pushing south towards the open sea. He'd risk one last shot from the top of the Round Tower at the harbour mouth, the conclusive evidence he might one day need. Then he'd be on his way. He stepped carefully off the boxes, hugging the shadows, reminded irresistibly of Belfast. A good night's work, he thought. The bastards well and truly slotted.

Goodman got out of the car and walked slowly across the gravel towards his front door. Evans watched him carefully from behind the wheel, watched him stumble and fall. He got quickly out of the car and ran across to help, but Goodman was already back on his feet, pushing him away. The wound on his forehead had begun to bleed again, and the scratch marks on his face looked livid in the light from the street lamps. He gazed at Evans, uncomprehending.

'I'm fine,' he said, 'fine.'

Evans helped him towards the door and rang the bell. He heard a door open inside, then footsteps down the hall. A shadow fell across the frosted glass. The door opened. He nodded at Mrs Goodman. They'd talked several times while he'd been waiting for her husband. She'd given him cups of tea. He'd given her a Marine beret for her son. They'd got a relationship of sorts. She stared at the figure beside him, her husband, the strange outfit, the face bloodied for the second time that day. Evans coughed apologetically. He could offer her no explanation, because there wasn't one. When he'd emerged from the flats, Goodman had said nothing, getting into the back of the car, telling Evans to drive him home. Evans had offered him a handkerchief, asked him what had happened, but he'd shaken his head, ignoring the question, slumped against the leather seat, holding his face, the blood showing black between his fingers. Now, Evans smiled at Joanna, trying to make light of it all.

'Been in the wars, ma'am,' he said, 'needs a bit of a wash.'

She looked at him, catching something in his voice, some tone she didn't quite understand, something jarring, something not quite right. Goodman blinked at her. Familiar wallpaper in the hall. Familiar smells. His wife. His house. He looked at Evans.

'Ten minutes,' he mumbled. 'Not five.'

Gillespie took only one shot from the Round Tower as the two boats nosed out through the harbour mouth. It was almost pitch black, no light at all, and the wind off the sea was too strong to risk a long exposure. Even 1000 ASA wouldn't penetrate that darkness.

He watched the boats leave, bow waves in the inky blackness, and then pulled his jacket around him, and retraced his steps down the Tower, unaware of the sudden activity in the darkness on the other side of the harbour, the footsteps running along the wooden jetty, the powerful inboards stirring into life, the hands on throttles, the heads already bent to radar screens. The first of the pursuit boats was already in the tidal stream by the time he was back on the ground.

Gillespie had parked the VW half a mile away, and now he was running fast, hugging the shadows, working the warmth back into his body. First call would be Ocean Towers, where he'd collect the girl. Then he'd pick up Sean and head for his own boat. By daybreak, with luck, they'd be riding at anchor, off the back of the island.

He got back to the car within minutes, stowing the camera on the floor, checking the roll of exposed film in his pocket. Then he drove back along the seafront, no lights, wary of the curfew. Ocean Towers was ahead of him, off to the left. He parked Suzanne's car under the trees, removed the camera, and ran across the road.

Upstairs, on the ninth floor, he found the right key first time, a big heavy Chubb, and let himself into her flat. He smelled the liquor at once, and smiled. He called her name, softly, not wanting to alarm her.

'Miss Wallace . . .'

There was no answer. He walked quickly through to the big lounge. One of the armchairs was overturned, and there was blood on the carpet. He put the camera down on a small occasional table, and picked up the empty glass. He sniffed it. Gin. He saw a heavy glass ashtray, upside down, on the carpet by the wall. He picked it up and examined it closely. There was blood, congealing on one lip. He looked around again. The room was cold. The door to the balcony was open, and the long velvet curtains were bellying in the wind. He drew his revolver and walked slowly out, checking left and right. The balcony was empty. He walked to the edge, and looked over. It took a second or two for his eyes to penetrate the darkness. Then he saw her. A bundle of rags on the concrete below. One leg splayed at an awkward angle. One hand outstretched. He felt the old, familiar chill of sudden death, and stepped inside the flat again, pulling the door shut behind him.

Quickly, he searched the other rooms. In the bedroom, under the pillow, he found a half-written letter. Big loopy script. *Darling, darling* . . . it began, *what can I say?* He read no further, sliding it back in the envelope, and replacing it under the pillow.

He returned to the lounge again, and picked up his camera.

Then he turned up the dimmer switch on the wall, adjusted the exposure ring, and took two shots of the room, exactly the way he'd found it, the armchair upturned, the ashtray on the carpet. Then he went to the balcony again, and hung over the edge, winding the zoom out, pulling the body towards him. Another shot.

Back inside the lounge, he shut the door, turned the key in the lock, readjusted the dimmer, and left. Outside, he followed the concrete path round the corner of the building.

Suzanne was lying on the path, face down. Her eyes were open, and there was blood on the concrete beside her ear. She looked startled, surprised, and strange, dark marks blotched her neck and shoulders. Her upper lip was split. He bent closer, smelling the alcohol again. Gin, he thought. He glanced up at the balcony. He had one shot left. He backed away, until he could frame the whole body, then pressed the shutter.

He rewound the film, and took it out of the camera. Then he stooped quickly to the flower bed. There were rose bushes in the thin soil. The roses looked black under the artificial light. He twisted a single rose off the stem, pricking his finger as he did so. Then he knelt by her body, and placed the rose gently on her cheek, close to the soft tender area beneath the ear. Her flesh was already cold, but except for a bruise around her temples, and those strange marks around her neck and throat, her face was barely touched. Poor cow, he thought again. Poor bloody cow.

Goodman was back in the Bunker by midnight. He'd let his wife wash him, sponging the blood from his forehead, drying him gently with a towel she'd warmed specially on the bathroom radiator. He'd refused to answer any of her questions, shaking his head, not wanting to listen, and when she'd suggested he stay, get a good night's rest, be fresh in the morning, he'd dismissed the suggestion with a gruff shake of the head. She'd helped him back to the door, disturbed and bewildered by what she'd seen, telling him to take care, to relax, to think of himself for a change. Come back soon, she'd said quietly, closing the front door, and hearing the big Rover crunching away across the gravel.

Now, back in the Bunker, Goodman sank into his chair behind the big desk and gazed at it. There was a note from the engineer about the air-conditioning. Evidently, it might soon fail completely. He shook his head and looked away. The gas mask was still there, sitting in the wire basket, malevolent as ever, the eyes uppermost. He reached for it, touched it, recoiled. Then he picked it up, and hung it dead centre over the waste-paper basket. He looked at it for a moment or two, his choice, his call. Then he let it go, plop, into the basket.

There was a polite cough behind him. He turned round very slowly in the chair, a movement of his whole body. Davidson was standing by the door. He looked almost apologetic, the intruder. He gestured at the latest roll of telex.

'There's a war on,' he said, 'if you're interested.'

Gillespie drove to Sandra's house from the flats on the seafront. En route, he saw no one. No cars. No shadows on the streets. He tried to rid his mind of the image of the dead girl, to tell himself it was none of his business, but he couldn't. At Sandra's, the lights were on behind the curtains in the front room. Sean heard Gillespie coming up the path and intercepted him in the hall. He nodded at the front room. The door was shut.

'She's in there,' he said, 'she's changed her mind. She wants to come.'

Gillespie frowned, surprised. The last conversation he'd had with his ex-wife had been far from amicable. He'd been a failure. He'd let her down. She had another life to lead. He stepped into the front room. Sandra was sitting in an armchair, reading a magazine. She looked up.

'I'm ready,' she said briefly, 'packed.'

Gillespie looked at her for a moment, wondering whether to ask why.

'OK,' he said instead, 'let's go.'

They drove away from the house in total silence. Sean didn't bother to ask about the new VW, and Gillespie didn't bother to explain. They all knew about the curfew. They all guessed the consequences of being caught.

At the eastern edge of the island, Gillespie turned north, bumping up the narrow dirt track that skirted the harbour. There was marshland on either side, tall banks of reeds, and he had to use dipped headlights to keep the car on track. Sean sat beside him, tense, body bent forward, trying to penetrate the darkness around them, trying to outguess whoever might be there, trying to give them all a better chance. In the back, Sandra was shivering even with her coat pulled around her. Gillespie watched her face in the mirror, dimly lit from the glare reflected back from the reeds. He was glad she'd decided to come. Their last conversation had depressed him more than he cared to admit.

A mile down the path, he slowed the car and then stopped. He switched off the engine, then the lights, winding down the window and listening carefully for a full half minute. Far away, he could hear the *chink-chink* of halyards against metal masts. Closer, the sigh of the wind in the reeds, and the mournful hoot of a night owl somewhere up ahead. He opened the door. A voice from the back. Sandra.

'Now what?' she said.

Gillespie hesitated.

'I need to take a look. Make sure the boat's OK.'

Sandra laughed, a short mirthless grunt of laughter.

'So what do we do?'

'Wait here. I'll be gone about half an hour.'

'Half an *hour*. Jesus Christ, Dave . . .'

He glanced back at her, and reached out, patting her on the cheek, encouragement. She muttered something incomprehensible, and curled herself even more tightly into the corner of the seat. Gillespie stepped round to the back of the car, and opened the boot. The can of diesel was still there, transferred from the Cortina. He took it out. He began to walk away, following the line of the dirt track, then he paused. Back, beside the car, he opened the front passenger door.

'Here,' he said to Sean, 'look after these. Keep them safe. And your mum, too.'

He gave the boy the rolls of exposed film from the dock, and patted him on the shoulder. Then he set off down the path again, into the darkness.

Ten minutes later, he was out of the reeds, and into the marshland at the water's edge. He could hear the lap of the rising tide against the mudbanks, taste the salt in the air.

He picked his way carefully through the tussock, trying to keep his feet dry. By now, he could make out the shape of his boat, still tied up beside the remains of the tiny landing stage. It was about fifty metres away, the sturdy, familiar swell of the hull, the small cuddy forward. He paused for a moment, getting his bearings, tracing the line of the channel, out into the harbour, out towards the open sea. For once in his life, he regretted not having a sail. The diesel would be noisy, attracting attention. Sail would be better. Or even a canoe. He smiled to himself, thinking of Sandra. Fifteen miles in a canoe. The final straw.

He began to move again, hauling the heavy can through the grass, hearing the slosh of diesel inside. He stumbled for a moment, and nearly fell, and as he did so he saw the first lick of flame curling up from the boat ahead, and then the fireball taking shape, climbing and swelling, and the huge roar of the explosion, the heat gusting and bubbling in his face, timber everywhere, falling around him, splintered wood. There were more lights suddenly, and voices, sharp barks of command. He stood quite still, pinioned by the lights. Part of him wanted to run, to give battle, anything. But he knew it was hopeless. He knew they'd shoot him dead.

A shape appeared from the darkness. A big man. Long hair. Flat face. Civvies. He held out his hand.

'Gillespie . . .' he said, 'our pleasure . . .'

Nine

It was ten minutes past midnight, GMT, when the squadron took off. Two of the Jaguars were unserviceable – a bird strike on one aircraft, and an avionics problem with the other – but the remaining nine eased off the runway at Bruggen, roared low over the guarded perimeter fence, and wheeled east at five hundred feet on yet another of the cat-and-mouse low-level runs along the line of the reconstituted Inner German Border.

Craddock was flying number two in the second flight of aircraft, and the concentration required was enormous. One eye for the head-up display, key items of data projected onto the windscreen, soft yellow lines against the black of the night, ordering the jet up or down in response to the folds of the landscape; another eye for the presence of the nearby lead aircraft, a shadow slightly thicker than the night, a spreading cone of turbulent air, felt rather than seen; and yet a third eye, somewhere deep in the very middle of his head, for what the Squadron Leader sometimes referred to as 'the overall', the bigger picture, where they were in relation to Bruggen, and other NATO airfields, and to hostile airspace the other side of the IGB. The latter extended east towards Magdeburg and Berlin, screened by radar, picketed by dense fields of SAM-7s, and patrolled by the hawklike MiG-29s Craddock had admired only the previous year. Farnborough. A glorious afternoon in September. His wife beside him on the roof of the car. Ice creams and laughter. Fizzy drinks, and world-class aerobatics, and his baby daughter learning for the first time to put her hands over her ears.

The Squadron Leader broke radio silence, the simplest of orders, his voice quiet, almost conversational.

'Break right,' he said, 'one-one-five.'

Craddock pulled his aircraft into a tight right-hand turn, increasing power as he did so, preserving his precious height, feeling the bladders on the G-suit tighten around his arms and legs. He watched the compass spinning in front of him, the plane taking up the new heading, one-one-five, a little south of due east. He remembered the chinagraphed attack lines on the big map in the briefing room, the lines that snaked out towards the IGB, weaving a carefully plotted path through the weaker points in the radar net, looking for the gate that would creak open in the night, and let them into the East, the enemy's pantry, amply stocked with big fat targets.

The Squadron Leader again.

'Zero-eight-five magnetic. In five . . . four . . . three . . .'

Craddock frowned. They were adjusting north, conforming exactly with the Attack Plan. He fingered the throttles, down in the left of the cockpit, his thin, leather gloves waiting for 'Zero', the Squadron Leader's cue, another step towards the unthinkable.

'Zero.'

Craddock eased the aircraft left. In forty seconds' time, according to the Doomsday brief, they'd route south again, a 34° turn that would put them on track for the tank parks north of Brandenburg, the squadron bellying out at one hundred feet, racing across the gentle foothills of the Harz Mountains, the screening F-16s up above, shadowing their every move, waiting to pick off the first of the big Fulcrums, blasting out of the forward airfields, eager to flame them.

Craddock tried to control his breathing, knowing that barely twenty seconds now stood between the squadron and that critical line on the map, thick red chinagraph, beyond which the exercises would be over. Normally, here, the Squadron Leader would wheel the aircraft in a tight 180° degree turn, pulling them back with barely kilometres to spare.

Ten seconds. Craddock swallowed hard. The bomb release levers were down on the right-hand side. The tank parks were nine minutes' flying time east of the border. Nine minutes at 95 per cent power. Nine minutes at one hundred feet. Nine minutes before he pulled the Jaguar into a steep climb, lobbing the two freefall bombs the last few kilometres to the target. The bombs were groundburst, deep penetration. A five-G turn and full afterburner would give him the fifteen precious miles he'd need to survive the fireball.

Craddock blinked. He was sweating. He could no longer sense the lead aircraft ahead. His compass was a blur. His left hand came up to his mask, adjusting the tight rubber mouthpiece. He needed air. He must breathe properly. Something horrible was happening to him.

There was a crackle of static, then the Squadron Leader's voice in his ear, indistinct. Craddock began to thumb the switch on his joy stick, the switch that opened communications. He needed clarification, he wanted a repeat, but then his brain caught up with his hands, and he told himself there was no argument, no way back.

'One-two-seven,' the Squadron Leader had said, 'one-two-seven.'

Craddock banked east, suddenly cool, the tension quite gone. End game, he thought curiously. What a shame.

Martin Goodman sat alone at his desk in the Bunker. By the clock on the wall it was 12.57. Through the thick plate-glass window, he could see the long line of desks, the figures bent over telephones and maps, shrouded in the thick green NBC suits. Someone, for reasons he couldn't possibly understand, was already wearing a face mask. It looked grotesque, a cartoon figure in three dimensions, and he had to guess an identity by working out who he couldn't see, who wasn't there. It was a game, and he played it with a mild curiosity born of total exhaustion. The last three hours had stretched him to breaking point and beyond. He had total recall. He knew exactly what had happened, what he'd done, cause and effect, that long remorseless chain of events that had ended so abruptly up there, out there, on her balcony.

He knew she must be dead, but he knew as well that it had been inevitable. He'd loved her like he'd never loved anyone in his life, but the fairy-tale had come to an end, and they'd collided head on with real life, and gravity, and cold concrete. Once or twice in the last hour he'd fought the temptation to try and imagine what it must have been like. What would she have been thinking? Those last thirty feet? That last split second? Would her face be intact? Her smile? Would she forgive him? Did she still love him? Would she ever understand?

The questions lodged in his brain, birds in a tree, ceaseless chatter, the babble of madness. His face hurt from the deep scratches she'd gouged in his cheek. His forehead had swollen around the gash from the ashtray, and his head throbbed inside, a dull, metronomic, empty pain. His wife had given him some balls of cotton wool, and a small bottle of TCP, and he dabbed at his forehead from time to time, looking curiously at his own blood on the damp cotton wool. There was more blood on the thick green fabric of the NBC suit, dark blobs of the stuff, already dry. His blood. Her blood. Their blood. He looked at it, fascinated.

Ironic, he thought. After all the letters, the phone calls, the times they'd shared, the memories they'd warmed with trinkets and keepsakes, the plans and the promises they'd made. Ironic that his last souvenir should be this: half a dozen balls of damp cotton wool, pinked with blood, smelling faintly of the bathroom cabinet. He poked one of the balls with his finger. It rolled across the desk. He blew on them, budding his mouth. They lifted in the current of air, drifting slowly towards the edge of the desk. One of them fell on the floor. He didn't bother to pick it up.

A door opened at the other end of the Bunker, and Davidson emerged from the telex room. There was yet another sheet of paper in his hand, more dispatches, but he moved slowly now, the urgency quite gone, threading his way past the desks, a smile here, a nod there. Quinn looked up at him, some unvoiced question, but he simply shook his head and passed on, a wholly neutral gesture, devoid of meaning.

Goodman heard his footsteps outside, watched the door open as he came in. In the space of an hour, the man seemed to have aged. His skin looked grey, the eyes dead, the movements leaden. He sat down without an invitation, and let the telex fall on the desk beside him. There was total silence between the two men. Goodman eyed the telex. He had little interest in the contents. He reached forward and rearranged the desk slightly, making better sense of the big bare spaces around his blotter. Then he looked out of the window, down the length of the Bunker. The figure in the gas mask still confounded him. Same instinct. Same passion for neatness and uniformity.

'Who's that?' he said.

Davidson followed his pointing finger.

'One of the secretaries.'

'Why's she wearing that thing?'

Davidson smiled wanly. 'She's crying,' he said, 'and she doesn't want anyone to know.'

Goodman nodded, the answer suddenly self-evident. The Bunker was a public place. It left you nowhere to hide. Tears were contagious. They might spread, cause undue alarm, even panic. Better, therefore, to contain them. He frowned, spotting the flaw in the argument.

'How do you know she's crying?' he said. 'How can you tell?'

Davidson said nothing for a moment or two, gazing out at the girl behind the desk. Then he looked at Goodman.

'You can hear her,' he said quietly, 'the length of the room.'

Goodman nodded again.

'Funny . . .' he said, 'you think they'd do some kind of psychological test. Make sure people can cope.'

Davidson eyed the balls of cotton wool on the desk, and the bottle of TCP, open beside them.

'Yes,' he said.

'Is there such a thing?'

'No.'

'Then perhaps there should be.'

Goodman reached forward, uninvited, and unrolled the latest telex. Davidson watched him. The bulk of Goodman's paperwork he'd already re-routed to Quinn. Since midnight the policeman had been Deputy Controller, his workload more than doubled. Soon, should the need arise, he'd take over from Goodman completely. Quinn had accepted the extra responsibility without comment. He'd never trusted Goodman, never liked him, and as events unrolled, he'd taken a dour satisfaction in the way the younger man was beginning to fold up under pressure. Some of this antagonism, Davidson was careful to discount. He recognized that the two men were very different. But the last couple of hours, he'd watched Goodman retreat almost entirely into a world of his own making, and when Evans had finally got through to him on the special 101 number, he knew that something had to be done.

Evans had apologized for making the call. He simply wanted to tell Davidson that his Controller was gone, a spent round. Davidson had pressed him for details – why the blood? The injuries on his face? – but the Marine had said no more. The circumstances were nobody else's business, his silence implied. Only the conclusion mattered. 'He's completely out of it,' he'd said, 'completely shot. You want to get rid of him.' Davidson had thanked him for his time and his information, courteous to a fault, and the Marine had put the phone down with a grunt.

Now, Davidson watched Goodman pick up the Telex, a perfunctory movement, chance curiousity. He scanned the three paragraphs of text. The telex was barely thirty minutes old. It featured a report from NATO HQ that an RAF Jaguar had been posted missing on a night sortie over the IGB. The plane had evidently strayed into Soviet airspace. MiG-29s had been scrambled from three airbases around Magdeburg. Radar Controllers aboard one of the big Boeing AWACS had reported an interception twenty-five kilometres east of Salzgitter. They'd watched the tell-tale smears of the air-to-air missiles. The Jaguar had disappeared from the radar screens seconds later. The rest of the squadron were safely back at Bruggen.

Goodman folded the telex and replaced it carefully on his desk.

'And?' he said.

Davidson looked at him, weighing up the exact limits of his remaining responsibilities to Goodman. In a sense, it was academic. Evans was right. The man was gone. Davidson picked up the telex and put it in his inside pocket.

'A-Taff are calling it a mistake,' he said.

'A-Taff?'

'Allied Tactical Air Force. In theory . . .' he smiled tiredly, 'they control the Jaguars.'

Goodman frowned. 'But why are they apologizing,' he said, 'if this plane of ours simply got lost?'

'It didn't.'

'No?'

Davidson shook his head. 'No,' he said, 'the Jaguar was on the way home. He'd done his job. Paid his visit . . .' He hesitated . . . 'there's a supplementary to the telex.'

'There is?'

Davidson nodded. 'Yes,' he said. 'Our RAF friend bombed a tank park near Brandenburg. The Russians are very upset.'

He paused. 'And under the circumstances, I don't blame them.'

'You don't?'

'No.' Davidson looked out, down the length of the Bunker. 'He was carrying two bombs,' he said bleakly. 'One of them was nuclear. Modest yield. But hardly the friendliest of gestures.'

He glanced at his watch and stooped quickly to the waste-paper bin, retrieving Goodman's gas mask which still lay on a litter of discarded paperwork. He put it carefully on the desk, dead centre, the perspex eyes uppermost.

'The shooting's started,' he said. 'You may need to set us all an example.'

He smiled briefly and left the office. As he opened the door, Goodman heard the noise for the first time, curiously faint, intermittent, an animal grief, muted by two millimetres of rubber and the Mark III charcoal filter. He looked out, through the plate glass, down at the scene below. The secretary had given up with the typewriter. She was sitting very still, her head in her hands, waiting.

A memo, Goodman thought. He reached for his notepad, wondering again why nobody had thought about psychological testing.

Gillespie lay on his back on the mattress, staring at the ceiling. The room was small, two iron beds, and a bare deal table beside each. The single window was barred, and the door was locked, and through the wire meshed window he could see the shadow of the guard outside in the corridor. Every time he moved, the plastic undersheet on the mattress crackled. The sound annoyed him. It was a nursery sound. It suggested infancy, helplessness. They think I'm going to piss myself, he thought grimly. They think I'm here for the taking.

He glanced at his watch. It was nearly two in the morning. From the remains of his boat, they'd taken him back to the dirt track, a different path, quicker. No one had said anything, no warnings, no drama, no questions, no explanations, just the tacit understanding that he knew the score, that he'd make no waves. There'd been a squaddie up ahead, full combat gear, SA80s, and a couple more behind. They'd moved fast through the tussock, leaving behind them the rich smell of charring timber and blistered paint, the hiss of salt water on the red hot embers. At the dirt track, he'd been bundled into the back of a Land-Rover, people who knew what they were doing, nothing unnecessary, nothing flash, and driven away. As they bumped back towards the main road, the engine whining in the low gears, he'd looked at the men opposite, flak jackets and combat helmets, silhouettes against the reflected glare of the headlights on the tall stands of reeds. The smell of it was hopelessly familiar – wet kit, and sweat, and rifle oil, and that special tang of mud on a hot exhaust pipe – and he knew all too well that it would be hopeless asking these men why and how and what next? For one thing, they'd never tell him. For another, they probably didn't know.

Back on tarmac, they'd driven at speed across the city, using the empty main roads, turning in through the gates of the big psychiatric hospital. He recognized the place at once. They'd taken him to one of the more remote villas, out near the perimeter wall. They'd marched him down the long bare corridor. And they'd bolted the door behind him.

Now, he stirred again, thinking of Sandra, of Sean. They'd have seen the fireball, heard the explosion, drawn their own conclusions. Sandra would have slid behind the wheel, resigned and capable, the usual mix. By now, they'd be back at home, Sandra probably asleep, Sean probably worrying at it all, this boy of his who always tested the strength of the current, the lie of the bait, the precise set of the tide. He'd want to know what had happened, where his dad was, and one day – please God – Gillespie would tell him.

He closed his eyes, flirting with sleep. Some time later, perhaps an hour, perhaps more, there were footsteps outside in the corridor. The footsteps paused. A female voice, gruff. Gillespie got up on one elbow, eyes suddenly open, blinking in the harsh overhead light. The door opened. Sean walked in. He was still wearing his jeans and anorak. He looked as if he'd just stepped out of the VW. He looked confused, wary, scared. He saw Gillespie. He smiled, fighting the urge to run across the room, making a fool of himself, being a child. Gillespie solved the problem for him, getting up off the bed, crossing the room, putting his arms around the boy, quite oblivious of the woman in the corridor and the men in the blue serge uniforms nodding good-night, pulling the door behind them.

'Son . . .' he said, 'you OK?'

The boy nodded, gulping back the tears.

'Yeah,' he said, 'yeah.'

'What did they do to you?'

'Nothing.' He shook his head, emphatic. 'Nothing.'

'You sure?'

'Yeah,' he nodded, same message. 'Promise.'

Gillespie gazed at him, arm's length, then hugged him. It was something he hadn't done for years, and they both knew it. Gillespie led him across the room, back towards the bed. They sat down, same bed, side by side.

'What happened?' Gillespie said. 'Where's your mum?'

'I dunno. Here somewhere.'

'She come back with you?'

'Yeah,' he nodded again, back with his dad, a feeling even better than freedom, 'they got us both.'

Gillespie listened while the story spilled out: the pair of them sitting in the freezing car, the noises all around them, Sandra fretful, nervous, waiting, she'd said, for the inevitable. Then abruptly, the shadows emerging from the darkness, wrenching open the door, motioning them out, gunpoint, the real thing. Sandra, Sean said, had given them a real earful, and Gillespie smiled, imagining the harsh Belfast brogue, the torrent of abuse, a half-forgotten reflex triggered by the uniforms, and the cam cream, and the infant fingers on the triggers.

Afterwards, with some respect, they'd been taken to a waiting car. The last he'd seen of his mother had been an hour or so back, outside the villa, she going one way, he another. Gillespie nodded, proud of her, proud of them both. Fuck the Russians, he thought. Fuck the world. He'd had it right first time round. Deep green eyes, and a wide, wide smile, and the best pair of legs he'd ever seen. Endless bottle, and a wicked sense of humour, and limitless patience with any other member of the human race. And the boy, too. Frightened out of his skull, totally stuffed, yet here, in one piece, beside him. He patted him on the leg.

'It's OK,' he said, 'OK.'

Sean looked up at him, smiling, lost for words, then Gillespie frowned, struck by a sudden thought.

'When did they get you?' he asked. 'When did all this happen?'

Sean looked startled, the wariness back in his face.

'Tonight,' he said, 'I just told you.'

'But when? Exactly? How long after I went?'

The boy hesitated. He was confused now, not sure of himself.

'After the explosion,' he said, 'ten minutes after. Maybe more.'

'So why didn't you go?'

'I wanted to. I said we should.'

'And Mum?'

'She said we should stay. In case you came back.'

'Yeah?'

Gillespie smiled, genuinely touched. Lying there, in the small barred room, he'd wondered how they'd found the boat, who'd told them. Sean had been one possibility. Maybe they'd come across the car first. Maybe they'd asked questions, made threats, torn the truth from him at gunpoint, hard-faced men on a very dark night. But here was Sean, telling him the way it was, the way it had been, giving his own squalid fantasies the lie. The boy was watching him carefully now, following the questions upstream, to their source.

'You think I told them?' he said. 'You think it was me?'

Gillespie shrugged, the old response.

'I didn't know,' he said.

The boy shook his head, emphatic again.

'No,' he said, 'I didn't. And I wouldn't.'

Gillespie nodded.

'They talk to you at all? Ask you any questions?'

'Yeah. A bit. Yeah.'

'About me?'

'Yeah.'

'And?' Sean looked at him a moment, not answering. 'Well?'

The boy shook his head again. 'No,' he said, 'I didn't tell them anything.'

He began to smile, a smile that spread wider, into a grin. Gillespie watched him, amused, relieved, the questions posed and answered, the weight off his mind. The boy had something else to say, a surprise, a bonus.

'Well?' Gillespie said again.

Sean looked pleased with himself, savouring the bond between them, old mates, comrades in arms.

'You know those rolls of film you gave me? Before you went?'

Gillespie frowned, dangerously slow on the uptake.

'Yeah . . . ?

'Well . . .' the boy bent forward, conspiratorial, 'I hid them in the car. I stuffed them down the side, under the —'

Gillespie cupped the rest of the sentence in his open hand, sealing the boy's mouth. Sean's eyes widened. Gillespie nodded up at the ceiling, the walls, signalling microphones, hidden ears, the whirr of a distant tape recorder. Sean caught on only slowly, resenting the hand over his mouth, thinking that – after all – he'd done rather well. Finally, he understood.

'Sorry, Dad,' he said quietly, 'sorry.'

Four rooms away a figure leaned back from the table and reached for the phone. The spools on the big Revox were still turning, seven and a half inches per second. The boy was fainter at the end than he'd have liked, the voice abruptly masked, but the drift of the conversation was very clear. Somewhere, in the abandoned VW, there were yet more rolls of film. The number answered. The man at the table lowered the volume on the tape recorder. Gillespie and his boy were just whispering now, silly talk, father and son, low grade stuff. He bent to the phone.

'Mr Ingle?' he said, 'a word . . .'

The *Timothy Lee* docked again at three-thirty in the morning, same slack oily water, same pitted iron ladder inset into the damp stones, same loop of heavy rope around the bollard on the quayside above. The passengers disembarked at gunpoint, the harbour master's men in makeshift uniforms under the arc-lights, the passengers lined up like refugees, family by family, no explanations, the few protests met with a grunt or a shake of the head. Last off the boat were Mick and Albie. They joined the other passengers, Mick embarrassed, Albie sullen, ignoring the whispered questions, the incipient outrage, a service paid for and manifestly not delivered.

The harbour master's men had found McNaught in the engine

room. He was blind drunk, barely capable of coherent speech, but he knew enough about human nature to recognize that these quiet men in their ribbed blue sweaters meant what they said about giving the money back, and when the conversation had turned to the real possibility of physical violence, he'd nodded quickly at the dark recess behind the gear box, watching them toss aside the heap of oily rags, exposing the biscuit tin behind.

Now, they redistributed the money on the quayside under the harbour master's careful gaze, £300 here, £700 there, big handfuls of high denomination notes, tens and twenties and fifties. At the end of it all, four in the morning, the families returned to their cars, reloaded their children and their dogs and their cardboard boxes, and drove away into the darkness, the party over. The last car gone, the dock deserted, the harbour master's men wiped their hands, and clambered back aboard their power boats, and burbled off into the first thin light of dawn, accounts settled, justice done.

Mick and Albie watched them go. Mick's head was beginning to throb, a combination of Stella Artois and Gillespie's well-aimed kick. Given a choice, he'd have settled for a hot bath and bed. Albie, though, had other ideas.

'That's robbery,' he said. 'Blind fucking robbery.'

Mick looked resigned.

'What is?' he said.

'What they just done.' He nodded down at the dock.

Bubbles in the oily water. The receding whine of the big two strokes in the chilly half light. Mick shook his head.

'Tough,' he said, 'win some . . .'

He shrugged. Albie looked at him.

'Win some?' he said. '*Win some?* You know what happened tonight? You know who screwed us?'

Mick shook his head, weary beyond belief. First the end of the world. Now this.

'Tell me,' he said, 'go on, surprise me.'

'Too fucking right, mate,' Albie said, 'your little friend. That's who. Bloody Cartwright. That's who. Off and away. Clean as a whistle. Wham . . .'

In lieu of anything else, Albie kicked the bollard, hands deep in the pockets of his bomber jacket, genuine outrage. Mick eyed the trawler, back beside the quay, higher now, the tide rising.

'Yeah . . .' he said, remembering Cartwright's flash motor yacht disappearing into the darkness as Albie pushed McNaught off the wheel, gunning the tired old diesels, doing his best to outrun the cone of light from the surrounding launches. They'd come from nowhere, no warning, no clues, and minutes later, when Albie had hit the sandbank on the seaward side of the dredged channel, the harbour master's launches had been alongside within seconds, shallow draught, the trawler's deck suddenly crowded with burly men with revolvers and set expressions. The harbour master had been with them, a shadowy figure in the background, white cap and gold epaulettes, trying to coax some sense from McNaught. But McNaught had been worse than useless, a man deprived of his precious bottle, and when he'd led them down to the engine room Mick knew that the game was up. No dosh. No Ireland. Just a tow off the sandbank, and the chilly twenty minutes back into the harbour.

Now, the dock deserted, the wind rising, Mick began to climb once again down the ladder. Albie watched him, wondering why. There was no prospect of a second chance. The punters had gone, and Cartwright had gone, and the harbour master's men had even taken the key McNaught used to start the engines. Knowing McNaught, there'd be no spare.

'What now?' Albie said.

Mick looked up at him, a small white face in the gloom.

'Three crates of Grolsch,' he said. 'Or had you forgotten?'

Annie awoke with a start, aware at once that something had changed. At the far end of the ward, light spilled in from the corridor. Annie peered closely at the next bed. A woman was lying on the single blanket. She looked about thirty-five, maybe forty. She was fully clothed and her eyes were wide open. She was looking at Annie, very direct, no attempt to disguise her gaze. Annie wondered for a moment whether she was mad, a regular inmate, but then she reached across, a touch of the fingertips, an accent Annie recognized at once. Northern Ireland. Probably Belfast. Definitely sane.

'My name's Sandra,' the woman said, 'who are you?'

Annie blinked, fighting the obvious conclusion.

'Annie,' she said, 'my name's Annie.' She paused. 'Sandra who?'

'Sandra Gillespie. As was.'

'Oh?'

The other woman nodded, a smile in the half-darkness. She'd recognized Annie from the start, the moment she'd clambered onto the big iron bed. She'd seen her four or five times, a silhouette in the Marina outside her house on nights when Dave dropped by, a blurred, out-of-focus background face in a photo she'd found in Sean's bedroom. Now she was here, the next bed. Vaguely, she supposed they'd been put together for a purpose, some clever ploy by the people Dave had always hinted at, the dim, nameless figures that had always lurked behind the headlines in Belfast, the kind of men her brothers would talk about after their sessions in Castlereagh. Deep down, she'd never really believed they existed, fantasy figures, men's talk. Now, she knew she'd been wrong. She looked at the girl in the next bed. Annie McPhee. Dave's current woman.

Annie was up on one elbow now, awake, alert, inquisitive.

'Why you?' she said. 'Why here?

Sandra shrugged, sounding more bitter than she really intended.

'What do you think?' she said. 'Bloody Dave again.'

It was dawn when Joanna heard the air-raid sirens. She was asleep, Charlie beside her in the cot. She blinked. There was a cold light filtering through the bedroom curtains. She turned over and got out of bed, still dreambound, still thinking that somehow she could turn down the volume, silence the world. She parted the curtains. The garden was empty, the city grey and lifeless. She pulled the curtains again, trying to shut it out, this hideous noise, rising and falling, wondering what on earth she should do. Her mother, she remembered, had once told stories about sitting out the blitz under the dining room table. The stories had always emerged at Christmas, a confection of memory and good port, the folklore of a whole generation. They'd lived in London. The nearest bomb had been half a mile away. The warden's name was Arthur. He'd been marvellous with children. On the worst night of all, the goldfish had died of fright. Belly up in the morning. Another corpse for Mr Hitler.

Now, Joanna padded across the room towards the door, meaning to check on the other children, quieten them down, still their fears, but when she got there they were both sound asleep, untroubled, unaffected, leaving her with that same hideous burden of decision: what to do?

She went back to the bedroom and sat on the bed, pulling on a dressing gown, shivering, none the wiser. Times had moved on, she thought bitterly. No more of those wonderful old-fashioned bombs, the sort that only killed in hundreds. No more dining room tables. No more husband. She eyed the telephone, trying not to succumb to the panic inside her, trying to contain it all, to keep it at arm's length, to die a decent death.

She closed her eyes a moment, felt herself swaying on the bed. Charlie stirred in his sleep, legs twitching, some private delight. She shivered again, and reached for the telephone. She'd scribbled Martin's new number on the back of an envelope. He'd told her the phone would be OK. She was on the list, whatever that meant. She could use it, but only in dire emergencies. She listened to the air-raid siren, the demented howl of a world gone barmy, dialling the first of the digits, wondering – absurdly – whether World War Three was serious enough to qualify for a call.

Martin Goodman sat behind his desk, transfixed by the flashing light. The light was red, a 500-watt bulb screwed into a fitting half-way up the wall in the centre of the Bunker. It was flanked by two large maps of the city, each with its separate quota of chinagraphed lines and scribbled annotations. The maps told the story of the last forty-eight hours – the arrests, the demos, the heavily guarded key points – while the blinking light brought the whole saga up to date. Underneath the light was a warning, stencilled in heavy black letters. The warning read: ATTACK IMMINENT.

The light had been flashing for no more than ten seconds or so when Quinn burst into Goodman's office. Goodman looked up, curious. The policeman crossed the room and picked up the gas mask on Goodman's desk.

'Put it on,' he said, 'now.'

Goodman frowned and began to protest, but Quinn was

already flexing the straps at the back of the mask. Goodman nodded.

'Yes,' he said, 'of course.'

He glanced out through the plate glass window, down at the Bunker below. One or two of the older men were already pulling on their masks, an automatic response to the two-tone alarm that Goodman could now hear through the open door, but the others were waiting for a positive command, faces turned towards him, not wanting to believe the evidence on the wall, the ICBMs already in flight, oblivion barely minutes away. Goodman glanced up at Quinn again, aware that the big policeman was on the brink of direct action, the kind he best understood, the kind Goodman most dreaded.

'Give it to me,' Goodman said, surprised at the authority in his voice. Quinn hesitated.

'You sure?'

'Quite sure.'

Quinn gave him the mask. Goodman looked at it for a second or two, a non-swimmer at the deep end, then shut his eyes and began to pull the mask over his head. He felt Quinn's hands close on his, and opened his eyes.

'Your glasses,' Quinn was saying. 'Take your bloody glasses off.'

Goodman grunted and did what he was told. Then he pulled the mask down over his face, smelled the sweet rubber smell, took his first shallow breath, felt the panic begin to rise inside him.

Quinn's hands, rough, were at his scalp, pulling back his hair, closing the airtight seal. Goodman adjusted the mask again, trying to fit it more comfortably on his face, the world closing in. He looked around, nearly blind, his field of vision restricted by the perspex lenses, details hopelessly blurred without his glasses. The faces down in the Bunker, the movements and the noise, no longer mattered. Nothing did. Only the huge imperative of climbing out of the swamp, of taking just one more breath, of somehow surviving.

Far away, he heard a telephone ring. He looked down at his desk, the dim shape of the phone. It was the first call in nearly an hour. He thought the thing had been cut off. He thought they were incommunicado. He watched the hand reach out, the fingers crabbing across the desk, wrinkled black rubber, no longer part of his body. The hand picked up the telephone. It cupped the receiver to his ear. It was Joanna.

'Martin?' she was saying, 'Martin?'

He closed his eyes. His breathing slowed. Her voice. His wife.

'My love . . .' he murmured.

At the other end of the phone, sitting on the bed, Joanna felt the coldest of hands on her heart. A voice she'd never heard before. Muffled. Metallic. Inhuman. A man with a megaphone four fields away.

'Martin?' she said again, 'is that you?'

Goodman nodded vigorously, the sweat beading under the hot rubber.

'Me,' he said, 'me.'

'But–'

'I'm in a mask. I've got a mask on. I'm wearing a mask.'

'What?'

'A mask. A bloody mask.'

'Martin . . . ?'

Goodman ripped the mask from his face, and threw it across the room. He saw Quinn in the Bunker below, look up and stare at him. He was putting on his own mask. Goodman bent to the telephone, ignoring the man, his voice low, urgent, confidential. He was crying now, sobbing, the child he'd never been.

'Darling . . .' he said, 'darling . . .'

Joanna blinked. Martin's voice. Definitely Martin. Normal again. But hurt. Distressed. Needful. Hers. At last she closed her ears to the wail of the siren.

'My love . . .' she said. 'My love . . .'

Goodman slumped back in the chair, drained, not caring any more, quite oblivious, his voice sinking even lower, the batteries gone. A figure in a gas mask was striding towards the office. He recognized the walk. It was Quinn.

'I'm sorry,' he said simply, 'I'm very, very sorry.'

He reached forward and let the phone fall the last inch or two onto the cradle. The door burst open and Quinn stood there, identified only by a name tag dangling from the clip on his chest. He strode across the office, hands outstretched. Goodman watched him, beginning to laugh, at last seeing the joke, the cosmic punch line, all of them in the Bunker no more than semi-colons in the grandest of plans, his own small paragraph utterly at an end. He began to get up, quite why he didn't know, but he was still laughing when Quinn hit him, the rubber-gloved knuckle slightly off centre, the left of his mouth, the taste of fresh blood, and the curious sight of the floor coming up to meet him, an entirely unplanned development, yet another of life's little surprises.

In the dim grey light of her bedroom, Joanna held the phone at arm's length. The end of the conversation had made no sense. Her husband had been rambling, his voice dying away. Robbed of contact, of clues, she could fit no pictures to the noises on the line. He might be in trouble. It might be worse than that. She simply didn't know.

The bedroom door opened. She looked up, startled. James stood there, in his Action Man pyjamas. He was wearing the Marine cadet beret Evans had given him, and he was carrying his favourite plastic gun. He was doing his best to look grown-up.

'What is it?' she said.

James took a step or two into the room, determined to maintain his cool, the man of the house, his daddy away, a terrible noise at the window, baddies everywhere.

'It's OK, Mum,' he said, 'I'll get them.'

Sean was asleep by the time they came to fetch Gillespie. At first, hearing the siren, the boy had panicked. His defences down, still shocked, he'd turned his face to the wall and started to cry, deep throaty sobs, wild gasps for air, an incoherent mix of grief and anger and raw fear. Gillespie had looked across at him in the darkness, tried to comfort the boy, told him it was yet another rehearsal, another try-on, some clown seeing whether the bloody things worked in the dark, but the boy had been inconsolable, calling for his mother, the bewilderment and the terror bridging the years back to his youth.

After a minute or two, Gillespie had got off his bed and stepped across to Sean, making enough space to lie beside him, gently taking the boy's head in his arms, pulling him into his own body, close, warm. Sean had responded at once, burying himself in his father's chest, blotting out the world and the terrible, terrible fear he'd been living with now for weeks. Not so much what it would feel like at the very end, the searing heat, and the blast, and the last swirling moments of life on earth; but what it would feel like now, six minutes, or six hours to go, the dreadful certainty of death.

An hour later, the siren silenced, the city still intact, the boy was calmer, his body slack in Gillespie's arms, his breathing deep and regular. Gillespie heard footsteps again, out in the corridor, a different walk, slower. The door opened softly. Gillespie looked at the door, recognizing the silhouette of the big man he'd seen by the boat, the man with the hair, the man in civvies. He heard a voice, soft, considerate, not wanting to disturb anything.

'Awake, are you?'

Gillespie swung carefully off the bed, pulling the blanket up around him.

'Yeah,' he said.

'Good.'

The man at the door stepped back into the corridor, the invitation obvious. Gillespie followed him, not bothering to pull on his shoes, blinking in the harsh neon. The big man led the way down the corridor. They went into a small, bare room. Window. Desk. Three chairs. There were two cups of tea on the table and a bowl of sugar. The big man sat down behind the table and motioned Gillespie into one of the other chairs. He didn't bother to shut the door. He reached for the sugar bowl.

'How many?' he said.

'Two.'

The big man tipped sugar into one of the cups and stirred it with the bitten end of a pencil. He pushed the tea towards Gillespie. Gillespie picked it up. It tasted foul. He drank half of it and put it back on the table. The big man was watching him, appraising him, a smile on his face. Gillespie felt faintly uncomfortable. This bloke was making the running without saying a thing. He'd never met it before, not as certain, as subtle, as this. He wiped his mouth with the back of his hand.

'I'll save you the trouble,' he said.

'Beg pardon?'

'I said I'll save you the trouble.' Gillespie leaned forward, a straight exchange, no bullshit, no nonsense. 'Yes . . .' he said, 'it was me who did your bloke tonight. And it was me who nicked his gun. And his I.D. And it was me . . .' he frowned, running through his mental check list, 'who was about to get in my boat and sod off,' he sniffed, 'before you blew it away.'

The big man looked at him, that same expression, completely oblivious of Gillespie's brisk tally of misdemeanours, the truth neatly packaged, laid out for inspection, word perfect.

'These photos . . .' he said after a while.

Gillespie frowned. 'What photos?'

'The photos your son mentioned. About an hour ago,' he smiled, 'before you shut him up.'

There was a silence. Gillespie stared at him, nonplussed.

'Photos?' he said woodenly.

The big man smiled again and leaned back in the chair, feet on the desk, hands clasped behind his neck. He had a conversational air about him, went to some pains to avoid the direct approach, the frontal assault. The threat, when it came, sounded almost speculative.

'Mr Gillespie . . .' he said, 'we can make this easy. Or we can make this hard.'

Gillespie shrugged.

'Yeah,' he said, 'I know.'

The smile widened, jowly. The man needed to lose weight.

'I'm talking about your son, Mr Gillespie. Not you . . .' He paused. 'Take your time. Think about it. The boy's still asleep. It's your choice.'

Davidson spooned the Largactil into Martin Goodman's open mouth while Quinn held his face steady, the two big rubber gloves cupping the dried blood and the stubble on Goodman's chin. Goodman swallowed the thick grey syrup without protest, watching Davidson screw the cap back on the bottle, and wipe the plastic spoon with a ball of Joanna's cotton wool. The Largactil had come from a charge nurse at St Ursula's. On the phone, Davidson had talked vaguely of a problem in the Bunker, spot of panic, and asked for something in the tranquillizer line, pretty strong. The charge nurse had complied at once, no names, no questions, readying the bottle for Evans, who'd been sent down to collect it. He'd told the Marine a maximum of 100 millilitres. Any more than that, he said, and you might as well use a cosh.

They carried Goodman's body from his office, down the steps, across the Bunker, and into the storeroom, now emptied of NBC suits. Davidson had already laid a mattress on the floor, amongst the boxes of dried marrowfat peas and the big catering tins of French onion soup, and now they lowered Goodman carefully onto it. They folded a blanket under his head, making sure his mouth was open, his breathing clear. Quinn checked quickly through his pockets, while Davidson looked on. In the breast pocket of his jacket, under the NBC suit, he found what he was looking for. It was a pair of Yale keys. He held them up, forefinger and thumb, Exhibit 'A'. Each key was tagged with a small blue plastic label. Davidson gazed at them.

'Storeroom?' he said. 'NBC suits?'

Quinn nodded, looking down at Goodman, his face full of contempt.

'Of course,' he said, 'what did you think?'

Back in the office, Davidson shut the door and motioned Quinn into Goodman's chair behind the desk. The Attack Imminent light was still blinking, but they'd managed to mute the two-tone alarm, returning a hot, uncomfortable silence to the Bunker. People sat behind their desks, not talking, barely looking at each other, masks off, NBC suits loosened at the neck, an overwhelming sense of collective exhaustion. One or two individuals were trying to sleep, heads nodding on their chests. Others were gazing out into the middle distance, passengers in some transit lounge, numb with expectation, still waiting.

Davidson sat on the corner of the desk. Quinn picked up the balls of cotton wool, one after the other, and dropped them into the waste-paper bin until the desk was finally bare. Then he looked up.

'Well?' he said.

Davidson shrugged. It was 06.16. They'd been expecting an attack for more than four hours. Plainly something had gone wrong. Maybe ghost missiles on the big early warning screens at Fylingdales. Maybe a test run, ordered by some over-zealous official in the quarries at Corsham. Maybe a simple fault in the alarm.

'I don't know,' Davidson said.

'Can we find out?'

'We can try.'

'Then I think we should.'

Davidson smiled. The contrast between Goodman and Quinn was complete. The big policeman had assumed control effortlessly, adapting the habits of a working lifetime to Martin Goodman's empty desk. Just another job. Just another set of problems to be resolved, methodically, one after another. Armageddon? Nothing that hard work and self-discipline couldn't sort out. Davidson stirred, shifting his weight on the desk.

'We have a problem,' he said.

Quinn looked at him, unamused.

'We have,' he said, 'you're right.'

'I mean locally.'

'Oh?'

Davidson nodded. 'There's a chance this thing may resolve itself.' He nodded out at the Bunker, the figures hunched over the desks, the red attack alarm still blinking. 'We should anticipate that.'

'And?'

Davidson glanced across at the big wall map that dominated the office.

'Your Mr Cartwright . . .' He paused. 'I understand he tried a spot of free enterprise.'

Quinn nodded. 'Stopped in his tracks,' he said. 'Turned back at the harbour mouth. We've had them taped since yesterday.'

'And the wives and children?'

'On their way. As agreed.'

'By whom?'

'By myself and . . .' he gestured at the empty desk, 'our friend here.'

Davidson nodded slowly.

'Have you considered the implications,' he said, 'should the facts come out? Mr Cartwright's little excursion? The city's businessmen? Buying their way out? With our blessing?' He frowned. 'Wouldn't look good, would it?'

'They were stopped,' Quinn said impatiently, 'I just told you.'

'That's hardly the point. The point is that our Controller

let them go in the first place.'

It was Quinn's turn to frown.

'That's his fault,' he said briskly, 'his pigeon.'

Davidson shook his head. 'No, my friend,' he said, 'it's ours.'

Quinn looked at Davidson and shrugged. He'd built a successful career on doing the obvious things very well, on confronting situations squarely, on taking the measure of men and applying to them his own brisk recipe of good sense and vigorous self-discipline. He had a provincial policeman's gut mistrust of metropolitan ways, and he had no time for Davidson's interest in the political nuances of situations, the half shadows cast by other men's actions. The thing was simple. Goodman had fouled up. He and the harbour master had put things right. Harry Cartwright's passengers were back where they belonged, back in their own beds back within the city's limits. Their money had been returned to them, and they'd been warned about the need for a discreet silence. In their own interests, they'd keep their mouths shut. He knew it.

He got up and turned his back on Davidson, realizing for the first time that the Attack Alarm was no longer blinking, that movement had returned to the Bunker, people circulating from desk to desk, the odd conversation, someone plugging in an electric kettle, even the steady wink of an incoming call on the minitelephone exchange. He glanced over his shoulder at Davidson.

'False alarm,' he said. 'Chance to get our act together.'

Davidson smiled at him.

'Exactly,' he said.

Ingle's men found the rolls of film tucked deep in the recess in the front of Gillespie's borrowed VW. They retrieved the film and returned to the hospital. Ingle was woken up and ordered priority development on the colour prints. Before he turned the light out again, he enquired whether the planet was still in one piece. Assured that it was, he grunted, turned over, and went back to sleep. Twenty years of CID work had given him a profound trust in the power of self-interest. If the world could find a way of not blowing itself up, he suspected it would.

*

Davidson sat over the telex machine, and keyed in the enquiry codes for the second time. Regional HQ had been silent since midnight and he guessed they were as much in the dark as he was. The home counties, in any case, had been swamped with refugees from London, and judging by the signals traffic he'd managed to intercept, they had bigger problems on the ground than the likelihood of a nuclear attack. The major arterial roads out of London had been blockaded by the locals, hundreds of families abandoning their cars and taking to the fields, finding food where they could, trying to avoid the squads of vigilantes, with their shotguns and their crossbows. There'd been reports of woundings, and several deaths. The situation, in a favourite Home Office phrase, was 'extremely fluid', yet another justification for the restrictions imposed here, in the city, where geography permitted a realistic chance of containing the situation.

On the whole, he thought, the experiment had worked rather well. The incident at the flats had been nasty, and there'd been worse to follow. But the city was quiet again now, and there was no indication of the trickier Queen's Gate scenarios ever coming to pass. The Cartwright affair was potentially awkward, but he was sure that Ingle could limit whatever damage had been done. In all, then, a satisfactory result, and if he ever got the chance he'd put together a comprehensive report, and make sure it found its way to the right desks. Brussels gossip about the British being a nation of donkeys, easily straddled, easily led, had – after all – been spot on. With a little guile, and a handful of sit-coms, you could make the Brits do practically anything.

He punched the last digit of the enquiry code into the small subsidiary keyboard interfaced with the telex machine. He heard the whirr of the decoder. A small, red light began to blink, then changed to green. Copy appeared. It was sourced from London. He nodded, thankful at least that the capital still existed. He read the lines of heavy black print. There'd been local exchanges in the Central Front, light casualties, but no major engagements. The rogue Jaguar had in fact missed the tank park by a comfortable ten kilometres, inflicting only light damage, and SACEUR had gone to considerable lengths to explain the incident. So far, then, the West had only one foot across the nuclear threshold, and the Soviets were showing a restraint which the author of the telex, in an understandably subjective moment, was calling 'quite remarkable'.

In the Barents Sea, meanwhile, there were confusing reports of a stand-off, with the Russians electing not to board the stricken submarine, and the US carrier battle group pausing on the edge of Soviet territorial waters. That put the *Kennan* squarely between the two, and reading between the lines Davidson suspected that something must have gone catastrophically wrong aboard the submarine itself. Perhaps a major radiation leak. Perhaps a problem with one of the Trident warheads. Ironic, he thought. The terrible mysteries of atomic fission take us to the brink, and the same ungovernable energy pulls us back again. For the first time, he permitted himself to think seriously about seeing his home again, the tiny riverside flat with a view across Steven's Eyot towards Hampton Court.

There was a knock at the door. Davidson glanced up. House rules dictated that no one but himself should be permitted access to the telex room. He leaned across and unlocked the door. Quinn was standing outside, his gas mask hanging loosely from a webbing belt around his NBC smock. Davidson could tell at a glance that he was playing his new role to the hilt, a bravura performance. He nodded grimly to the Telex machine, now quiet.

'Well?' he said.

Davidson thought a moment about the paragraph from London, careful not to overstate the case, conscious yet again of the perils of optimism. It was like talking about a sick friend or relative, stricken with serious illness. No one was really sure whether it would be terminal or not, so it paid to be cautious. Everything, after all, depended on an accurate diagnosis.

'It's difficult to be certain,' Davidson said carefully, 'but I'd say there were signs of slight improvement.'

Quinn shifted impatiently from foot to foot.

'Fine,' he said, 'but what do we do about the city?'

'The city?'

'The all-clear.' He paused. 'Everyone's still waiting for the roof to fall in. It might be kinder to let them know otherwise.'

Davidson stared at him for a moment. He'd completely forgotten about the carefully rehearsed series of siren blasts –

up and down the scale for Attack Imminent, one long sustained note for all-clear. He thought about the telex again, the total absence of instructions or analysis, just the raw data passed on down the line for his own interpretation. He turned back to Quinn, and as he did so, the telex began to chatter. The two men looked at each other, then Quinn turned away, obeying Davidson's rules to the letter, denying himself first glimpse of the latest news.

Davidson stooped to the machine, reading the text, line by line, as the paper rolled out. He began to smile. The machine stopped. He tore off the message and gave it to Quinn without comment. In the light of the Jaguar débâcle, the Americans and the Soviets had struck a bilateral agreement on the Washington/Moscow hot line. No first-use of ICBMS. Status quo in Western Europe. The *Kennan* to be towed to the deepest part of the Barents Sea and scuttled under joint Soviet/American supervision. The crew already en route to specialist facilities in Reykjavik. There was more. Cautious rumours of bilateral negotiations. Some kind of reference to the Security Council. Talks about talks. Quinn folded the Telex and returned it to Davidson. He was clearly bemused.

'Status quo?' he said. 'Bilateral negotiations? What does that mean?' Davidson reached over and put the telex machine on standby. Then he looked up. Quinn was still waiting for an answer.

'It means the game's not worth the candle,' he said wearily, 'Never was, never will be . . .'

He paused wishing suddenly that there was a window to stare out through, fresh air at the turn of a handle, the wind on his face. He looked at Quinn again. The man was still bewildered, still trying to make sense of it all.

'So how long have we got?' he said.

Davidson shrugged, and then smiled, picking up his jacket from the back of his chair.

'Thirty years?' he said. 'Forty? Who knows? It'll be a while before they get this close again.'

Quinn stepped back as Davidson left the room, locking the door behind him. He'd been Controller for barely an hour, and there was the faintest hint of disappointment in his face when

Davidson took him by the arm and began to walk him the length of the Bunker. They paused by the desk of the secretary who'd earlier been sobbing into her gas mask. Davidson looked down at her. The girl was composed now, back in control again, though there was the slightest tremor when the pencil paused in mid-sentence over the memo pad. Davidson reached down and touched her lightly on the shoulder.

'Break out the brandy snaps,' he said, 'and ask the siren chap to join us in the office.'

He looked up, aware of the eyes watching him, the faces upturned, the collective unvoiced question: when does all this end? He hesitated a moment, then reached into his pocket and produced the Telex. He unfolded the sheet of copy paper and cleared his throat. He hated making any kind of public statement, hated committing himself, but he knew that there was no humane alternative.

'This is strictly subjective . . .' he paused, '. . . but I think we're through the worst.'

There was absolute silence for a second or two, then one of Lipscombe's staff officers at a desk at the far end began to applaud, smacking the flat of his hand on the desktop. This strange rhythm, bang bang bang, was taken up around the room, gleeful, insistent, capturing Davidson's news, his cautious prognosis, and turning it into something solid and public, a buttress against anything ever going wrong again, an impregnable dam against groundbursts, and radiation, and the terrible prospect of it all coming true. They'd been in the front line, all of them. They'd sited dressing stations, and discussed the theory of triage, and stockpiled bodybags, and read morbid reports on the properties of industrial quicklime, and now – unilaterally – they'd decided that it was all over.

Davidson waited until the noise began to die down. Then he glanced at the telex again.

'Weather report's pretty good, too,' he said, 'if anybody's interested.'

Dawn found Mick and Albie on a small crescent of pebble beach in the shadow of the harbour walls. It was a place they'd both known since childhood, a place where you went as a kid on the hotter days in high summer, a place they now went back to, common consent, half a crate of Grolsch down, six bottles to go. They took with them a big ghetto blaster, and a couple of picnic chairs, and a collection of ancient cassettes they'd retrieved from Mick's pad. Early Eighties stuff, David Bowie, and UB40, and Roberta Flack. They set the chairs up at the water's edge, and rolled up the bottoms of their jeans, daring the tide to come in. They coaxed another ten decibels from the big stereo speakers while the grey metallic light stole up from the east, and the sky began to purple, and the big cumulus clouds made way for the first rays of the rising sun.

By the time they'd emptied another couple of bottles each, they were into a serious helping of Tina Turner.

'*Right now I need your loving*,' sang Albie, totally tuneless, big delivery, '*Right now . . .*'

'La la . . .' sang Mick, 'La la . . .'

The record came to an end and Mick looked sideways at Albie.

'You never could fucking sing,' he said fondly, 'never.'

'Yeah,' agreed Albie, 'but at least I can remember the fucking words.'

Mick respooled the cassette, catching the end of *Overnight Sensation* before the big raunchy voice came out again. Albie sat back, giving her centre stage, mouthing the words, a box of stale crisps on his lap, his feet in the sea. Mick sat beside him humming along, throwing pebbles at the flotilla of empty bottles bobbing in the flood tide. Now and again, he'd hit one, the sound of breaking glass, and Albie would scowl and remind him again that there was fifteen pence on each bottle, good money wasted, typical of the endless lost opportunities, small fortunes they'd pissed away in the wind, millionaires in the making, rich for an hour.

The sun up now, long shadows on the beach; the music came to an end, and then at last they heard the air raid sirens wailing out over the city, one long sustained note. Mick looked at Albie again, his sixth and last bottle raised in salute. The end had come and they'd judged it to perfection.

'Cheers, mate,' he said, 'happy fucking landings.'

Albie eyed him, smiling.

'Yeah,' he said, 'Go for it.'

They both closed their eyes while Tina Turner launched into *I'll be Thunder* and after a while Mick glanced at his watch and put his hands over his ears. Ever since he could remember, he'd hated bangs.

Ten

Gillespie was still listening to the last dying note of the all-clear when he heard the footsteps again. He glanced across at Sean. The boy looked asleep, face to the wall, his chest rising and falling. The footsteps paused outside in the corridor, and the door opened. A middle-aged man in a blue uniform was standing in the grey half-light from the window. He motioned Gillespie to his feet. Gillespie followed him down the corridor, and they stopped for a moment outside a yellow panelled door while the guard knocked twice and waited for an answer. Gillespie recognised the door from his earlier visit, the same NO SMOKING sticker, half ripped off. A voice called from inside. They went in. The same big man glanced up from the table. He looked as if he'd just been roused. He was eating a bowl of cornflakes. Gillespie could smell burnt toast. There were crumbs on the table. The big man nodded at the guard.

'Thanks,' he said.

The guard grunted and left the room. The big man transferred his spoon to his left hand and extended his right. There were blobs of milk on his sweater. He smelled of cheap cigars.

'Name's Ingle,' he said briefly. 'Should have told you last time.'

Gillespie nodded, shaking his hand briefly and settling into the chair across the desk. Ingle resumed his breakfast, spooning the last of the soggy flakes into his mouth. He wiped his chin with the back of his hand. Gillespie watched him carefully.

'War over, is it?' he said. 'All clear?'

'Postponed,' Ingle said. 'Till next time.'

'Oh,' Gillespie nodded, 'I see.'

Ingle pushed the empty bowl to one side, and reached back for a large brown envelope on the radiator. He opened the envelope and shook the contents out onto the desk. Upside down, Gillespie recognized his evening's work at the dock: the faces in close-up, fathers, mothers, kids, the dim shape of the boat behind, the dense black of the night. Ingle spread a handful of the photos on the desk, taking his time. Finally he looked up, curious, conversational, a man expressing a purely passing interest.

'You took these?'

Gillespie nodded.

'Yeah.'

'Where?'

'At the dock.'

'When?'

'Tonight.' He paused. 'Last night.' He nodded at the trawler. 'Before she sailed.'

'I see.'

Ingle selected a photograph and picked it up. It showed a family of five bent over a small mountain of suitcases. Mick Rendall was clearly visible in the background, gazing at the eldest daughter's bum. Ingle looked up.

'There by invitation, were you?'

Gillespie looked at him for a moment, wondering whether to bother with an answer, this big untidy man with his scruffy sweater and his unwashed hands.

'No,' he said at last.

'No?'

'No.'

'Ah.'

Ingle let the air escape from the word, trailing off into silence. He sorted through more of the photos, looking for one in particular. He found it. He passed it across to Gillespie. A woman lay sprawled on cold concrete, one hand outstretched. Gillespie looked at it. Her face had come out well. Perfect focus. Ingle shifted his weight in the chair and picked a shred of cornflake from his teeth.

'So what's all that about?' he said matter-of-factly.

Gillespie looked at it a little longer.

'That's a lady with a flat on the seafront,' he said slowly, 'and she's dead.'

'Dead?'

Ingle raised an eyebrow, and retrieved the picture, checking for himself. He looked up.

'You sure she's dead?' he said.

'Positive. She fell from a balcony. Nine floors up.'

'You checked that, too?'

'Yeah.'

Ingle nodded, reaching for a pen.

'Address?' he said.

Gillespie gave him the address. Ingle wrote it on the back of the photo. Then he looked up again.

'What's her name?' he said. 'This friend of yours?'

Gillespie smiled at him, recognizing the old trick. He didn't answer. Ingle repeated the question, bemused, holding the photo between his big white fingers. Finally Gillespie leaned back in his chair.

'Why don't you ask your Controller?' he said.

Ingle frowned. 'You what?'

'I said, why not ask your Controller? Who the lady is?'

'You mean Mr Goodman?'

Gillespie nodded. 'Yeah,' he said, 'I mean Mr Goodman.'

'Why would I want to do that?'

Gillespie shrugged, patient, taking his time.

'Try. . .' he said, 'and you might find out.'

Ingle nodded, looked at his watch, and began to tidy the photos into a pile on his desk.

'Not going to tell me?' he said, yawning.

Gillespie shook his head, smiling, enjoying himself.

'No. . .' he said, 'but he might.'

The big man nodded and produced a pack of small Dutch cigars. He lit one, and extended the open packet towards Gillespie before hesitating, the apology just a little too fulsome.

'Sorry. . .' he said, 'sorry . . . I forgot. You don't smoke, do you?'

Gillespie looked him in the eye, acknowledging the real message, so carefully wrapped in the loose, easy, conversational phrase. The file read, war declared, hostilities under way.

'No,' he said carefully, 'I don't.'

Davidson took Ingle's phone call in Goodman's old office. Quinn was down in the well of the Bunker, moving from desk to desk, explaining individual parts of the big jigsaw, the jobs to be done next, now that the worst of the crisis hid evidently passed.

Since dawn, he'd received word from Corsham that both sides were willing to discuss a formula for starting talks, exploring proposals that would withdraw half a million men from the Central Front, and restore much of the status quo. There were the normal precautionary warnings about 'early days' and 'continued vigilance', but even the terse Whitehall prose had found room for a postscript. *So much for CND*, Corsham had signed off, *God Save Edward Teller*.

Now, Davidson answered the phone, recognizing Ingle's hoarse voice at once.

'Morning,' he said cheerfully, 'happy Wednesday.'

Ingle grunted something unintelligible, then changed the subject.

'This bloke Gillespie. . .' he said.

Davidson frowned, remembering Ingle's briefing. The man with the camera. The man who'd followed Goodman.

'Yes?' he said.

Ingle briefly described his exchanges with Gillespie, the rolls of film retrieved from the VW, the pictures spread on the desk. Davidson's frown deepened, news he didn't want to hear, the euphoria of the past hour or so quite gone.

'He was at the dock?' he queried. 'Last night?'

'Yeah.'

'Took photos?'

'Yeah.'

'Why?'

'Dunno.'

Davidson nodded, thinking at once of the other girl, Gillespie's little friend, the reporter sprawled in the dust at the roadblock.

'These photos. . .' he said carefully, 'how . . . ah . . . comprehensive are they?'

'Very. He did well.'

'Do you recognize any of the faces?'

'No. But there's a list to go with them.'

'A list?'

'Yeah. A fax. We took it off him after we brought him in. Chapter and verse. Who paid who.' He paused. 'There's serious money involved.'

'Ah. . .' Davidson winced, the worst confirmed. Harry Cartwright's private excursion, courtesy Martin Goodman. He looked out at the Bunker, at Quinn bent over a desk talking to the Transport Chief. The policeman's wife and kids were in those pictures. Bound to be. Prime targets for a bright young investigative reporter with scores to settle and a reputation to make.

'The girl. . .' he began, 'the reporter. . .' Ingle interrupted.

'There's a couple of other shots,' he said, 'not taken at the dock.'

Davidson frowned again. 'Oh?'

'Yeah. We've got a body.'

There was a silence. Through the open door, Davidson could hear laughter, female, the first for nearly a day. Someone was telling a joke about something that had happened during the small hours, something involving fear, flatulence, and the hated NBC suits. Davidson fingered the pad on Quinn's desk.

'A body?' he repeated.

'Yeah.'

'Anyone we know?'

There was another silence. In the distance, at the other end, Davidson could hear Ingle talking to someone else. Then, abruptly, he was back again.

'You'd better come and have a look,' he said. 'Tell Evans to go to the flats on the seafront. The usual place. He'll know where you mean.'

Evans drove Davidson down to the city in Goodman's official car. Davidson sat in the back of the big Rover, gazing out. The streets were still empty, but soon, he knew, they'd have to share the news from London, the prospect of a hot war receding, the tensions easing, both blocs laying aside their weapons, unbuckling their armour, asking themselves exactly what kind of mistakes had taken the world so close to the brink.

For now, though, it was probably best to wait a little longer, to plan the thing properly, this difficult transition back to a world of traffic jams, and interest rates, and football violence, and the countless other daily irritations that had become so suddenly precious.

Evans threaded his way through the back streets towards the

seafront. There were one or two kids about, squatting in the gutters with a football or a skateboard, but otherwise it felt like the deadest of Sundays. The car slowed to a halt outside a modern block of flats a hundred yards or so from the seafront. Evans glanced back, over his shoulder.

'I think this is the one, sir,' he said drily.

Davidson nodded.

'Thanks,' he said.

He hesitated a moment before getting out of the car. Evans had said nothing during the journey down, choosing not to add to the telephone call he'd made only hours earlier. Davidson had been tempted to enquire further, to ask exactly what had prompted his concern about Goodman, but there was something forbidding in the Marine's silence, something which kept Davidson at arm's length.

Davidson got out of the car. There was a police van at the kerbside, and a young WPC standing by the open passenger door. Davidson reached for his Home Office pass. She looked at it briefly, and nodded across the rectangles of grass towards the path that skirted the foot of the building. Davidson could see white tapes flapping in the wind.

'Round the corner, sir,' she said. 'The pathologist's already there.'

Davidson thanked her and walked towards the tapes. The wind was cold off the sea. Davidson rounded the corner of the building. Twenty yards down the path was a small group of people. A photographer was setting up a tripod. A uniformed officer was gazing up at a balcony and making notes on a small pad. A woman in a tweed jacket was bending over a body sprawled across the concrete path. Davidson walked towards her. The woman glanced up, then returned to the body. It had rained overnight, and there was wet hair matted over the girl's face. She looked young. She might have been asleep after ten minutes or so in the shower. There was very little blood. Davidson glanced up at the balconies above, following the policeman's eyeline.

'She fell?' he said.

The woman, a pathologist, nodded. 'Yes.'

'How far?'

'A long way.'

Davidson nodded.

'Mr Ingle about?' he asked.

The uniformed officer glanced across at Davidson.

'Mr Ingle sends his apologies, sir,' he said. 'He says he won't be coming down.'

'No?'

'No.'

'I see.'

Davidson frowned, wondering exactly what this body on the concrete had to do with him, what part his own presence served in the plans that Ingle was evidently hatching. Perhaps it was simply a question of involvement, of giving him a taste of the sharp end, flesh and blood and the remorseless pull of gravity.

The woman in the tweed jacket was taking careful swabs, sealing them in polythene bags. Davidson watched her for a moment, the pathologist building the case, trying to script the final five minutes of this young woman's life, the events that had led her out onto the balcony, and beyond.

'Anything obvious?' he asked.

The woman looked up again.

'Yes,' she said. 'She'd been drinking.'

'I see. . . ' Davidson paused. 'Anything else?'

The woman began to answer, but then her eyes flicked left, some sudden distraction, and Davidson turned in time to see Evans coming to a halt behind him, staring down at the girl on the concrete, the forceps and the collection bags and the pile of unused swabs. There was pity there, certainly, and revulsion. But something even more obvious. Disgust.

Evans looked at Davidson. He was slightly out of breath.

'It's Mr Quinn, sir. On the car phone. Needs to talk to you urgently.'

Davidson nodded. 'Fine,' he said bleakly, 'I think I've seen enough.'

It was Ingle who suggested the walk. Annie fell into step beside him, the sun warm on her face after the overnight rain, the first of the autumn's leaves rustling softly beneath her feet.

The big detective had come to her bedside at nine in the

morning. He'd given her a cup of black coffee with two custard creams in the saucer. He'd said it was a nice day. He'd said they ought to walk. The overnight promise of instant oblivion, the wail of the siren, appeared to be history.

Now, mid-morning, they paused by an empty bench. Ingle nodded at it. Annie sat down. There were squirrels in the long grass beneath the big chestnuts, foraging for food. Ingle lay down on the grass. He was wearing an old corduroy jacket, torn under one arm. He produced a slice of white bread from his pocket and tore off a corner. A squirrel sat up, looking at him, small brown eyes shining.

'Your friend. . .' he began, 'Gillespie.'

'Yes?'

'How well do you know him?'

Annie looked at him, trying to gauge the weight of the question, the direction it represented, the precise door he was trying to open.

'Quite well,' she said carefully.

Ingle glanced up at her, shredding the bread, crumbs in his lap.

'You sleep with him?'

Annie nodded. 'Sometimes,' she said.

'You love him?'

Annie gazed at him, thoughtful.

'Strange question,' she said at last.

Ingle shrugged, coaxing the squirrel towards him. 'Not really,' he said.

The squirrel seized the first piece of bread and began to nibble at the edges. Annie watched it, thinking of Gillespie, the cropped hair, the sudden smile, his careful private ways. She and Sandra had spent half the night talking about him, a strange conversation, fond and affectionate, shadowed by Sandra's conviction that he might well be dead.

Now, she thought about Ingle's question again. Love was a complex proposition. She wasn't sure what the word really meant.

'I dunno,' she said finally, 'I'm not sure.'

Ingle nodded. There were crumbs all over his lap. The squirrel had gone.

'But you'd share everything with him?' he said. 'And vice versa?'

Annie looked at him, finally understanding the drift of his questions, the sudden plunge into intimacy, the hook tied neatly at the end.

'Ah. . .' she said, grinning, 'do we kiss and tell?'

Ingle looked up at her, returned the grin.

'Yeah,' he said, 'something like that.'

Annie laughed.

'What do you think?' she said. 'Is he here? Have you met him?' Ingle said nothing. Annie drew the obvious conclusion. 'You have met him,' she said, 'and he is here. Only he won't tell you what you want to know.' She paused. 'Is that it?'

Ingle lay back on the warm grass and closed his eyes.

'Might be,' he said, 'might not.'

'So you think you might get it out of me instead.' She paused again. 'Yes?'

Ingle got up on one elbow, and looked at her, thoughtful.

'Yes,' he said.

Annie shrugged.

'OK,' she said, 'what is it you want to know? Give us a clue.'

Ingle began to tear holes in the bread again, not bothering to answer. The girl was sharper than he'd thought. Much sharper. She'd turned his key question on its head, offering it back with exactly the same casual innocence. The way she played it, alert, amused, he was no closer to knowing whether she'd been party to the business at the dock. She might know everything. She might not. It all depended on her relationship with the man Gillespie. And that, for the time being, was a mystery.

He tossed the last of the bread into the shadows, and got to his feet. The back of his jacket was covered in grass.

'Shame,' he said regretfully, 'this could have been a doddle.'

Davidson went straight to Quinn's office when he got back to the Bunker. The atmosphere, at once, was very different. The engineers had managed to fix the air-conditioning, and the place was cooler, less stuffy. There was fresh milk in the fridge in the tiny galley, and the NBC suits were piled neatly in a corner beside the biggest of the fire extinguishers.

Except for the lack of windows, they could have been back in the Civic Centre. Just another working day. Tea, biscuits, and the usual mountain of paperwork.

Davidson tapped on Quinn's office door and stepped in. The policeman, back in civilian clothes, was bent over his desk. He waved Davidson into a chair.

'Home Office have been on,' he said, 'your lot.'

Davidson raised an eyebrow.

'Oh?'

'Yes. If peace breaks out, they want us back to normal as soon as possible.'

'Any particular reason?'

'Yes. The feeling is that we might have overplayed our hand.' He paused. 'They were remarkably frank.'

Davidson frowned, remembering the months of careful planning, the long process of selecting the key city, the one they'd button up really tight. At the time, there'd been no mention of afterwards.

'What are they worried about?' he said.

Quinn looked up at him, impatient to finish his work.

'The media,' he said briskly. 'I think they want us all to be friends again.'

'I see.' Davidson nodded, thinking of Bullock. So far, the body count had been remarkably low, a single death, a mistake, an understandably nervous finger on a trigger, simple to explain, easy to justify. The body he'd seen this morning had been something else completely, a private death, nothing to do with him, or the regime his masters had imposed upon the city. Later, he'd talk to Ingle about it, find out why the girl was so important. In the meantime, though, his Queen's Gate colleagues were evidently in a lather.

'So how did they leave it?' he said.

Quinn frowned. He, more than anyone, wanted Davidson back where he belonged. In London.

'I said you'd phone them back as soon as you could,' he said. 'They gave me a number.' He paused. 'Evans back yet?'

Davidson nodded. 'Yes,' he said.

'Good.' He looked at his watch. 'We've got a little problem on the seafront. Girl found dead.'

Davidson frowned. 'I know,' he said.

'Do you?' Quinn scribbled his signature on a last sheet of paper, and clipped the silver biro into the top pocket of his jacket. 'Then you'll bear with me,' he said, 'it's a question of formal identification. She appears to have no relatives.'

'So?'

'So. . .?' Quinn echoed the question, looking Davidson in the eyes. 'So we take him down to the mortuary.'

Davidson looked blank for a moment. 'Take who?' he said.

Quinn paused, not quite sure whether Davidson was joking. He nodded out, into the well of the Bunker, out towards the storeroom.

'Goodman,' he said, 'your precious Controller.' He smiled. 'Her boyfriend.'

Davidson gazed at him, remembering Ingle on the telephone, the conversation cut short, and Evans in the car, picking his way so surely to the seafront block of flats. Been there before. All part of the job. He closed his eyes for a moment, trying to assess the damage, drawing together the looser ends. Ingle's surveillance on Gillespie. The photos of Goodman and his girlfriend on the bench. The phrase of Reese's he'd used in the report. *Distraught*, the man had said. They'd both looked 'distraught'. And now this: Goodman on the edge of a nervous breakdown, blood all over his NBC suit, his girlfriend dead.

Davidson opened his eyes.

'She lived in the flats?'

Quinn nodded. 'Number 913.'

Davidson shook his head slowly. The jigsaw, quite suddenly, made all too much sense. God knows what they'd find in the flat. In Goodman's car. On his NBC suit. At best, already, the thing was a shambles. At worst, it was a catastrophe. Their showpiece Controller, embroiled with a racketeer, involved in sudden death. Absolute power, abused absolutely. If the details ever leaked, the press would have a field day. Even the gentler papers would tear the experiment to pieces, and him with it, a shattering blow from which no career could possibly recover.

Davidson looked up at Quinn again. The big policeman tore the top sheet off a yellow legal pad and offered it to Davidson. Davidson looked at it.

'What's that?' he said numbly.

Quinn smiled, sweetest revenge. 'The Home Office number,' he said. 'I told them you'd lots of ideas.'

Quinn got up from the desk and retrieved a file from his in-tray and left the office without further comment. Davidson watched him walk down the Bunker to the main exit at the end. He glanced at the number Quinn had given him, and reached for the phone. After a moment's thought, he dialled six digits, and waited a second or two before the number answered.

'Inspector Ingle,' he said briefly.

There was brief pause. Then a man's voice. Apologetic.

'I'm afraid Mr Ingle's very busy,' he said. 'He's not to be disturbed.'

Ingle chewed at the end of his pencil, listening to Gillespie spelling it all out. The photographs were back on the table between them, the faces at the dock. Ingle nodded at the photos, feigning bemusement, wanting to be sure.

'Again,' he said, 'tell me again.'

Gillespie nodded, leaning forward, eager to remove the last shreds of ambiguity.

'OK,' he said, 'let me take you through it. It's really quite neat. What you have is a wall around the city. Not a real wall, but roadblocks and policemen, and the odd squaddie with an SA 80 to put the shits up the punters. That means that most of us stay put and do what we're told. Except, of course, those who can afford to leg it. Now who might they be...?' He paused, surveying the faces on the desk in front of him, spoiled for choice. He reached across and pointed to a middle-aged man with blow dried hair and a sharp blazer. He had a baby in his arms. Gillespie tapped the photo. 'Him for a start...' he said, 'he's a property developer.' His finger moved to another photo, another face. 'And him. String of garages. And her. She runs the classier tarts for the business crowd. And Lennie Bishop, here. He's got the gaming machines...' He paused, looking up. 'Now what do this lot have in common? Eh?' He nodded, vigorous, remorseless, answering his own questions. 'Money. Bent money, legit money, but money all the same...' He paused again, pulling Ingle along, inviting him to share his outrage. 'Sick, isn't it? While you and me and Fanny down the road sit and wait for the Big One, these comedians have bought themselves some kind of second chance. They're laughing, mate . . .' he reached for yet another photo, 'and so is he.'

Ingle peered at the face in the photograph, small, white, glasses and a neatly trimmed moustache.

'Who's that?' he said.

'Harry Cartwright. He's the brains. He's the one who's cleaned them all out. Dog eat dog. The old story. Mind you. . .' He paused for a moment.

Ingle looked up. 'What?'

Gillespie frowned. 'There are some other faces here that don't really belong.'

'Yeah?'

'Yeah.' He pointed to an ample woman standing beside a minibus, surrounded by children. 'Her for instance. Her name's Molly Quinn. She's our Police Chief's wife. Now what would she be doing with this bunch of animals?'

Ingle looked at him, committing the names to memory. Cartwright. Quinn. God knows who else. 'You tell me,' he said.

Gillespie shrugged.

'OK,' he said, 'so you're Harry Cartwright. You're frightened. Like we're all frightened. So you want out of the city. Like we all want out of the city. But you're greedy too. Because you can never resist a deal. With me?' Ingle nodded, still chewing the end of the pencil. 'OK, so you find yourself a boat. And you find yourself some cargo. Friends and clients and the odd business associate. And you charge them what you think they'll pay. Not money, of course. Not readies. But some fancy deal you've cooked up with your lawyer. Some deal that lets you help yourself for the next couple of years. Big fat slice of the profits of all these businesses here.' He paused. 'You read the fax?' Ingle nodded again but said nothing. 'OK,' Gillespie smiled, 'but you're still left with one problem. Getting away's against the law. Or it is for most of us. So what do you do?' Gillespie leaned forward, returning to the photo of the big woman with the children. 'You take Molly Quinn. And you take her. She's the Chief Medico's wife. And these two. They're the City Treasurer's kids. You charge them some nominal fee. Or maybe you even take them for free. Kindness of your heart. Act of civic duty. Either way it makes no difference because you've made your money and you've broken out. And what's even sweeter, you've done it all with official blessing. Totally corrupt. Totally above board. Neat isn't it?'

Gillespie came to a halt, his case stated. Ingle studied him carefully. Then he nodded at the photos.

'What would you say if I told you these punters got no further than the harbour mouth?'

'I wouldn't believe you.'

'And what if it were true?'

Gillespie hesitated.

'It wouldn't make any difference. . .' he said. 'Nothing would have changed. The principle's the same. Like I said, dog eat dog.'

Ingle nodded, paused, looked at the ceiling. One more question, he thought, one more nail in the coffin. Then it's time to do a little thinking. He and Davidson. The outlaws from the Smoke.

'So why were *you* here?' he said finally, reaching forward and tapping the photos. 'Why these?'

Gillespie looked at him for a moment. Then he smiled.

'I have a friend,' he said, 'in the media. She likes this kind of thing. Turns her on. She'll make a meal of it. Give it the treatment it deserves.'

Ingle nodded. 'Annie McPhee,' he said. A statement, not a question. Gillespie hesitated a moment, off-guard.

'You've got her too?'

Ingle nodded again. 'Of course,' he said.

'Here?'

'Up the corridor.'

Gillespie leaned back in the chair, genuine admiration in his voice, the government machine working the way it should.

'Nice one,' he said.

Evans and Goodman arrived at the city mortuary shortly before noon. The mortuary was a small, single-storey, red-brick building, attached to the city's busiest hospital. Big vents, with extractor fans, were inset into the grey slate roof, and there was a tiny Chapel of Rest at one end.

Evans parked the car, and helped Goodman out of the back seat. Goodman had been awake for several hours, drowsy at first with Largactil, but better after a wash. Fiona, his secretary, had sponged the congealed blood from his chin, and bathed the deep gash in his forehead, sealing it up with a wide strip of Elastoplast from the bunker medical chest. Goodman had watched her hands in the mirror, marvelling at how deft she was, his mind otherwise blank.

He remembered everything that had happened over the last day or so, every last detail, but he felt no responsibility for any of it. It was simply something that had happened, as inevitable as rain, utterly removed from any notion of right or wrong. He didn't want to talk about it. He didn't even want to acknowledge that it had happened. It was already remote, a set of events in an ethical void.

He followed Evans towards the mortuary. His mouth still hurt, and Fiona had found another swelling on the back of his head where he must have hit a chair, or the side of the desk, as he fell. Otherwise, physically, he didn't feel too bad. From Evans, he'd gathered that the international crisis had receded, that there was some prospect of peace breaking out, and that too, met with his approval. Perhaps, after all, there'd be a world to go back to, and a life to lead.

A small woman in a white coat emerged from the mortuary, and came across to greet them. She extended a hand. Goodman shook it.

'Dr Mossiter,' she said, 'I'm the pathologist.'

Goodman nodded.

'Martin Goodman,' he said vaguely. 'I hope this won't take too long.'

The woman looked at him for a moment, and Goodman was aware of her eyes on the bandage on his forehead. Then she turned on her heel and led the way to the mortuary. The ante-room was small, no more than a lobby. There was a large pile of folded bags against one wall, black shiny material, big dull metal zips. Goodman looked at them, fascinated.

'What on earth are they?' he said.

The woman paused for a moment, one hand on the door.

'Body bags,' she said, 'our entire NHS allotment.'

Goodman frowned, trying to remember the exact figure, one of the hundreds of pre-war statistics he'd tried to file away. Already, it seemed like years ago, relics from some previous existence. He gave up, following the woman into another room. It was tiled white, big and bare and shiny. Tall fridges lined one wall, and there was a faint smell of bleach. There were no windows. Goodman paused. A policeman in uniform was waiting at the far end of the room. He was young, fresh-faced, slightly hesitant, and there was a clipboard in his hand. Another man stood beside him, much older, buttons missing on his stained white coat. The pathologist nodded at the older man.

'Yes, please,' she said.

The older man, a mortuary attendant, stepped forward and opened one of the fridge doors. The whine of the fridge motor got abruptly louder. There were bodies on metal racks, one above the other. They were shrouded in white, heads towards the door. The attendant pulled at one of the lower racks. A body slid into the room. Goodman gazed down. Unlike the bodies above and below, this one was wrapped in clear polythene, sealed with sellotape. The hands inside the polythene were covered in plastic bags. The head lay to one side. There was bruising around the eyes and temples, dark blotches on the neck. Goodman stared at the face. Suzy, he thought absently. My Suzy. He felt the pathologist's hand on his arm, the lightest of touches. He looked up at her.

'Miss Wallace?' she said.

He nodded. 'Yes.'

'Are you sure it's her?'

'Quite sure. . .' He hesitated, looking down at her face, her lips, the surprising lack of damage, thinking briefly of her bathroom, the smell of the lotions she used, the way she wound the dental floss around her index finger, sawing back and forth. He looked up again.

'Will you be doing a post-mortem?' he said.

The pathologist nodded. 'Of course,' she said, 'circumstances like these.'

Goodman looked at Suzanne one last time, then turned away. The policeman stepped forward with his clipboard. There was a form attached. Suzanne's full name. Her address. A place for him to sign beside a formal declaration. Suzanne Wallace. The figure in the plastic bag. One and the very same. The policeman handed him a pen, and he checked the details against his own name before he began to scribble his signature. He heard the rattle of metal rollers as Suzanne was returned to the fridge. The door closed with a bang.

'Do you have any ideas. . .?'

He handed back the pen and the clipboard to the policeman, and looked at the pathologist, the rest of the sentence unfinished. She shook her head.

'No,' she said, 'except that she obviously fell.'

Goodman nodded. 'Yes,' he said, 'obviously.'

He turned away from the fridges. Evans was waiting for him by the door. He thanked the pathologist and returned to the car. Only when they were back on the main road, clear of the hospital, did it really begin to hit him.

'She's dead,' he said to no one in particular. 'Gone away.'

Davidson met Ingle on the seafront, Ingle's idea. The back end of a big Atlantic front was moving through the area, and the sky was full of fat tumbling cumulus clouds. The wind was chill, and Davidson turned up the collar of his coat, stepping out of his car and meeting Ingle on the long stretch of promenade. The seafront was quite empty, the city still hours behind the news from the Central Front and the Barents Sea.

Davidson thrust his hands deep in his pockets.

'Bit melodramatic, aren't we?' he said.

Ingle ignored the comment, telling Davidson the gist of the exchanges with Gillespie, the man's obsession with what had happened at the dock, the depth of his knowledge, the detail in the pictures, his anger, his determination to share the news with as wide an audience as possible. At this, Davidson interrupted, pausing in mid-step.

'How?' he said.

'The girl,' Ingle said, 'his little friend. McPhee. The reporter.'

'Does she know?'

Ingle looked at him for a moment.

'I'm not sure,' he said, 'but probably not.'

'*Probably* not?'

'Yes,' Ingle acknowledged the distinction with a wry smile,

'probably not.'

'Do we get to know? For sure?'

Ingle nodded. 'Yes,' he said, 'of course.'

There was a silence between them. Then they walked west again, into the sunshine.

'So tell me...' Davidson began, 'how do we dissuade Gillespie?'

Ingle smiled and produced a manila file from the depths of his anorak. The file was creased. Someone had written WALLACE on the outside, big, clumsy capital letters. He opened the file and extracted a sheet of paper. Davidson recognized the preliminary Scenes of Crime Report, a précis of the basic facts: location, obvious clues, fingerprints, relevant circumstantial detail.

'Quinn sent this round,' he said. 'He thought it might help.'

Davidson nodded and read it quickly. Then again, taking his time. When he looked up, he was smiling.

'Fine,' he said, 'me or you?'

Ingle stopped again. The sun had gone in.

'You,' he said.

'And the girl?'

Ingle smiled. 'Me,' he said.

Goodman elected, in the end, to go home. He'd spent a chilly five minutes with Quinn in what had once been his own office, listening to the big policeman recommending a spell in hospital, extolling the virtues of proper psychiatric care. The exchange had all the trappings of an interrogation, Quinn sitting on the edge of the desk, looking down at him, emotionless, cold, tabulating the pros and cons on the fingers of his left hand. In hospital, he said, they'd know what to do. In hospital, they'd put things right. In hospital, they'd get him better, quicker, than any other form of treatment. What he referred to as Goodman's 'little turn' had been entirely understandable. Impossible demands on his time. No sleep. The pressures growing hour by hour. To be frank, said Quinn, he'd been lucky to get away so lightly.

Goodman had listened to it all, letting it wash over his head, all too aware of what a spell in a psychiatric ward would do to his career prospects. The past few days had been bloody, and he'd come very close to a total collapse, but whatever they'd given him had begun to work. He felt much better, calmer inside, and now he wanted to go home. There, he'd be safe. There, he could recover at his own pace. There he could begin to rebuild a life with Jo-Jo and the kids. Pleading madness would be a convenience for Quinn. It would be used against him. He knew it.

Finally, he shook his head, and looked at Quinn.

'Thanks all the same,' he said, 'but I think I'll go home.'

Quinn hesitated a moment, then shrugged.

'Use the phone outside,' he said briefly, nodding at the door. 'I expect you remember the number.'

Joanna answered the phone. He said he loved her. He said he wanted to come home. And he smiled when she said she'd come and get him. School, he thought. Just like school.

Ingle came at it again, different angle, different point of the compass, different mind set. Annie sat in front of him. He wasn't messing, and she knew it, and it frightened her.

'We picked you up with the film,' he reminded her, 'and you say you don't know where it came from?'

'No.' Annie shook her head, tired of it all, the incessant questions, the way his voice had changed, flinty hard, no prisoners. 'I've no idea.'

'Then whose film was it?'

'Gillespie's.'

'And what was on the film?'

'I don't know.'

Ingle hesitated a moment, then launched in again.

'Suppose I told you they were films of his boat. Some fishing trip. Cod. Salmon. Whatever he catches.'

'I wouldn't believe you.'

'Why not?'

'Because he went out specifically. I tried to –'

She stopped abruptly, aware of the mistake. Ingle pounced at once, seized the admission, prising it open, laying it on the table between them.

'He went out where?'

Annie shook her head.

'Nowhere,' she said.

'You said he went out specially. Out specially where?'

She shook her head again.

'Nowhere. I made a mistake. I'm tired. All this. . .'

Ingle bent very close to her, over the table, the huge white face, the warm, yeasty smell of his breath.

'Where?' he said, '*where*?'

Annie closed her eyes. Soon, she knew, he'd hit her. She could feel it. The impatience. The anger. She opened her eyes again.

'I don't know,' she said.

'You don't know where he went?'

'No.'

'He wouldn't tell you?'

'No.'

'This man you kip with?'

She nodded. 'Yes,' she said, 'sounds daft, doesn't it?'

Ingle said nothing for a moment, the dog with the bone, pushing it around with his nose, looking for the last shreds of meat.

'You say you don't know what's on the film,' he said slowly, 'you say you don't know where he went, what he did. Yet here you are, in a relationship with the man.' He paused. 'That make sense to you?'

Anne shook her head. 'No,' she said, 'but then you don't know Gillespie. He hates journalists. Television. He thinks it's all crap. He does what he does. Not my business. Not yours. Simple as that.' She smiled at Ingle, genuine sympathy. 'I'm no wiser than you are,' she said. 'Frustrating, isn't it?'

At the other end of the building, on the floor above, Davidson let himself into the small bare room with the table and the three chairs. He carried a large black briefcase. He put the briefcase on the table, and opened it. He took out three manila envelopes, foolscap size, and laid them carefully beside the briefcase. Then he sat down.

Gillespie looked at him. The sun was in his eyes.

'Who are you?' he said.

Davidson ignored the question. He put the briefcase on the floor, and opened each of the three envelopes, careful, deliberate movements. He extracted a single photograph from each. He laid the three photos in a line, side by side, facing Gillespie, the conjuror, the magician, playing games with reality.

Gillespie, at first, refused to look at the photos.

'Your name,' he said, 'I want your name.'

Davidson cleared his throat, adjusted the middle of the three photographs, and looked Gillespie in the eye, taking his time. His tone, when he spoke, was utterly reasonable, the voice of a man for whom life held few surprises.

'Mr Gillespie . . .' he began, 'contrary to public belief, we civil servants are very much in favour of keeping things simple. So. . .' he smiled, 'here goes. First of all, we find a body. Next, we are obliged to conduct an investigation. Finally, we must try and identify the person, or persons, responsible. But to do that, we need to establish a chain of events. With me so far?'

Gillespie nodded, his eyes still fixed on Davidson's face. Davidson hesitated a moment, then pushed the first of the photographs towards Gillespie. Gillespie looked at it. It showed Goodman and Suzanne on a bench in the Botanical Gardens. Gillespie blinked. It was his own shot. From his own camera. He heard Davidson beginning to talk again, the voice a little softer, a little warmer, more confidential.

'A Mr Goodman is having an affair with a Miss Wallace,' he said. 'Nice photo, if I may say so.'

His fingers moved onto the second of the three photos, the one in the middle. Gillespie looked at it. A telephoto shot of himself on the seafront with the woman with the red scarf. Mrs Goodman. Money was changing hands. Gillespie was frowning. He looked up. Davidson nodded, smiling, building the case, step by step, image by image, the voice silky now, persuasive, amused.

'Now Mrs Goodman is very upset by this situation,' he said. 'So upset, she hires a man to take care of the problem.' The smile widened. 'That's you. On the right.' The finger moved again, tracking across to the last of the photos, Suzanne lying dead on the concrete.

'And this one. . .' he said, 'shows the unfortunate Miss Wallace. . . well and truly taken care of.' He paused, letting the smile die on his lips. 'Get my drift?'

Gillespie looked up, his brain numbed, only one question left. He nodded at the photos on the table. Two of them were obvious. The shot of him and Mrs Goodman was their own, a straightforward surveillance job. The shot of Suzanne on the concrete came from the film they'd retrieved from the VW. But what of the other shot? Goodman and the girl on the bench? Last time he'd seen the exposed roll, it had been still loaded in his camera in his living room at home. The camera had then disappeared. Now the film prints were lying on the table, the key link in Davidson's careful exposition, graphic evidence of the situation that had started it all.

'That one,' he said, 'where did you get that one?'

Davidson looked at him, amused again.

'Where do you think?'

Gillespie gazed at him, not wanting to put the answer into words, but knowing that it had to be done.

'Annie,' he said, 'Annie McPhee.'

Annie looked at Ingle. Ingle was standing by the window, picking his teeth with a matchstick. She asked him again, a second time, not believing it.

'Now?' she said.

Ingle shrugged. 'Why not?'

'After all this?'

'Sure.'

'Just walk out the door?'

'Why not?'

'I thought there was a war on?'

'There was. But they cancelled it.'

'Very funny.'

Ingle turned back from the window, the matchstick still in his mouth.

'It's true,' he said simply, 'everybody bottled out.'

Annie looked bewildered. Eighteen hours behind a locked door had conditioned her more quickly than she'd have thought possible. She'd already accepted that she'd be stuck in the place for days, even months. There was nothing she could do about it, no possible redress, no place to lodge an appeal, and the future itself had become nothing more than an act of faith. Yet here was Ingle, the Grand Inquisitor, telling her that the war was over, and that she was free to leave.

'So what do I do?' she said. 'Where do I go?'

Ingle shrugged. 'Dunno,' he said, 'it's up to you. The curfew's off. The squaddies are back in the box. If you can find petrol, you can go wherever you want.'

'Simple as that?'

He nodded. 'Simple as that.'

Annie hesitated a moment and then got up. She was trying to sort out how she felt, and she realized that whatever it was included disappointment, a sense of acute anti-climax.

'What about you?' she said. 'All this?'

She gestured at the table, the two chairs, the last hour and a half, the questions piling up around her, most of them answered, some of them not. Ingle shrugged.

'It's OK,' he said, 'no problem.'

'You got what you wanted?'

'Oh yeah. . .' he nodded, letting the phrase expire between them.

Annie turned on her heel and made for the door. Then she paused again. She turned round. Ingle was back in the seat, behind the desk, looking up at her. He said nothing. Not goodbye. Not good luck. Nothing.

'What *did* you want?' she said.

Ingle didn't reply, but slumped deeper into the chair, his chin on his chest, his hair falling lank around his shoulders.

'Gillespie's alive,' he said, 'in case you were wondering.'

'Is he here?'

'Yes.'

'Will he stay here?'

'Depends.'

'On what?'

He looked at her, and yawned, and for the first time she realized how tired he was. He said nothing for a while.

Then he shrugged.

'It's a game,' he said vaguely. 'Always was. Always will be.'

Gillespie accepted the second cup of tea, but left the soggy custard creams in the saucer. Outside, the shadows were lengthening in the late afternoon sun. Davidson sat opposite, across the desk, dropping Sweetex into his own tea. His jacket was off, hung carefully over the back of his chair. The atmosphere was quiet, even intimate, two old friends discussing a mutual problem.

Gillespie sipped at the tea and then put the saucer down beside the pile of photos. The contents of all three envelopes were strewn across the desk. Uppermost, was one of the closer studies of Suzanne, lying on the concrete. He gazed at it for a moment. He'd been alone with Davidson for more than two hours, circling the evidence, the fingerprints in Suzanne's flat, the photographs he'd taken there, the shots below, beside the body, on the concrete path, even the tiny tell-tale trace of his blood on her cheek. He'd volunteered a blood sample without protest, expressing no surprise when the phone rang, and a voice told Davidson that it was a perfect match.

'I left a flower,' he said, 'a rose. I pricked my finger picking it.'

Davidson had nodded, regretful, a sympathetic listener burdened by the sheer awkwardness of the facts.

'Pity,' he said.

'I felt sorry for her. Poor bitch.'

'Of course.'

There was a long silence. At first, confronted with Davidson's accusation, Gillespie had just laughed. Davidson had said nothing, letting the laughter turn to disbelief, and then to outrage, and then – when the anger had spent itself – to a kind of watchful silence, a refusal to commit himself any further, to risk the scene turning any more surreal.

Throughout this first hour or so, Davidson had remained carefully neutral. Only when it was clear that Gillespie understood it all, the sheer weight of the case against him, did he attempt to build any kind of relationship between them. That relationship, Davidson knew, was critical. What he required from Gillespie at the end of it all was a careful calculation, a decision governed not by emotion, or by principle, but by raw self-interest.

Now, Davidson leaned back in the chair, his saucer cradled carefully in his lap. He'd spent lunchtime browsing through Gillespie's file. Names. Dates. His last month and a half in the Service. Everything would help. Especially the latter.

'McMullen,' he said, 'tell me about him. . .'

Gillespie looked at him, guarded, wary.

'You'll know about McMullen. Must do.'

Davidson conceded the point with a nod.

'Yes,' he said, 'of course.' He paused. 'Lucky not to go down for that, weren't you. . .?'

He let the question trail away, looking once again at the photo of Suzanne on the desk. Gillespie was still gazing at him, refusing to be cornered.

'Who says I did it?'

Davidson didn't answer the question but sipped slowly at his tea. Then he frowned.

'McMullen was a rapist, wasn't he?'

Gillespie looked at him, saying nothing. Davidson sipped at his tea.

'Tell me. . .' he said finally, 'did you assess the risk before you pulled the trigger? Or did you have a rush of blood to the head?'

Gillespie blinked, stung.

'The man was an animal,' he said, 'he liked little girls.' He paused. 'Very little girls.'

'You knew that?'

'Yes.'

'You saw it happen?'

'Yes,' he paused again, 'once.'

'Up in your sangar, were you? Some field or other? Some stake-out? Some hide?'

Gillespie nodded. 'Something like that.'

Davidson looked at him over the rim of the teacup.

'So you executed him,' he said.

Gillespie shrugged.

'He was blown away.'

'But you did it. Judge and jury.'

There was a long silence. Then Gillespie moved in the chair, more relaxed now, back in a chain of events he understood, facts, not fantasy.

'What does the file say?'

'It says you did it.'

'Nothing was ever proved.'

Davidson smiled. 'Yes. . .' he said, 'it says that too.' He paused. 'But you resigned, all the same.'

'Had to.'

'Quite.'

There was another silence. On the floor above, Gillespie could hear laughter and the sound of crockery. Warm, domestic noises. A world getting back to normal. Davidson laid his cup and saucer carefully to one side and leaned forward over the desk. He picked up one of the photos of Suzanne.

'Tell me...' he said, 'this girl here... Miss Wallace...' he looked up. 'What was she like?'

Gillespie thought about the question, what little he knew, a couple of conversations, a couple of miles in the car.

'She was terrified,' he said, 'out of her depth. Just like a kid...'

'Did you feel sorry for her?'

Gillespie nodded.

'Yes,' he said, 'in a way, I did.'

'Like the little girls at Ballycombe?'

Gillespie looked at him for a long time, and then shook his head.

'No,' he said, 'that's stupid. It wasn't like that at all.' He paused, nodding at the photo in Davidson's hand, taking the conversation back to where it belonged, to the reality of her flat, the up-turned armchair, the spilled blood. 'She'd got in with some pretty heavy people,' he said, 'and she knew too much for her own good.' He hesitated for a moment, scanning the other photos, littered across the desk. He selected a couple, both featuring Mick and Albie. Cartwright was there, too. A face in the wheelhouse window. He slid the photos across towards Davidson. 'You should start talking to some of these guys,' he suggested.

Davidson eyed the photos with little visible interest.

'Why should I do that?'

'Because they could *really* help you...' he paused, 'assuming you're interested, of course.'

It was early morning before Joanna Goodman collected her husband from the Bunker. He looked much better than she'd expected, sitting beside her in the battered old Metro, the kids in the back. They had the radio on, real news again, the old familiar voices. NATO armies were withdrawing to defensive positions the length of the Central Front. Norway was having second thoughts about cosy deals with Moscow. Sudden as it was, it all sounded very promising, and although Joanna barely understood most of the jargon, she knew for certain that the portents were good.

The news over, she patted her husband on the knee.

'So. . .' she said, 'we might make it after all.'

He looked at her, then leaned across and kissed her gently on the cheek.

'I hope so,' he said softly.

Back at the house, she helped him out of the car while the kids danced round in the garden.

Inside, Goodman collapsed into one of the big armchairs in the lounge. He'd left his NBC suit in the Bunker, but he could smell it on his clothes, a musty, slightly sweet smell, sweat and rubber and the charcoal-like deposit it left on his hands. Soon, he'd have a bath. Afterwards, dog tired, he'd probably go to bed.

Joanna was at the phone, dialling a number from memory. He looked across at her. As far as he knew, the telephone system was still non-operational, cut off as part of the Emergency Regulations.

'Can you get a line?' he queried.

She nodded.

'Yes.'

'And is the number ringing?'

She nodded again, grinning at him.

'Yes,' she said, 'just leave it to me.'

She bent to the telephone and began to talk. It was their GP at the other end. She was telling him about Martin. The stresses. The strains. She'd be grateful if he could come over. Nothing desperately urgent. Just a precautionary check. A sleeping tablet, perhaps. Or a mild tranquillizer. She smiled, and thanked him, and put down the phone, another brick in the wall she was building around them.

She crossed the room and bent low over the back of the chair. She was wearing an old T-shirt, loose at the neck. He could see the swell of her breasts, smell the perfume she wore. She kissed him on the forehead, lightly, along the line of the Elastoplast. He felt her hands on his face. He smiled up at her.

'Tea?' she mouthed.

He nodded.

'Please.'

She kissed him once more and left the room. He lay back, eyes closed, mind empty, treasuring the silence and the peace. He'd lived through the worst three days of his life. He'd faced the impossible, confronted it, kept his nerve, and now – like everyone else in the city – the nightmare was nearly over. Three days. Seventy-two hours. The world performing a giant loop, and then righting itself again, ready for the next ten thousand years. Perhaps now they'd really do something serious about disarmament, revive the spirit of glasnost and the memory of the dead Gorbachev. Perhaps now they'd sort the whole thing out. No more call for new generations of weapons. No more need for holes in the ground.

Outside, in the street, he heard the whine of a car changing down through the gears. It sounded familiar. He got up and moved slowly to the window. A pair of headlights were nosing in through the gate. Tyres crunching over the gravel. The low, sleek, familiar shape of the Rover. The car stopped outside the front door. The engine died. A face turned towards him. Evans.

Goodman went to the front door, and out, into the darkness. He bent to the driver's window, heard the whine of the electric motor deep in the door. Evans looked out.

'Sir?' he said. Flat. Neutral.

Goodman frowned.

'What are you doing here?' he said. 'What do you want?'

His voice sounded more hostile than he'd intended. Hostile and a little anxious. Evans looked up at him curiously, taking his time.

'Mr Quinn's idea,' he said. 'Thought I might keep an eye on you.' He smiled coldly. 'Just in case.'

By the time Davidson found Quinn, the policeman was back in his office in the city's Central Police Station. The office was up on the fourth floor, a wide, spacious room, browns and creams, with framed photos on the wall: Quinn in the class shot at the Bramshill Staff Command Course, Quinn the captain of the CID football team, Quinn the city's new Police Chief, an official portrait commissioned the week he'd been appointed.

Now, he sat behind his desk, studying an open file. He'd managed a shower and a change of shirt since Davidson had last seen him, and there was a tumbler of whisky at his elbow. He looked up. In his own office, he seemed even more solid, even more sure of himself. The alpha male. Unquestionably in charge.

He waved Davidson into a chair beside the desk. Davidson didn't bother with the formalities.

'This body of yours. . .' he said, 'the girl at the flats. . .'

Quinn nodded. 'Yes?'

'What's going to happen?'

Quinn frowned, fingering the glass of Scotch.

'Have you seen the report? The one I sent round?' Davidson nodded. 'Then the answer's academic.' He glanced down at the file. 'She'd been drinking. There was some kind of fight. She fell from the ninth floor.' He shrugged. 'We have prints. Blood. Forensic.' He paused. 'You're looking at a murder inquiry.'

Davidson nodded.

'Suspects?'

'Naturally.'

'Goodman?'

'Of course.'

'Anyone else?'

Quinn hesitated a moment, returning to the file.

'Maybe the other chap,' he said, 'Gillespie.' He paused. 'Though I doubt it.'

'Why?'

Quinn shrugged.

'Wrong profile,' he said, 'no motive.'

'So what was he doing at the flat?'

'I don't know.' He hesitated again. 'But it's hardly relevant, given the state of our friend in the Bunker. Did you see him last night?' He laughed, a short, mirthless bark of laughter. 'Looked like a man who'd fallen out with his mistress?' He paused, the laughter turning to contempt. 'Didn't he?'

Davidson didn't answer for a moment. Then he leaned back in the chair.

'So where is he now? Our ex-Controller?'

'At home. With his wife.' Quinn paused. 'Evans is outside. Keeping an eye on him.'

Davidson nodded, reaching for his briefcase. He slipped open the catch on the side, then looked up, as if struck by a sudden thought, pure chance, the longest shot.

'Maybe she committed suicide,' he suggested lightly.

Quinn frowned again.

'Chairs upturned? Blood on the carpet? Bruises all over her?'

Davidson shrugged.

'She was depressed,' he suggested, 'she was drunk. She thought the world was going to blow up.'

Quinn's frown deepened. 'I'm not with you,' he said. 'I'm a policeman, not some bloody novelist. It's facts you have to deal with. Not suppositions.'

'Of course.'

Davidson smiled, apologetic, and slid a photograph from the briefcase.

'What's that?' Quinn said.

'A little souvenir.' Davidson offered him the photograph. 'Your wife's the one in the middle.'

Quinn picked up the photograph, recognizing his wife and children at the quayside, Harry Cartwright shaking her hand.

'Where did you get this?' he said.

'Gillespie. He took them at the dock. He collects them. He's got the whole set.'

'And what does he want to do with them?'

'He wants to publish them. He wants to put them in the papers. On television. He wants the whole world to know.' He smiled. 'He thinks the thing stinks. He's quite old-fashioned that way.'

Quinn paused, gazing at the photo. He took the tiniest sip of whisky, his tongue moistening his lips.

'So what are you saying?' he said, looking up again.

Davidson took his time.

'I'm suggesting it's not in your interests to have these published,' he said slowly. 'At best it looks inefficient. At worst. . .' he shrugged, letting the sentence trail away. 'Cartwright was in for six figures,' he said, 'and Gillespie has the evidence to prove it.'

'What evidence?'

'A fax.'

'I see.' Quinn nodded slowly, gazing at the photograph again. Finally he looked up. 'And you?'

'Me?' Davidson smiled. 'I'm less than eager to see Martin Goodman arrested for murder. Circumstances being what they are.'

Quinn nodded.

'So?'

'So. . .?' Davidson shrugged, eyeing the open file, his voice edged with a faint regret. 'So I suggest she committed suicide.' He reached down for the briefcase and snapped the lock shut. '*N'est-ce pas?*'

The GP had come and gone by the time Goodman put Evans to the test. The doctor had given Goodman a thorough physical examination – pulse, blood pressure, chest, eyes, ears – and had asked him a series of questions, trying to establish the exact degree of stress. Goodman had explained the abrupt transition to war, the administration uprooted, the Bunker suddenly operational, and the GP had nodded, smiling, saying he was lucky not to have suffered a complete breakdown.

The GP had departed after forty minutes, leaving a supply of Valium – high dosage for two days, low dosage for ten – and strict instructions not to return to work for at least a month. After that, fingers crossed, all should be well.

'It's a question of confidence,' he told Joanna, before stepping out into the dark. 'He's had a bad knock or two. It'll all come right if we're careful. Oh. . .' he smiled, 'and no booze.'

Now, downstairs again, slacks and an old pullover, Goodman could hear his wife singing in the kitchen. She'd promised him scrambled eggs on toast. She said she was determined to look after him. The TV was on, and the news was uniformly good. Negotiations in New York were to start at once. The Security Council would sit in all-night session. The President was back in the White House, and there was footage of spontaneous street celebrations in Moscow. Regrets, relief, and goodwill on every side. Maybe even a second chance for Glasnost.

Goodman got up and walked to the window. Evans was still

there. Goodman hesitated a moment, then crossed the room and went into the hall. He took a coat from the hook on the wall, and stepped out into the night. He'd barely walked five yards on the gravel towards the gate when he heard the door of the Rover open. He stopped. Evans came towards him. He was wearing civilian clothes, a light jacket, dark trousers.

'Sir?' he said. A question.

Goodman looked surprised.

'I'm going for a walk,' he said. 'Any objections?'

Evans shifted a little, the gravel noisy beneath his feet.

'No, sir.'

Goodman nodded.

'Good.'

Evans didn't move. Goodman tried to resume the walk. Evans didn't let him. Goodman frowned.

'What's the matter?' he said. 'Am I under arrest?'

Evans looked at him, eye to eye, cold, impassive, blocking the path.

'I don't know, sir,' he paused, 'it's just Mr Quinn. Thinks you'd be better off in bed.'

'Then I am under arrest. Effectively.'

Evans shrugged. 'I don't know, sir,' he said again, 'I don't know what you are.'

The two men looked at each other for a moment, no ambiguities left. Then Goodman turned on his heel and went back to the house. Evans didn't return to the car until he was sure that Goodman was back in the lounge, settled in the chair, taking the first exploratory sip at a large gin and tonic.

Gillespie had finished his supper by the time Davidson returned to the small bare room on the first floor. His empty plate lay on the table, a small pile of carrots heaped neatly on one side.

He looked up as Davidson stepped into the room. Davidson was still carrying the briefcase, and Gillespie wondered how many copies of the photographs they'd bothered to print. If they were sensible, they'd keep the prints to the minimum, and the more he saw of Ingle and Davidson, the more sensible he realized they were. He'd met class operators before, men and women who knew exactly what they were doing, but these two were something special. In a curious way, he felt flattered. Whatever he'd stumbled on, down at the dock, evidently mattered a great deal.

Davidson sat down. He was more businesslike this time, brisker, a travelling rep with a quality product. He opened the briefcase, and extracted a single photograph. A wide shot of the dock. Cars. People. Both boats. The whole story, condensed into a single grainy image.

He looked up and coughed, preparing the pitch.

'Everything's a question of interpretation. . .' he began, 'as you well know.'

Gillespie nodded, said nothing. Davidson leaned back in the chair.

'Take the unfortunate Miss Wallace. . .' he said, 'drunk, lonely, depressed, frightened. . .' He paused.

Gillespie looked at him.

'So?'

'So?' Davidson shrugged. 'So she takes one drink too many. She walks out onto the balcony. She thinks it's all too awful. And she throws herself off.'

Gillespie smiled.

'Pathetic,' he said.

'I agree.'

'I mean you. Your lot.'

'I know you do.'

There was a long pause, then Davidson picked up the photo on the desk. The dock. Gillespie's scoop. The news he wanted so badly to share with the world.

'Then there's this,' he said slowly.

Gillespie nodded.

'Yeah,' he said, 'there is.'

'A handful of people,' he said, 'going nowhere.'

Gillespie shook his head.

'Nearly a hundred. Copping out. With a great deal of money, and a little help from your friends.'

Davidson looked at him for a long time, saying nothing.

'Murder carries life,' he said. 'They probably told you that before.'

Gillespie nodded.

'Yeah,' he said, 'they did.'

'Be a shame, wouldn't it?'

There was another silence. Gillespie looked beyond him, out of the window, into the dark. Then he glanced down at the photo.

'You want me to forget it,' he said, 'that lot.'

'Yes.'

'In return for what?'

'Your freedom.'

'Otherwise?'

'Otherwise?' Davidson laid the photo carefully on the desk, and leaned back in his chair. 'Otherwise justice, I'm afraid, will take its course.' He paused. 'Fingerprints. Photographs. Motive. Opportunity.' He paused again. 'Theft.'

'Theft?'

Davidson smiled.

'Her car,' he said. 'You know the way it goes.'

Gillespie looked at him, eye to eye.

'But I didn't do it.'

Davidson nodded.

'So you keep saying.' He got up, leaving the photograph on the desk. He picked up his briefcase and put his hand lightly on Gillespie's shoulder. 'Take your time, Sergeant,' he said, 'it's your choice. Your call.'

When Mick Rendall finally woke up, it was dark again. He tried opening his eyes. His eyes hurt. He tried to swallow. His mouth was parched, fuzzy with something unspeakable. Then the pain hit him, a sharp insistent throb that began somewhere deep in his skull, and blossomed outwards, breaking in waves against the insides of his face, nauseous, making the dim outlines of the room sway and bend.

He groaned and tried to turn over. Nothing happened. He called out, beginning to remember, wondering what was supposed to happen after the first bomb, the one that tore whole cities apart. What was he doing in bed? Was he still alive?

He swung one leg out of bed and felt the thick shag carpet between his toes. He tried to sit upright, then fell over. He crawled across the room to the door. On the landing, for the first time, he heard the noise.

He looked round. His landing. His Athena prints on the wall. He listened hard. Something was happening down below, in the living room. Something rhythmic, the squeal of metal against metal. A spring somewhere. Creaking.

He felt his way slowly to the head of the stairs, knowing he was going to throw up, wondering about radiation sickness, whether or not you died before your hair fell out. He paused on all fours at the top step, gazing down.

The lights were on in the living room. Albie was sitting on the rowing machine, naked except for his boxer shorts, rowing fast, back and forth, in and out, the sweat glistening on his chest, his eyes locked on some imaginary point half-way up the opposite wall.

Mick began to fumble his way downstairs, lost his balance, and fell. At the bottom, he let the room stop spinning, then slowly disentangled himself, one limb at a time. The noise had gone away. Albie had stopped rowing.

Mick looked at him, trying to get the words together, the right order, not too fast. There was an empty litre of vodka, upside down in the magazine rack. The sight of it made him feel giddy.

'What are you doing?'

Albie sniffed and wiped his nose on the angle of his shoulder. Then he was off again, the same rhythm, the same expression, deadly earnest.

'Harry fucking Cartwright,' he said at last. 'When I find him, I'm gonna kill him.'

Annie McPhee met Duggie Bullock at nine in the evening at a pub on the mainland. The roadblocks had been lifted to the north of the city, and the only trace of the last three days were sets of caterpillar tracks scored by the big APCs in the soft mud on the roadside verges. Petrol was still impossible to find, but Annie's car was intact outside Gillespie's house, and there was enough fuel left in the tank to carry her the six miles to the rendezvous. Before she'd driven away, she'd checked through Gillespie's place. The house had obviously been searched. Drawers had been emptied onto the carpet, cupboards ransacked, even the side of the bath levered off. But of Gillespie himself there was no sign. Still at the hospital, she thought. Still under questioning.

Probably in trouble, but doubtless still very much alive.

At the pub, she found Bullock sitting at a table in the corner, nursing a soft drink. The pub had long since run out of alcohol, but there was plenty of fruit juice on sale from big jugs behind the bar.

'Welcome back,' Bullock said, raising his glass of orange in a toast. 'Here's to Armageddon.'

Annie smiled. 'Cheers,' she said.

She told him what had happened in the city, the riot outside the flats, Goodman arriving, the flying wedge of troops, the man on the balcony, the rocks and the rubble, the riot squads kneeling carefully in the flower beds, the baton rounds skeetering across the dusty concrete. Afterwards, a big policeman, someone powerful, someone important, standing over Goodman, visibly outraged.

'I got some great shots,' she told him, 'great stills. Only they took them off me.'

Bullock nodded.

'Useful,' he said drily.

She told him the rest. About Davidson, the hospital, the detainees, the atmosphere of the place, pages from some Russian novel. She told him about the sessions with Ingle, his incessant questions, her abrupt release.

'What did he want?' Bullock asked at the end of it all. 'What was the point?'

Annie frowned, no wiser now than then. Already, it seemed like weeks ago, a strange, lost episode, inexplicable, gone.

'I don't know,' she said, 'I just don't know.'

Bullock nodded. 'They've stripped the library,' he said. 'There's nothing left.'

Annie frowned. 'What do you mean?'

Bullock fingered the beer mat, the closest he was likely to get to a real drink. Then he told her about the television network closing down, central control from London, a nightly diet of sit-coms and game shows, a pre-med for the big operation. The viewing figures, he said, would be sensational, the best ever, but what little chance was left to do a real documentary, the kind they understood, had gone for ever. Two officers from Special Branch had arrived only that morning with a sworn warrant, and removed every video cassette shot since the beginning of the Emergency. A week and a half of pictures – refugees from France, bread queues, arms convoys, demonstrations, roadblocks – had disappeared on a trolley into the back of a hired Transit van. Bullock had phoned for legal help, done his best to protest, but the two men had ignored him, and the last he'd seen of his precious archive – the raw material they'd need to anchor any investigation – was a cloud of dust as the van accelerated out of the car park, back towards the motorway.

By now, the phones back on, he'd had a chance to talk to colleagues up and down the country, and he knew that the situation on his own patch had been unique. Nowhere else had the Government tried to corral an entire city. Nowhere else had they so shamelessly revealed their hand. But the evidence had gone – his video, her stills – and that made their job near impossible. People could still write about it all, of course, but the history that really mattered was now television, and the Government's finger was firmly on the Erase button.

He looked up at her, and shrugged.

'Still. . .' he said, 'I suppose we should be grateful.'

'Why?'

'Well. . .' he smiled wearily, 'it all worked. We all survived. We're still here.'

Annie nodded. 'Yes,' she said, unconvinced. 'But that's hardly the point, is it?'

Gillespie lay in the darkness, back in his room, his head on the pillow, his shoes on the floor, his feet on the big iron rail at the end of the bed. When they brought him back, Sean had gone. He'd seen the empty bed, and turned to ask what had happened to the boy, but the door was already shut, the key scraping in the lock, and when his patience snapped, and he threw himself across the room, beating on the door, splintering the wooden panels, there was only the sound of footsteps receding down the corridor.

Now, an hour or so later, he stared up at the ceiling. He'd given half his life to the service of the Crown. Lots of it had been boring. Some of it had been tough. Once or twice, in the Falklands especially, he'd nearly died. But never, not once, had he thought to question the pact he'd made, the oath he'd taken, the act of faith he'd turned into a way of life. For Queen and

Country, they'd told him. For Queen and Country, he'd agreed.

Now, though, he wasn't so sure. He sensed the power, the sheer reach of the animal he'd angered, the massive state apparatus behind the pale-faced man at the desk, with his big brown envelopes, and his photographs, and his godless proposition, and he realized for the first time what older and wiser men had often told him. That there was no such thing as honour. No such thing as principle. Only expediency. Means and ends.

He stirred in the darkness. There were new footsteps out in the corridor, lighter. They paused outside the door. The door opened. A figure stepped into the room, silhouetted against the light outside. The head tilted. For a moment there was total silence. Then Davidson spoke. The voice was barely audible.

'Well, Sergeant. . .' he said, 'what's it to be?'

Eleven

The Service of Deliverance was announced exactly four weeks later.

Gillespie read about it first in the local paper. The local paper had already published a special 'Front Line' souvenir edition, prefaced on the front page with a black outline of the city, circled and cross-haired. 'Ground Zero', it read, 'Seventy-Two Hours When the City Held Its Breath'. Inside, amongst the stirring articles on the city's strategic importance, and the Navy going to war, was a brief chronology of events, and Gillespie recognized at once the fingerprints of the official line. No mention of police excesses, or the unfortunate Jason Duffy. No mention of the black market in bread and petrol. No mention of the busy night at the dock when those who could afford it prepared to open the city's door, and make a bolt for the open sea. Instead, a mish-mash of nostalgia and cheap sentiment and 'blitz recipes'. As an exercise in collective amnesia, Gillespie thought, 'Front Line Special' already deserved an award. Now, though, it was evidently to go one better. Instead of an award, an official blessing.

Gillespie studied the brief announcement. The Service of Deliverance would be held in the city's cathedral. The Lord Mayor and city dignitaries would attend. Gillespie ringed the date and the time, and laid the paper carefully aside. Deliverance from what? he thought bleakly.

He went upstairs and lay down in the darkened bedroom. It was October now, fully autumn, but the weather was still superb, the sun warm, the gentlest of breezes stirring in the early afternoon, in off the sea. He'd been afloat once or twice, a boat borrowed from a friend, alone, without the boy, trying to shift the dead weight that lay inside him, the knowledge of exactly what had happened that last night in the hospital, Davidson sitting on the other bed, all too understanding, all too real. He'd said yes to the offer, agreed the deal, and now he, too, was part of this charade, this careful filleting of history. In a way it was the same old story, the Falklands all over again, telling the people what they wanted to hear. Don't bother them with the small print, the hypocrisies, the duplicity, the thousand ugly details that compose the real picture.

On the table, beside his bed, the phone began to trill. Gillespie turned over, ignoring it, shutting it out of his head. For the last month, he'd seen barely anyone. Annie had left countless messages on the ansaphone, asking him to get in touch, imploring him to return her calls. Sean had come round, telling him the sea bass were on the feed, gorging on the slipper limpets in the deep channel off the harbour mouth, the fish better than ever. Sandra had invited him over for Sunday lunch, an invitation he couldn't even be bothered to acknowledge. And although Jenner was allegedly back in the city, back from the Scilly Isles, Gillespie had yet to make contact. For now, he told himself, he could get by on what little cash he'd managed to stuff away in the savings account. For now, he'd simply rest up a while, and let his head sort itself out. For now, he'd stay low, totally camouflaged, totally hidden, safe behind his own front door.

But it hadn't worked. None of it. The days had simply begun to slide into each other, a seamless wilderness of dead time, and when he'd stopped running in the mornings, he knew he was in real trouble. At first he'd told himself it was simple exhaustion. His body wouldn't do it, no matter how firm his resolve. But deep inside, he knew that this was bullshit, and after a week or two of doing nothing – no running, no fishing, no anything – he'd begun to wonder about his mental state. Maybe, after all, they'd been right to take him to the nuthouse. Maybe he was going barmy. Maybe they were even cleverer than he'd thought.

The phone stopped ringing, and he turned over again. Tomorrow, according to the paper, was the Service of Deliverance. In the interests of fiction, and what little sanity he'd managed to preserve, he decided he ought to attend.

Duggie Bullock sat in the tiny restaurant, studying the menu. Philip Cussins, Vice-Chairman of the TV Wessex Board, sat opposite, sipping a glass of kir. The meal had been Cussins' idea, an abrupt invitation that Bullock's secretary had fielded only this morning. The Vice-Chairman of the company had always fascinated Bullock. He was younger than most successful businessmen he'd worked under, no more than 37 or 38. A tall man, quiet, watchful, he was always exquisitely dressed with perfect manners and a smile that was all the more effective because he used it so rarely. He'd made his money in property development outside London, trading estates and business parks on the margins of the major motorways, and then come south to oversee the building of a big marina on the east side of the city. The area in general had appealed to him, and he'd stayed, acquiring a large modern house in the country, and a new wife called Sabine. He'd been living in the south now for nearly four years, and had an important finger in a number of the city's fatter pies.

From the start, Cussins had viewed TV Wessex as simply another vehicle for profit and for profile, paying lip service to other members of the Board with more serious programme aspirations. With his business contacts, and his large personal shareholding, and his sheer intelligence, he'd quickly become the one member who really mattered. The retired admiral who chaired the Board routinely deferred to his judgement. Other Board members rarely raised their heads above the parapet. Even Bullock made very sure of his facts before pursuing any kind of independent line.

Now, the order taken, the waiter gone, Bullock sat back and lit a cigarette. One of Cussins' qualities was his limited patience for small talk. An invitation to lunch was simply a business meeting with a pause for refreshments.

'So . . .' Bullock said, 'you're back.'

Cussins nodded, fingering the glass of kir beside his plate. Recently, he'd developed a taste for long-distance sailing. The latest voyage had been to Florida where – coincidentally or otherwise – he had substantial property interests. The blackest days of mid-September had found him 1,500 miles west of the Azores, a typical tribute to his luck, or his judgement. He'd returned only days ago, tanned and fit, his hair bleached white by the sun. The Emergency had clearly passed him by, though he appeared to have been briefed since.

'I understand you had your troubles,' he said carefully.

Bullock nodded.

'Yes,' he said.

'Exciting times?'

'Yes.'

Cussins paused. 'Shouldn't we be doing something?'

Bullock frowned. For all his clout, Cussins had rarely interfered on the programme side. In fact in a year and a half, Bullock couldn't remember a single serious proposal. Once or twice he'd raised an eyebrow about conflicts of local interest – major advertisers under the spotlight in some three-minute news report or other – but that was about the limit of his programme involvement. Now, he evidently had other ideas.

'What do you mean?' Bullock said.

Cussins looked at him. Very direct. Not a trace of a smile.

'From what I hear, we were pretty much unique. A one-off. . . That would apply on the programme side, wouldn't it? The story no one else can tell? The city that stood alone? Wouldn't there be a market for that kind of film? Wouldn't that be something we could sell? Nationwide? Break into that network you keep missing so badly?'

Bullock smiled, acknowledging the dig. The last time the two men had met for lunch, he'd drunk a little too much for his own good, keeping Cussins at the table until mid-afternoon with his stories of the way it used to be, both feet in the network door, high-profile documentaries, awards in San Francisco and New York. Even, nearly, a BAFTA.

'Sure,' he said, 'I'm with you.'

'So why don't we do it?'

'Are you serious?'

'Perfectly.'

'Do you know what it would take?'

'No?' Cussins shook his head and reached for the kir again. 'Tell me.'

Bullock ducked his head a moment, and then began to run through the areas they'd need to cover, the research they'd need to commission, the pressures they'd need to exert to expedite the return of the library film, the arms they'd need to bend, the countless city-wide relationships they'd inevitably jeopardize. He'd had a girl in there himself. Sharp operator. Lots of experience. But she, like the rest, had simply collided head-on with the powers-that-be. She'd taken pictures. Made notes. Yet all she had at the end of it was a scar on the back of her skull, and a determination never to spend another day of her life in a mental hospital.

Bullock paused here, warming to his theme, flattered in some strange and unexpected way by Cussins' interest. It was a great idea, he said. Absolutely spot on. In fact he'd been toying with something similar himself. But there were hard realities to take into account. What was at issue here was the raw authority of the State, and the lengths it was prepared to go to to preserve that authority. For a brief period, in unprecedented circumstances, in a single city, the State had revealed its hand, and every official conversation he'd had since convinced him that they were now keen to forget the whole business. The sooner the city's lost three days were buried, the better. Digging the whole thing up, piecing together the real story behind it all, would be wholly honourable, and he'd love to do it, but that meant doing it properly, and under these circumstances it would be foolish to underestimate the risks, both legal and financial.

He paused again, his attention briefly caught by the waiter returning with the Chablis in a bucket of ice. When he turned back to Cussins, the man was looking at the table cloth.

'There might be another way. . .' he said slowly.

Bullock frowned.

'Yes.' He paused while the waiter deposited the ice bucket on the table and began to uncork the bottle. Cussins tasted the wine and nodded. The waiter poured two glasses. Bullock left his beside his plate, still gazing at Cussins.

'Well?' he said.

Cussins looked up.

'I've been talking to some friends,' he said. 'They're keen to give us all the help they can.'

'Oh?'

'Yes.' He looked out of the window, the magician with the white rabbit. 'What would you say to an interview with Martin Goodman?'

'Our ex-Controller?'

'Yes.'

'I thought he was ill? *Hors de combat*?'

'He was,' Cussins shrugged. 'Exhaustion. He's back now. Fit as a fiddle.' He paused. 'We could get access, too.'

'Access to what?'

'That bunker of theirs. . .' he smiled. 'The daily logs. Interviews with the other key players. Insights into what they had to do. Just to keep the city going. . .' He paused again. 'I dare say we can get your film back too, if that's what you need.' He ran a finger around the rim of his glass. Then he looked up. 'I just thought it might make something special. . .' He shrugged. 'Back from the Brink. The Inside Story. World exclusive. Isn't that the way you people work?'

Bullock hesitated a moment, scenting at last the way it was really going, the old stench, buddies and influence and a determination to keep the cap on the bottle.

'Fascinating,' he said slowly.

'You think so?'

'Yes. . .' He paused, reaching for his own glass. 'But tell me something.'

'Of course.'

'On whose terms would we do this thing? Ours or theirs?'

'Ah. . .' Cussins smiled again, and raised his glass. 'That's something you and I will have to discuss.'

Bullock looked at him, his own glass still on the table.

'Will or would?' he said.

Cussins acknowledged the distinction with a nod. The smile had gone.

'Will,' he said, 'I want the thing done.'

By the time Mick and Albie emerged from the Ensign, it was mid-afternoon. Mick hadn't seen Albie for more than three weeks. Albie had been out of the city for a while, working for a scrap merchant on a big site somewhere in north London, living in the back of his van, saving every penny he could, building a modest war chest, buying himself time for something he now chose to call 'the business'. After three pints of Stella, Mick knew all too well what Albie meant.

They walked across the cobbles and paused at the quayside. The *Timothy Lee* was moored against a clutter of fishing smacks and harbour runabouts, tied up alongside the big stone wall. The deck was still littered with ropes and tackle, and empty cardboard boxes, debris from the abortive excursion. There was a summons taped onto the wheelhouse window, a demand for three months' mooring dues. Nobody had seen McNaught since the Harbour Restrictions were lifted, weeks back, but there was a persistent rumour that he'd gone down Channel, Cornwall way, with a pocketful of notes and a vague determination to retire.

Mick glanced at Albie's face and knew what was coming. Albie, as usual, had spent lunchtime assaulting the fruit machine, refusing to soften his anger with anything but pineapple juice. Mick put his hand on Albie's shoulder, an almost paternal gesture.

'Most people,' he said thoughtfully, 'would be grateful.'

Albie looked at him.

'*Grateful*,' he repeated, 'for what?'

Mick nodded, out towards the water. Boats. Seagulls. Life itself.

'We're alive, mate. We made it. We ain't pork kebabs. Ain't that something?'

Albie looked unconvinced. They walked on towards the *Timothy Lee*, stopping above the wheelhouse. Through the dirty salt-caked windows, Mick could see the empty biscuit tin Cartwright had used to store the cash the night they'd tried to leave harbour. It was wedged between the wheel and the thick plate glass of the window. Albie was looking at it, too.

'We were robbed,' he said, 'conned rotten. You thought it up. We made it work. And your little mate ran off with the ackers.' He glanced across at Mick. 'That's bad business, mate, and you know it.'

Mick shrugged. 'He'll be back,' he said. 'Bound to be.'

'Yeah? When?'

'Soon. You'll see.'

Albie looked at him.

'Been in touch, have you? Nice cosy little phone calls? Kiss and make up?'

Mick shook his head and turned away.

'Give it a rest, Alb,' he said.

Albie stepped in front of him, a refusal to be fobbed off, a gesture of intent.

'How d'you know, then?' he said. 'How d'you know he'll be back?'

'I just do.'

'Yeah. But how?'

Mick looked at Albie a moment. The boat scam was yesterday's deal. The world had moved on. Yet trying to coax Albie into accepting these simple facts was pissing in the wind. He smiled.

'Listen, mate. . .' he said, 'I'm sorry the paint thing didn't work out. I know you worked your bollocks off. . . Maybe we can do something there, too.'

Albie stepped towards him, very close. The suspicion had hardened on his face.

'We?' he said, 'who's we?'

Mick grinned at him, uneasy. Albie would be a bad man to cross, and he knew it.

'You and me, Alb,' he said hastily, 'you and me.'

The Service of Deliverance took place next day, twelve noon, in the city's cathedral, a smallish building, no bigger than a good-sized parish church, tucked away in the oldest quarter of the city. Annie McPhee arrived forty minutes early, in the front of the Wessex TV Volvo estate car. While the two-man crew unpacked the equipment, she walked slowly around the cathedral, looking for establishing shots, wondering again exactly what Bullock had really meant.

He'd phoned her the previous evening at her flat in Kensal Rise. It was the first time she'd spoken to him since leaving the city. He asked about her holiday, and she'd said it had been fine, three weeks with friends in a cottage in mid-Wales. She'd hesitated then, knowing she owed him some work on the Falklands project, a proper filming schedule, a plan for post-production, but he'd dismissed her apologies. There was another film, he'd said, closer to home. Something about which he was sure she had a great deal to say.

She'd asked him to expand, knowing already what it must be, but surprised at how imprecise he was, how little guidance he offered her. The inside story, he'd kept saying. The real McCoy. City Under Siege. Back from the Brink. She'd pushed him further. Who was she to go for? How much time did she have?

The first question he deflected, telling her she had unlimited access to Martin Goodman, plus the offer of interviews with other heroes of the Emergency.

His response to the second question was more straightforward.

'A week,' he'd said simply.

Annie had blinked.

'A week's filming?' she'd said. 'Is that all?'

Bullock had laughed at the other end of the phone.

'No,' he'd told her, 'a week until transmission.'

Then he'd put the phone down.

Now, sixteen hours later, she was only a little wiser. She'd phoned him back, of course, his home number bullied from his secretary. He'd confirmed the transmission date, and assured her that she'd have every post-production facility she'd need. The lot. No expense spared. She'd dismissed this largess with a grunt, telling him it was irrelevant. It was research and shooting time that really mattered, getting the story straight, finding out what had really happened. How could she possibly do that in the three or four days she could afford to spend out on the road?

To this, Bullock had no real answer. He flannelled about the public appetite for a look inside the Bunker. He emphasized the exclusive nature of the access and told her time and time again that they had a network slot on offer, just seven days away, contingent on their ability to produce.

'We have no choice, love,' he'd said. 'Either we grab it with both hands, or we pack up. This could lead to something great.'

'This *is* something great.'

'Exactly. Go for it.'

She'd paused, sitting in the tiny window of her upstairs flat. Given this schedule, she'd no choice but to accept the official line, the hook buried deep in all this lovely access they were being offered. It was an impossible brief, and Bullock must have known it before he'd said yes.

'You're mad,' she'd said, 'this is crazy.'

'You don't want to do it?'

'That's not what I said. I just remember all those conversations, you know, pre-war. . .' she'd paused, 'the secret state. Goodman. All that.' She'd paused again. 'Amazing what a network slot can do.'

'That's cheap.'

'Yeah. But true.'

She'd asked him again, as nicely as she knew how, then a third time, forceful, stopping just this side of abuse, a major row. But at the end of it all, Bullock exhausted, she'd simply shrugged and said she'd do her best. Twelve noon at the cathedral, he'd reminded her. Goodman will be expecting you.

Now, she returned to the car. The cameraman had readied the camera, a new lightweight Sony. She explained the shots she needed, the wide angle framed by the big oak tree, the tilt-down from the tower to the stained glass window at the other end of the transept. The cameraman nodded, shouldering the tripod and camera and wandering away. The sound recordist followed, tethered by a length of umbilical cable.

Annie ducked into the cathedral, a big, cool, dark space smelling faintly of incense. A verger in a long black cassock was distributing hymn books and an Order of Service to each chair. There was a spare pile of the Service sheets on a long refectory table. She took one. *A Service of Deliverance* it read, *And of Thanksgiving*. She glanced down at the lines of careful type. Martin Goodman was reading the second lesson. Samuel II, 22. She folded the single sheet of paper and put it in her pocket. Maybe there was some reference in the biblical text, some subtle irony or other, unintended, undetected, some tiny chink in the man's official armour. She caught the thought as it began to develop, realizing how tightly they'd sealed it all up, how desperate she must be if it had truly come to this.

She shook her head, dismissing the thought. Tomorrow, Bullock had scheduled the major interview: four whole hours with the ex-Controller in the Bunker, hers to use as she pleased. A series of action sequences and reconstructs to give her pictures for the Emergency itself, plus a long, in-depth interview. She smiled, heading for the door again, feeling a little better. Then, at least she could pin him down, put him on the spot: about her own experiences, the roadblock, the mental hospital, plus the still unexplained death of Jason Duffy. Tomorrow, at least, she'd be on home ground. Tomorrow, who knows, she might even crack it.

Gillespie left home deliberately late, forcing himself to hurry the mile and a half to the cathedral. His mind, for once, was totally blank. He was wearing a pair of slacks and an old blazer, and a tie and shirt he'd found in a long-discarded holdall. Dressed this way, Gillespie felt like a stranger, someone he didn't know, someone he'd never known. A penance, he thought, rounding the corner into the High Street, watching the first of the official cars sweep past on its way to the cathedral, and thinking, quite suddenly, of the dead girl at Ocean Towers.

Annie McPhee saw the big Daimler in the distance, the mayoral pennant on the bonnet, and told the cameraman to start filming. He did so, pulling the shiny black car towards him with the telephoto lens, his fingers twitching on the focus. Behind the Mayor's car, he could see a low, sleek Jaguar, also black, and he became aware of Annie's whispered instruction in his ear.

'Second car,' she said, 'tall bloke with glasses.'

The Mayor's car glided to a halt at the kerbside, and the Bishop stepped forward to offer an official welcome. A crowd had gathered by now, kids, mums, dads, some just passing by, simply curious, others clad in suits and formal dresses, waiting to file in behind the big wigs and take their seats in the cathedral.

The Mayor emerged from the Daimler. The Bishop shook him by the hand and turned towards the cathedral in a swirl of purple. The other car stopped. A door opened. Goodman stepped out.

'Left,' hissed Annie, 'go left.'

The cameraman did so, a slow gentle movement riding the focus all the way, introducing a new player to the scene. Annie followed the pan. The last time she'd seen Goodman had been at the flats, a face in her own viewfinder, a man in a black suit trying to make sense of the noise, and the anger, and the dull ugly thud of falling rocks and rubble. Then, he'd looked first bewildered, then frightened. When the soldier closest to him had fallen, he'd stayed with him, and Annie remembered admiring the man, the folly and the blindness of his courage.

Now, he looked very different. He was composed, serious, but he'd been somewhere hot, somewhere relaxing, and it showed. His face was tanned brown. The eyes were alert, flicking left and right, a gleam of recognition here, a nod there, the faintest hint of a smile for someone he recognized in the Bishop's entourage. In the four weeks since she'd left the city, something had happened to this man, something that gave the lie to Bullock's conviction that he'd suffered some kind of breakdown. The man had calm, poise, self-assurance. He was playing the scene for all it was worth, a slight stoop, a hint of some mysterious wound or other, a man who'd felt the heat, a leader baptized by fire, a star in the making.

At a lifted finger from the cameraman, Annie stepped towards Goodman, smiled a greeting, and guided him deftly into camera range. The sound recordist passed her a microphone. The cameraman adjusted the shot.

'Mr Controller. . .' Annie began, 'before you go in. . .' She let the sentence trail away, and Goodman accepted the invitation with practised ease.

'Controller's an awful word,' he said, 'and redundant, too, thank God.' He glanced at his watch and smiled at her. 'We're here to give thanks,' he said. 'We've all been through it, every one of us, and my only sadness is that the cathedral isn't bigger. We should all be here. We should all be bearing witness. The whole city. It's been a kind of miracle, a kind of rebirth. It's time to look forward. And thank God we still can.'

He stopped, the tone perfectly pitched, the message perfectly articulated. In the realm of the sound bite, those little ten-second quotations so beloved by news editors, Goodman was clearly king. He looked apologetic and glanced up the path towards the door. The Bishop's party, and the Mayor, had disappeared into the cathedral. Annie smiled her thanks, and watched Goodman shepherd his wife towards the open door. His wife was much smaller than he was, slight, attractive, well-dressed, the same expensive tan. The perfect couple, she thought, turning away to look for a handful of other shots to bridge the gaps in their brief conversation, to make the scene come alive.

Across the road was a line of spectators, the beginnings of a thin crowd. Annie reached back to nudge the cameraman, then stopped. Standing apart, slightly to one side, was Gillespie.

She didn't recognize him at first. He was wearing a collar and tie. An ill-fitting blazer, and a pair of slacks. She half-raised her hand, began to call his name, but he'd been looking at her all the time, taking it in, the camera, Goodman, the exchange of smiles at the kerbside, and now he turned away, refusing to acknowledge her. She stepped out into the road, starting to go after him, but the cameraman was calling her name, a query about shot numbers, and by the time she'd given him the information he needed, Gillespie had gone.

Gillespie was back home twenty minutes later. He went straight to the bathroom. He tore off the blazer, wrenched at the tie. He stepped out of the slacks, leaving them in a pile on the floor. Then, in vest and briefs, he walked through to the living room.

The first set of press-ups helped, deep dips, his chest touching the carpet. Every tenth press-up he pushed hard off the floor, clapping his hands once, then catching himself as his chest fell once again towards the carpet, hands outspread. At seventy, he lost count, the muscles in his shoulders and his upper arms beginning to burn, his strength ebbing away, leaving only that tight knot of determination inside himself, that absolute disregard for gravity and pain that was finally his only resource.

Another thirty seconds, and he was finished, fighting his way upright on the carpet, refusing to lie down, refusing to let his body rest, turning over, sitting upright, pushing himself into the next set of exercises, stomach curls, flat on his back, hands behind his head, hinging upright, elbows touching his knees, grunting each time he did it, driving away the demons, pushing Annie out of his head, the terrible suspicion at last confirmed. He did fifty to begin with. Then fifty more. Then, when his stomach began to cramp, the beginnings of another set.

The door bell rang, Gillespie's rhythm slowed. The bell rang again. He stopped, sitting on the carpet, hands behind his head. For a moment or two he did nothing, thinking of Annie again, standing outside the cathedral, ringed by her precious film crew, cosying up to Goodman, a smile on her face. He glanced at his watch. Forty minutes had gone by since he'd left the cathedral. Just enough time for her to finish what she was doing, tidy up, and come round. She never gave up. Never stopped trying. It was bound to be her. He got to his feet, glad that the worst of the anger had gone, glad that he could say his piece, seal the whole thing off, without losing control. Ten minutes earlier, he'd probably have killed her. Now, he'd simply tell her what he thought.

He walked down the hall. There was a shadow at the door. He pulled it open, feeling the fresh air raise the sweat on his face. He blinked. It was Sean.

'Yeah?' he said gruffly, robbed of a different conversation.

Sean looked startled.

'Hi, Dad,' he said, uncertain.

Gillespie looked at him a moment, then turned away and walked back along the hall. Sean followed him, closing the door. They both went into the kitchen. Gillespie wiped his face on a tea-towel. He hadn't seen the boy for more than a week, and even then there'd been little to say. Both Sandra and Sean had made the running, closing the door on what had happened out in the marshes, out by the boat, the guns to their heads, the faces daubed with camouflage cream, the ride to the hospital, the incessant round of questions. All that had gone, no blame, no bitterness, no need even to hang onto the memory. Dave, their Dave had done his best and the only outcome worth a mention was the fact that he was still alive. The rest was a nightmare, devoid of plot, empty of meaning. A day or so later, the world had woken up, and here they all were again, a living to make, chores to attend, business as usual. Except that Dave had changed, gone funny, withdrawn so totally that it was impossible to even see him.

Sandra, at first, thought that they must have hurt him. Drugs. Shock treatment. A beating or two. White noise. The sort they'd used on her brothers. But when she finally managed to coax him to the telephone, he said they'd done nothing of the sort. On the contrary, he said, they'd behaved like perfect gentlemen. She'd remembered the phrase for days, the way he said it, the bitterness in his voice, the sense of personal injury. She'd worried about it. She'd phoned him again, to no effect. She'd even written to him, telling him to take it easy, to relax, to be like everyone else in the city and simply forget it all. Gillespie had read the letter early one morning, the postman's footsteps receding down the pavement in the street outside. He'd left it on a shelf in the kitchen, tucked behind a mug where he kept the broken fishing traces he was always meaning to mend. Sean looked at it now, recognizing his mother's handwriting, the careful backward slope to the capital letters.

'She wants to see you again,' he said. 'She wants you to come round.'

'Yeah?'

Gillespie folded the tea-towel over the edge of the sink. He was still thinking about Annie. The things he would have said to her. The way he would have put it. The boy was a distraction. The wrong face. The wrong day.

'Listen – ' he said. 'I'm pretty busy.'

Sean looked round. The pile of unwashed plates on the draining board. The empty Guinness tins. Leavings from a life going nowhere. It was like walking into some stranger's kitchen. His father had always been methodical and tidy. Not fussy. Not worrying about it all the time. Simply neat. Ship shape. The way he liked it afloat. This place belonged to someone else. He tried again.

'She's really upset. . .' he began.

Gillespie grunted, cutting him off, not wanting to listen.

'Yeah,' he said, 'I bet.'

'She is. . .' he paused.

'So?' Gillespie spun round, swamped again by the anger and the pain, the world on his back. 'What the fuck do I do about it?'

Sean blinked and backed away, and Gillespie saw the shock in the boy's face, and then the fear. He stopped himself, realizing what he was doing, where the conversation was heading. His own son. In his own kitchen. Scared witless. He sank into a chair and gazed at his hands. To his surprise, they were shaking.

'Son. . .' he began, 'I'm sorry. . . '

Sean looked nervous, not knowing quite how to react. First the flash of explosive temper. Now this.

'It's OK,' he said uncertainly.

'No,' Gillespie shook his head, 'it's not OK. It's not OK at all.'

He looked up, trying to coax a smile from the boy, but all he saw was wariness and a growing sense of bewilderment. Gillespie got up and reached for the kettle, knowing that at last the time had come to make yet another decision.

The first, four weeks back, had been forced upon him. He'd been offered a simple choice, yes or no, freedom at the turn of a key, or prosecution for murder. The latter was by no means a foregone conclusion but the evidence was strong and they were obviously prepared to play the Ballycomble card: McMullen lying dead in the gravel with a 7.62mm hole in his head. This man has killed before. This man has killed again. He has a taste for it. A talent for it. Lock this man up. He'd thought hard about the prospect, the way the man in the suit had meant him to, and in the end he'd elected for freedom, and for silence. Set me free, he'd said, and your precious secret – Harry Cartwright's little racket – will be safe. The man in the suit had concurred with a nod. Wise move, his smile had suggested. Good lad.

He'd known then that it was a hopeless decision, the worst sort of compromise, but he thought he might be able to live with it. Now, a month later, he knew that he couldn't. The evidence was there in front of him, Sean reaching for the door handle, his own son, the one relationship that really mattered, looking for a way out. At this rate, unless he did something radical, took a risk or two, there wouldn't be a relationship left. He'd end up like his own dad. Dead in the water.

He looked up at Sean and smiled.

'You won't understand this, son. . .' he began.

Sean hesitated by the door, detecting a tone in his father's voice, conciliatory.

'No?' he said.

Gillespie shook his head.

'No,' he said, 'but I think I do.'

The boy frowned.

'What does that mean?'

'It means I screwed up. Dropped a big one.' He shrugged. 'Happens sometimes.'

Sean looked at him, the uncertainty still there.

'And?' he said, wanting only the good news.

Gillespie was silent for a moment, toying with the big knife he used to gut fish. The kettle began to boil. Finally, he looked up, the decision made, a sense of marvellous calm spreading inside him. Peace at last, at whatever price.

'We get another boat,' he said, 'after I'm through.'

Annie McPhee left the camera car at the foot of the tower block while she went up to arrange the interview. The last time she'd been here, there'd been a riot in progress. Now, it was quite deserted, sixteen storeys of curtained windows in a wasteland of abandoned supermarket trolleys.

Annie took the lift to the twelfth floor. The woman's address she'd acquired from the young reporter on the local paper. 'Hudson Towers,' he'd told her, 'No. 1204'. He'd hung onto the conversation for a moment or two, curious about her interest, but she'd been deliberately vague. My story, she'd told herself. My chance.

The lift stopped and she got out. Number 1204 was at the end of the corridor, an orange door. She rang the bell and waited. Nothing happened. She rang the bell again. Another door opened across the hall. A woman emerged, old, running to fat. She was wearing a housecoat, quilted nylon, pink. She looked hostile. Annie introduced herself.

'I'm after Mrs Duffy,' she said.

'She's gone.'

'Left?'

'Yeah.' The old woman sniffed. 'Gave her a transfer, didn't they? Brand new place.' She looked closely at Annie. 'You from the Social?'

'No.'

'Friend, are you?'

'No.' She paused. 'It's personal.'

'Oh.' The old woman nodded. 'Then maybe you can tell me what she'd want with four bedrooms? Just her and the two kids? Eh?'

Annie nodded, beginning to understand. Like everyone else in the block, Mrs Duffy probably hated the flats. What she'd want would be a transfer, somewhere ground level, somewhere with a bit of space, and a garden. Somewhere half decent to bring up the remains of her family. In this vision of a better life, Mrs Duffy wouldn't be alone. There'd be thousands like her on the waiting list, resigned to a wait of years before they amassed enough points to take them to the head of the queue. Miraculously, though, in the space of a month, Mrs Duffy had gone. Annie looked at the orange front door, wondering what kind of price Mrs Duffy had offered to pay, what kind of deal had been struck. She glanced back at the old woman.

'I'm press,' she said idly, 'I was wondering about that boy of hers. The one that got killed.'

'Jason?'

'Yes. Jason.'

'You want to talk to Mrs Duffy about Jason?'

'Yes.'

The old woman shook her head and began to step back into her flat.

'Fat chance,' she said.

'Why's that?'

'Because Mrs Duffy ain't talking. Not now. Not ever.'

Annie nodded, thanking her, stepping back towards the lift. No interview, she thought. Not now. Not ever.

Mick and Albie finished up at Mick's place, gone seven in the evening, that strange twilight interlude between the working day and an evening of serious drinking. Albie, at last, had abandoned his pineapple juice and was into his second can of Special Brew. Mick watched him, recognizing the old problem, all or nothing, totally slaughtered or totally sane. He grinned to himself and lay back in the big leather armchair, half closing his eyes. Time for a gentle piss-take, he thought. Time for a few laughs. He proffered the can, a toast.

'The Albie Curtis Home Defence System,' he said. 'Fifty gallons of nicked emulsion and a load of old cobblers about the Space Shuttle.' He paused, making room for the punch line. 'Should have done a bomb, shouldn't it? Eh, Alb?'

Albie looked at him, tipped the can of lager half an inch, a small dangerous movement that should have told Mick a great deal.

'Ha, ha,' he said, totally mirthless.

Mick lifted his own can in acknowledgement.

'Listen. . .' he said grandly, the big gesture, 'I'll take a couple of tins, old times' sake.'

Albie nodded.

'Sure,' he said, 'but what do *you* want paint for?'

'Thought I might cheer this place up.'

Albie nodded again.

'You staying here?'

Mick frowned.

'Of course,' he said, 'where else?'

'I thought you were on notice? I thought Cartwright was sending the bailiffs in?'

Mick looked confused.

'What?' he said.

Albie paused. He was talking slowly now, not a trace of the Special Brew, plenty of space between the words, no ambiguities.

'You told me, a month back, before all the bother. . .that we were skint.' He paused, took a long attentive drag from the can. Then he wiped his mouth on the back of his hand. 'That's why we went into boats.' He paused again. '*Isn't it?*'

Mick nodded, automatic reflex movement.

'Yes,' he said.

'Only the boats didn't work out, did they?'

'No.'

'And we didn't see a penny, did we?'

'No.'

'Because Cartwright disappeared. . .' He smiled, a bad sign. 'Or at least that's what you told me. . .'

Mick swallowed hard.

'It's true,' he said defensively.

Albie looked at him, said nothing. Mick tried hard to think of something funny. Nothing happened. Albie smiled again, totally in control.

'So when's he back?' he said softly. 'Mate?'

Mick nodded, understanding him perfectly, the situation, the Special Brew, twenty-odd years of obligation.

'Tomorrow morning,' he said quietly, 'on the Jersey boat.'

Gillespie drove into the Wessex TV compound at dusk. The security guards stopped him at the gate. He gave them Annie's name. He said he was expected. He sat behind the wheel, waiting. They conferred on a phone and let him in. He drove around the studio block and parked outside the main reception door. The parking space was labelled 'Managing Director'. He got out.

Annie met him at the front door. She was in a T-shirt and jeans. She had a pencil tucked behind her ear.

'Where've you been?' she said.

Gillespie shrugged.

'Away,' he said, smiling to himself, a private joke. 'Out of touch.'

'I've been worried,' she said, 'more than worried.'

'Yeah. I gathered.'

'You picked up the messages?'

'Yeah.'

'Didn't phone me back?'

'No.'

'Why not?'

Gillespie shrugged.

'I thought it was better this way,' he said, 'face to face.'

Annie looked at him a moment, then glanced at her watch.

'Right now it's difficult,' she said, 'I'm running late.' She paused, expecting him to accept the tacit invitation, take the hint, make a date for later and leave. He smiled at her.

'Fine,' he said, 'I'll come in.'

She hesitated a moment, then shrugged and led the way into the studio. They walked along a series of corridors, then into a small editing suite. A young man with glasses turned from the control console, nodding at Gillespie, directing Annie's attention to the middle of three monitor screens.

'What do you think of this?' he said. 'Watch.'

He punched a button. Goodman appeared on screen, getting out of a large black Jaguar. Gillespie recognized the scene outside the cathedral. Goodman approached the camera, acknowledged Annie's whispered question, delivered the perfect answer. Something was missing in the middle, bridged by a shot of a young mother across the road, watching with her baby in a pushchair. The sequence came to an end. Annie nodded, her hand on Gillespie's arm.

'It's fine,' she said. 'He sounds quite plausible.' She turned to

Gillespie. 'Don't you think?'

Gillespie shrugged.

'Depends. . .' he said.

Annie looked at him, a new look, a professional curiosity. Smoke in the wind. New information. New source. The photo she'd found in the living room. This man she could never control.

'Depends on what?' she said.

Gillespie looked at the screen, Goodman arrested in mid-smile. The glasses. The eyes. Four weeks earlier, he'd been a face in his own viewfinder, sitting on a bench in the Botanical Gardens, at odds with his mistress. Now, very evidently, he was on the edge of stardom, this week's TV personality. His ever-loyal wife, Gillespie's ex-client, beside him.

'What are you doing?' Gillespie said. 'What is all this?'

Annie didn't answer for a moment, telling the editor to run into the next roll of rushes. Only when the screen was blank again, the editor looking for the right cassette, did she turn back to him. He recognized the change in her voice at once. She was defensive. She was uneasy. She didn't know quite what to say.

'It's a kind of profile,' she said, 'warts and all.'

Gillespie nodded, looking at her, leaving her no place to hide.

'Profile of who?'

'Goodman.'

'Ah.' He smiled. 'Our Controller. The man in the middle.'

Annie glanced up at him, uncertain.

'Sure,' she said, 'it must have been difficult for him.'

Gillespie nodded, the smile widening. 'Yeah,' he said, 'you're right.'

There was a long silence. The editor loaded another cassette. Pictures of the dockyard. Shots of the deep water channel. Annie leaned forward, her hand on the editor's shoulder.

'Five minutes,' she said apologetically, 'I'll be back.'

She opened the door and stepped outside. Gillespie followed. The corridor was empty. He looked at Annie. She was still preoccupied. She led him along the corridor. At the end there was a door. She opened the door, and pulled him inside. When she found the wall switch, there were shelves and shelves of theatrical props, kitchen implements, cups, saucers, books, vases, trivia, each tagged with the name of a programme. It looked like a department store, the place where you shopped for the TV version of reality. Gillespie gazed round, fascinated.

'Wonderland,' he said, softly.

Annie ignored him. 'Tell me,' she said urgently, 'I have to know.'

Gillespie looked at her, enjoying the moment, knowing at last that he'd made the right decision. He smiled.

'Nice of you to ask,' he said, 'but I'm OK.'

Annie gazed at him.

'That's not what I meant.'

'I know.' He smiled again. 'But it's still true.'

Annie hesitated a moment, time ticking on. Then, quite suddenly, she relaxed. She smiled.

'You know what I want,' she said, 'you know why it matters.'

'I do?'

'Yes.' She reached out for him, one finger up the lapel of his denim jacket, up the line of his throat, to his chin. 'So tell me,' she said.

'Tell you what?'

'Tell me why you were interested in the man? Tell me why you took the photos. I've got a week to get this thing right.' She paused. 'Do you know what that means?'

Gillespie shook his head.

'No,' he said.

'Do you care?'

'No.' He paused. 'Should I?'

'Yes.'

'Why?'

'Because it matters. Because I'm interested in the truth.'

'Ah. . .' he nodded, 'the truth.'

Gillespie looked at her for a moment, then cupped his hands behind her head, pulling her gently towards him. He hadn't felt so good for months. It was a feeling of wholeness, of renewal. He was back where he belonged. In command.

'You took the film,' he said slowly, 'you should know.'

'I did,' she admitted.

'So. . .' he shrugged, 'you tell me.'

'I can't.'

'Why not?'

'Because I never saw the prints.'

Gillespie kissed her softly.

'No?' he said.

She shook her head, her tongue sliding between his lips, her hands falling away, down, over the denim jacket.

Gillespie said nothing, letting the conversation find its own path, her hands at the waistband of his jeans, pulling gently at the buckle on his belt, easing the loop of leather wider and wider.

'You going to tell me, or not?' she said.

He smiled.

'No,' he said, 'I'm not.'

She sank to her knees, easing the tongue of leather back through the buckle.

'You're a difficult bastard,' she said, looking up. 'Always were.'

'I am?'

'Yes,' she said.

She undid the belt, and tugged at the zip on his jeans. He felt her hands exploring inside, fingers teasing up towards his crutch, lips and hot flesh and the long slow curl of her tongue. He leaned back, transferring the weight of his body against the wall, feeling the hard ridges of the shelving against his back. Her fingertips began to dance, way down, underneath, the subtlest rhythm, while she licked and licked, cat-like, and took him in, as deep as she could. He looked down, watching her head, the slow rhythm, the noises she made. Then, very gently, he sank to his knees, his face to hers. She looked at him, blinking.

'Nothing personal. . .' he said, 'but don't think. . .'

She put a finger to his lips.

'I know what you're going to say,' she said, 'and you're quite wrong.'

She looked at him, her hands beginning to dig again, her fingers exploring the moistness between his thighs.

'This is because I love you,' she said. 'The rest of it is shit.'

Annie finished at the studio at eleven. Gillespie had long gone, walking out through the big double doors, his point made, some kind of relationship back on offer. Annie couldn't be sure where the latest encounter would take them, but she knew enough about this man to recognize that he meant what he said. Business was business. Friendship was friendship. Whatever he knew about Goodman was strictly confidential. No kiss and tell. No pillow talk. No short cuts to get her off the hook.

She rang Bullock's home number from a phone in reception. It answered after about a minute. He sounded groggy. He'd probably been asleep.

'Annie,' she said tersely, 'your fearless sleuth.'

'Oh,' he said.

She told him what she'd been up to, the progress she'd made, the fact – now confirmed – that the dead boy's mother had no interest in talking to the media. When she'd finally traced the woman to her new council house, a quiet estate in the north of the city, she'd simply said that the incident was over. Her Jason was dead, and she just wanted to be left in peace. She wasn't bitter. She didn't blame anyone. She was just tired of it all. Annie had done her best, getting as close as she could to the woman in the ten brief minutes they'd shared in the tiny back kitchen, giving her every opportunity to open up, to sound off, to heap the blame at Goodman's feet, but the woman refused to even discuss it. Her washing was flapping on the line outside, there was a casserole in the oven for lunch, and she was far too busy getting on with it all to worry about fancy interviews with the press. The boy was dead and buried. So be it.

Bullock listened to her on the other end of the phone. He shared her disappointment. It showed in his voice. Despite the absurd deadlines, she thought, despite the evasions, he obviously still cared. Whatever pressures he was under hadn't quite killed off the journalist within him. She hesitated on the phone, gazing out at the darkened car park.

'So that's it,' she said, 'Goodman still calls the shots.'

There was a silence. Bullock was obviously thinking.

'What about your friend?' he said. 'Your ex-Marine?'

'Gillespie?'

'Yes,' he paused. 'Would he know anything?'

Annie nodded.

'Yes,' she said, 'he would.'

'Is he worth a tickle?'

Annie smiled, the sweetest of memories.

'Definitely.'

'Will he come across?'

'No chance.'

'Why not?'

She hesitated again, interested herself in the answer, as uncomfortable as it might be.

'Because he thinks we're schmucks,' she said finally. 'Because he thinks we've sold out.'

Martin Goodman was the last into bed. He cleaned his teeth in the bathroom, cupping his hand under the tap and sluicing the cold water around his mouth. Then he dipped a finger into Joanna's jar of Astral, and rubbed the cream into his face. At the hospital, they'd told him that the gash in his forehead would probably leave a permanent scar, but already it was barely visible, the faintest track running obliquely towards the hairline above his right eye. Long afternoons on the beach at Lavagna had helped. So had Joanna and this new life of theirs, an unspoken agreement to begin again, to bury the last few years, his weakness and his greed, and simply level the ground between them. Total honesty. Total frankness. A life they could truly call their own.

He dried his hands on the towel and walked through to the bedroom. Joanna was sitting up in the big double bed reading a book about alternative medicine. They'd discussed it on holiday, something new, something to share. She'd explained about homoeopathy, and the extraordinary benefits of tricking the body into healing itself. She'd taken to carrying a small supply of the more important remedies, Arnica, and Rhus Tox, and Sulphur, tiny white tablets in small patterned boxes, and one morning, when Goodman had awoken with a headache and the beginnings of a temperature, she'd made him submit to treatment. By lunchtime, at a favourite restaurant in a narrow shadowed alleyway three streets from their hotel, he'd felt better, and she'd been delighted, reaching across, patting him on the arm, doctor and patient. He'd smiled at her, indulged her, enjoying her simple delight, not bothering to explain about the two Paracetamols he'd taken when she was in the shower.

Now, while Goodman shed his dressing gown, she laid her

book on the bedspread. He glanced down at it. The chapter heading read 'Understanding Acupuncture'. Goodman folded the dressing gown over the back of a chair, and climbed into bed, mentally preparing himself for a discussion on Chinese medicine. His wife was watching him carefully, speculative, curious.

'Tell me something,' she said.

Goodman nodded.

'Of course,' he said.

She looked at him for a moment.

'Do you *ever* see her?'

Goodman blinked. For a month, they'd never mentioned Suzanne. Neither by name. Nor in any other way. She had become dead ground between them. A locked box. By pretending she had never happened, she had simply ceased to exist. He shook his head.

'No,' he said, 'I don't.' He paused. 'In fact I can't.'

'Can't?'

'No.'

'Why not?'

Goodman didn't answer for a moment, wondering what had prompted the question, wondering how far to go, how many risks to take with the reality of what had happened.

'She's gone away,' he said finally. 'She's not around any more.'

Gillespie got to the cemetery past midnight. It lay off the main road out of the city, acres of headstones and withered bunches of flowers, and a dark, gloomy chapel in the middle surrounded by trees. The area reserved for welfare funerals lay close to the wall, within range of the street lamps. He'd been there three weeks before, the only mourner at the burial. There'd been a bald, two-line announcement in the paper two days earlier. Suzanne Wallace. Recently deceased. To be buried at 2 p.m.

Gillespie had gone along in the rain, an act of simple respect. A vicar had arrived on a bicycle, a small thin man in glasses, removing his cycle clips under the sodden cassock, leaning the old black Raleigh against the iron railings. He'd taken a prayer book from his saddle bag, and intoned the simple service over the grave as the undertaker's men lowered the coffin into the earth.

Gillespie had bowed his head, muttering 'Amen,' wishing her luck and a safe journey.

Afterwards, the vicar had pedalled away again, one hand for the bike, the other hitching up the long cassock, while the undertaker's men returned to the empty hearse, and the cemetery staff rolled up the plastic grass. At the time, Gillespie had wondered at the absence of mourners, the grim austerity of the ten-minute commital. There'd been no wreaths, no bouquets of flowers, no eyes to dry. Just a single bunch of freesias, laid carefully to one side while the men from the council buried their spades in the mound of loose earth, and began to shovel soil back into the grave. He'd glanced down at the freesias before he'd left. There were a dozen of them, wrapped in cellophane. A hand-written note had smudged in the rain. All he could read were three words: *Chagrin*, and *Pitié*, and *Paix*. They looked French. They'd stuck in his brain. One day, he promised himself, he'd get hold of a dictionary.

Now, he walked carefully between the rows of headstones, looking for her grave. Across the main road, on the other side of the wall, he remembered a shop selling electrical goods, and a telephone box. He saw them now. He stopped. He looked down. At the spot where they'd buried her, there was a new headstone. It was small, and plain, gold letters inlaid on the black marble. . . SUZANNE WALLACE, it read, BORN 29 JUNE 1962 LOVED AND MISSED.

He stooped and briefly touched the headstone. It felt cold and damp. He stood there in the darkness for a moment, hearing the vicar again, the old assurances, the soft patter of the rain on the wet earth. Then he stepped carefully away.

Albie Curtis glanced at his watch and yawned. The Jersey boat was late. At the desk, in the Ferryport, they'd said an hour at least. A labour situation in St Helier, wildcat stoppages amongst the stevedores. He'd grunted at them, asking about a Mr Cartwright. Was he on board? Did they have a passenger list? The girl behind the desk had tapped the name into a computer, and nodded. Yes, she'd said, a Mr H. Cartwright, travelling alone, vehicle registration HC 179.

Now, Albie watched the big white boat easing slowly backwards into the berth. The rear door was already opening, and ten minutes later the first cars began to roll off onto the dockside. Cartwright's white Mercedes was the third car to appear and Albie recognized the small, familiar figure behind the wheel. He saw the Mercedes drive into the Customs shed and reappear seconds later. The car came to a halt outside the main terminal. Cartwright disappeared inside.

Albie sauntered across the road and got into the Mercedes. He could see Cartwright through the thick plate-glass windows. He was buying a paper. Albie reached forward and turned on the cassette player. Something classical. Some opera or other. Big voices. Nice tune. Cartwright hurried across the pavement, head buried in the paper. He opened the door, only aware of Albie sitting beside him once he'd slid in beside the wheel. He looked at him. If he was surprised, it didn't show. Albie nodded.

'Morning,' he said affably. 'Good trip?'

On Albie's instructions, they drove south, across the city, to the tiny dock near the harbour mouth. Albie indicated his white van, parked near the pub.

'There,' he said, 'park there.'

Cartwright did what he was told, an air of slight irritation. Whatever he'd been up to in Jersey hadn't included days on the beach. He was as pale and white as ever. He pulled the car beside Albie's van and switched off the engine. The tide was high, and the *Timothy Lee* was clearly visible at the quayside. Albie nodded at it.

'You owe us,' he said simply, 'and I'm here to it collect.'

Cartwright looked at him, a busy schoolteacher with a difficult pupil.

'What do you want?' he said.

'Only money.'

'There is no money.' He paused, choosing his words carefully. 'In fact we're in a refund situation.'

Albie gazed at him. 'A what?'

'A refund situation.' He paused again. 'As you know, things didn't quite work out the way we planned. The cash we took at the dock, the up-front money, that all went back.'

'I know,' Albie nodded, 'I was there. I'm talking about the rest of it.'

'Rest of it?' Cartwright looked pained. 'What rest of it?'

'The rest of the ticket price.' He bent towards Cartwright, crowding him towards the door. 'We're talking thousands. Remember?'

Cartwright looked at him. 'We were. But we didn't deliver.' He smiled. 'Remember?'

Albie shrugged. 'Makes no difference. You did some kind of deal. Must have done. All I'm asking for is our cut. As agreed.'

Cartwright shook his head, the action of a man in the presence of an imbecile. He began to reach back, one hand stretching for the briefcase on the back seat. Albie stopped him.

'Do you want to see the figures or not?' Cartwright said. 'Only I'm a little busy.'

Albie shook his head. 'I'm a bit old for fairy-tales,' he said. 'Thanks all the same.'

Cartwright shrugged, his duty done.

'Suit yourself.'

There was a silence. Albie eyed the dashboard. The milometer read 276 miles.

'Nice new motor,' he said.

Cartwright ignored the comment, reaching for the ignition keys, the conversation over. Albie stopped him.

'I've got some white paint I'd like you to buy,' he said.

'Some what?'

'White paint. Quite a lot of white paint. You can have it cheap.' He smiled. 'Old times' sake. I want it paid personally. In cash. To me. To this address. By tomorrow lunchtime. OK?'

He produced an old envelope with an address pencilled on the back. He put it on the dashboard, in front of Cartwright. He began to get out of the car. Then he paused, looking back.

'Ten grand,' he said, 'non-refundable.' He smiled again. 'OK?'

He got out of the car and slammed the door behind him. Cartwright started the engine, not looking up. The car purred away, and Albie watched it disappear around the corner of the pub. Only when it had gone did he associate the hand that had emerged briefly from the driver's window, and the ball of crumpled paper on the cobbles, with the address he'd just left on Cartwright's dashboard. He shrugged, kicking the remains of the envelope into the water. Fine, he thought. If Cartwright wants to play games, that was his affair. One way or another, he'd get his money. If not ten grand, then something close. He strolled across to his van and wrenched open the door. The lock had long gone, and he'd stopped worrying about it years ago. His most valuable cargo for months had been the big drums of white emulsion, and even then no one had bothered to nick them. Pity, he thought, climbing into the driver's seat.

He started the engine and kicked it into gear. He glanced in the remains of the wing mirror, and pulled the van into a tight three-point turn. The van was barely a yard from the edge of the dock when he felt the arm circle his throat and tighten. He stamped on the brake and tried to struggle, but it was hopeless. He opened his mouth to shout. Nothing happened. He began to choke. There were red spots in front of his eyes, then the colour drained away, and everything turned into the same shade of grey, and he knew he was losing consciousness.

His body went slack, and the pressure around his throat loosened. Gradually, very slowly, he was able to take in air again. His vision cleared. He looked up at the rear-view mirror. Gillespie's face was next to his, his breath hot on Albie's ear. He was wearing a combat jacket and a small woollen cap. He had gloves on.

'Over there,' Gillespie said, 'by the boat.'

Albie looked at him again, and pushed up, hard, from the seat, trying to catch him under the chin, the nose, token resistance, a sop to his pride. The choke hold tightened again.

'Do it,' Gillespie said. 'Now.'

Albie did his best to nod, to signal he'd had enough, but Gillespie's eyes were elsewhere, looking out through the windshield, checking left and right. Albie let the clutch out, and backed the van very slowly away from the quayside. Then he inched it forwards until it was abreast of McNaught's trawler.

'Switch off the engine,'Gillespie said.

Albie did what he was told. The engine coughed and died. There was silence. Gillespie again, inches from his ear.

'Tell me about the girl,' he said, 'I want to know about the girl.'

'What girl?'

Gillespie laughed, a brief expulsion of stale air. Then he pushed hard on the back of Albie's head, without warning. Albie saw the steering wheel coming up to meet him, then there was darkness as he shut his eyes, and an excruciating pain around his nose. Gillespie took a handful of his hair and pulled his head back and did it again. Albie tasted blood.

'The girl who was working for Cartwright,' Gillespie said, 'the one who was on the ladder the night you gave me the diesel.' He paused. 'Remember?'

Albie nodded. 'Yeah.'

A tooth had loosened. He nudged it with his tongue. Gillespie was still there, inches away, the voice in his ear.

'So what happened to her?' he said. 'Tell me.'

Albie shook his head, wincing with the pain.

'I dunno,' he said, 'ask Cartwright.'

'Did *he* kill her?'

Albie looked up to the mirror, genuinely astonished.

'What?'

'Did *he* kill her?'

'Kill her?'

'Yeah,' Gillespie nodded. 'She's dead.'

'No. Of course he didn't.'

'Did you?'

Albie gazed at Gillespie, completely out of his depth. The arm began to tighten again, and he kicked hard against the floor panels, arching his body, twisting to the left, throwing Gillespie momentarily off balance. There was a heavy rubber torch on the dashboard, and Albie seized it, lashing out behind him. Gillespie was too close for him to do real damage, but he felt the lens of the torch shatter on something bony, something hard, and when Gillespie emerged from his left, diving in over the back of the seat, there was blood running down his face.

He lashed out again, using his fists, as Gillespie closed on him, forcing him back against the door. Gillespie was on top of him now, the two bodies wedged together between the steering wheel and the back of the seat. Albie brought his knee up, as hard as he could, feeling the bony arch at the bottom of Gillespie's pelvis. Gillespie gasped with pain, his hands closing again around

Albie's neck, going for the jugular.

Abruptly, Albie went limp. He began to make gurgling noises. His eyes started to widen. Gillespie held him a second or two longer, then let go, falling back against the passenger door, fumbling with the window, winding it down, leaning out in time to be sick over the cobbles. He wiped his mouth with the back of his hand. Albie was still flat on his back, his chest heaving, forcing the air deep into his lungs.

'Yes or no?' Gillespie said.

Albie tried to struggle upright, but gave up and sank back on the scuffed vinyl.

'No,' he said in a croak.

'You hurt?'

Albie nodded. 'Yeah,' he said.

There was a silence. Gillespie wiped his mouth again. The last five minutes had taken more out of him than he liked to admit. More running, he thought. Get back out there. Into shape. Albie got up on his elbows. He looked terrible. There was blood all over the bottom half of his face and his nose changed direction half-way down. He ran his tongue around his mouth in pursuit of something small and hard, and finally produced a tooth. He took it out and looked at it. Then up at Gillespie.

'You done, then, have you?'

Gillespie nodded, feeling behind him for the door handle.

'Yeah,' he said, opening the door, 'for now.'

He got out of the van and glanced briefly back inside. Albie was sitting upright, examining the damage in the mirror, aware of Gillespie at the open window. He fingered the area around his nose, very gently, scowling at the pain.

'They're right about you, Gillespie,' he said, 'you're off your fucking head.'

Annie McPhee had been in the Bunker for most of the morning before she realized what was happening.

She'd decided to split the filming into three parts. First, she did a preliminary interview with Goodman, covering the nuts and bolts of the period underground, who sat where, who did what, how the procedures worked, how one man could possibly orchestrate the life of an entire city.

This part of the filming went moderately well. Goodman sat in front of the Situations Board, describing the command structures, the careful division of responsibility, the enormous task addressed by a tiny corps of local government officers, most of them too young even to have done National Service. It was, he said, a triumph of teamwork, a round-the-clock effort by a selfless group of dedicated professionals. Annie had taken this line a little further, probing the effects of claustrophobia, and anxiety, and sheer exhaustion. These were men and women, after all, who must have been a lot closer than the rest of the population to incoming reports from Central Europe and the Barents Sea. They knew how critical the situation had become. They'd every reason to expect the call from Fylingdales, the inbound blips on the big radar screens, the first airbursts blossoming over the city. Hadn't they been worried about their families? Their loved ones? How could they possibly cope?

At this, Goodman smiled and nodded, agreeing that it had been a problem. Annie had explored the question further. Were there special arrangements for wives and kids? Some way of lessening the tensions? Easing the burden? Goodman had smiled again. Yes, he'd said, there'd naturally been provision for Bunker dependants. It would have been foolish not to have anticipated the problem. But thankfully, the Emergency had been over before he'd had time to properly action the plan. When Annie asked for details – a destination, say – he'd shaken his head, statesman-like, maintaining a proper reticence, and said he'd prefer these arrangements to remain confidential.

After this first interview, Annie set up a series of shots around the Bunker. Most of the key officers had been told to attend. They sat at their desks, shrouded in their NBC suits, wooden faced, awkward, pretending to discharge their civic duties, doing again what all of them preferred to forget. Annie did her best, trying to create a genuine feeling of tension, trying to ensure the tiniest details were right, the NBC masks in the in-trays, the half drunk cups of coffee, the litter of old memos, the red winking eye of the Attack Imminent alarm.

Some of it, she thought, might work. With the right sound effects, and a chord or two of music, it might begin to suggest the way it must have been. But the harder she tried, and the more ambitious the shots she set up, the more she became aware of the watching eyes of Goodman, and the young assistant he'd introduced, in a casual aside, as Mr Jones. The latter was supposed to be local, some functionary from the Civic Centre, but Annie found this line increasingly hard to swallow. On one or two occasions, he seemed vague about the city's geography, and when – mid-morning over coffee and biscuits – she asked him point blank where he lived, he offered her an uneasy smile and side-stepped the question. It was a bit tricky, he said. He was in transit just now between addresses. In fact he often asked himself the same question: where *did* he live? Annie laughed dutifully into her coffee, knowing full well that he actually came from somewhere else, probably London, probably sent down to keep an eye on things. What were they frightened of? She began to wonder. What had really happened?

The last part of the filming should have given her the answer. She set up another interview with Goodman, different location, up in his office, the man in charge, the focus tighter, the questions sharper. The success of this kind of interview always depended on research, little pockets of prior knowledge acquired by stealth or diligence, concealed from the interviewee, the necessary antidote to the usual evasions and bluster and half truths. On this occasion, though, Annie knew that much of the material she could rely on was already public knowledge: the arms convoys, the rationing of food and fuel, the curfew. To this, admittedly, she could add her own experience – the assault at the roadblock, summary arrest, hospital wards full of detainees – but even so, it didn't really add up to very much. The situation plainly warranted emergency measures. As Controller, Goodman would have been irresponsible not to have implemented them.

Even so, she tried her best again, seating Goodman behind the big desk, lighting him in a certain way, heavy key light, minimal fill, more than a hint of Leni Riefenstahl. She put the questions to him as artfully as she knew how, trying to voice the surprise that ordinary people must have felt, glimpsing the extent of the power they'd handed to this man, the limitless sweep of the actions he could take. Goodman sensed at once what she was trying to do, and rode the interrogation with ease, giving each question careful thought, deflecting it with the kind of sincere concern politicians reserve for the trickier issues. It was wholly convincing, the purest reassurance, and Annie soon recognized that she was getting nowhere. What had begun as an investigation, was fast turning into a whitewash. At this rate, she thought grimly, she might just as well try interior decoration.

She shifted in her chair, trying to retrieve the initiative. Goodman watched her from behind the desk, composed, at ease, a man with absolutely nothing to hide. A man who'd simply done the job he'd been paid for. A man, in short, you could trust.

'So why did you impose a curfew?' Annie asked.

Goodman acknowledged the question with a nod.

'To keep people at home. It was a matter of. . .' He paused, frowning, feeling his way towards a conclusion, doing his thinking on camera, the way they taught you at the £400-a-day TV schooling sessions.

'Control?' suggested Annie.

He smiled. Cheap point.

'Information,' he said. 'It was important that people kept in touch.'

'Is that why you took over radio and television?'

'Yes, it was.' He paused again. 'Can you suggest a better alternative?'

Annie looked at him, driven to the frontal assault.

'How about telling people the truth?' she suggested. 'For a change?'

'That's exactly what we did.'

'All those game shows? Cartoons? Sit coms? All that pap?'

Goodman smiled at her earnestness, playing the man in the street.

'Oh, I don't know. . .' he said, 'our job was to offer as much information, and as much reassurance, as we could. Information, as it happened, was hard to come by. Reassurance was on the shelf. Is there something wrong in making people laugh?' He paused, the smile broadening. 'Have you seen the viewing figures for that week? They were sensational.'

Annie blinked.

'Are you suggesting people prefer game shows to the truth?' she said.

Goodman spread his hands wide, the mock innocent, the

interview falling into his lap.

'I'm not suggesting anything,' he said. 'I'm simply telling you that we tried to keep life as normal as possible.' He paused again. 'Who knows?' he said finally. 'Perhaps that amounts to the same thing.'

Gillespie met the estate agent outside the seafront block of flats, as arranged. Since leaving Albie at the dock, he'd had time to go home, shower and change. He'd done his best with the gash on his forehead, but the swelling was already there, and he knew there was no way of disguising it.

The agent arrived late, a young man in a suit and a tie, stepping out of a smart new Honda, glancing apologetically at his Swatch watch, and shaking Gillespie by the hand. They took the lift to the ninth floor, while the agent extracted the particulars from a file, and ran through what he termed 'the major features'.

Gillespie nodded, not listening, wondering who'd got in that night, who'd tempted the girl to the door and talked her into opening it. He'd seen no evidence of a forced entry, no splintered wood, none of the scars from a wrecking bar or a sledgehammer. At first, he'd assumed her death had some connection with events at the dock – Cartwright, Rendall, Curtis – but five minutes in the back of Albie's van had made him wonder. Men under extreme physical pressure rarely lie, and he'd seen the expression on Albie's face when he'd told him about the girl's death. He'd been astounded. More important, he'd been insulted. Whoever killed Suzanne Wallace, it certainly wasn't Albie Curtis.

The lift began to slow. The agent was returning the particulars to his briefcase. The door opened and they stepped out onto the landing. Gillespie nodded at Suzanne's door. Number 913.

'Place vacant?' he said.

The agent nodded, fumbling in his pocket for the keys.

'Yes,' he said, 'you're lucky.'

'Who was the previous owner?'

The agent frowned, coaxing the key into the lower lock.

'I don't know. To tell you the truth,' he turned the key, 'we're handling the sale for the Treasury Solicitor. I gather it's a liquidation case.'

'Oh?'

Gillespie frowned. The Treasury Solicitor normally dealt with estates where there was no known next-of-kin. He remembered the funeral, the vicar and his bicycle at the graveside, the total absence of mourners. Maybe this was the explanation. The girl died without relatives. No one, quite literally, to wave her goodbye.

The agent turned the key in the second lock and stepped into the flat. Gillespie followed. The place smelled of fresh paint. They walked through to the lounge. The walls were white. He remembered a different colour, a hint of blue. He looked round. The carpet was spotless. No trace of the blood spills near the window. He crossed slowly to the big sliding doors that led out onto the balcony.

'Nice view,' he said automatically.

The agent nodded, glancing at his watch again.

'Magnificent,' he said.

Gillespie paused at the window. He unlocked the catch on the door and glanced over his shoulder.

'May I?'

'Of course.'

He slid the door open and walked out onto the balcony. The morning was bright, but cool, the wind off the sea. The island was very clear, an arm's reach away, and a gusting wind was slicing the tops off the bigger waves. Gillespie ran a thoughtful finger along the top of the parapet. He glanced over. Same drop. Same concrete. Same spread-eagled figure imprinted on his memory. He looked out to sea again, feeling the old tug, the old affection, and then turned away and went back into the flat. The agent, a busy young man, was obviously eager to get away. Gillespie sank into one of the armchairs. Last time he'd seen it, it had been on its side, by the wall. He leaned back, made himself comfortable. The loose covers felt newly washed and ironed. Someone had done a thorough job.

'What happens to all this stuff?' he enquired. 'The furniture? The pictures?'

The agent glanced round.

'I gather it's all on offer. We'd negotiate separately on that.'

'I see.' Gillespie paused, fingering the linen of the loose covers. 'Good condition, isn't it?'

'Yes,' the agent nodded. 'We think presentation's important.'

'We?'

The young man caught the inflection in Gillespie's voice, the tiny shift of emphasis, a definite question.

'Yes,' he said.

'You had this place cleaned?'

'Of course.'

'Bit of a state, was it?'

The agent frowned.

'I'm not sure,' he said, 'to tell you the truth. I know there's money in the estate.' He smiled. 'You can see it. It's a nice place.' He shrugged. 'So I imagine we spent a penny or two really getting it up together.' He paused. 'Do I take it you're interested?'

Gillespie nodded. 'Very.' He got up and circled the room. 'This cleaning up business. . .' he said slowly, 'on whose instructions would you have done that?'

The agent frowned, not following the logic of Gillespie's questions. Clients normally asked about the central heating and the rates. Not stuff like this.

'I don't know,' he said, 'to tell you the truth.'

'But it would have been somebody? Somebody outside the firm?'

'Maybe,' he shrugged, 'maybe not.'

Gillespie nodded.

'Who instructed you?'

'I've told you. The Treasury Solicitors.'

'In London?'

'Yes.'

'And who instructed them?'

'I'm afraid I've no idea.'

Gillespie nodded again, kneeling by the wall, and running a finger along the skirting board. New paintwork. Thick gloss. He looked up.

'What happened to the vendor?' he said.

The agent opened the file again. He was clearly getting tired of it all.

'A Miss Wallace,' he said finally.

'That's her name. I asked you what happened to her.'

The agent looked down at him.

'I've no idea,' he said. 'Though I imagine she's dead.'

Gillespie said goodbye to the agent at the kerbside, keeping a copy of the particulars and thanking him for his time. The young man got in his car, and sped away, the uncertainty and the suspicion evident beneath the automatic smile. Gillespie returned to the ninth floor, choosing the door opposite Suzanne's flat. He knocked twice and rang the bell. After a while, the door opened. A man in his mid-sixties stood there. He was wearing monogrammed pyjamas under a silk dressing gown, and he smelled of aftershave. Down the hall behind him, Gillespie could see a line of framed regimental photographs.

'My name's Gillespie,' he said, 'I've come about the flat opposite.'

The man nodded and looked vague.

'Gas, are you?' he said. A refined accent. Clipped. Ex-military.

Gillespie shook his head.

'Number 913,' he said again, 'Miss Wallace. That was.'

'Oh?'

'Yes. . .' He paused. 'Did you know her at all? Were you friends?'

The man looked confused again.

'I'm on the electric,' he said, 'I haven't got gas.'

Gillespie gazed at him for a moment, and tried again, trying to tease some sense out of the man, but the conversation went nowhere, and in the end Gillespie gave up. The man was clearly shot. A lifetime of cheap booze in the mess had seen off the last of his white cells, and there was no point prolonging the exchange. Gillespie thanked him for his time and turned away.

At the other two flats on the hallway, he drew more blanks. One flat was evidently empty, while the woman at the other refused to even come to the door.

He took the lift again and walked out into the sunshine. At the corner of the flats, he glanced up, checking the line from the ninth-floor balcony. The concrete path beneath was quite bare. The intervening month had removed whatever the forensic men might have overlooked. Gillespie hesitated a moment, deep in thought. Then he turned on his heel and headed for the seafront. There were two phone booths by the

Pier. One, at least, might have survived the vandals.

Annie said goodbye to Goodman outside the Bunker. She'd been tempted to forgo the normal courtesies, the handshakes and the assurance that all had gone well, but she knew that she'd have to go back to this man, with his softly spoken good manners and his permanent hint of a smile, and she knew it was wiser to wrap the whole thing up properly.

She paused in the sunshine while the video crew filed past with the heavier bits of equipment. She extended a hand.

'Thanks very much,' she said, 'for your time.'

Goodman shrugged.

'I'm glad we could help,' he said. 'Did you get what you wanted?'

Annie looked at him, weighing up the merits of an honest answer, deciding against it.

'Yes,' she said, 'more or less.'

He nodded, pleased.

'Good,' he said. He took out a diary, small, thin, bound in red leather. He looked up at her. 'When do we expect to see the results?'

'Next week. Tuesday.'

'Really? As soon as that?'

She looked at him, knowing for a fact that he was lying, that he'd known the transmission date for days. Bullock had already agreed the terms of the arrangement: a preview forty-eight hours before transmission, the hospitality suite booked for Sunday evening, the champagne already on ice. Some celebration, she thought, watching the camera assistant loading a box of recorded cassettes into the back of the Volvo. An hour of bland nothings. The authorized version. Stamped, sealed, and utterly meaningless. She blinked. Goodman still had the diary open, his finger anchored on a particular day.

'I've just had a thought,' he said. 'It may be of some use.'

Annie smiled politely.

'Oh?'

Goodman glanced down at the diary.

'Tomorrow night,' he said, 'I'm speaking at Rotary.'

'Are you?'

'Yes.' He smiled at her. 'The speech won't be anything special, but they're going to give me an award. I only mention it because it might give you something extra. It's obviously up to you.'

Annie frowned. 'What sort of award?'

'Oh,' he shrugged, master of the subtle boast, 'services to the city. A thank-you for what happened during the Emergency.' He smiled again. 'It's not for me, really. It's for all of us.' He nodded back towards the Bunker. 'The whole team. That's why I'm suggesting it . . . but it's probably irrelevant. I'm not sure what you're really after. . .'

Annie glanced at her watch.

'It sounds fascinating,' she said. 'Can I take a rain check?'

'Of course,' he said, 'of course. Just let me know. OK?'

'I will.'

She smiled at him and extended a hand for the second time. He shook it, maintaining contact for a second longer than the occasion demanded. His touch fascinated her. Dry, cool, total self-assurance.

'Give me a ring,' he said, looking her in the eye. 'We might have a spot of lunch.'

Gillespie met his CID friend in a pub near the Civic Centre. The man was half an hour late. He picked his way through the crowd of lunchtime drinkers and joined Gillespie at a table in the corner. Gillespie slid the beer-mat off the top of his pint. The man sat down and acknowledged the drink with a nod. He took a mouthful and glanced at his watch.

'I've got ten minutes,' he said. 'Been in the wars, have we?'

Gillespie fingered the bruise over his eye.

'Yeah,' he said, not bothering to explain further.

He looked at the man across the table, and lifted his drink in salute. He'd known the detective for the best part of three years. He'd been a Redcap before leaving the Army, serving ten years in the Military Police, most of it in West Germany. Now he was a constable with the local CID, bored witless by the back-biting, and the gossip, and the daily mountain of paperwork. The two men understood each other, shared a similar outlook on life. A mutual friend had once suspected they were brothers. Gillespie took another mouthful of lime juice.

'There's a file I want,' he said.

The other man nodded.

'No problem,' he said. 'What's the urgency?'

'As soon as you can.'

The detective nodded.

'OK,' he said. He reached inside his anorak and produced a pen.

'Photocopy do?' he said drily. 'Or would you prefer the original?'

Gillespie sipped at the lime juice.

'Photocopy,' he said, 'bird called Suzanne.'

The other man hesitated, his pen in mid-air.

'Suzanne?' he queried. 'Suzanne Wallace?'

Gillespie nodded. 'That's right.'

The other man put his pen down.

'What do you want that for?' he said.

Gillespie shrugged.

'I just do,' he said. 'Is there a problem?'

'She's dead.' He paused. 'And it ain't that simple.'

'Yes,' Gillespie smiled, wholly innocent. 'Committed suicide, didn't she? Fell off some balcony?'

The detective leaned back, wary now.

'How much do you know?' he said at last.

There was a long silence, and then the other man picked up his pen and returned it to his pocket. He pushed back his chair and stood up. Gillespie watched him backing away.

'You haven't finished your drink,' he pointed out quietly.

The detective shook his head.

'Don't need it,' he said. 'Thanks all the same.'

He turned to go, but Gillespie called him back.

'By tonight,' he said. 'If it's OK by you.'

'It isn't.'

'No?'

'No.'

'Oh,' Gillespie shook his head, reaching for the beer-mat, and sliding it once again over the half-empty glass. 'Shame. . .' he said thoughtfully, looking up, '. . .about all those other little drinks. Still. . .' he shrugged, 'I expect you'll find some story or other.'

The other man looked down at him.

'You wouldn't?' he said. 'Would you?'

Gillespie smiled. 'Yeah,' he said, 'for this one, I would.'

Annie sat in the studio canteen, nursing a glass of Coke. It was the first time she'd stopped for nearly a day, and Bullock had joined her in time to answer the harder questions. He put a plateful of spaghetti on the table and returned his tray to the rack. Then he sat down.

'How goes it?' he said.

Annie looked at him without enthusiasm. Sleep obviously agreed with him. Lucky man.

'It doesn't,' she said.

'Oh.' Bullock frowned, reaching for the black pepper.

Annie shook her head.

'It's game, set and match,' she said. 'We haven't got a prayer.'

'Oh? Why not?'

'You know why not.'

'I do?'

'Yes.' Annie pushed the glass to one side, angry at the hours of wasted time, the mute compliance forced upon her by impossible deadlines, and Bullock's precious network slot. In two brief, busy days she'd become just one more arm of the Government machine, the voice in the nation's living rooms, the assurance that all was well, that everything had been for the best. 'It'll be crap,' she said, 'and you know it.'

Bullock wound a strand of spaghetti around his fork, and coated it in bolognese.

'Really?' he said mildly.

'Yes. Really.'

Annie bent forward over the table. Time for a few home truths.

'Number one,' she said. 'They're calling the shots. They decide the agenda. Nothing obvious. Nothing I can I put my finger on, stamp my foot about, have a good shout. Nothing like that.' She shook her head. 'Oh no. They're much too clever. They know bloody well that we've no time, no research, no pictures, nothing.'

'The pictures are coming back,' Bullock said. 'This afternoon.'

'Oh?' Annie paused. 'Are they?'

'Yes. They're returning the stuff they seized.'

'All of it?'

'So they say.'

'Well. . .' Annie sniffed, the wind spilling out of her sails, 'even so . . . it's still a joke.'

Bullock looked at her, another hundred calories on his fork.

'It'll be OK,' he said, 'just you wait.'

'I can't.'

'You can. You have to.'

She stared at him, trying to make sense of what he was saying, the space between the words.

'What is this?' she said. 'What haven't you told me?' Bullock shook his head, innocent, the benign editor with nerves of steel and a passion for stodgy Italian food.

'Nothing,' he said. 'Absolutely nothing.'

Annie nodded, unconvinced, looking for further ammunition. She found it, remembering her final exchange with Goodman outside the Bunker. She bent forward again, earnest, outraged.

'You know what he's offering now?' she said. 'Goodman?'

'No?'

'His speech to the Rotary Club. It's prize-giving. He's getting some award.'

Bullock looked amused.

'Sounds great,' he said, 'you should go.'

Annie stared at him. 'You serious?'

Bullock nodded. 'Perfectly,' he said, eyeing another forkful of spaghetti. 'Do it.'

Gillespie sat in the big armchair in his living room, feet up on the low table, phone to his ear, big foolscap pad propped up on his lap. Through the net curtains at the front, he could see the Bengali kids across the street learning how to skateboard off the kerb. He bent to the phone, beginning to write.

'Say again,' he said.

The voice at the other end spelled the name. Gillespie wrote it down, looked at it.

'Bowyer?' he said. 'With a "y"?'

'Correct.'

'Thanks.'

He put the phone down and stared at the name. The man from the Environmental Health Department had been more than helpful. They'd acquired responsibility for Suzanne's body from the Coroner. An inquest had been opened four weeks back. The Coroner's Officer had reported the circumstances in which her body had been found – a fall from a balcony, evidence of heavy drinking – and there'd been a formal identification by a friend. A post-mortem had taken place, and he understood that the police were still making inquiries. In the meantime, in the absence of any known relatives, Suzanne's body had been released to the Environmental Health Department for burial.

It was an unusual situation, the official had admitted. He himself had been to the flat. It was his job to assess the estate, and to pass on the details to the Treasury Solicitor. Normally, in these cases, he'd be dealing with the destitute, men and women eking out the last of their lives in some squalid bedsit, but in this case, the young lady, it had been very different. The place was spotless, beautifully tidy, neat as a pin, and the flat itself was in a prime position with seventy-five years left on the lease. The estate could easily run to six figures. It was all highly unusual. Gillespie had stopped him there.

'Neat as a what?' he said, backtracking.

'A pin.'

'Nothing disturbed?'

'No. Nothing. In fact it had only just been painted.'

'Oh?' Gillespie reached for his pen. 'When was this?'

At the other end of the phone, he could hear the man leafing through a diary. Then he was back, ever helpful, ever precise.

'Three weeks ago,' he said, 'exactly.'

Gillespie frowned.

'But the funeral was before that. The 5th. Monday.'

'That's right.'

'Why the delay? In getting into the flat?'

The official hesitated, sensing for the first time the depth of Gillespie's interest.

'I don't know,' he said at last. 'You'll have to ask the Coroner.'

'Sure.' Gillespie made another note, leant back in the chair.

'But you're telling me it was ten days before you got into the flat?'

'Yes.'

Gillespie nodded and thanked the official, and hung up. Time to repaint it, he thought. Time to cover tracks, tidy up. No wonder the young man from the estate agent had been so vague. He simply hadn't known. Gillespie studied the name on his pad. Mr Bowyer. 862561. Ran a funeral parlour. Had the Council contract for welfare burials. He'd know about the headstone, the man from the Environmental Health had said. He'd know where it came from.

Gillespie reached for the phone again and dialled the number. A receptionist answered, a querulous woman with a middle-aged voice. Gillespie asked for Mr Bowyer. There was a pause. Then a male voice. Very local, very gruff.

'Yes?'

Gillespie introduced himself as a close friend of poor Suzanne. He'd just come back from Greece. He was distressed to have heard the news. He understood there'd been a welfare burial. He'd been to the cemetery. He wanted to know who to thank for the headstone. There was a long pause at the other end.

'It's not in the price,' Bowyer said at last, 'we never quoted for that.'

'I know you didn't,' Gillespie said patiently. 'That's why I'm asking.'

Bowyer grunted. 'Only don't you go telling people the Council pay for fancy headstones.'

'No.'

'Because they don't.' He paused. 'You live here?'

'Yes.'

'Well, then. . .' he sniffed, very self-righteous, 'it's your money too. Ratepayers' money.'

Gillespie gazed at the phone, promising himself one last bid for the simplest of facts. A name. Nothing else. There was a long pause. Bowyer clearly hated discussing welfare burials. He came back on the phone, even gruffer.

'Middle-aged gent,' he said, 'paid cash.'

'You know his name?'

'He never left any name.'

'That wasn't my question.' Gillespie paused. 'I asked you if you knew who he was.'

Gillespie waited, wondering whether he'd been too direct, too forceful. In the Corps, they always taught you to take control, to dominate the situation. In Civvy Street, it wasn't always so simple. Mr Bowyer again.

'Yeah,' he said, 'happen I do know who he was.'

Gillespie smiled, knowing that he'd made the right decision after all. Nice and easy now, reeling in.

'Oh yeah?' he said lightly. 'So who was he?'

'Goodman,' he said, 'that Controller bloke we had.'

Gillespie thanked him and put the phone down. He hesitated a moment, thinking hard. Then he got up and went across to the small bookshelf beside the fireplace. He found the pocket French dictionary at once. He thumbed through it, remembering the smudged blue scrawl on the card with the freesias at Suzanne's graveside. The three words had stuck in his brain. He found *chagrin*. He found *pitié*. He found *paix*. He listed the words carefully, on a pad, one under the other. *Sorrow* . . . it went, and *pity*, and *peace*. He looked at the words, scarcely believing it, at last beginning to understand.

Twelve

Martin Goodman left work at four that afternoon, driving out of the underground car park, and turning east at the big main road. James' first football match had begun only half an hour earlier. With luck, by the time he got to the recreation ground, the kids would still be playing.

He drove fast through the city, the sun streaming in through the open roof. The morning in the Bunker had gone well, far better than he'd expected. When Davidson had first phoned him about the film, he'd been cautious. He saw no point in disinterring the whole episode. His own brief war had been far from distinguished, and he sensed no appetite amongst his colleagues for going through the whole thing again. Better, surely, to simply forget it.

Davidson had been sympathetic. He understood Goodman's reservations. He was glad he'd had such a successful holiday. He was delighted he was back at work. But there were anxieties at national level that the Government had been seen to be rather forceful in this one key city. The blockade and the curfew and one or two other measures might well become *causes célèbres* in certain left-wing circles. Better, went the official line, to come clean at once, to get the whole thing out in the open. To pre-empt any criticism of the kind he'd described.

As it happened, there was an ideal vehicle available, in the shape of the local TV station, their good friend Duggie Bullock, and his remarkably compliant Vice-Chairman, a Mr Cussins. The latter, it seemed, was seeking a DoE ruling on yet another marina site. He needed all the ministerial goodwill he could get. He was more than happy to shepherd the programme through. In fact he thought it was an excellent idea.

Goodman had read the clear message behind Davidson's casual asides. The film is to be done. The programme is to be made. The journalists will be taken care of. No hard questions. No real investigation. Nothing to get anxious about. Just another dollop of helpful propaganda in the ceaseless battle to get the Government's policies truly understood for what they were: short-term measures for the long-term good.

The conversation had ended amicably enough. Davidson had thanked Goodman for his support. One day, he said, he'd have to pop down again. He'd stand Goodman a dinner, reminisce a little, stroll round some of the old locations. It would be very pleasant. He'd look forward to it.

Now, turning into the recreation ground, Goodman knew there wasn't the remotest possibility of Davidson ever doing any such thing. Once the film was out, the case made, all criticism safely sealed off, Goodman's usefulness would be at an end. He'd go back into the drawer with all the other duds. His name would be circulated on some confidential list or other. Be careful about this man, senior officials would warn each other, he's not quite up to it, can't quite cut the mustard.

Goodman smiled, parking the car outside the tiny playing field and watching James dive wildly at the feet of the opposing centre forward. He wasn't sure he cared any more about all that. Once upon a time he'd fantasized about it, dreaming of the day when he could leave local government, and step into the higher realms of national administration, but after twenty years of worrying about it, two whole decades of trying to reach the top of the pile, he was no longer sure it was even worth the effort.

He got out of the car and strolled through the gate of the recreation ground. Joanna was jumping up and down on the touchline, Caroline on one side, Charlie in the buggy on the other. He took them by surprise, putting his arm round his wife's shoulders, watching her turn, seeing the delight on her face, kissing her softly on both cheeks, a continental gesture, a souvenir from Tuscany. She smiled up at him, while Charlie went frantic in the buggy, straining up against the reins, demanding his share of the kisses.

'How was it?' she said. 'How did it go?'

He shrugged, and returned her smile, nodding at the kids on the pitch, with their striped team shirts, and their tiny Puma boots, their faces contorted with concentration and effort.

'Piece of cake,' he said. 'Another home win.'

Gillespie took the detective's call at home. He was still in the living room, drawing lines on the big foolscap page, testing one possibility against another, wondering quite where to head next. When the phone rang, he picked it up at once. The detective sounded far from friendly.

'John,' Gillespie said, 'take it easy.'

The voice on the phone paused for a moment, then came back. He named a big department store about half a mile from the central police station.

'Menswear,' he said briefly, 'second floor. Be there in fifteen minutes. I'll wait for five. Don't talk to me. Just take what I give you. OK?'

The phone went dead, and Gillespie gazed at the pad one final time before heading for the door. His latest line petered out in mid-page, leaving a wilderness of empty white space. He tore off the sheet, screwed it into a ball and lobbed it into the waste paper basket. Then he collected his jacket and walked the length of the hall. Only when he was out on the street, did he realize he was whistling.

The department store was a mile or so away. Gillespie got there with five minutes to spare, taking the escalator to the second floor. The menswear department occupied about half the floor space, rack after rack of suits and jackets, anoraks and sweaters. Gillespie gazed round. The detective had already arrived. He was standing alone in a far corner under a pair of surveillance cameras, safely out of shot. He was sorting carefully through a rack of long-sleeved shirts, designer colours, pinks and yellows and delicate shades of green. Gillespie skirted the display area, approaching him from behind.

'Suits you,' he said, 'angel face.'

The detective spun round and Gillespie put his finger to his lips.

'Moscow rules,' he whispered.

The other man began to say something but thought better of it. Instead, he reached into his pocket and produced a long brown envelope. He gave it to Gillespie. Gillespie studied it.

'What's this?' he said.

'Path report.'

Gillespie looked up at him.

'What about the Scene of Crime?'

'It's gone.'

'What do you mean it's gone?'

'It's not there.' He paused. 'Something wrong with your ears?'

Gillespie ignored the sarcasm.

'I don't believe you,' he said.

The other man shrugged, already turning away, hands amongst the shirts, the browsing shopper spoiled for choice.

'Believe what you fucking like,' he said, 'it's true.'

Gillespie drove home with the envelope. He didn't open it until he was back inside his house, the front door shut, the kettle on the stove, the tea-bags in the pot. He sat down in the kitchen at the big old table and made a space for himself amongst the litter of bills, and newspapers, and assorted ovenware. Then, at last, he opened the envelope.

Inside, there was a typed three-page report from the pathologist. It was dated October 2nd, three-and-a-half weeks back. The name at the top read SUZANNE MARGARET WALLACE. It began with a brief four-line paragraph headed *History*.

Gillespie scanned it quickly. Suzanne had been found lying on her left side on the ground at the foot of a block of flats. Investigations suggested a fall from a balcony on the ninth floor. Gillespie nodded. So far, so good. Then he read on, quickly at first, then more slowly as the final paragraph sank in. '*No further police action is anticipated*,' it read, '*and a routine Coroner's post-mortem has been requested*.'

Gillespie shook his head, remembering the lounge, the big armchair tipped on its side, the ashtray lying on the carpet, blood on the cold glass. He remembered the door open to the balcony, the curtains bellying in the wind. He remembered the girl sprawled on the concrete, the blood pooling around her ear. And he remembered the other marks on her neck, on the other side of her face. He was no pathologist, but these details told the most obvious of stories. There'd been a fight. Someone else was involved. The girl had been murdered.

He returned to the report. The paragraph was headed *External Injuries*. It listed superficial abrasions on the front temporal region below the left eye. It said there was a depression of the left zygomatic arch. It mentioned blood in the left ear. Of the other injuries – the right-hand side of the face and the neck – there was no mention. They'd simply disappeared, cured at the stroke of the pathologist's pen.

He leaned back in the chair and turned off the kettle. He read quickly through the rest of the report. Under *Internal Injuries*, it listed fractures of the skull and the upper arm. There was another fracture of the ribs, and a substantial quantity of blood in the lung cavity. Stomach contents smelled of alcohol, and there was something called *extravasation of blood* around the left kidney. He paused. Towards the end of the second page, under *Genito-urinary System*, there was a single sentence. It read *The uterus contained a gestational sac with a small foetus 8 cm crown – rump length, foot length 1.3 cm, consistent with a gestation of 13 – 14 weeks.* He looked up. He was no expert on the longer words, but the drift was all too plain. Suzanne Wallace had been pregnant. He was investigating a double murder.

He read on to the end. Under *Cause of Death*, the report listed *subarachnoid haemorrhage and cerebral contusions*, followed by *fractured skull.* These injuries, the report concluded, were consistent with a fall from a great height. Gillespie's eye drifted slowly to the foot of the page. The pathologist's name was Mossiter. He pulled the envelope towards him, and wrote the name in heavy capital letters. Then he sat back in the chair for a while, staring at the opposite wall, wondering about the scale of the cover-up, what it really masked, who it really protected. He picked up the report again. A single sentence caught his eye. *The brain*, it said bleakly, *weighed 1310 grammes.*

He got up and went through to the living room. The phone directory had no listing for Mossiter, but he found the hospital number in seconds.

Albie Curtis was waiting for Cartwright when the secretaries began to emerge from his office, their working day at an end. He sat behind the wheel of his van, watching them hurrying away down the street. Soon, he'd go in and collect. Soon, he'd put the day back on the rails.

He swung his legs up onto the long bench seat and lay back

against the door. After his encounter with Gillespie, he'd toyed with going to hospital. He knew his nose was broken, and he'd found three teeth on the floor under the steering wheel, but in the end he'd settled for a couple of aspirin, and a treble Bacardi from the pub at the end of the road. The combination had made him slightly light-headed, and when he'd finally run Mick to earth, three in the afternoon at a busy traffic intersection near the railway station, he'd had a lot of trouble getting things in quite the right order.

That it was Mick behind the steering wheel, he'd no doubt. But what was he doing driving Cartwright's old car? He'd parked the van in the middle of the road, and run through the traffic to find out, but then the lights had changed, red to green, and by the time he was abreast of the big white Jaguar, it was already easing away. He'd banged on the boot, and he was certain that Mick had recognized him in the mirror, but it had made no difference. The car had accelerated away, leaving Albie surrounded by angry punters. He'd turned on his heel, two-fingering the lot of them, and when the traffic warden had arrived to remonstrate about the van, he'd told him to fuck off.

Now, half-past five, the last of the secretaries had gone. Albie swung his legs off the seat and got out of the van. He crossed the road and pushed in through the office door. The big outer area was empty. There was a flight of stairs in one corner. He went up them. Cartwright's office was on the first floor. The door was open and he went in. Cartwright was sitting at his desk, eating a packet of crisps and absently looking at a copy of the *Radio Times*. He looked up as Albie walked in, unsurprised, unimpressed.

'What happened to your face?' he said.

Albie sniffed. It wasn't the reaction he wanted. He'd have preferred something a little more anxious, a little more apprehensive. Not a man eating crisps. Not this. He stood in front of the desk, leaning over it, hands flat on the polished rosewood.

'Pay day,' he said, 'like we agreed.'

Cartwright took another crisp and put it in his mouth. Then he shook his head.

'There is no money,' he said, 'and there never will be. You should understand that. Save us both a lot of time.'

'Bullshit.'

Cartwright shrugged, a vague, regretful twitch of his upper body. He picked tiny flakes of crisp off his jacket. Albie glared down at him, beginning to lose his temper.

'The paint's still at my place,' he said. 'Where do you want it?'

'I don't want it.'

'You haven't got a choice, mate. It's yours. You've paid for it. Or you will have in a minute or two.'

Cartwright adjusted his glasses and sat back in the big leather chair.

'You're threatening me,' he said carefully, 'and we have three options. One, you can leave. Two, I can call the police. Three, you can do whatever you have in mind, and later – assuming I survive – friends of mine will break your legs . . .' He smiled. 'Slowly.'

Albie hesitated. Threats of the police had never bothered him. He knew most of them on first-name terms, and two brief spells in prison had given him a mild affection for lukewarm porridge and powdered eggs. The third option, though, was very different. He'd acknowledged from the start that Cartwright had some very heavy friends. He'd known most of them for years, and respected their talents, but it had never occurred to him that his own name would ever figure in any job they'd take on. It just didn't work that way. Not in this city.

Now, though, he wasn't so sure. Cartwright had big money. Big money talked. The boat scam proved it. So maybe he should listen to the little man, while he still had a nose at all. Albie looked at him a moment, then he changed his mind again. Bollocks, he thought. Bollocks to it all. He lifted a heavy glass paperweight and brought it down, crash, on the desk. One last try.

'Ten grand,' he said, 'now.'

Cartwright didn't move. Then he rubbed his eyes, both hands, and yawned. Long day at the office. One last problem to deal with. He opened his eyes.

'Go on then,' he said, 'do it if you must.'

Albie looked at him for a long time, his hand closing on the paperweight again. He had a lot to get off his chest. Then a thought occurred to him. Yet more aggro.

'Mick Rendall,' he said, 'how come he's got your motor?'

Cartwright shrugged.

'Is that any of your business?' he said.

'Yeah. Too right it is.'

'He bought it.'

'He can't have. He's got no money.'

Cartwright smiled.

'Who's talking about money?' he said.

Albie frowned. There was one last flake of crisp, an inch below Cartwright's tie knot.

'You're bullshitting again,' he said at last.

'Am I? Then why don't you go and ask him yourself?'

Albie lifted the paperweight. It fitted smugly into his hand. Right shape. Right size. He measured the distance between himself and the little accountant, wondering whether to go for the head straight off, or to confine himself to the body, nasty, short little jabs, bang, bang, bang, thirty seconds' worth. He hesitated a moment longer, until the last of the fantasy melted, then he turned away and stormed out of the office, dropping the paperweight into the waste bin as he went. Cartwright watched him go, reaching for the crisps again.

Gillespie was already in bed, drifting slowly into sleep, when he first heard the noise downstairs. He'd been reviewing the day's events in his head, planning the next steps forward. Tomorrow, he told himself, he'd go running. Tomorrow, he'd find the pathologist. Tomorrow he'd follow the smoke slowly upwind, no matter how difficult the country, until he found the source of the fire. Already, in his own mind, he'd narrowed the field to two names. By the end of tomorrow, with patience, and with luck, he'd be down to one. Only then could he confront the real problem. Evidence.

Now, he lay quite still, in the dark, listening. The noise again. Metal against metal. The front door creaking open. He swung his legs slowly out of bed. He padded softly across the room, and onto the top landing. Albie Curtis, he thought, come to help himself. He stepped briefly into the spare room, the one that Sean used when he stayed over. There was a short length of solid mahogany hanging on a strap behind the door. He used it to stun the bigger fish. Congers. Rays. He reached for the baton, wound the strap round his wrist.

There were footsteps on the stairs, hesitant, light. He positioned himself behind the door. The footsteps paused a moment. A shadow fell across the carpet, someone smallish, Albie's size. Gillespie took a shallow breath, winding himself up, then kicked the door and swung left. His arm was already plunging down, a short, definitive blow, when he became dimly aware of the big Afro haircut, and the pale, sallow face. Annie screamed and covered her head with both arms. Gillespie stopped dead, and let the baton fall to the floor.

'You,' he said.

Annie nodded, peering out under her arms.

'Me,' she agreed.

Gillespie kicked the baton back into Sean's room. He heard it roll across the carpet and clatter against the skirting board. He put his arms round Annie.

'Just pretending,' he said. 'Come with me.'

Gillespie had gone, next morning, when Annie woke up. She blinked at the bedside alarm clock and swore softly. Seven-thirty. Most of the filming was now finished, but she'd promised the editor they'd make an early start. Eight o'clock, she'd said. On the dot.

She got out of bed and went downstairs, half-hoping to find Gillespie in the kitchen, or the bath. She'd never got the relationship quite straight in her head, but she knew that it worked whenever they met, and if neither of them chose to put it at risk by sticking a label on it, then that was probably just as well. He appeared to have forgiven her for taking the roll of film. In fact, he'd dropped the subject completely, rolling her over in the big double bed and attending to her with some skill when she'd mumbled yet another apology for being so crass. Afterwards, she'd fallen asleep, and now she realized how badly she'd needed the rest.

She walked into the kitchen, and smiled. There was a single bowl on the table, with a small white plate beside it. There was a spoon, and a knife, and half a pound of butter, and a choice of three cereals. There was a loaf of bread on the bread board, and a jar of thick-cut marmalade. It was very Gillespie.

She got milk from the fridge and sat down at the table. Then she saw the note, propped against the cereal boxes. It was written on a brown envelope. It said *Good Morning*, and called her a lazy cow. It hoped she'd slept well and asked her to feed the cat. There was a big *G* at the end, and a single scrawled kiss.

She turned the envelope over. There was a name with a line under it, big capital letters. She peered at it, MOSSITER. She turned the envelope over again, looking for a postmark, some other clue, but there was nothing. She gazed across the kitchen through the open door, up the hall. He was at it again. She knew he was. And he wasn't telling a soul. She shook her head. Mossiter, she thought. Where the fuck does that get me?

Gillespie was still waiting in the car at half-past nine. He was parked against a wall within the grounds of the city's main hospital. Across a narrow strip of tarmac road was a long low building, the Department of Histopathology, modern, wood and glass, already falling apart. There were parking spaces in front of the building. Each one carried a name. Dr Mossiter's was closest to the door.

Gillespie looked at his watch again. Another hour, he thought, then he'd have to find a different way. He folded his copy of the *Daily Telegraph* and glanced up at the rear-view mirror. A yellow Montego had appeared round the corner with a woman at the wheel. Gillespie watched closely as the car turned into the parking space marked Mossiter and stopped. The woman reached into the back seat, collected a shopping bag, and got out of the car. Gillespie did the same. The post-mortem report was folded in his pocket. He walked quickly across the narrow strip of tarmac and intercepted the woman as she turned from the car and began to walk towards the door. She looked briefly startled. She was small, with a kind thoughtful face, and a stocky build. Her hair was starting to grey around the temples. Gillespie gave her the report. She looked at it, uncomprehending.

'What's this?' she said. 'Who are you?'

Gillespie nodded at his own car, parked beside the flower bed.

'I'm over there,' he said, 'and that's a report of yours.' He paused. 'Do you have an office?'

She nodded.

'Yes,' she said.

'I'll be over in ten minutes,' Gillespie smiled, 'after you've read it.'

He turned away before she had a chance to answer. By the time he was back in the car, she'd gone.

Ten minutes later, Gillespie tapped softly on the open door of her office.

'Come in,' she said tonelessly.

Gillespie walked in and shut the door behind him. He sat down, uninvited, on the other office chair. The report lay open on the woman's lap. She looked up at him.

'Are you a relative?' she said.

Gillespie shook his head.

'She had no relatives,' he said.

'A friend then?'

'I knew her.'

'Well?'

Gillespie looked at her. He liked her manner. Direct. No messing. 'No,' he said.

There was a pause. The woman folded the report and laid it carefully to one side.

'Why me?' she said at last. 'Why are you here?'

'You wrote the thing,' Gillespie frowned, 'didn't you?'

'Yes,' she said, 'it's my job.'

Gillespie hesitated. The woman was watching him closely.

'I saw the body,' he said at last, nodding at the report on the desk, 'and I know that's incomplete. There were other marks . . .' He touched his neck, the right side of his face. 'Here and here . . .'

'I know.'

'So why didn't you mention them?'

The woman looked at him a moment longer, tussling with some private decision. Then she got up and walked across to one of the big grey filing cabinets that lined one wall. She opened a drawer and extracted a file. From the file, she slid another report. She handed it to Gillespie without comment. Gillespie glanced at it. It was identical to the first report, except longer. He read it more carefully. Under *External Injuries,* it listed a 3-cm laceration about the right eyebrow, and a right peri-orbital haematoma.

Gillespie glanced up.

'What's a haematoma?' he asked.

'A bruise.'

Gillespie nodded, returning to the report. Suzanne's upper right lip had been torn laterally, and there were bruises on her neck and shoulders. These bruises, the report said, *were associated with a deposit of a greenish pigment on the skin surface.* He nodded to himself, picturing the girl on the concrete, the strange dark shadows on her neck. He read the rest of the report. At the end, under *Comment*, he found what he'd been expecting. The report confirmed that the fractured skull was consistent with a fall from a great height. Then came an additional note. *The other facial injuries are probably not consistent with this unless the body struck some object during its fall. The marks on the neck would not seem to be explained by a simple fall.* Gillespie read the sentence again, then he looked up. The woman was gazing at him.

'Does that make sense?' she said. 'Is that what you saw?'

Gillespie nodded.

'Yes,' he said, 'it makes perfect sense, so why the difference?'

The woman extended her hand, wanting the longer report back. Gillespie gave it to her. She picked up the old one, the one Gillespie had given her, and flicked through it briefly.

'You got this from the police or the Coroner's office,' she said, 'must have done.'

Gillespie looked at her, but made no comment.

'What about the inquest?' he said. 'Why the delay?'

The woman glanced up and smiled at him.

'There's a problem,' she said.

'About what?'

'Me.' She handed him back the shorter report. 'Look at the last page.'

'Why?'

'Just look.'

Gillespie did so. Her name was at the foot of the page. Dr Kathryn Mossiter.

'Have I signed it?' she said.

'No.' Gillespie looked up. 'Will you sign it?'

There was a long silence. The woman turned away, gazing out

through the venetian blinds.

'Are you some kind of detective? Enquiry agent?'

Gillespie shook his head.

'Friend,' he said, 'ally.' He paused. 'My name's Gillespie.'

She nodded, and hesitated again. Another decision. Another corner to turn.

'Have you seen the Scene of Crime report?' she said at last. 'I imagine you probably have.'

Gillespie shook his head again. No point in pretending, he thought. Not with this woman.

'No,' he said, 'I haven't.'

'You should,' she said. 'One of the CID boys showed me the draft. I think he's as worried as I am . . .' She paused, then glanced across at him. 'I've got a copy. Just in case. You should read it.'

She opened a drawer in her desk and took out a yellow envelope. She gave it to Gillespie. Gillespie opened it. There were four sheets of paper inside, handwritten. He read them quickly, then again, letting the loopy, careful hand bring back the scene in the lounge, the upturned armchair, the ashtray, the blood on the carpet. Towards the foot of the second page, he found it, the one detail he'd missed, the key to it all. He looked up, finger on the line. The woman had been watching him. She obviously knew the report inside out, word perfect.

'Really?' he said.

She nodded.

'Really.'

'Are they sure?'

'Quite sure.' She paused. 'That's why I won't sign the report.'

Gillespie nodded.

'So who doctored your report?' he said. 'Who censored the injuries?'

The woman looked at him for a long time, then stood up and extended a hand.

'Goodbye, Mr Gillespie,' she said, nodding at the door.

Joanna Goodman was back from the morning school run by the time Gillespie turned in from the main road and pulled the ancient Marina to a stop outside her house. Joanna looked up from the sink, hearing the crunch of gravel under the wheels, recognizing the tall, lean figure stepping out of the car. She stopped, frowned, rinsed her hands under the tap.

The front door bell began to ring. Joanna dried her hands and walked through to the hall. She could see Gillespie through the frosted glass panels, and she felt a vague irritation. This man belonged to a past she no longer wanted to think about. He had no right to come up here, to barge in, to intrude. All that was over. Paid for, and over.

She opened the front door. Gillespie nodded at her.

'Mrs Goodman,' he said.

She looked at him, a cool appraising look she reserved for the lesser tradesmen.

'Mr Gillespie,' she said, 'can I help you?'

Gilliespie smiled.

'Yes,' he said, 'I think you can.'

There was a long moment of indecision, then Joanna shrugged and opened the door wide, letting him in. She led him into the living room. He stood awkwardly by the door. She looked pointedly at her watch.

'I have to go out in a minute,' she said, 'I'm on playgroup duty.'

Gillespie nodded.

'I never gave you the photographs,' he said.

Joanna shook her head quickly.

'I don't want them,' she said.

'They were paid for.'

'I know. Burn them.' She paused, frowning. 'Is that what you've come up here for? To tell me that?'

Gillespie gazed round. The framed family groups on the polished walnut cabinet. The smell of the place. Fresh air and beeswax.

'No,' he said, 'it isn't.'

'What, then? What do you want?'

Gillespie turned back to her, taking his time.

'You went to see her, didn't you?' he said slowly.

Joanna looked briefly startled, then annoyed.

'Yes,' she said, 'I did.'

Gillespie nodded.

'There was a row,' he suggested.

Joanna frowned again, her arms folded across her chest, the blood rising in her face.

'What is this?' she said.

Gillespie looked at her.

'Was there a row?'

'Yes, there was,' she said, 'but –'

'She was upset.'

'So was I, Mr Gillespie.' She paused, not wanting to remember it, not wanting to bring it all back. She looked at her watch again, not understanding where the conversation was headed, wanting it to stop. 'I really must be going . . .' she began.

Gillespie was still looking at her.

'Did she attack you?' he said. 'Is that how it started?'

'How what started?' she said. 'She'd been drinking. She was drunk.'

Gillespie nodded. 'Yes . . .' He paused. 'That's what they said at the post-mortem.'

Joanna stared at him. There was a long silence. Gillespie could hear the steady tick of the clock in the hall.

'She's dead?' she said at last.

Gillespie watched her carefully. 'Yes,' he said, 'she was killed. Murdered.' He paused. 'The night you went to see her.'

'I don't believe you.'

Gillespie shrugged. He pulled out the post-mortem report and laid it on the small sofa-table between them.

'It's true,' he said, 'you can read all about it.'

Joanna looked down at the report but didn't pick it up. When she spoke again it was in a small, low voice, a private conversation.

'Why didn't I know about it?' she said. 'Why wasn't I told?'

Gillespie said nothing. He picked up the post-mortem report.

'Did she offer you a drink,' he asked, 'the night you went round?'

Joanna looked at him, not hearing the question. He repeated it. She nodded.

'Yes,' she said. 'Why do you ask?'

'Because they found the glasses,' he said, 'hers and yours.' He paused again. 'Same drink. But different lipsticks.'

Joanna nodded, her face quite blank.

'So what?' she said.

Gillespie hesitated a moment, returning the report to his jacket pocket.

'It means you probably killed her,' he said, stepping back towards the door.

Albie found Mick Rendall at the scrap yard, three acres of rusty old iron, empty boilers, engine blocks and the crushed remains of hundreds of abandoned cars. Mick was talking to the foreman of the yard, an ex-merchant seaman who occasionally flogged Albie choice bits of non-ferrous when the yard's owner was otherwise engaged. Albie pulled his van to a halt, and got out. Mick gave him an uneasy smile. Cartwright's old car, an F-registration Jaguar, was parked near by.

'Hi, Alb . . .' Mick began, 'sold any paint lately?'

Albie didn't smile. The other man, the foreman, sensed the atmosphere at once and withdrew, leaving them to it. Albie nodded briefly at the Jaguar.

'Nice motor,' he said.

'Yeah,' Mick smiled again, 'good innit? Sweet as a nut.' He paused. 'What happened to your face, Alb? Someone cop a moody?'

Albie ignored the dig. He was still looking at the car.

'So what was it then? Services rendered? Little divi on the proceeds?'

Mick frowned, affecting confusion.

'What are you on about?' he said. 'Brain OK in there?'

Albie stepped up to Mick, very close. Mick blinked. One of Albie's eyes was almost completely bloodshot. It made him look like a relic from a Hammer film. Albie picked a thread of cotton from the lapel of Mick's suit, an intimate thoughtful gesture. Mates.

'You know what hurts me most?' he said.

Mick frowned. 'What?' he said.

'You. Doing this to me . . .' He nodded at the car. 'You, of all people.'

Mick shook his head, starting to protest, going through the motions.

'Alb—' he began.

Albie caught him by the collar.

'Do us a favour, Mick,' he said. 'I might be pretty thick. But not *that* thick.'

Mick tried again, changing the tone of his voice, bringing it down, low, confidential, wheedling, persuasive.

'Alb . . .' he said.

Albie pushed him away.

'You know what,' he said, 'you're not even worth loafing. You're dogshit on my shoe. And you know it.' He spat on the ground at Mick's feet. 'So bollocks to you.'

He turned on his heel and began to walk away. Then he spotted a length of angle iron lying in the dust. He stooped and picked it up. He glanced contemptuously at Mick, just the once, and walked to the Jaguar. The headlights went first, a straight jab into each, the thick glass splintering. Then the sidelights and one of the wing mirrors. Finally he lifted the angle iron above his head and heaved it through the windscreen. The windscreen shattered and went opaque. Albie wiped his hands on his jeans and got back into the van. The engine started first time. He drove away, bumping over the rutted track. Mick watched him go, shaking his head. Albie had been right. Nice motor.

Joanna sat in the church hall, watching Charlie. The play group had been going now for more than an hour, and she'd said sorry to everyone she could think of for being so late. After Gillespie had gone, getting into his Marina and driving slowly out of the gate, she'd sat for a long time in the lounge, oblivious of Charlie's fretful cries. The news about Suzanne had shattered her, destroyed whatever peace of mind she'd won from the last four weeks. She'd no idea the girl had died. On the contrary, Martin had talked about her going away, out of their lives, the kind of tactful retreat she'd always hoped might happen.

Now, though, it wasn't like that at all. The girl was dead. Worse, she'd been killed. Worse still, Gillespie appeared to have evidence that implicated her. She thought back to the evening in the flat, walking into the lounge, how hard it had been, Martin's picture on the television, the girl bleating on about her pregnancy. She'd told herself at the time that accepting the drink was a right and proper gesture. It demonstrated her self-control, her composure. It confirmed that she was in charge, an older, wiser woman for whom a situation like this held no fears. In reality, of course, she'd felt no such thing, but oddly enough the drink had helped. It had calmed her. It had given her strength. Now, though, far too late, she was beginning to regret accepting it.

She tried to think the situation through again, tried to imagine what might happen next. She knew nothing about the legal process, except Charles Jenner's phone number, but she'd read enough papers in her life to know that murders were seldom ignored. It was the one crime that really mattered. It was the one occasion when the police really pulled their fingers out. All the more curious, then, that nothing appeared to have happened. No investigation. No publicity. Nothing. Except Jenner's wretched private eye turning up on her doorstep with a copy of a post-mortem report. Perhaps he'd invented the whole thing. Perhaps he'd imagined it. Perhaps he got his kicks from frightening middle-aged housewives with rumours of homicide. She closed her eyes a moment and shook her head. Martin had promised to take her out to lunch. Before she met him, she'd phone Charles. He, at least, might know what to do.

Gillespie parked the Marina outside Jenner's office, and walked in. The receptionist glanced up and smiled as he passed her desk. She already had the kettle on, she said. Would he be staying for coffee? Gillespie said yes, and nodded at Jenner's door. 'He's free,' she said, 'go right in.'

Gillespie tapped on the door and walked in. Jenner was sitting behind the desk, wrestling with a small portable dictaphone. He looked at him, and smiled. A couple of weeks away had done him the world of good. He looked fitter, tanned. He'd lost at least one of the chins, and he'd had a modest haircut. He looked up, and saw Gillespie by the door.

'For God's sake,' he said, putting the dictaphone back on the desk. 'I thought you'd emigrated.'

Gillespie shook his head, picking up the dictaphone and sliding back the cover. The battery compartment was empty. He showed it to Jenner.

'No batteries,' he said, 'no work.'

Jenner looked vague, pushing a fresh set of batteries across the desk.

'Please,' he said, 'you do it.'

Gillespie fitted the batteries and tested the dictaphone. It worked. He returned it to Jenner, who watched with open admiration.

'Marvellous,' he said, 'quite marvellous.'

The door opened and the receptionist appeared with two coffees. She put them on the desk. Jenner produced a small tin of sweeteners, and dropped two in his cup, a recent innovation. He looked up, beaming.

'Now then,' he said, 'I assume you're well?'

'Very well.'

'So when do we start?'

Gillespie hesitated, then produced the post-mortem report. He slid it across the desk towards Jenner. Jenner picked it up. He read it.

'So?' he said.

Gillespie sipped the coffee.

'I need some affidavits,' he said, 'starting with the lady that drew up this report.'

Jenner nodded, glancing again at the last page. Then he looked up, knowing Gillespie too well to bother with any of the obvious questions.

'Fine,' he said, tapping the dictaphone, 'my pleasure.'

Joanna Goodman met her husband for lunch at a new Thai restaurant which had recently opened near the pier. He'd asked her to turn up at half-past twelve, a little earlier than usual, because he had important meetings all afternoon, but she was there ten minutes early. She sat by herself at a table near the back. It was a quiet, discreet little place, fresh flowers on the table, and a waiter so tactfully unobtrusive that he was barely there at all.

She sipped at her drink, gazing down the room, out onto the street. She'd phoned Charles Jenner fifteen minutes earlier. She'd explained a little about the situation. She'd mentioned the man Gillespie. There'd been a pause. Then Jenner had asked her for the girl's name. She'd told him, Suzanne Wallace, and there'd been another pause, and a rustle or two of paper, before he was back again to tell her that, yes, Miss Wallace was indeed dead, and that, yes, there was some question of foul play. Joanna had thanked him and hung up, feeling a chill steal over her, the ambiguities evaporating, the situation slipping remorselessly into focus. On both counts, Gillespie had been right. Where did that leave her?

A shadow fell over the door, and her husband pushed into the restaurant. He spotted her at once and smiled. She got up, kissed him. He sat down. He looked pleased with himself.

'Eric sends his best,' he said, 'he's just been in.'

'Oh?'

'Looked marvellous. Amazing really.'

'Is he coming back?'

'No,' he smiled again, 'that was the whole point. That's why he came in. He's throwing in the towel. Officially.'

She lifted her glass. 'Congratulations,' she said. 'Your dream come true.'

Goodman shrugged, signalling the waiter.

'Early days,' he said. 'The job could go to anybody.'

Joanna looked at him, quizzical.

'I'm confused,' she said. 'Yesterday you'd had enough of it all. You told me so. At the football. You said it wasn't worth a candle.'

'Ah . . .' Goodman nodded darkly, 'yesterday.'

'Was I wrong to believe you?'

'No.'

'Was it true?'

He looked up at her, catching the inflection in her voice, the slightly tempered edge that cut through all the banter.

'Well . . .' he shrugged again, 'we all have a living to make.'

'That wasn't my question. I asked you whether you meant it or not.'

Goodman looked up.

'Yes,' he said, 'I did. At the time.'

'But not any more?'

'I'm not sure.' He fingered the menu. 'It'd be a fascinating challenge.'

'That's not what you said yesterday.'

'No, I know.' He opened the menu, not looking at her. 'Confusing, isn't it?'

Joanna watched him, the head bent over the menu, the finger running down the list of entrées. She remembered the night he'd come back, out of the dark, blood all over his face, nearly incoherent. She remembered Evans at the door beside him, the embarrassed half-smile, the coldness in his eyes. And she knew, in that moment, exactly what had happened. She realized how empty the last four weeks had been, and the years before that. She realized how easily, how wilfully, she'd confused what she wanted, with what she'd got. And she realized with extraordinary clarity, exactly what she must do about it. For now, she'd play along. But very soon, it would be all over.

Her husband looked up.

'Number seventeen,' he said, 'Heavenly Chicken.'

She glanced at him over her menu, suddenly free of it all, suddenly wise.

'Fine,' she said, 'whatever you say.'

It was early afternoon before Gillespie got the call. He was in the kitchen, sawing the end off a fresh loaf. He walked through to the living room, and picked up the phone.

'Gillespie,' he said briefly.

There was a woman's voice at the other end. He recognized it at once. She'd taken longer than he'd expected to call back.

'It's Mrs Goodman,' the voice said.

'I know.'

'I thought I ought to give you a ring. About this morning.'

'Yeah?'

'There's someone you ought to talk to.'

'Who's that?'

'A man called Evans. He used to drive my husband around. During the troubles.' She paused. 'I think you'll find he knows a great deal about . . . ah . . . what happened . . .'

Gillespie hesitated a moment, frowning. He'd braced himself for a long conversation, awkward, difficult, the woman's loyalty to her husband in conflict with her need to cover her own back. But here she was, as clipped and decisive as ever, giving him chapter and verse. He wrote down the name and looked at it.

'Evans . . .' He paused. 'You wouldn't have a Christian name, would you? Or a phone number?'

'I'm afraid not.' She hesitated 'I think he was a Marine of some sort. A corporal. Would that make any sense to you?'

'A Marine?'

Gillespie started to laugh, gazing out of the window, his head tilted back. It was raining now, big splodges trickling down the dusty glass.

'I'm sorry?' he could hear her saying. 'I'm sorry?'

He put the phone down, very slowly, the laughter louder, deeper, full-bodied. After all this, he thought. The boat, the girl, the man in the suit in the small bare room. After all the heartache, all the nausea. After everything he'd tried to do, all the mistakes he'd made. After all this, it simply boiled down to a Marine. Not him. Not Gillespie. Someone else. Someone current. He fingered the pad. Evans.

Gillespie met Dawkins at the barracks gate. He'd phoned the RSM an hour before. The two men had served in the Falklands together, same Commando, both corporals. They'd shared the Arctic Warfare course, drunk themselves insensible in Tromso bars, shivered together in iceholes up near the Finnish border. He knew the man like a brother, and Dawkins's had been the last hand he'd shaken the day he left the Corps. On the phone, he'd kept it simple.

'Bloke called Evans,' he'd said. 'One of yours?'

'Clive Evans? Tall bugger? Local boy?'

'Could be.' Gillespie had paused. 'Attached to the civvy set-up during the recent troubles.'

'That's him.'

Gillespie had rung off a minute or two later, an arrangement made. Dawkins would meet him at the gate. Evans was on base. Piece of cake.

Now, the rain still falling, Gillespie shook Dawkins's hand, and walked with him back into the Barracks. Dawkins was in his last year. Soon he'd be retiring, taking his chances in Civvy Street. They joked about it, bodies running to fat, marriages collapsing under the weight of unaccustomed daily contact, and Gillespie got the strongest possible whiff of the world he'd left behind, its camaraderie, its order, its sense of cheerful self-discipline. He still missed it. Even now.

They paused by a big red brick building. Inside, through the open windows, Gillespie could hear the thunder of heavy men doing something brutal. Feet on a wooden floor. The slap of flesh on flesh. Gasps, and curses, and an occasional yelp of laughter.

They walked in, out of the rain. A dozen or so men in singlets and shorts were wrestling a big medicine ball across a gymnasium. There were low goals at each end. The object was to put the ball between the posts. There were no rules. Anything went. Dawkins and Gillespie had watched for a minute or so. Every time the ball stopped, it disappeared beneath a ruck of bodies. Fists. Feet. An arm locked around a neck. Someone driving a knee deep into the nearest face. Dawkins smiled.

'Doesn't change much, does it?'

'No,' Gillespie grinned, 'which one's Evans?' Dawkins peered into the mountains of bodies. Finally he found the face he wanted. He pointed Evans out. Tall. Wiry. Someone else's blood smeared across the front of his singlet. He spotted the ball in a gap. He dived in, head first, regardless.

'Game, isn't he?' Gillespie said. 'Your corporal?'

Dawkins shook his head.

'*Sergeant* Evans,' he said. 'Get it right.'

'Really?'

'Yeah,' he nodded. 'Since Monday.'

Ten minutes later, Gillespie was standing in the changing rooms, waiting for Evans to emerge from the shower. The room was thick with steam, the white tiles gleaming in the light from the overhead neons. Evans appeared, towelling himself dry. He saw Gillespie, and paused.

'You Dawkins's mate?' he said. Gillespie nodded. Evans stared at him, unimpressed.

'What's the name again?'

'Gillespie.'

'Dave Gillespie?'

'Yeah.'

'What's this then, Dave? Some kind of investigation, is it?'

'Yeah,' Gillespie said again.

He gave Evans the bare facts. A girl had died. A friend of a

Mr Goodman's. There was some doubt about the circumstances. He needed a little help. He understood Evans had been with Goodman most of the time. Perhaps there were things they could discuss. Evans listened without comment. When other men drifted in from the shower, they walked next door, to the urinal. Evans leaned back against the row of hand basins, rubbing his hair dry, not taking his eyes off Gillespie's face. Finally he shook his head.

'I don't know a thing,' he said, 'I can't help you.'

'No?'

'No.'

'Saw nothing?'

'No.' Evans sounded irritated. 'Nothing.'

Gillespie frowned, remembering Goodman's wife on the phone, the certainty in her voice.

'But you must have known about the girlfriend,' he said, 'must have done.'

Evans began to towel his shoulders, both hands, sawing back and forth.

'Look . . .' he said at last, 'I'm a soldier. I did a job. Drove the bloke around. Kept an eye on him. And that's about it. I've got a life to lead, mate. Wife, kids . . .' He paused. 'Know what I mean?'

Gillespie nodded, ignoring the overt message behind the terse phrases. Leave me alone. Sod off out of it.

'So you're not telling?' he said. 'Even though you obviously know?'

Evans looked him in the eye.

'Know what?' he said.

Gillespie nodded, a slow sardonic curl of the lips. There was a long silence. Next door, someone was telling a joke about a priest with bad habits. Gillespie stepped a little closer, a message of his own to deliver.

'Listen, son,' he said softly, 'don't think I'm giving up, will you. Don't kid yourself I won't come looking.' He paused. 'As long as it takes. You hear me?'

Evans shrugged.

'Suit yourself, mate,' he said. 'But you haven't got much time.'

'Oh?'

'No,' he smiled. 'I'm off to Belize next week. For a whole fucking year.'

Bullock sat in the tiny editing suite, watching the final scene of the film. Annie had phoned him an hour or so earlier, telling him she'd finished the first rough cut, a crude assembly of shots, overlength, no music, no finesse, no polish, and he was welcome to take a look. She normally tried to avoid these rituals, preferring to keep everyone away until she could run something she was proud of, but on this occasion she decided it was the only practical solution. Bullock, at the very least, should share some of the blame. The film was truly awful.

Bullock let the final image fade, sunset over the harbour, city voices in the background, ordinary men and women saying their separate thank-yous that the whole thing was over, that everyone had survived. Annie had focused in the end on two families – an unemployed couple from a big housing estate, and a young computer programmer with a pretty wife and a three-month-old baby. The social contrasts were stark, but the concerns they voiced were almost identical. The world, they both said, was crazy. Only now, perhaps, would the politicians realize what they were really putting at risk. The message, if obvious, was nicely phrased, and intercut with footage from the Bunker – hands on phones, chinagraphs advancing across huge maps of the city, the two-tone buzz of the Attack Alarm – it made compulsive viewing. Of Goodman, the putative subject of the film, there was surprisingly little, and when he appeared at all it was simply to help the story along. A detail here. A time reference there. An admission, late in the film, that yes, tension had at times been unbearable.

The screen went to black and Bullock leaned back in his chair.

'Bloody good,' he said. 'Bloody excellent.'

Annie gazed at him in the half-darkness.

'Wrong,' she said. 'It's terrible.'

He looked across at her.

'Why do you say that?'

'It's bland. It's obvious. And it says absolutely zilch.'

'About what?'

'About the issue that matters. What they did. What they

got away with.'

Bullock shook his head.

'That's not what we're about,' he said.

'No?' Annie got up and switched on the light. 'It used to be.'

Bullock ignored the comment, running a finger down a pad on his lap. He'd made a couple of notes during the viewing. He frowned, trying to decipher his own shorthand.

'Our friend Goodman,' he said, 'he's practically invisible.'

'I know.'

'Why's that?'

'He didn't say anything worth using.'

'Are you sure?'

'Positive.' She paused. 'I was there. Remember?'

Bullock nodded and thought about it a moment. Then he got up.

'You're still going to the Rotary thing,' he said, 'that'll fit nicely. Have another go at him afterwards. Find somewhere quiet. I'll give him a ring. Tell him there's nothing to worry about.' He smiled. 'You probably frightened the life out of him. Be gentle. He's easily flattered.'

He reached for the door handle and opened the door. Before Annie could begin to protest, he was gone.

It was dark before Evans realized that it was Gillespie in the car outside his house. His wife had twice mentioned the old Marina, peering out between the bedroom curtains, but Evans had dismissed her worries with a grunt. Now, though, looking out for the first time himself, he recognized the face behind the steering wheel, a perfect view of the house, the man making good his promise, not giving up.

At first, he'd done nothing about it, going back to the endless lists of kit he was trying to draw up for his move to Belize. The posting had come as a total surprise, a brief ten-minute interview with his colonel, all plans cancelled for the coming year, the move explained as an urgent response to something the colonel termed 'a personnel glitch'. The pill had been sugared by his promotion to sergeant, another surprise, but even so he was less than pleased to be going. He'd already done two stints in the place, routine training assignments, and he hated it. The flies, the heat, and the sheer boredom acquired an almost physical dimension. The posting had put him in a bad mood for nearly a week, and now – quite suddenly – he began to boil over. The bloke across the road evidently didn't understand plain English. Time to try the shorter words.

He put the list to one side and left the bedroom. He clattered downstairs and tore open the front door. He walked across the road and stood by the car, hands on hips, waiting. Gillespie glanced up at him, and wound the window down. Evans bent towards him.

'Listen, mate,' he said slowly, 'I'm serious. I don't know what your game is, but you're wasting your time.'

Gillespie gazed up at him, recognizing the tone of voice, the explicit threat. Fuck off or face the consequences.

'I'm serious too,' he said mildly, 'believe it or not.'

The two men looked at each other. Then Evans stepped a little closer.

'Are you going?' he said. 'Or not?'

Gillespie smiled.

'Little woman been on at you?' he said. 'Worried about the neighbours?'

He reached inside his jacket. Evans watched him carefully. Gillespie produced a card. He offered it to Evans. Evans took it.

'What's that?' he said.

'My address and phone number. Think about it.' Gillespie started the engine. 'I'll be back tomorrow.'

Martin Goodman and his wife went to bed early. Goodman had watched the mid-evening news, made a phone call or two, poured himself a drink before supper, and had been more than complimentary about Joanna's Spanish omelettes. When he started yawning at ten o'clock, and suggested bed, she'd nodded and agreed it was a good idea.

Now, past midnight, they lay quite still in the darkness. Beside her, she could hear the regular sigh of Martin's breathing, and she knew he must be asleep. The day had seemed the longest in her entire life, longer even than the day she'd found the postcard. The two events were linked, of course, inextricably, but what she'd done today carried with it a finality that she found truly awesome. She was still quite sure of herself, quite certain that she was making the right decision, but she felt somehow cheap, and a little cowardly. She ought to tell him what she thought. She ought to come clean.

She inched her body towards the edge of the bed, and slipped noiselessly onto the carpet. She moved slowly across the bedroom and stood by the window. She parted the curtains. The last of the rain had gone now, and the night was very clear. The glow of the city was bright, and she could see the frieze of ornamental coloured lights along the promenade, and the inky blackness of the sea beyond. She heard Martin stirring behind her, and she wondered briefly what would happen to him. Would they lock him up? Would they put him on trial? Would it go badly for him? She thought about it for a moment or two, then put it out of her head, happy that she knew so little, and surprised that she cared even less. Martin Goodman had ceased to be her husband. He'd become, instead, a total stranger.

Goodman stirred again, turning over in the bed, reaching out for her. His eyes opened. He saw the sheets pulled back. He felt the hollow in the mattress, still warm from her body. He rolled over, seeing her standing by the window.

'Darling . . .' he murmured, 'you're up.'

She said nothing for a long moment. Then she opened the small top window.

'She's dead, isn't she?' she said.

Goodman looked at her for a long time.

'Yes,' he said, finally.

'And you never told me.'

'No . . .' He paused, his voice still low. 'How did you find out?'

She turned back into the room and shivered, putting her arms around herself.

'A man called Gillespie,' she said. 'He thought I ought to know.'

Gillespie was back at the hospital at nine. He'd been on the phone to the pathologist since seven. She lived out in the country. He'd got her number from his detective friend, destroying what little there was left of the friendship. The pathologist had been sceptical at first, reluctant to commit herself, but he'd laid it all out for her, the last detail, and she'd finally agreed to give him a statement. She'd only talk about what she knew, the marks on the body, her own findings, typed up in the longer report she'd shown him in the office. The rest of it, the Scenes of Crime draft, the edited version of the report that Gillespie had shown her, were off limits. She'd talk about the facts. Nothing else.

They met in the car park. She got into Gillespie's car, and they drove through the rush hour traffic to Jenner's office. Jenner was already waiting, deep in the book of instructions that went with the new dictaphone. The woman sat down at the desk, and Jenner pushed the record button, and Gillespie supplied the few prompts she needed. She'd brought with her a copy of her own post-mortem report, and she quoted from it verbatim, dictation speed, spelling one or two of the longer words. At the end, she refused Gillespie's invitation to enlarge on the implication of the injuries, what they might indicate about cause and effect, and politely declined Jenner's offer of coffee.

'Sorry,' she said, 'but I have to get on.'

Gillespie drove her back to the hospital. Before she got out of the car, she opened her bag and produced a small white envelope. She gave it to him. He opened it. There were two photographs inside. They were both shots of Suzanne, close-ups, head and shoulders. Her eyes were closed, and a line of heavy stitches ran from the base of her neck to the foot of the print. The injuries on the right-hand side of her face, and the curious dark marks around her throat, were clearly visible. Gillespie studied the prints carefully. Cheap camera, he thought. Too much flash.

'Who took these?' he said.

The woman reached for the door handle.

'I did.'

'When?'

'After the post-mortem.'

Gillespie looked at them again.

'You must have been worried,' he said.

'I was.' She opened the door. 'And I still am. They should have called the Home Office in. Forensic post-mortem. Done it properly. The way I suggested.'

'But they didn't?'

'No.' She shook her head. 'That's why you got your statement.'

Goodman sat alone in his office. Fiona, as usual, had typed out a neat list of the day's engagements: meetings in the morning, a lunch date with the city's Publicity Chief, housing accounts review all afternoon, the Rotary Award in the evening. On each occasion, once again, he would be playing the Acting Chief Executive, Eric's able young stand-in, the man hotly tipped for the very top.

Already, he suspected that the word was out around the office. Eric had finally gone. The job would be advertised, of course. There'd be interviews, a short list, a brief but decent interval for consultation. But the final outcome, the name at the top of the list on the big board by the lifts on the ground floor, was never in doubt. His name might be mud in Whitehall. Quinn might rubbish him behind his back. But here, in the Civic Centre, he was king. The succession was secure. The job would be his.

He reached for his coffee, smiling at the thought, trying again to rid his mind of that one single image that had haunted him since he'd woken up: his wife standing in the darkened room, reaching up for the top window. Gillespie, she'd said. A man called Gillespie.

He reached for his pad, and a pen. He wrote the name down, studied it for a moment, wondering exactly what she'd meant. This morning over breakfast, his wife hadn't said a word. He'd thought about a direct question, asking her straight out, but the kids were there, and in any case, he wasn't even sure he wanted to know. Like toothache, it might just go away. Like rain, this gnawing sense of imminent disaster might simply stop.

The phone began to trill on his desk. He picked it up. It was Bullock.

'Morning,' he said briskly.

The other man grunted, coming at once to the point. He'd seen the film that Annie was making. He was pleased with the results. It was perceptive, and sympathetic, and profoundly moving. His only reservation was Goodman's contribution. In all candour, he didn't think he'd done himself justice. Perhaps he and Annie should try again, one last interview. There was a pause.

Goodman looked out of the window. The rain was back again.

'When?' he said at last.

'Tonight. After the Rotary thing.'

'Where?'

'Where do you suggest?'

Goodman looked round the office.

'Here?' he said. 'Civic Centre?'

'Done.'

There was a pause. Goodman could hear the peck of typewriters in the background, and a woman's voice yelling for some phone number. Then Bullock was back again. Annie would be in touch. He was, as ever, deeply grateful. The phone went dead. Goodman gazed down at his desk, still holding the receiver. Then he returned it to the base set and reached for his pad. That name again. Gillespie. He frowned, sure that the name was familiar. Davidson had mentioned it once. Something about a 'K' reference. A three-figure number. Two something. He tried to bring the number back, digging deep into his memory, then he shook his head, annoyed with himself. The name was a distraction. He had other things to think about. He looked down again at the pad, ripped off the top sheet of paper, screwed it into a tight ball, and dropped it neatly into the bin.

By mid-morning, Gillespie was back outside Evans' house. He parked opposite, very obvious, and sat in the car for a minute or two. The house was brand new, one of hundreds on a big private estate on the site of the city's old airport. There were thick net curtains in the upstairs windows and a hanging basket outside the front door. A child's tricycle lay upturned on the tiny drive.

Gillespie got out of the car and walked across to the house. He rang the door bell twice and waited. The rain had stopped, but the concrete was wet underfoot. The door opened. A woman stood there. She was blonde, small, pretty. She was wearing a T-shirt. The T-shirt said 'Marines Do It By Numbers'. Gillespie looked at it, wondering whether it was a joke.

'Yes?' she said. 'Can I help you?'

Gillespie knew at once that she'd recognized him. The voice told him so. Flat and nasal, and very hostile. She must have seen him the previous evening. She must have been looking.

'Name's Gillespie,' he said. 'I'm after your husband.'

'He's gone to work.'

'Oh.' He paused. 'When's he back?'

There was a silence. The woman looked at him. Within a minute or so, she'd be back onto the barracks. That bloke again, she'd be saying. That weirdo. For God's sake. As if we haven't got enough on our plates. She folded her arms.

'I dunno,' she said, 'but I wouldn't chance your arm, if I were you. I think he's had enough.'

'I'm sure.'

'So do us a favour, eh?' She began to shut the door. 'Just leave us alone.'

Gillespie put his foot in the door. Inside, he could hear a baby crying. There was a new expression on the woman's face. It was fear.

'Fuck off,' she said, 'whoever you are.'

Gillespie nodded.

'Sure,' he said. 'But tell him I called, will you?'

He looked at her one final time, making sure that she understood, then turned and walked away. Back in his car, reaching for the ignition key, he could see her in the front room, the phone already to her ear, a small baby tucked into the other arm. Evans, he thought, a trickier proposition than he'd expected.

Goodman walked quickly along the corridor, glancing over his shoulder. At the end of the corridor, he stopped outside an office door. The sign on the door, black letters on a yellow background, said simply *Liaison*.

He knocked softly. Hearing no reply, he turned the handle, very slowly, taking his time. The door began to open. He glanced over his shoulder again, and stepped inside.

The office was bare. There was a plain desk and a chair. There was a filing cabinet against the opposite wall. There was a row of telephone directories on a bookshelf, and a large map of the south of England. On the table was a monitor screen and a computer keyboard.

Goodman sat down in front of the keyboard, and slid out a sheet of paper from his inside jacket pocket. He unfolded the paper and laid it carefully on the desk. He eyed the keyboard and located the power switch. There was a flicker of static on the screen, and then a steady green glow.

Glancing at the sheet of paper, he began to type instructions onto the keyboard, one serial after another, pausing to check as he went. Once, hearing footsteps in the corridor outside, he paused, hands immobile over the keyboard, the sweat beginning to bead on his forehead. The footsteps receded, then disappeared. Silence again. He bent to the keyboard.

The instructions complete, he leaned back in the chair and waited. There was a delay of perhaps fifteen seconds as the computer interfaced with the big mainframe in the basement at Queens Gate. Then lines of type began to strip across the screen. He read them as they appeared, avidly, relieved the 'K' reference had been correct, thankful his memory hadn't, after all, let him down.

The copy came to an end, a whole paragraph, twelve or so lines. He read it again, carefully, committing the details to memory. The Christian names, the date of the man's birth, the date of his marriage, the name of his son. He read about the Falklands, the incidents on Mount Harriet, the MoD decision to countermand the medal. His eye raced on, the months in barracks at Plymouth, the Arctic exercises in Norway, the last full tour in Northern Ireland. He paused, the man's career hitting the buffers in a small, remote country lane in County Armagh, a body lying dead at the roadside, furious activity at Lisburn, damage limitation, quiet precautionary briefings, and a collective sigh of relief when the man took the point and packed his bags and headed back to civilian life.

Goodman blinked, scanning the details one final time, making quite sure there were no ambiguities. K reference 211. Sergeant David Gillespie. Commended on the Sniper Course. Applauded for his Falklands War. Schooled in the disciplined application of extreme violence. He switched off the screen and returned the sheet of paper to his pocket. The footsteps were there again, closer, but when he opened the door and checked the corridor outside, it was quite empty.

Goodman returned to the fifth floor, hurried along the corridor, and in through the big outer office where Fiona had her desk.

'Get me Harry Cartwright,' he said, 'right away.' He paused. 'Then the Marine Barracks. A Sergeant Evans.'

Gillespie finally chose the flag irises, a huge bunch, more flowers than he'd ever bought in his life. He returned to the car and laid them carefully beside the bottle of Moët. He drove out of the multi-storey, away from the city centre, back into the maze of side streets, whistling his tuneless whistle. He parked across the street, collected the flowers and champagne, and rang the front door bell.

For a minute or so, waiting, he wondered if he'd chosen the wrong morning. Then there were footsteps in the hall, and the scrape of bolts, and the door opened, and Sandra was standing there, blinking in the first sunshine of the day. She was wearing a long T-shirt and not much else. She looked as if Gillespie had interrupted something important. He beamed at her, holding out the flowers and the champagne. He felt about three years old.

'Cheers,' he said, 'little present.'

Sandra looked at him, looked at the flowers, at the champagne, not quite able to believe it. She ran a hand through her hair. She smelled of bed.

'What's all that for?' she said, dazed.

'Nothing,' he said, 'in particular.' He looked her up and down, then looked beyond her, along the hall. A man's jacket hung on the banisters at the foot of the stairs. 'I thought medics worked day and night,' he said cheerfully. 'Never got time off. What's the matter with the man?'

He pushed the presents into her arms, and reached forward, and kissed her on the lips.

'Sorry to intrude,' he said, 'nothing personal.'

He grinned at her again, and turned away, and walked down the path towards the car. Even after he'd crossed the road, and got in, and shut the door after him, Sandra could still hear the old tuneless whistle. Colonel Bogey, she thought, looking at the flowers. Nothing ever changes.

Goodman met Harry Cartwright in a car park behind the Civic Centre. The little accountant was sitting behind the wheel of the big Mercedes, listening to an edition of *Gardeners' Question Time* on the car radio. Goodman spotted him at once, picking his way between the rows of parked cars.

Cartwright lowered his window and nodded a greeting. He wasn't smiling.

'Good morning,' he said.

'Morning.'

Goodman glanced down. There was a small brown parcel on the passenger seat, cocooned in sellotape. Cartwright picked it up and handed it out through the window.

'Thanks,' said Goodman.

'My pleasure,' said Cartwright drily. 'Seven days, please.'

'Of course.'

'Thank you.'

The little man reached for the ignition. The engine started. The car pulled away. He hadn't bothered to say goodbye. Goodman looked down at the parcel, weighing it in his hand. It was heavier than he'd expected. He smiled, and turned on his heel, and walked away.

The calls to Evans finally found the Marine in a small, airless room in the barracks armoury. He looked up when the duty clerk called his name. He was holding out a telephone.

Evans took the phone. He'd already had a brief conversation with his wife, telling her to lock the door and ignore all callers. If he saw the bloke in the Marina again, he told her, he'd sort him out. Now, he bent to the telephone. A girl's voice, refined, hoity-toity.

'Mr Goodman's secretary here,' she said. 'Thank goodness we've found you.'

Evans frowned. He'd never liked Goodman, not then, not now, and he resented people who tracked him down. He asked her what she wanted. The secretary said that Mr Goodman was out of the office, but had asked her to check whether Mr Evans was free for lunch. She named a pub on the harbourside. The invitation had a peremptory ring to it. He was clearly expected to accept. Evans glanced at his watch, wondering what on earth the man wanted.

'When?' he said.

'One o'clock.'

'OK,' he said, 'I'll be there.'

Evans arrived at the rendezvous five minutes early. The pub had a small discreet restaurant with a fine view of the harbour mouth and a reputation for good seafood. Evans, still in uniform, sat at a table in the corner, reading a copy of the *Daily Mirror*, feeling vaguely uncomfortable. He'd already made a private decision to consign whatever he knew about Goodman to the waste bin. He was glad of the promotion, and far too cynical not to suspect a tacit link with the events of a month back, but beyond that he wasn't prepared to speculate. A year in Belize was enough penance for anyone. He didn't see the point in inviting further attention.

Goodman arrived minutes later. He looked leaner than Evans remembered, fitter, suntanned. He was carrying a small brown parcel. He smiled a greeting and put a hand on Evans' shoulder as the Marine began to get up.

'Stay there,' he said. 'It's good to see you.'

Goodman sat down, and they talked for a minute or two about nothing in particular, an awkward conversation, their lives divided rather than bonded by the three days and nights they'd spent together. Evans began to regret accepting the invitation, eyeing the parcel, wondering exactly what Goodman had in mind.

Finally, once the waitress had fetched drinks from the bar and taken the order, Goodman raised his glass.

'Congratulations,' he said. 'I understand you made Sergeant.'

Evans hesitated a moment, catching the tiny nuance in his voice, a suggestion that Goodman, somehow, might have had a hand in the promotion, a confirmation of his own hunch.

'Thank you, sir,' he said guardedly. 'Bit of a surprise, actually.'

Goodman smiled.

'Cheers,' he said.

Evans raised his glass.

'Cheers.'

They drank in silence. A ferry churned past the window, one of the big, slab-sided boats that went to France. Goodman picked up the parcel, and offered it to Evans.

'A little present,' Goodman said lightly. 'A personal thank-you.'

Evans looked at it.

'A present?' he said blankly.

'Yes.' Goodman paused, choosing his words carefully. 'The Council, in their wisdom, have voted to give me . . . ah . . . a little gift. A token of their esteem, services rendered to the city during the recent . . . ah . . . troubles . . .' He hesitated again. 'Under the circumstances, I thought it only fair to . . . ah . . . share it . . .' He smiled. 'Comrades in arms . . .'

Evans was still looking at the parcel.

'What is it?'

'Money, Sergeant.'

'Oh?' He glanced up at Goodman. 'How much money?'

'Six thousand . . .' He paused. 'That's three thousand for me . . .' he nodded at the parcel, 'and three thousand for you . . .'

Evans sat back and looked out of the window. The ferry had gone. The harbour mouth was quite empty.

'And *where* does this money come from?' he said quietly.

Goodman leaned forward over the table, shaking the creases out of his napkin, very casual, full of bonhomie.

'The city, Sergeant . . .' He pushed the parcel towards Evans. 'Here. Take it. It's yours. And very well earned, if I may say so.'

Evans got up, and retrieved his paper from the window-sill. His beer was barely touched. He looked down at Goodman, at the parcel, the disgust and the contempt self-evident.

'No thanks,' he said.

He turned and walked away, bodychecking around the waitress juggling with a laden tray. Goodman watched him go, knowing that he'd made a terrible mistake, hearing the footsteps again, closer still.

Annie was back in the city by five-thirty, driving against the traffic flow. She let herself into the house. Gillespie was in the kitchen, reading a copy of the evening paper. He looked up as she walked in.

'Short day again?' he said. 'I'm surrounded by women who do sod all.'

Annie ignored the dig, wondering who the other women might be, putting the kettle on, emptying the teapot. When she turned round, Gillespie was reaching for his jacket.

'Something I said?' she asked him.

Gillespie shook his head.

'How's that film of yours?'

Annie pulled a face, and told him what had happened, the compromises she'd had to make, the questions she hadn't asked, the sheer ordinariness of it all. Goodman, she said, had been as unctuous as ever, an hour or so of pure flannel, answers so empty of meaning that even Bullock had noticed.

'So what do you do about that?' Gillespie asked, breaking off the crusty bits from a loaf he'd just bought.

'We try again.'

'When?'

'Tonight. After another wonderful sequence.'

'Oh yeah?' He looked up. 'What's that then?'

She told him about the Rotary Club, and the award they were making to Goodman. Dedication in the service of the city. With love and kisses and grateful thanks. Gillespie nodded.

'It's in the paper,' he said. 'Page three.'

'I bet.'

Gillespie smiled. 'This interview of yours,' he said, 'afterwards.'

'Yes?'

'Where would you do that?'

Annie looked at him, puzzled.

'His office,' she said, 'why?'

Gillespie shrugged and made for the door.

'Just wondered,' he said.

He opened the door, and stepped back to let the cat in.

'I'm round the corner,' he said, 'Digger's Arms. If anyone calls.'

Joanna Goodman sat at her dressing table in the bedroom, putting on the last of her make-up. Marge was already downstairs, giving the children their tea. Across the landing she could hear Martin in the bathroom, listening to *The Archers*, splashing around with the sponge. He said they should be there by seven-thirty. It was already quarter-past.

She checked her make-up in the small hand-mirror, and reached across to open the wardrobe doors. There was a rackful of dresses inside, and she sifted through looking for something suitable, not too formal, not too casual, something to complement the occasion, something that would permit her to play the loyal consort for just one more night. Tomorrow, she'd decided, she would leave him. By tomorrow, it would all be over. Until then, though, she owed him a certain mute support.

She got up and pulled out a dress she'd had for years. It was black, nicely cut, with padded shoulders, and jet buttons she'd bought specially. She put it on and studied the effect in the full-length mirror. It made her look quietly attractive, cool, a woman in her own right, sure of herself. More important, it made her feel somehow safe, imposing a mood of its own, buffering her from the world outside.

She heard the bathroom door open. Footsteps crossed the landing. Martin appeared at the bedroom door. He was wearing a dressing gown. He looked preoccupied. He paused by the door, catching sight of her by the window. He smiled.

'You look terrific,' he said, 'truly.'

She looked at him, realizing again what a child he was, how unaffected he could be. If only she could be sure of this Martin of hers. If only she could trust him to overcome all the silliness, and the greed, and the ambition, and the insecurity. If only he'd accept life in small portions, not reach out all the time for second helpings. She returned his smile, rueful, knowing that it would never be.

'I'm glad you like it,' she said, 'I chose it for you.'

He slipped off the dressing gown, and opened his own wardrobe.

'It's black,' he pointed out.

'I know,' she said.

Gillespie sat in the public bar in the Digger's Arms. He'd borrowed the house copy of the local paper, picking up where he'd left off. He ran a finger down the classified ads, looking for likely boats, something to replace his beloved *Harriet*, once the insurance money came in. There was a seventeen-foot Dory for sale. It had a cabin and a new outboard. He shook his head. Small, he thought, limited range. Poor sea boat. He needed something bigger, something he could trust.

Gillespie glanced at his watch. It was already gone seven. Evans should have arrived by now. He'd have been home, talked to his wife, heard more about the incident on the doorstep, come looking. He'd be angry. He wouldn't bother about the formalities. It would be strictly private, limited dialogue, Corps style. He carefully folded the paper, wondering whether he was still up to it. He'd watched Evans in the gym, seen him in action, acknowledged his strength and his courage. The boy had a real appetite for it. He could tell.

He called the barman, and ordered another bottle of Guinness. Afterwards, assuming they were both conscious, it might be different. Evans might ease up a little, the worst of it off his chest, might be prepared to look at the whole thing afresh. Back home, Annie gone, they might even sit down and talk, establish ground rules, see what might be possible. The sudden posting to Belize was obviously no coincidence. They wanted him gone, out of it, off the plot, and Evans would know it. Maybe he preferred it that way. Promotion in return for a discreet silence. Maybe not.

The barman finished pouring the Guinness, and Gillespie rummaged for the money for the drink. As he did so, he felt a pressure on his arm. He paused on the bar stool, easing it back, giving himself room. Evans stood there, civvies, light-weight shirt, well-cut slacks. He nodded, gruff, brisk.

'Keep it,' he said. 'My shout.'

Albie Curtis carried the last of the big tins of white emulsion into Cartwright's office, and put it on the carpet beside the other six. The cleaner in the corridor looked at him curiously.

'He never mentioned any decorating,' she said. 'Not to me.'

Albie shrugged.

'Not my problem, love,' he said. 'Don't worry about locking up.'

The woman hesitated a moment longer, not quite sure what to do, then unplugged the vacuum cleaner and went downstairs. Albie heard her moving around the big working area, straightening chairs, turning off lights, tidying up. Then came the click of the front door. He crossed to the window, watching her buttoning her coat, and putting up her umbrella against the thin rain drifting in again from the west.

Albie waited for her to walk away, then turned to the tins of paint. Using a silver letter opener from Cartwright's desk, he prised the tops off all the tins, one after another. He let the tin lids topple onto the carpet, paint side down, neat white circles on the tasteful sea-green Wilton.

He picked up the first of the tins of paint, heavy, and then clambered onto Cartwright's antique desk. Then he poured the tin vertically down, watching it splash over the polished walnut veneer and over the big leather chair, dripping down, onto the carpet below. He emptied the first tin and got off the desk. He opened Cartwright's drawers, white footprints on the carpet, and stooped for the second tin. He filled both drawers, watching the pens and the diaries and the small collection of calculators disappear under a sea of white emulsion.

He circled the desk, the tin up-ended, a line of heavy drips. He pulled out the drawers in the filing cabinets, working from the top downwards, half a tin in each, the stuff cascading down through the files, puddling in the drawers. He threw an entire tinful at one wall, swamping the expensive wooden panelling. He threw another at the window, masking the remains of the daylight.

Finally, he threw what was left of the last tin at a picture on the other wall, a framed photo of Goodman and Cartwright at some official function or other, Goodman smiling at the camera, Cartwright presenting him with a cheque. The tin caught the print high on one side, shattering the glass. It hung drunkenly down, still secured to the wall, dripping white emulsion.

Albie looked at it, his head cocked to one side. A shard of glass had penetrated the photograph, severing Cartwright's head from his body. Albie smiled. He rather like the effect. He wiped his hands on his jeans, and made for the door. By the door, he paused, retrieving Cartwright's silver letter opener from the carpet. It was bent nearly double from opening the tins. He wiped off most of the paint on the curtain, and laid it carefully on Cartwright's blotter. Dead centre.

Then he left.

Goodman's address to the Rotary Club was short and graceful. He thanked the assembled members for giving him the award, and said that he accepted it on behalf of his entire team. He said that it was neither the time nor the place for political speeches, but he was glad that the deterrent had worked, and that the world had finally woken up to the folly of tempting providence. Never again, he hoped, would there ever be a call for a bunker and a curfew. What was needed now was a permanent reminder of the days they'd all lived through, of just how close a flirtation they'd all had with oblivion. The award they'd given him, and the feelings it represented, might be just such a reminder. He was glad to accept it, and gladder still to have survived.

He sat down. There was a wave of applause, the women clapping, the men banging the supper tables in approval. From her camera position at the back of the hall, Annie had to admit that it was a good piece, beautifully judged, and would make a fitting coda to her film. Bullock, God bless him, had been right. She watched Goodman up at the top table, accepting a congratulatory kiss from his wife. Perhaps the interview would go well, too. Perhaps, after all, there was still hope.

The cameraman was panning slowly across the packed tables, easing the faces into focus, capturing the pride, the satisfaction, their Controller, their city, their salvation, giving Annie a handsome shot to complete the sequence. When he'd finished, he nodded at the door.

'We should set up in his office,' she said, 'he'll be out of here soon.'

Gillespie and Evans sat in Gillespie's car, thirty yards up the road, watching Annie and the cameraman emerging from the hall. They'd been talking for more than an hour. Evans had told him everything he knew. He'd told him about the days and nights with Goodman, the calls to the car phone, the half-hours outside the wine bar, the visits to the seafront flat. He'd put together the relationship in his own head, drawn his own conclusions from the evidence he'd seen first hand. The man had wanted out, he said. He'd had his nose in the trough, and he'd taken everything he could get, and now he was moving on. A month or two with his own family, his own missus, before something else turned up. Pathetic.

Gillespie had queried some of this, curious at the depth of Evans's feelings, but the big Marine had simply shaken his head, confirming it all. The man was a right bastard, he said. He was cold, and he was callous, and when the going got really tough he'd pushed the poor bitch off the balcony. There'd obviously been some kind of fight. The bloke had come out of the flats in a right state, goon suit covered in blood, shaking like a leaf.

'You remember those?' Evans had said, 'goon suits?'

Gillespie had nodded.

'Don't I just,' he said, remembering the NBC gear he'd worn in the Corps, and his own hands, covered in the greasy dark green deposit, and the photos he'd seen that morning, those same dark marks blotching the girl's throat and shoulders. Silly of him not to have made the connection before. Obvious really.

They'd driven to the hall in silence. Only when they were parked, waiting for the Rotary meeting to end, did Evans ask what Gillespie expected him to do, what he really wanted. Gillespie told him. A sworn statement, he'd said, a formal affidavit, admissible in court. Evans had looked at him and told him it was out of the question. No statements. No interviews. Nothing in cold print. He'd do what he could to help, but it had to be low profile, and it had to happen in the next three days. After that, he'd be away. Gillespie had thought about it, acknowledging Evans' qualms with a grunt, masking his own disappointment. At first, he'd thought he was back to square one, nothing really solid, no proof, but now, watching Annie helping the cameraman stow equipment in the back of the Volvo, he wasn't so sure. There might, just conceivably, be a way.

He glanced across at Evans. The windows were down in the car, and they could hear more applause, filling the hall. The doors onto the street opened, and Goodman appeared. Evans watched him carefully, the smile, the handshakes, the born politician easing his way out of yet another triumph.

'Did you see the girl at all?' Evans said quietly. 'Afterwards?'

Gillespie nodded. 'Yes,' he said.

'Pathetic, wasn't it? Poor bitch.'

'Yes.' Gillespie watched Annie conferring briefly with Goodman before getting in the Volvo and driving away. She looked pleased with herself. She was laughing. It must have gone well. He leaned forward and started the engine. Evans frowned.

'What now?' he said.

Gillespie looked across at him, pulling out onto the road.

'One more call,' he said, 'then we're through.'

Annie and the cameraman arrived at the Civic Centre and walked into the reception area. The security guard behind the desk had been warned about the filming and directed them to Goodman's office on the fifth floor. There'd be others to come, she told him. She wasn't quite sure how many.

In Goodman's office, Annie chose the angle she wanted, while the cameraman prowled around, looking for power points for the lights. The other Volvo had arrived by now, and they both returned to the kerbside to help unload the gear.

Gillespie and Evans watched them from a side road fifty yards away. Gillespie had seen the lights go on in Goodman's office, and knew more or less what would happen next. Soon, Goodman would arrive. His wife would probably be with him. They'd join the film crew in his office. And then they'd shoot that one last interview.

Evans lit another cigarette. Under the circumstances, Gillespie thought he was being remarkably patient. He glanced across at him.

'Tell me,' he said, 'what made you change your mind?'

'About what?'

'This. You. Me.'

Evans didn't answer for a moment. Goodman's car had arrived, parking behind the Volvos. Goodman got out and walked around the car to hold the door open for his wife. Evans was watching him.

'Real gent,' he said softly. 'Look at him.'

Gillespie laughed.

'Yeah,' he said, 'all part of the service.'

There was a silence. Goodman walked slowly across the square towards the Civic Centre, his footsteps on the flagstones echoing back from the surrounding buildings. He and his wife mounted the steps and disappeared through the revolving door. Evans flicked the remains of his cigarette into the darkness, prepared at last to answer Gillespie's question.

'He tried to bung me,' he said. 'Three thousand quid.' He looked across at Gillespie. 'The prat.'

Annie was almost ready to shoot by the time Goodman and his wife arrived in the office. The lights were set up, the desk bathed in a soft tungsten glow. The tripod was levelled, and there was a new twenty-minute cassette on board. All that remained was a brief white balance for the camera, and a microphone to be attached to the lapel of Goodman's suit. With luck, fingers crossed, they'd be away within half an hour.

Goodman stepped into the room, and introduced his wife. Annie shook her hand and showed her to a seat in the shadows at the edge of the room. It was the first time the two women had met. She'd originally asked Goodman for permission to approach his wife for a quite separate interview, but he'd said at once that he'd rather she didn't. His wife had had a difficult time, he'd said. She'd been rather shaken by the experience, and he'd no desire to put her through it all over again. Now, looking at her, Annie wondered why. She seemed perfectly at ease, an attractive woman in a well-cut dress. A little quiet, perhaps. A little withdrawn. But utterly self-assured.

Goodman sat down behind the desk. The sound recordist clipped on a tiny Sony mike, and returned to the camera to adjust the sound levels. Annie checked the shot, making sure it gave her what she wanted. Through the viewfinder, in extreme close-up, Goodman looked strangely vulnerable. He kept glancing out to the left, out into the shadows, towards his wife. Annie lifted her head from the camera and followed his eyeline. His wife was watching him, totally expressionless. There was something wrong between them, but Annie had no way of knowing quite what it was. The sound recordist caught her eye and gave her the thumbs up. Annie reached for the clipboard and kicked the cameraman's ankles.

'Roll,' she said softly.

The clipboard contained few surprises. She fed Goodman the simplest of questions, seeking the emotional response Bullock was so fond of, and he returned the compliment with a bravura performance. He spoke in a low, reflective voice, pausing to search for the right phrase, the difficult thought, opening himself up for the first time.

He talked about going to the brink, to the very edge, and looking over. He talked about pressure and pain, and the awful knowledge that you might soon have to lose what you most loved in life. Not life itself. Not the chore of living from day to day.

But that handful of relationships that made life worth living. In that sense, he said quietly, those few days in September had been almost worthwhile. Because only then, in the bleakest of times, did you begin to learn the really hard things about yourself. What you'd done well, and what you'd done badly. How, in short, you'd chosen to conduct your life. The Emergency had been, for him, a profound experience. He'd hated most of it, but he'd treasured the lessons he'd learned since. There'd be a new start, he said. A new beginning.

He paused for a moment, his voice sinking lower and lower, and Annie bent forward, willing him to continue, not wanting to interrupt him with anything as crass as a question or a prompt. She couldn't believe her ears. What had started as a sop to Bullock, had turned into a profound piece of self-revelation, almost confessional in its intensity. Whether it was genuine, or simply a performance, Annie didn't know. What mattered was that the camera was suddenly eavesdropping on an intimate conversation, a private settling of accounts. Annie had been making films long enough to recognize gold dust, and this was certainly it.

Goodman had fallen silent now, gazing down at his hands. Annie glanced back towards his wife. She was crying, silently, one hand over her face. Goodman looked up and began to talk again. His voice had almost gone, no more than a whisper. He cleared his throat. The future, he was saying, belongs to all of us. We've inherited it. It's ours, inescapably, the one real bequest of those terrible, terrible days. We must do in the future what we haven't done before. We must be stronger. Kinder. Less selfish. More content. We must learn our limitations. Know what we can't do, as well as what we can.

Annie heard the door opening, very softly. She looked up. There was a figure silhouetted against the light from the corridor, someone else, slightly taller, behind. Two men stepped into the room.

Annie frowned. Goodman had stopped again. He was looking at the intruders in the shadows. One of the two men eased forward, the light spilling onto his face. He was smiling. Goodman took his glasses off, and rubbed his eyes. He suddenly looked very tired.

'You're Gillespie,' he said quietly, 'I know you are.'

Annie gazed at him, then looked at the men in the shadows. He was right. One of them was Gillespie. She stared at him.

'Dave . . ?' she began.

Goodman interrupted her. Annie, and the camera, could have been a million miles away.

'What do you want?' he said to Gillespie.

Gillespie studied him a moment, taking his time.

'I want you to meet a friend of mine,' he said at last.

The other man stepped forward, slightly taller, same build, lean, good face. Goodman nodded at him.

'Evans,' he said, 'what a surprise.'

The cameraman eased back from the viewfinder, wanting to know what was going on. Gillespie glanced across at him.

'Keep filming,' he said.

The cameraman looked at Annie. Annie shrugged, helplessly.

'Why not?' she said, quite lost, suddenly a stranger at her own party, aware that something momentous was happening, but not knowing what.

There was another long silence. Goodman was examining his hands again. His hands were shaking.

'Take your time,' Gillespie said, 'don't rush it.'

Goodman didn't look up.

'What do you want?' he said for the second time.

'All of it. The boat. The girl. Everything . . .' Gillespie paused. 'Why don't you start with the girl?'

Goodman nodded, an actor taking his prompt. When he finally looked up, the voice was quite dead.

'I killed a girl called Suzanne Wallace . . .' he began. 'I killed her about half-past eleven on a Tuesday night. I killed her because I loved her . . .'

An hour later. The square outside the Civic Centre. The rain stopped. The air fresher. Low, broken clouds racing over a young moon.

First out of the revolving door, out onto the flagstones, were Gillespie and Evans. They walked in silence to the head of the steps. They paused. Gillespie held out a hand. Evans shook it. Gillespie looked at him.

'Thanks,' he said.

Evans hesitated a moment. Goodman was visible in his office on the fifth floor, standing at the window, staring out.

'My pleasure,' Evans said.

He glanced at Gillespie. The door behind them began to revolve again, and Joanna Goodman appeared. Her face looked white in the moonlight. She walked past them, staring straight ahead, saying nothing. She began to descend the steps.

'Poor cow,' Evans said softly, 'poor bloody cow.'

'Yeah.'

There was another silence. Joanna Goodman paused at the kerbside by her car, opening the door. They watched the car drive away. Evans shrugged.

'Cheers,' he said to Gillespie.

Gillespie nodded.

'Cheers,' he said.

The two men parted, Evans walking in the other direction, in towards the city centre, hugging the shadows. Gillespie was down at the bottom of the steps, crossing the square, by the time Annie caught him up. She was slightly out of breath. She was holding a video cassette, tightly, against her chest. She stood in front of him. She was smiling.

'I owe you,' she said.

Gillespie looked at her for a long time. Then he nodded.

'You're right,' he said, 'you do.'

He glanced up at the office on the fifth floor. The light was out. Goodman had gone. Gillespie shook his head, and looked at Annie for a moment. Then he turned, and plunged his hands in his pockets, and walked away. Annie watched him, uncertain.

'Dave . . .' she began.

Then she stopped, and glanced at her watch, and carried on towards the Volvo, running.

Don Anderson
Heatshield £3.99

He escaped the earth's gravity.
But could he escape the IRA?

Stukalin stared immobile at the screens, stabbing the reset buttons in the hope that the warning mechanisms were at fault. But they were telling an awful truth: his space shuttle was dying . . .

When a Soviet shuttle crash lands off the Irish coast, Major Petr Stukalin survives. His mission now is to return to Moscow, whatever the cost. But Stukalin hasn't calculated for one vital factor: capture by the IRA.

The crash sets in motion a terrifying sequence of events. In the United States Irish operative Patrick Faloon is engaged in a deadly game of counter-terrorism against the Provos – particularly Martin Riley, whose ruthless sense of purpose will make him stop at nothing.

As Ireland becomes the lethal stage for a superpower confrontation, Faloon must channel his hatred in a desperate race for the priceless secrets of the stricken Russian craft.

But it is a race without rules, and not all the runners are what they seem . . .

Carl Hiaasen

Double Whammy £3.99

'Sharp humour, energetic action, and a supporting cast of well-drawn weirdos make this one of the most imaginative, zippy, and fun to read capers of the year' THE TIMES

Dennis Gault, tycoon and fishing fanatic was only the first of Private Eye R. J. Decker's problems. Hired by Gault to investigate cheating on the Florida bass-fishing circuit, Decker found himself surrounded by murder, obsession, and a plethora of characters from beyond the fringe, to whom catching bass was more fun than sex. Pretty soon, Decker's own neck is on the line as he discovers that fishing in Florida doesn't involve killing just bass . . .

'A careful reading of DOUBLE WHAMMY will do more to damage the Florida tourist trade than anything except an actual visit to Florida' P. J. O'ROURKE

'I went for DOUBLE WHAMMY hook, line and sinker, and I think you will too' WASHINGTON POST

'An outrageously entertaining high-protein experience' CHRISTOPHER WORDSWORTH, OBSERVER

'A savagely funny crime adventure . . . DOUBLE WHAMMY bristles all over' MIAMI HERALD

Jonathan Franzen
The 27th City £4.99

St Louis had sung the blues for a century. Once America's fourth city, now the 27th, change had been a long time coming.

Now, with the arrival of S. Jammu, things are happening fast. She's a police chief with a plan – and it's got nothing to do with law enforcement. After a monsoon of charm, bribery and violence, most of the city is where she wants it – on her side.

Except Martin Probst. He's reached the top the hard way, the legal way. He believes in the spirit of St. Louis, something an outsider could never understand. For S. Jammu to build her 27th heaven, Probst must be seduced – or destroyed . . .

'Like *Bonfire of the Vanities* with its wide scope and lush realism . . . laced with a subtle, icy, unforgiving humour, a debut novel that will make quite a splash' KIRKUS REVIEWS

'A big lavish novel of creepy realism, and as gripping as a detective story . . . it teems with energy, wit and invention' NEWSWEEK

All Pan books are available at your local bookshop or newsagent, or can be ordered direct from the publisher. Indicate the number of copies required and fill in the form below.

Send to: **CS Department, Pan Books Ltd., P.O. Box 40, Basingstoke, Hants. RG21 2YT.**

or phone: 0256 469551 (Ansaphone), quoting title, author and Credit Card number.

Please enclose a remittance* to the value of the cover price plus: 60p for the first book plus 30p per copy for each additional book ordered to a maximum charge of £2.40 to cover postage and packing.

*Payment may be made in sterling by UK personal cheque, postal order, sterling draft or international money order, made payable to Pan Books Ltd.

Alternatively by Barclaycard/Access:

Card No. | | | | | | | | | | | | | | | | |

Signature:

Applicable only in the UK and Republic of Ireland.

While every effort is made to keep prices low, it is sometimes necessary to increase prices at short notice. Pan Books reserve the right to show on covers and charge new retail prices which may differ from those advertised in the text or elsewhere.

NAME AND ADDRESS IN BLOCK LETTERS PLEASE:

....

Name ____

Address ____

____

____

____

3/87